Goosebumps™

SECRETS OF THE SWAMP

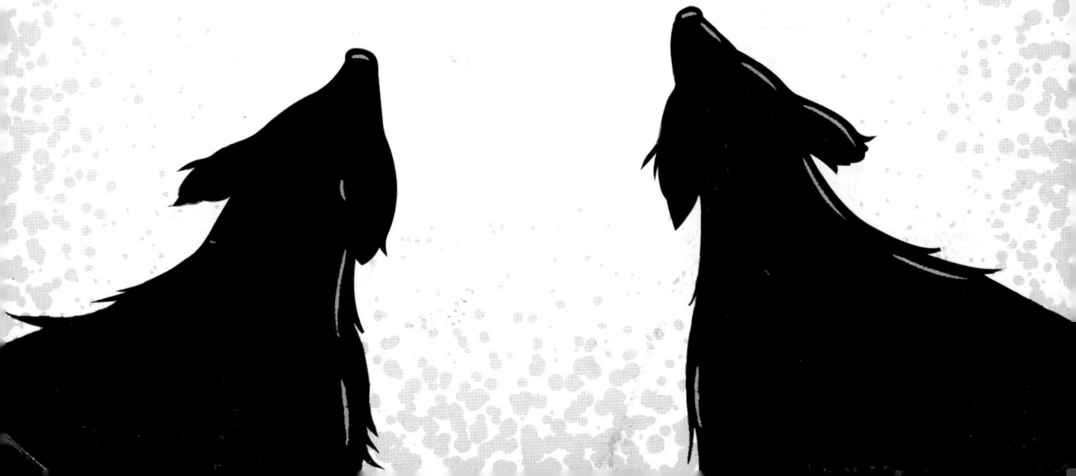

Goosebumps

COVER ARTIST:
CLARA MEATH

COVER COLORIST:
DJ CHAVIS

SERIES EDITORS:
ELIZABETH BREI &
CHASE MAROTZ

COLLECTION EDITORS:
ALONZO SIMON &
ZAC BOONE

COLLECTION DESIGNER:
JESSICA GONZALEZ

IDW ■SCHOLASTIC

Special thanks to R.L. Stine.

Originally published as GOOSEBUMPS: SECRETS OF THE SWAMP issues #1–5.

ISBN: 978-1-68405-813-6   24 23 22 21   2 3 4 5

Nachie Marsham, Publisher
Blake Kobashigawa, VP of Sales
Tara McCrillis, VP Publishing Operations
John Barber, Editor-in-Chief
Mark Doyle, Editorial Director, Originals
Erika Turner, Executive Editor
Scott Dunbier, Director, Special Projects
Mark Irwin, Editorial Director, Consumer Products Mgr
Joe Hughes, Director, Talent Relations
Anna Morrow, Sr. Marketing Director
Alexandra Hargett, Book & Mass Market Sales Director
Keith Davidsen, Senior Manager, PR
Topher Alford, Sr Digital Marketing Manager
Shauna Monteforte, Sr. Director of Manufacturing Operations
Jamie Miller, Sr. Operations Manager
Nathan Widick, Sr. Art Director, Head of Design
Neil Uyetake, Sr. Art Director Design & Production
Shawn Lee, Art Director Design & Production
Jack Rivera, Art Director, Marketing

Ted Adams and Robbie Robbins, IDW Founders

Facebook: **facebook.com/idwpublishing**
Twitter: **@idwpublishing**
YouTube: **youtube.com/idwpublishing**
Instagram: **@idwpublishing**

WRITER:

Marieke Nijkamp

ARTIST:

Yasmin Flores Montanez

COLORIST:

Rebecca Nalty

LETTERER:

Danny Djeljosevic

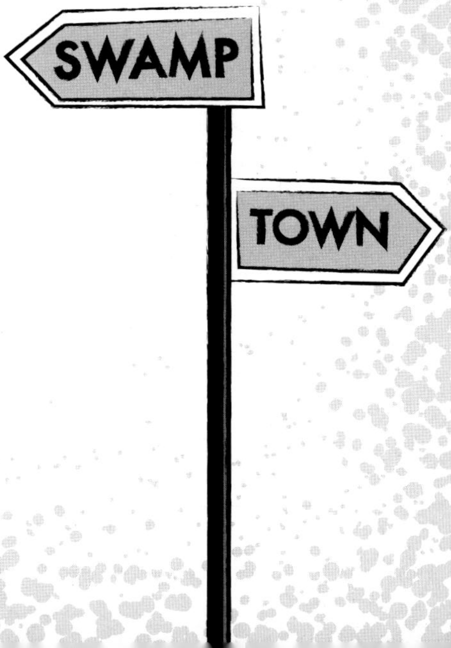

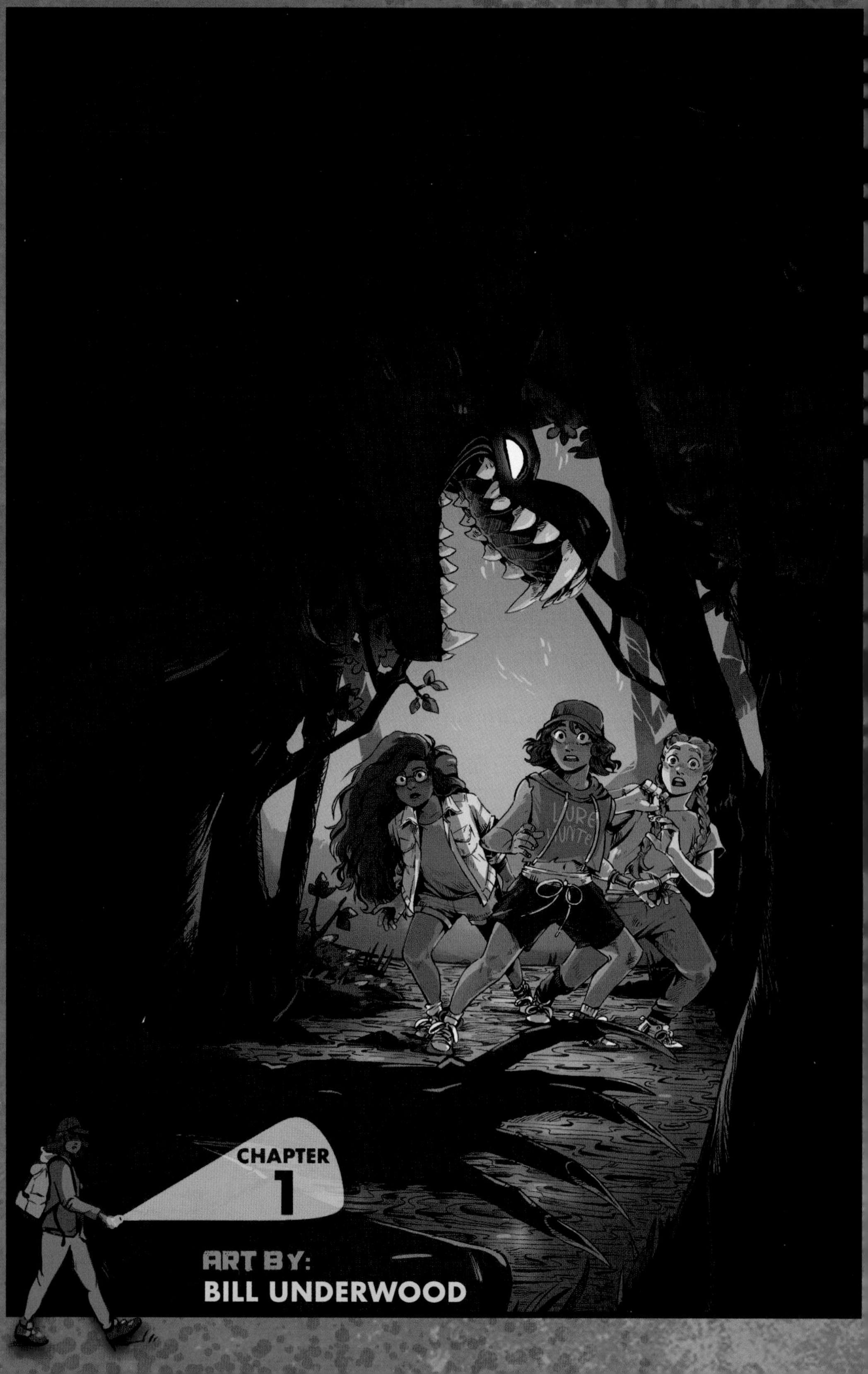

CHAPTER 1

ART BY:
BILL UNDERWOOD

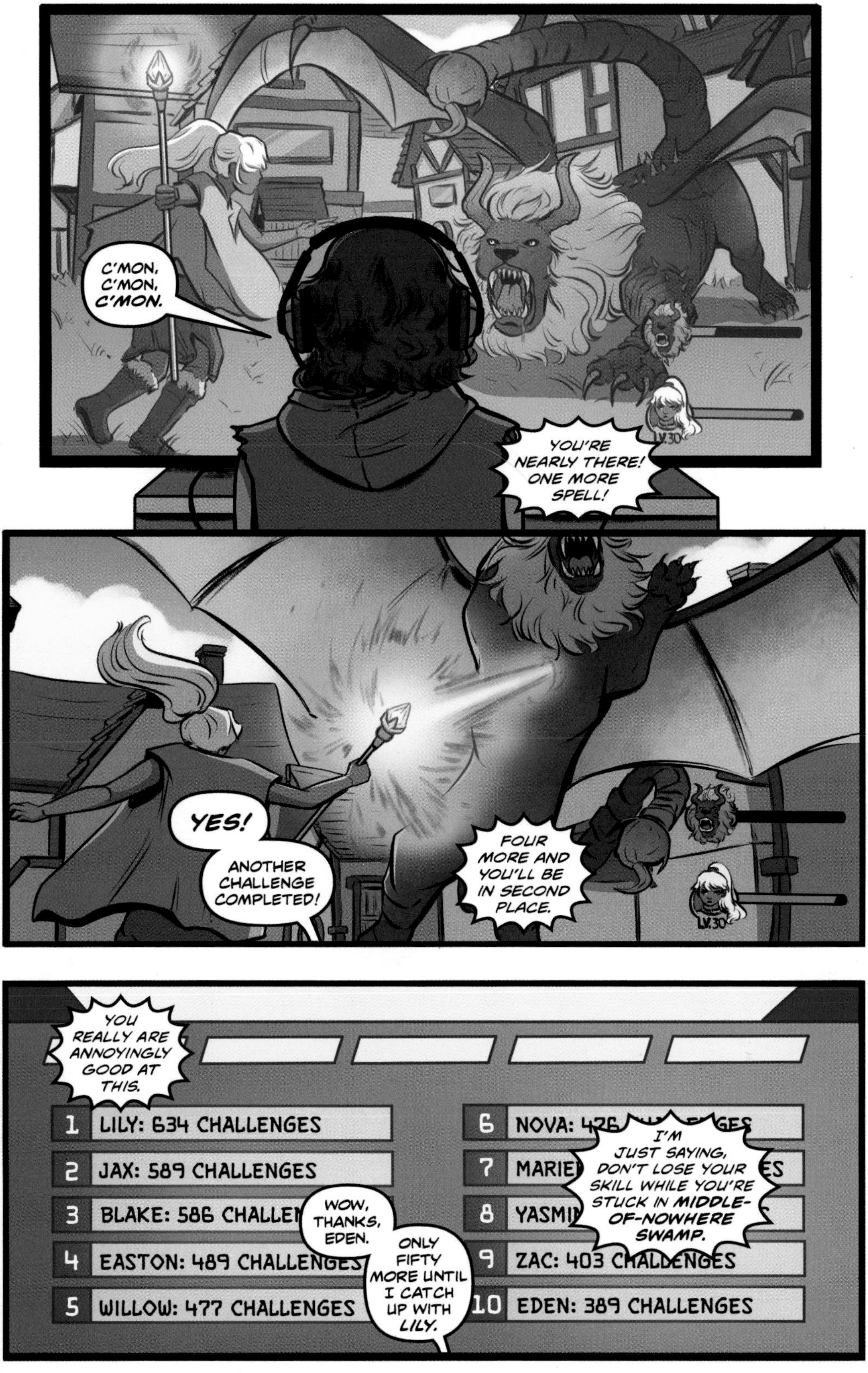
C'MON, C'MON, C'MON.
YOU'RE NEARLY THERE! ONE MORE SPELL!
LV.30
YES!
ANOTHER CHALLENGE COMPLETED!
FOUR MORE AND YOU'LL BE IN SECOND PLACE.
LV.30
YOU REALLY ARE ANNOYINGLY GOOD AT THIS.
1 LILY: 634 CHALLENGES
2 JAX: 589 CHALLENGES
3 BLAKE: 586 CHALLEN
4 EASTON: 489 CHALLENGES
5 WILLOW: 477 CHALLENGES
6 NOVA:
7 MARIE
8 YASMI
9 ZAC: 403 CHALLENGES
10 EDEN: 389 CHALLENGES
WOW, THANKS, EDEN.
ONLY FIFTY MORE UNTIL I CATCH UP WITH LILY.
I'M JUST SAYING, DON'T LOSE YOUR SKILL WHILE YOU'RE STUCK IN MIDDLE-OF-NOWHERE SWAMP.

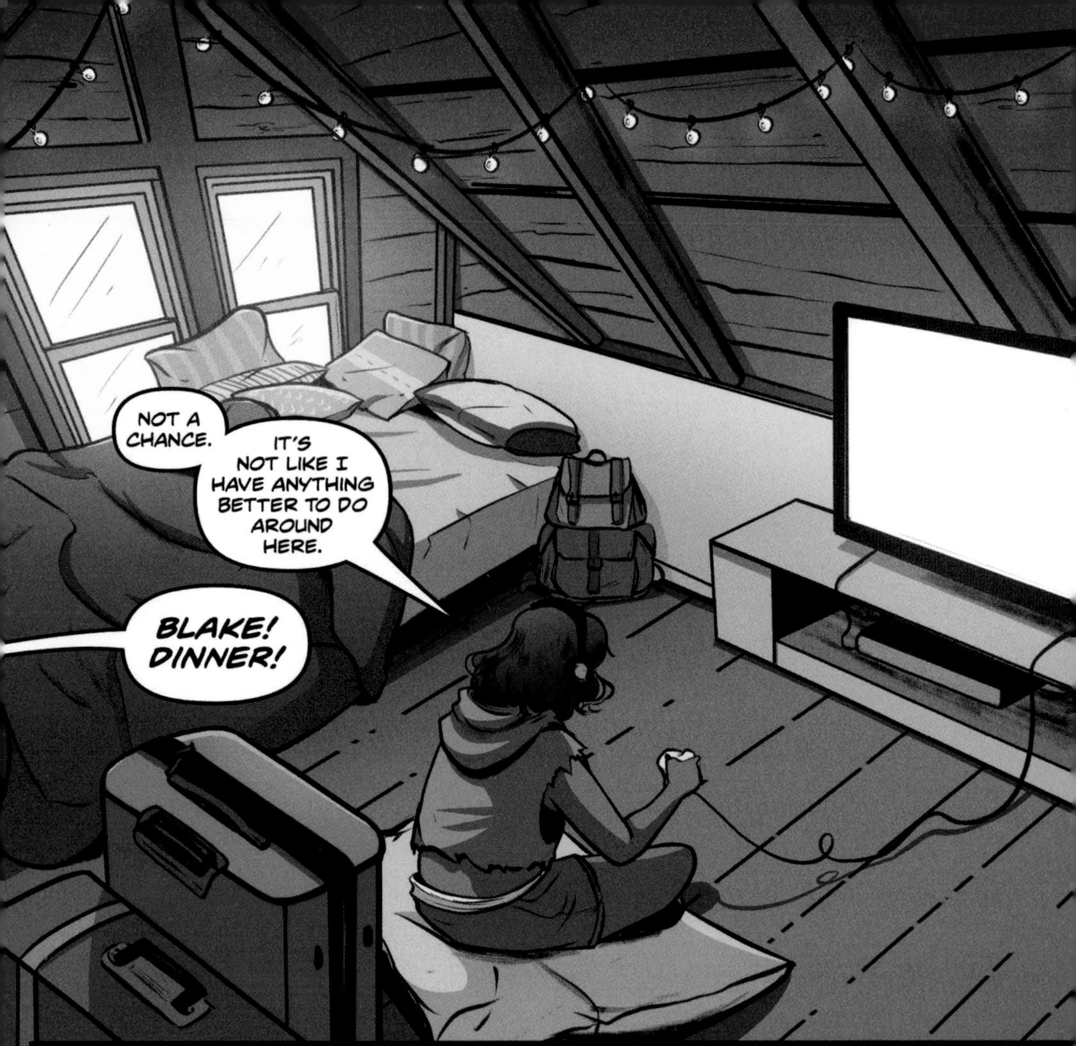
NOT A CHANCE.
IT'S NOT LIKE I HAVE ANYTHING BETTER TO DO AROUND HERE.
BLAKE! DINNER!
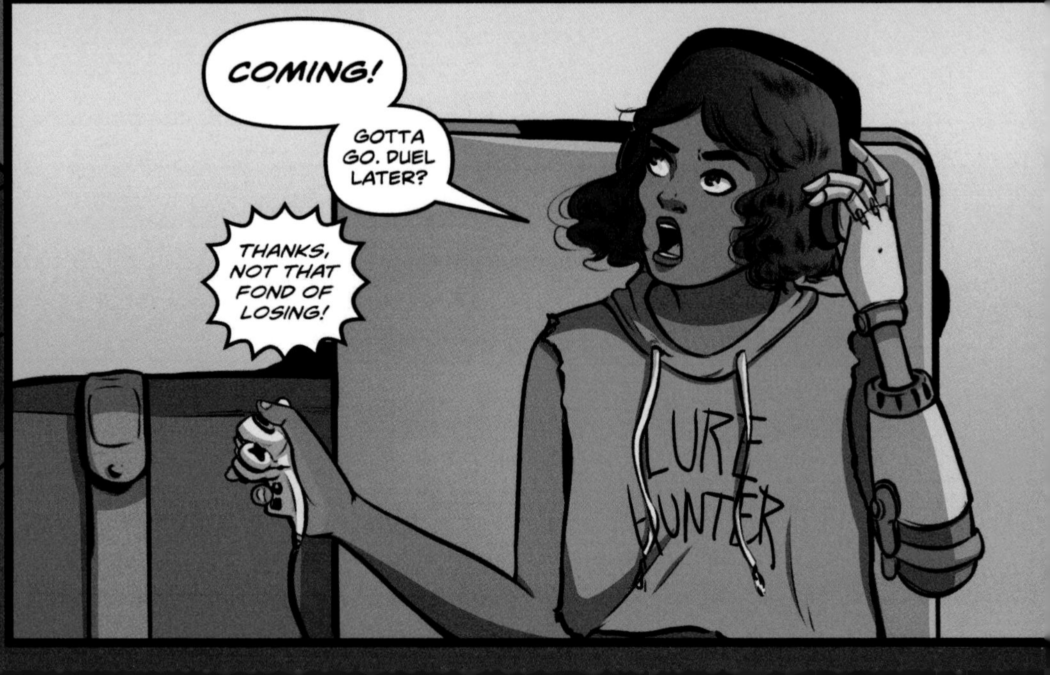
COMING!
GOTTA GO. DUEL LATER?
THANKS, NOT THAT FOND OF LOSING!
LURE HUNTER

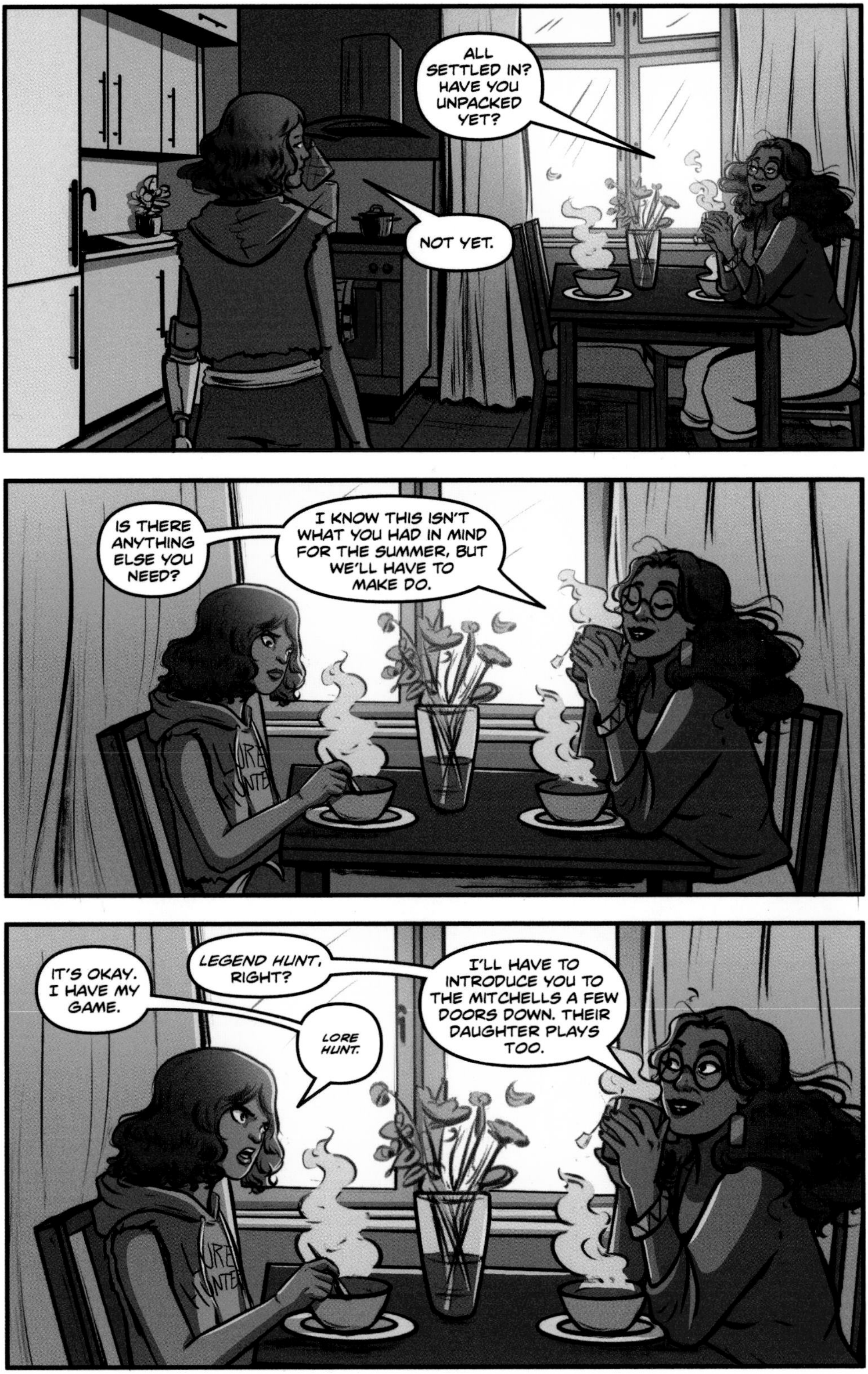
ALL SETTLED IN? HAVE YOU UNPACKED YET?
NOT YET.
IS THERE ANYTHING ELSE YOU NEED?
I KNOW THIS ISN'T WHAT YOU HAD IN MIND FOR THE SUMMER, BUT WE'LL HAVE TO MAKE DO.
IT'S OKAY. I HAVE MY GAME.
LEGEND HUNT, RIGHT?
LORE HUNT.
I'LL HAVE TO INTRODUCE YOU TO THE MITCHELLS A FEW DOORS DOWN. THEIR DAUGHTER PLAYS TOO.

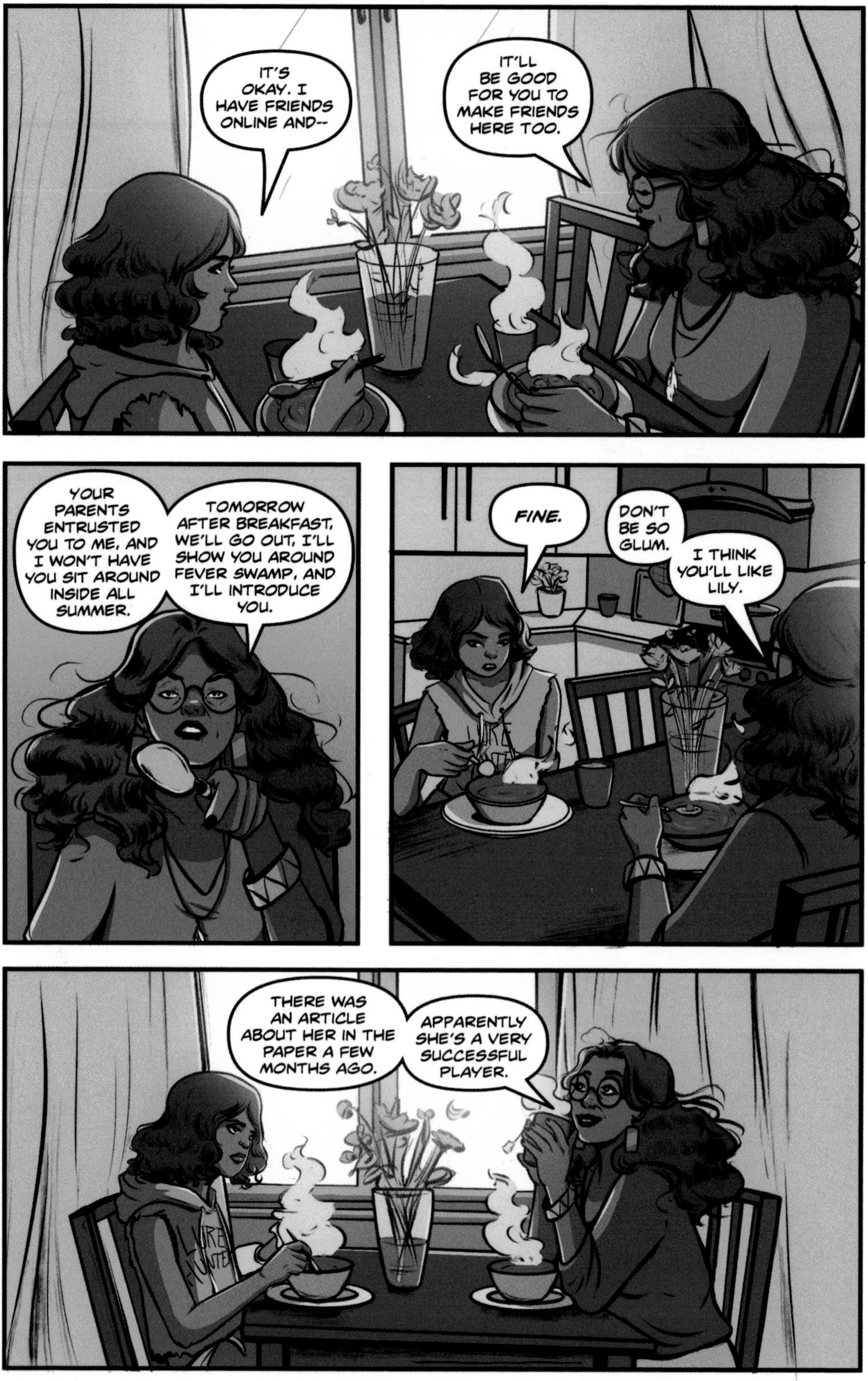
IT'S OKAY. I HAVE FRIENDS ONLINE AND--
IT'LL BE GOOD FOR YOU TO MAKE FRIENDS HERE TOO.
YOUR PARENTS ENTRUSTED YOU TO ME, AND I WON'T HAVE YOU SIT AROUND INSIDE ALL SUMMER.
TOMORROW AFTER BREAKFAST, WE'LL GO OUT, I'LL SHOW YOU AROUND FEVER SWAMP, AND I'LL INTRODUCE YOU.
FINE.
DON'T BE SO GLUM.
I THINK YOU'LL LIKE LILY.
THERE WAS AN ARTICLE ABOUT HER IN THE PAPER A FEW MONTHS AGO.
APPARENTLY SHE'S A VERY SUCCESSFUL PLAYER.

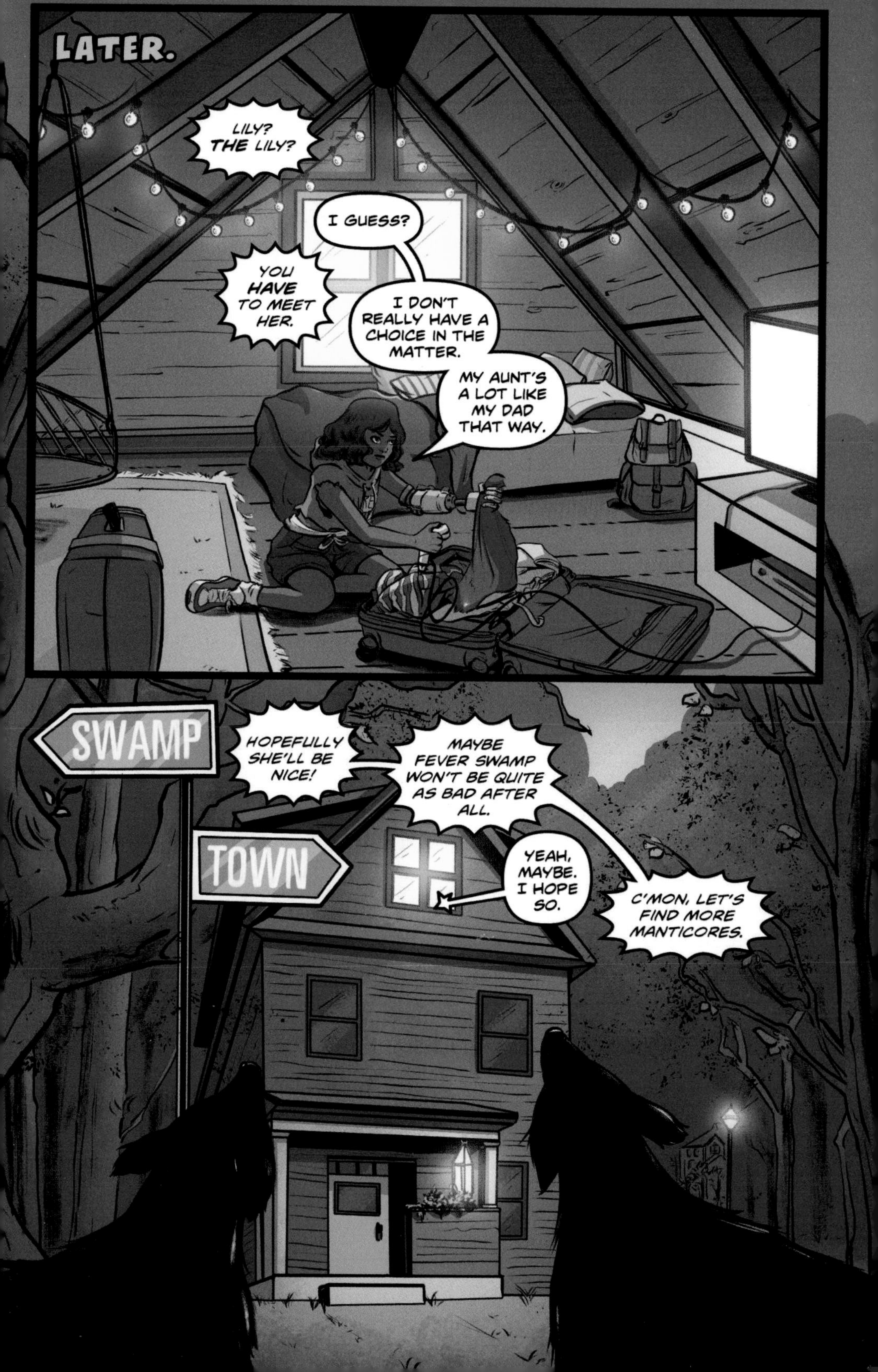
LATER.
LILY? THE LILY?
I GUESS?
YOU HAVE TO MEET HER.
I DON'T REALLY HAVE A CHOICE IN THE MATTER.
MY AUNT'S A LOT LIKE MY DAD THAT WAY.
SWAMP
TOWN
HOPEFULLY SHE'LL BE NICE!
MAYBE FEVER SWAMP WON'T BE QUITE AS BAD AFTER ALL.
YEAH, MAYBE. I HOPE SO.
C'MON, LET'S FIND MORE MANTICORES.

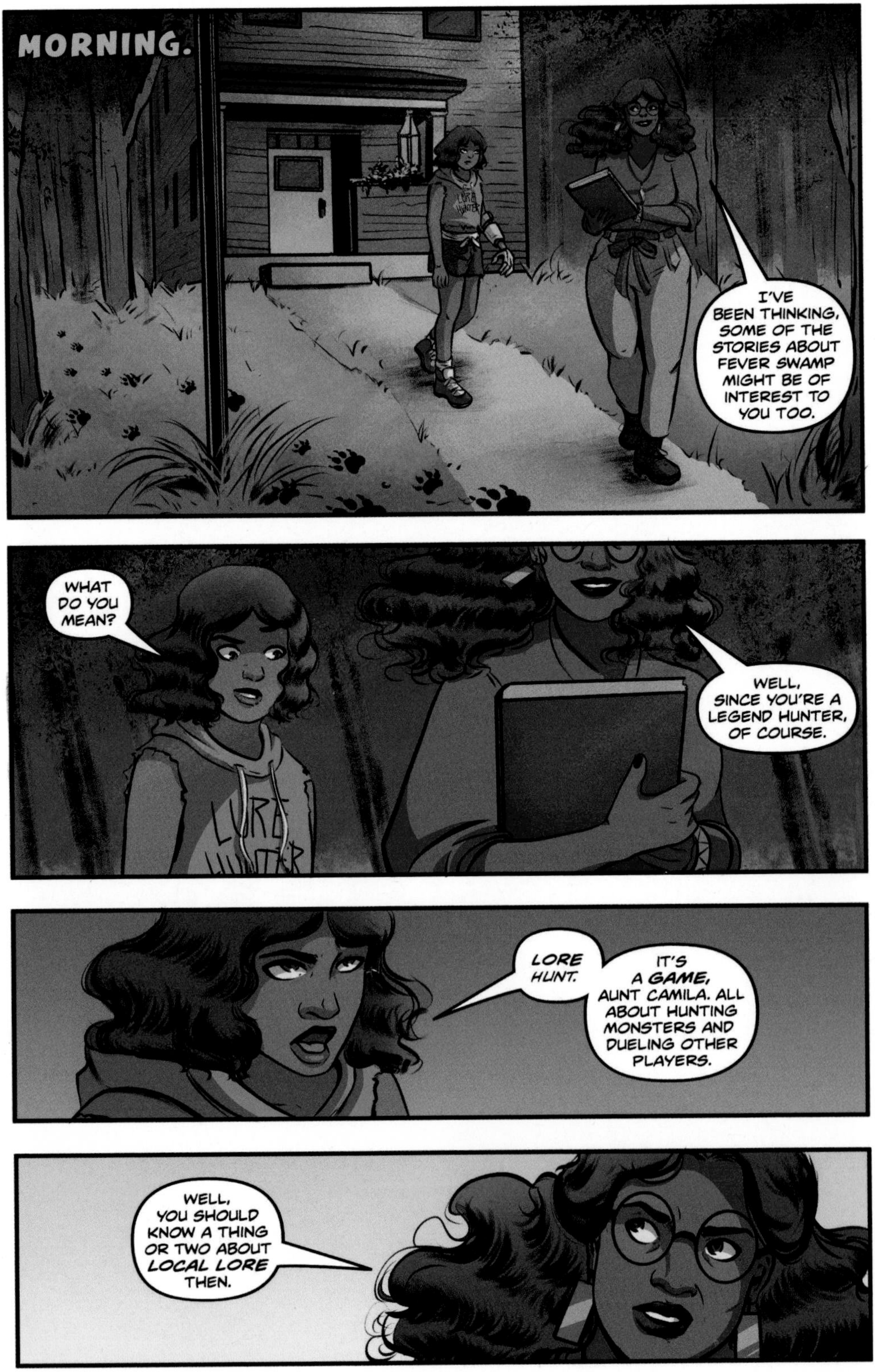
MORNING.
I'VE BEEN THINKING, SOME OF THE STORIES ABOUT FEVER SWAMP MIGHT BE OF INTEREST TO YOU TOO.
WHAT DO YOU MEAN?
WELL, SINCE YOU'RE A LEGEND HUNTER, OF COURSE.
LORE HUNT.
IT'S A GAME, AUNT CAMILA. ALL ABOUT HUNTING MONSTERS AND DUELING OTHER PLAYERS.
WELL, YOU SHOULD KNOW A THING OR TWO ABOUT LOCAL LORE THEN.

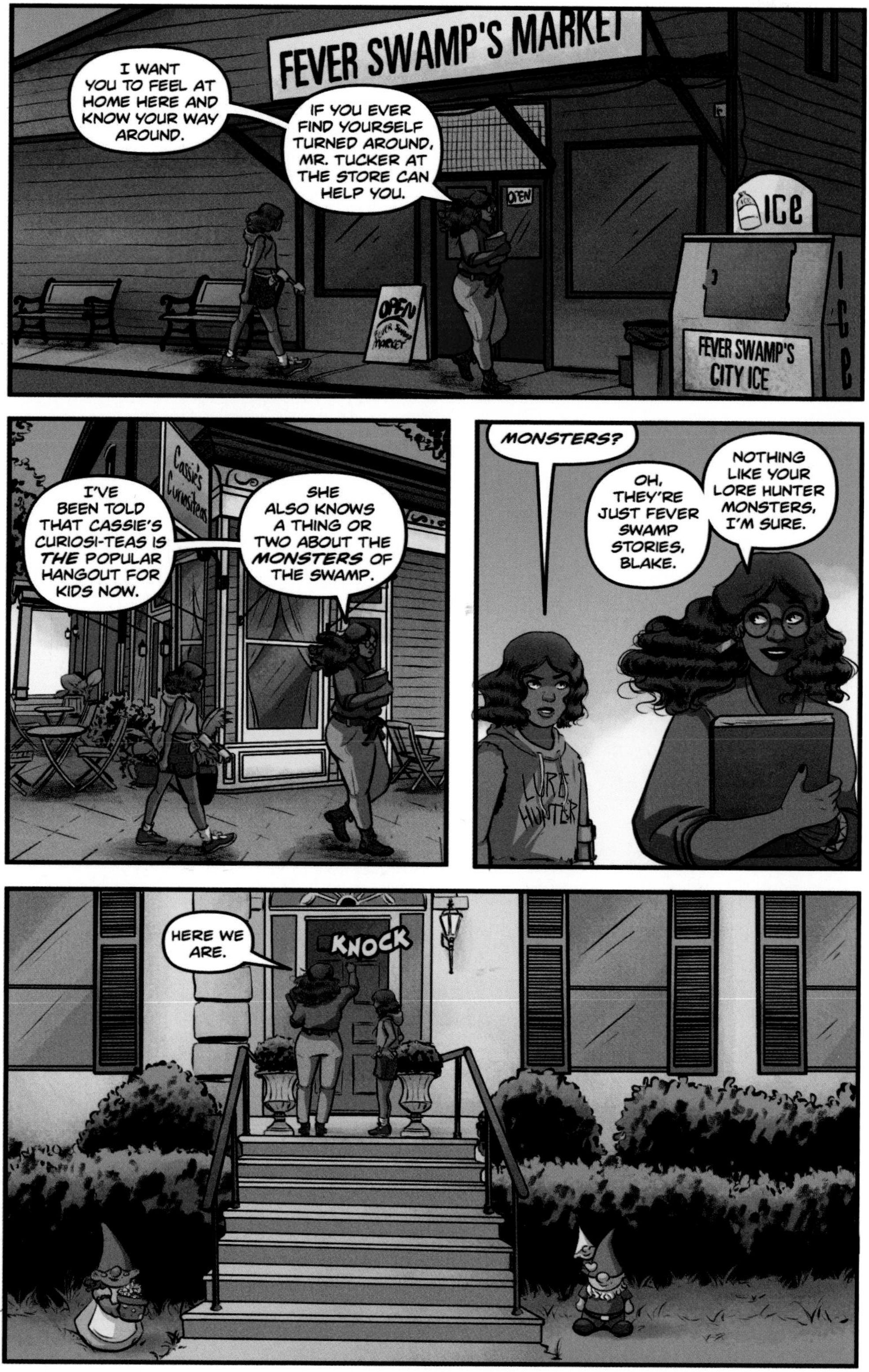
FEVER SWAMP'S MARKET
I WANT YOU TO FEEL AT HOME HERE AND KNOW YOUR WAY AROUND.
IF YOU EVER FIND YOURSELF TURNED AROUND, MR. TUCKER AT THE STORE CAN HELP YOU.
OPEN
ICE
FEVER SWAMP'S CITY ICE
ICE
I'VE BEEN TOLD THAT CASSIE'S CURIOSI-TEAS IS *THE* POPULAR HANGOUT FOR KIDS NOW.
SHE ALSO KNOWS A THING OR TWO ABOUT THE *MONSTERS* OF THE SWAMP.
Cassie's Curiositeas
MONSTERS?
OH, THEY'RE JUST FEVER SWAMP STORIES, BLAKE.
NOTHING LIKE YOUR LORE HUNTER MONSTERS, I'M SURE.
LORE HUNTER
HERE WE ARE.
KNOCK

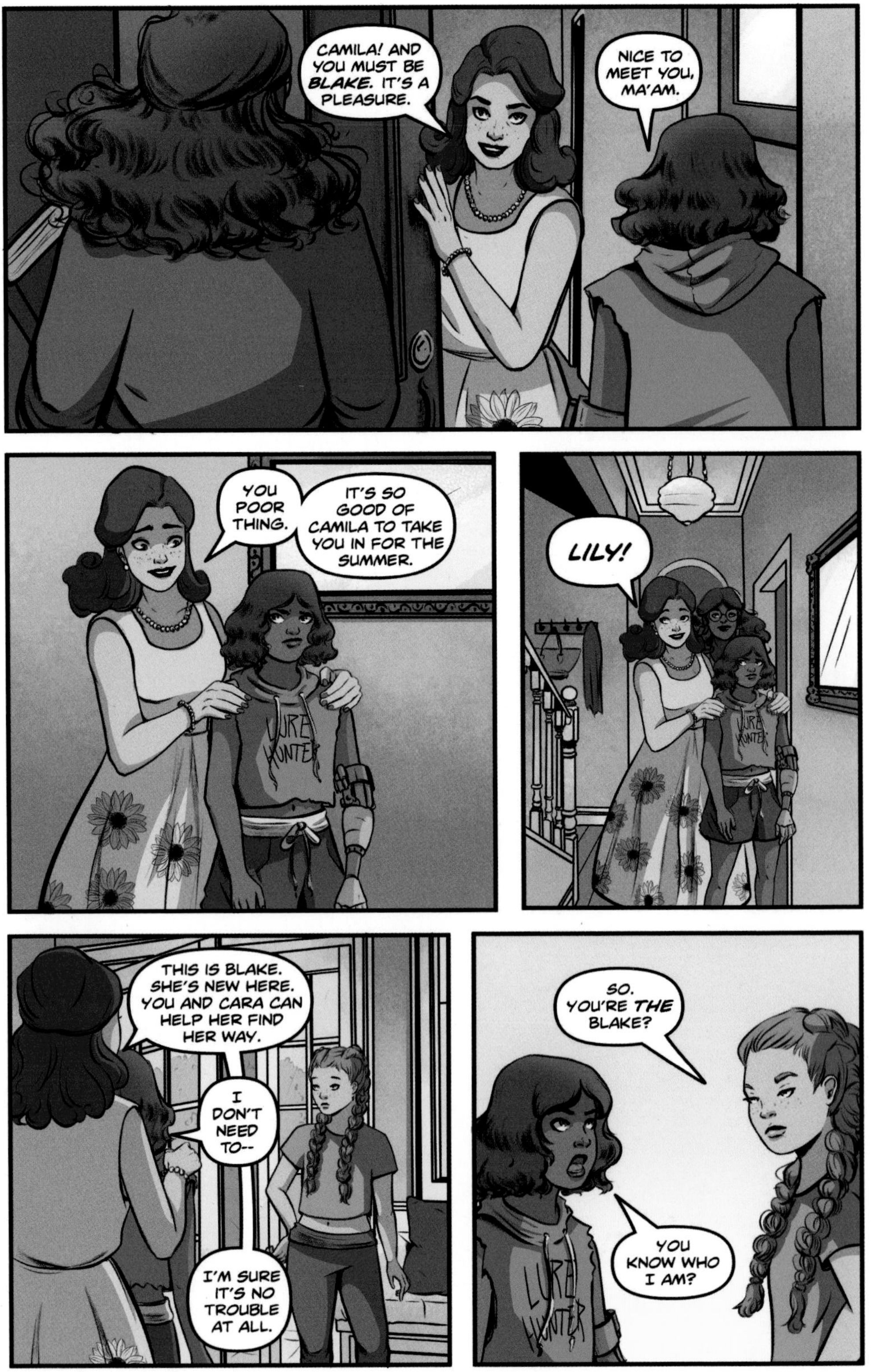
CAMILA! AND YOU MUST BE *BLAKE*. IT'S A PLEASURE.
NICE TO MEET YOU, MA'AM.
YOU POOR THING.
IT'S SO GOOD OF CAMILA TO TAKE YOU IN FOR THE SUMMER.
LILY!
THIS IS BLAKE. SHE'S NEW HERE. YOU AND CARA CAN HELP HER FIND HER WAY.
I DON'T NEED TO--
I'M SURE IT'S NO TROUBLE AT ALL.
SO. YOU'RE *THE* BLAKE?
YOU KNOW WHO I AM?

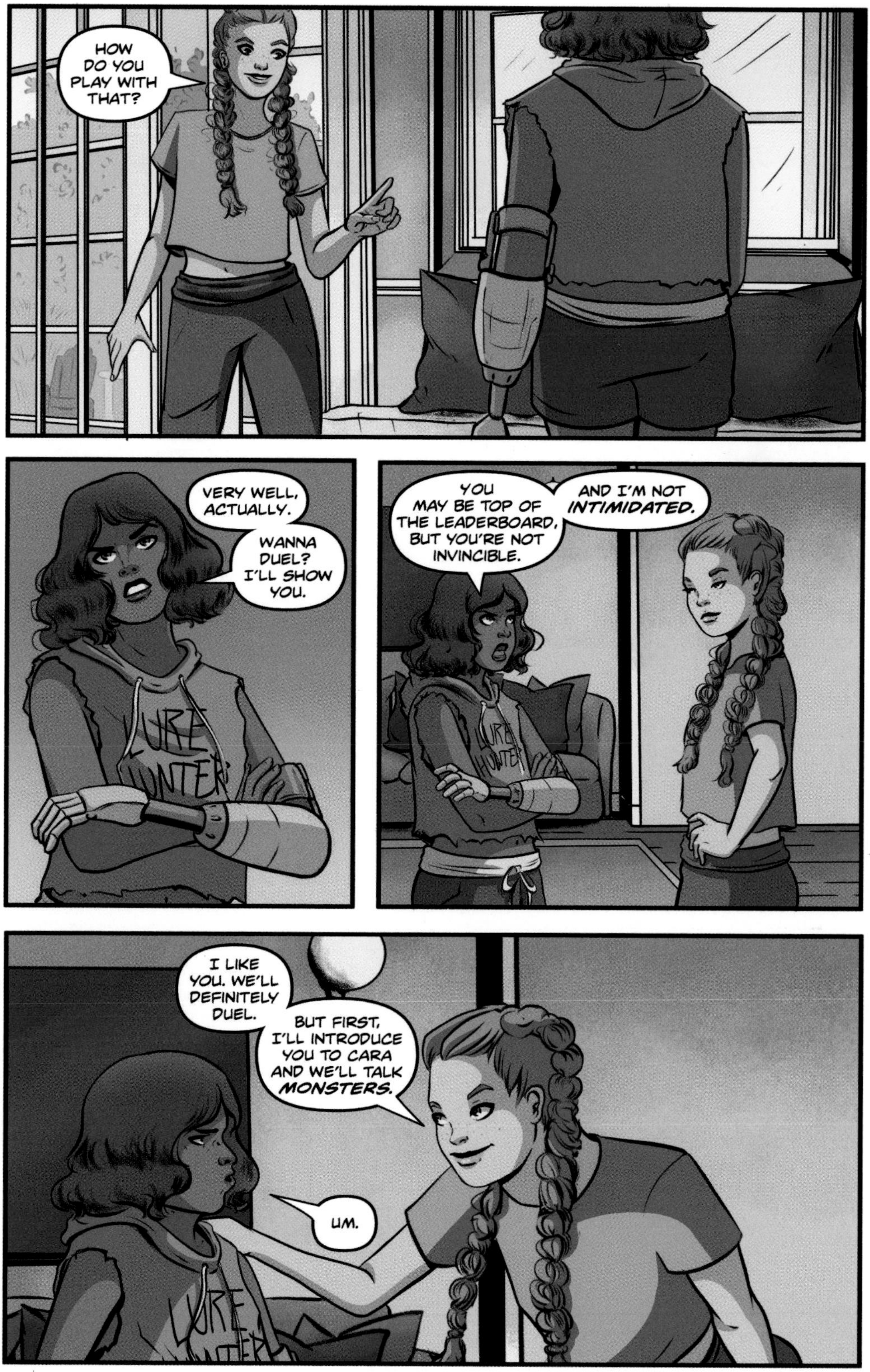
HOW DO YOU PLAY WITH THAT?
VERY WELL, ACTUALLY.
WANNA DUEL? I'LL SHOW YOU.
YOU MAY BE TOP OF THE LEADERBOARD, BUT YOU'RE NOT INVINCIBLE.
AND I'M NOT *INTIMIDATED.*
I LIKE YOU. WE'LL DEFINITELY DUEL.
BUT FIRST, I'LL INTRODUCE YOU TO CARA AND WE'LL TALK *MONSTERS.*
UM.

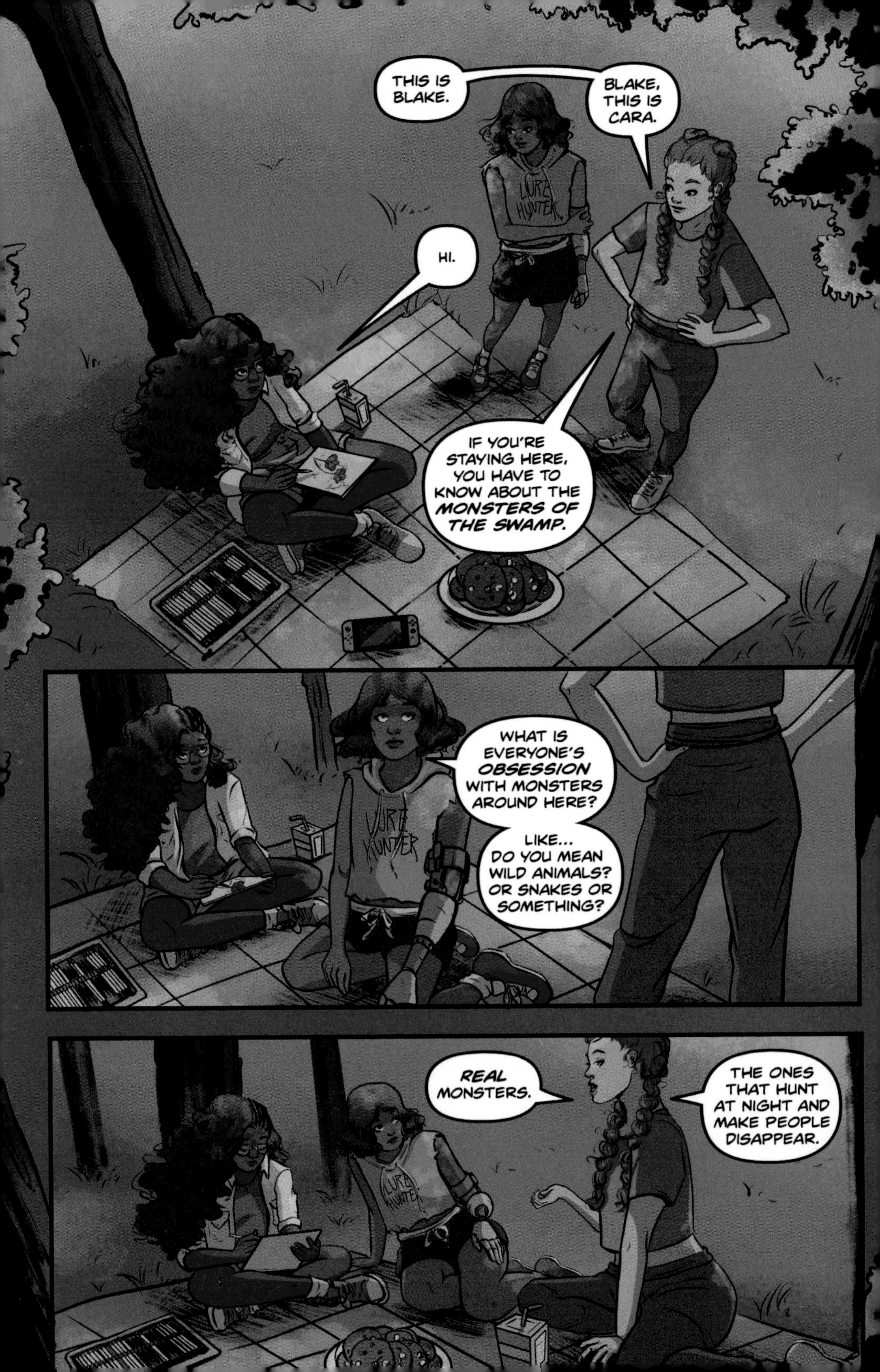
THIS IS BLAKE.
BLAKE, THIS IS CARA.
HI.
IF YOU'RE STAYING HERE, YOU HAVE TO KNOW ABOUT THE *MONSTERS OF THE SWAMP.*
WHAT IS EVERYONE'S *OBSESSION* WITH MONSTERS AROUND HERE?
LIKE... DO YOU MEAN WILD ANIMALS? OR SNAKES OR SOMETHING?
REAL MONSTERS.
THE ONES THAT HUNT AT NIGHT AND MAKE PEOPLE DISAPPEAR.
LURE HUNTER

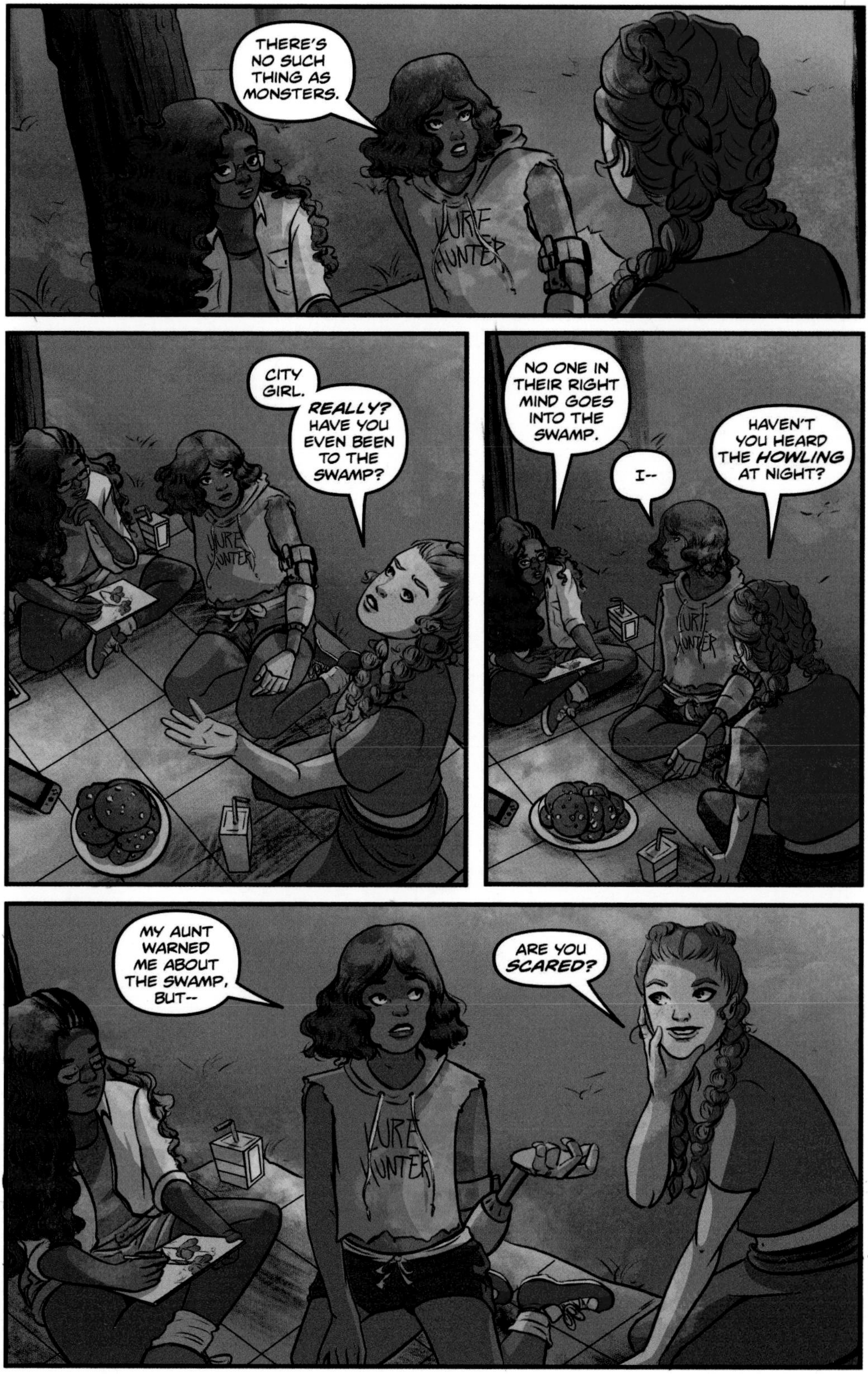
THERE'S NO SUCH THING AS MONSTERS.
LURE HUNTER
CITY GIRL.
REALLY? HAVE YOU EVEN BEEN TO THE SWAMP?
NO ONE IN THEIR RIGHT MIND GOES INTO THE SWAMP.
I--
HAVEN'T YOU HEARD THE HOWLING AT NIGHT?
MY AUNT WARNED ME ABOUT THE SWAMP, BUT--
ARE YOU SCARED?

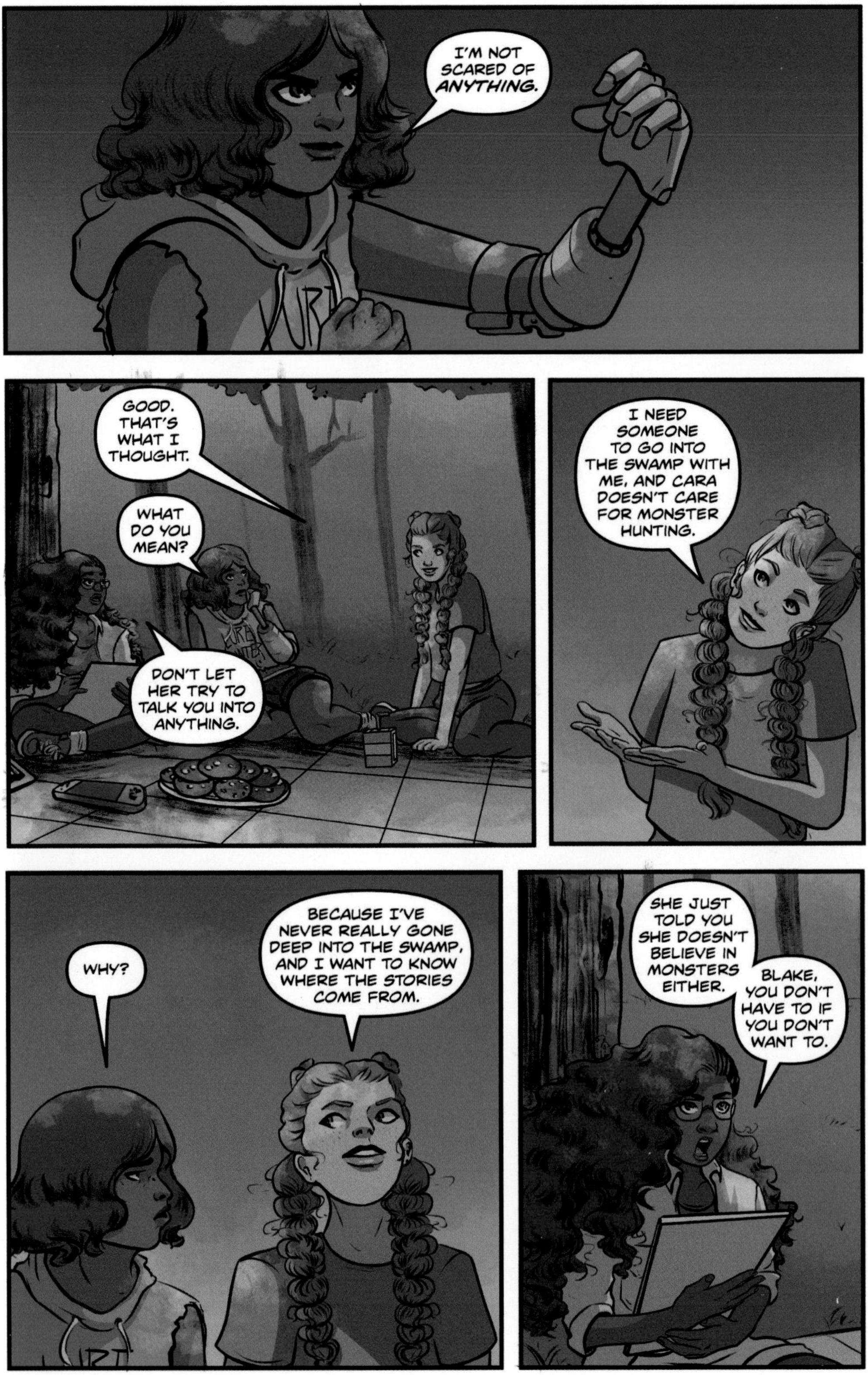
I'M NOT SCARED OF ANYTHING.
GOOD. THAT'S WHAT I THOUGHT.
WHAT DO YOU MEAN?
DON'T LET HER TRY TO TALK YOU INTO ANYTHING.
I NEED SOMEONE TO GO INTO THE SWAMP WITH ME, AND CARA DOESN'T CARE FOR MONSTER HUNTING.
WHY?
BECAUSE I'VE NEVER REALLY GONE DEEP INTO THE SWAMP, AND I WANT TO KNOW WHERE THE STORIES COME FROM.
SHE JUST TOLD YOU SHE DOESN'T BELIEVE IN MONSTERS EITHER.
BLAKE, YOU DON'T HAVE TO IF YOU DON'T WANT TO.

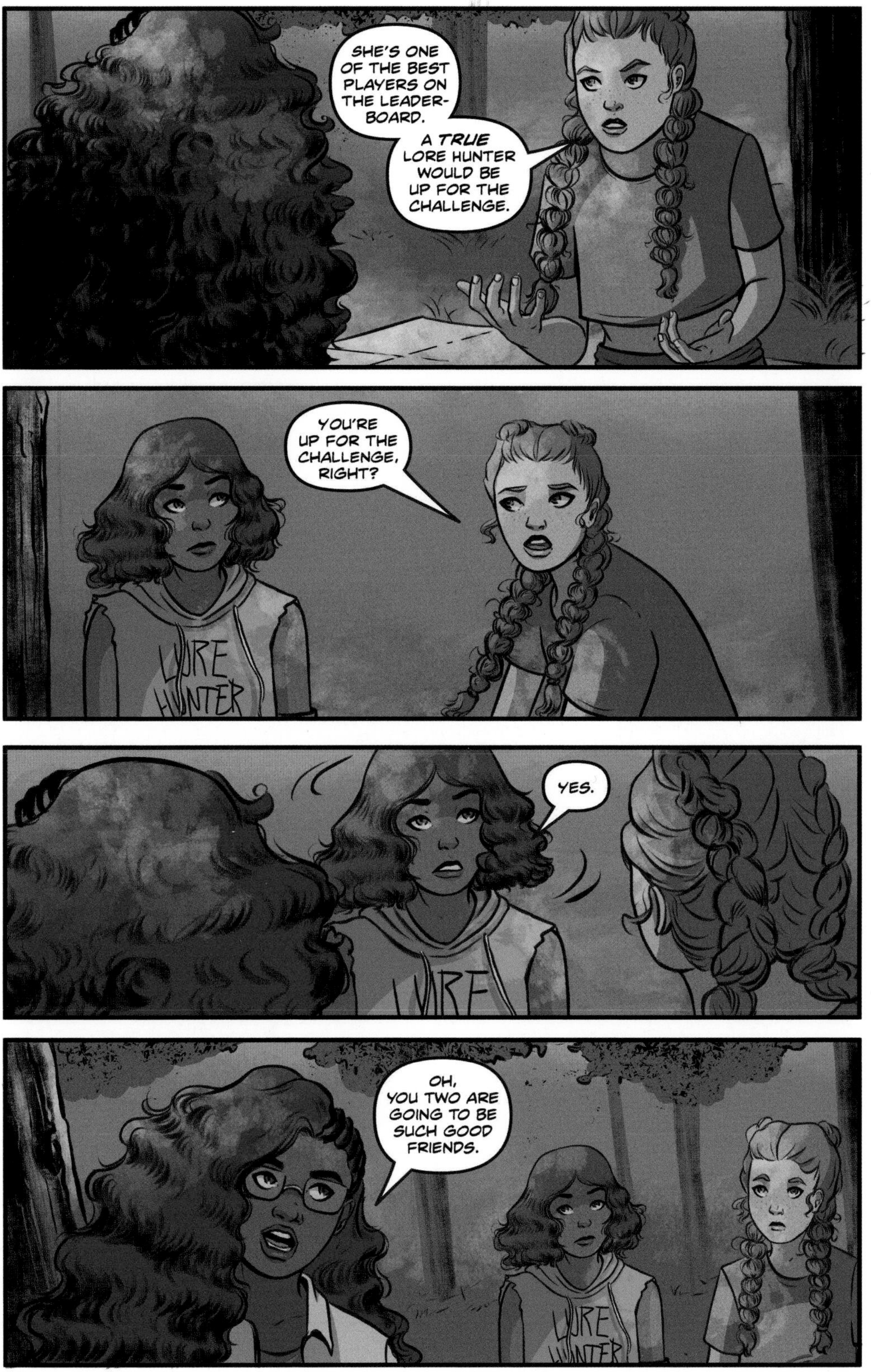
SHE'S ONE OF THE BEST PLAYERS ON THE LEADER-BOARD.
A *TRUE* LORE HUNTER WOULD BE UP FOR THE CHALLENGE.
LORE HUNTER
YOU'RE UP FOR THE CHALLENGE, RIGHT?
YES.
OH, YOU TWO ARE GOING TO BE SUCH GOOD FRIENDS.
LORE HUNTER

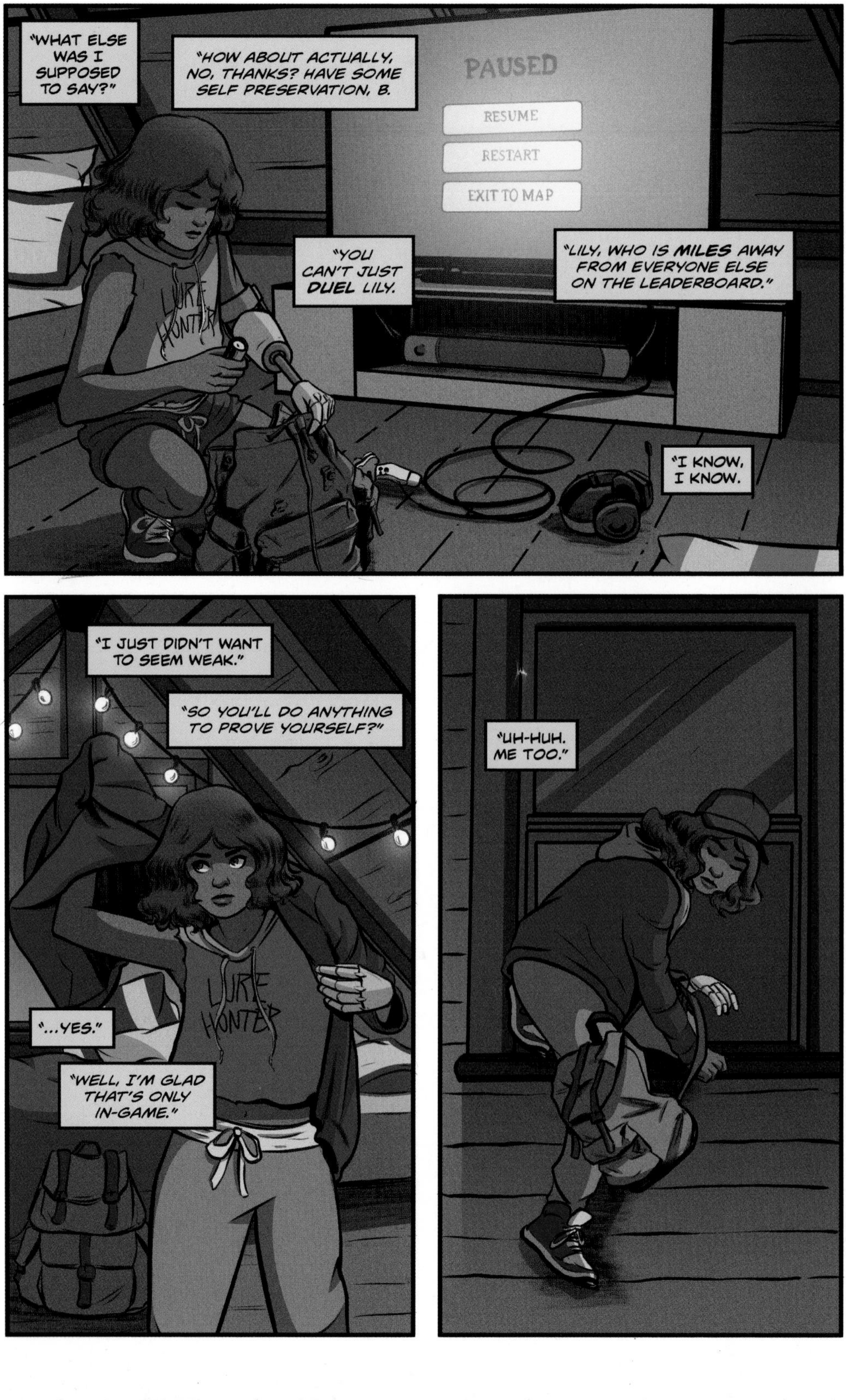
"WHAT ELSE WAS I SUPPOSED TO SAY?"
"HOW ABOUT ACTUALLY, NO, THANKS? HAVE SOME SELF PRESERVATION, B.
PAUSED
RESUME
RESTART
EXIT TO MAP
"YOU CAN'T JUST **DUEL** LILY.
"LILY, WHO IS **MILES** AWAY FROM EVERYONE ELSE ON THE LEADERBOARD."
"I KNOW, I KNOW.
"I JUST DIDN'T WANT TO SEEM WEAK."
"SO YOU'LL DO ANYTHING TO PROVE YOURSELF?"
"...YES."
"WELL, I'M GLAD THAT'S ONLY IN-GAME."
"UH-HUH. ME TOO."

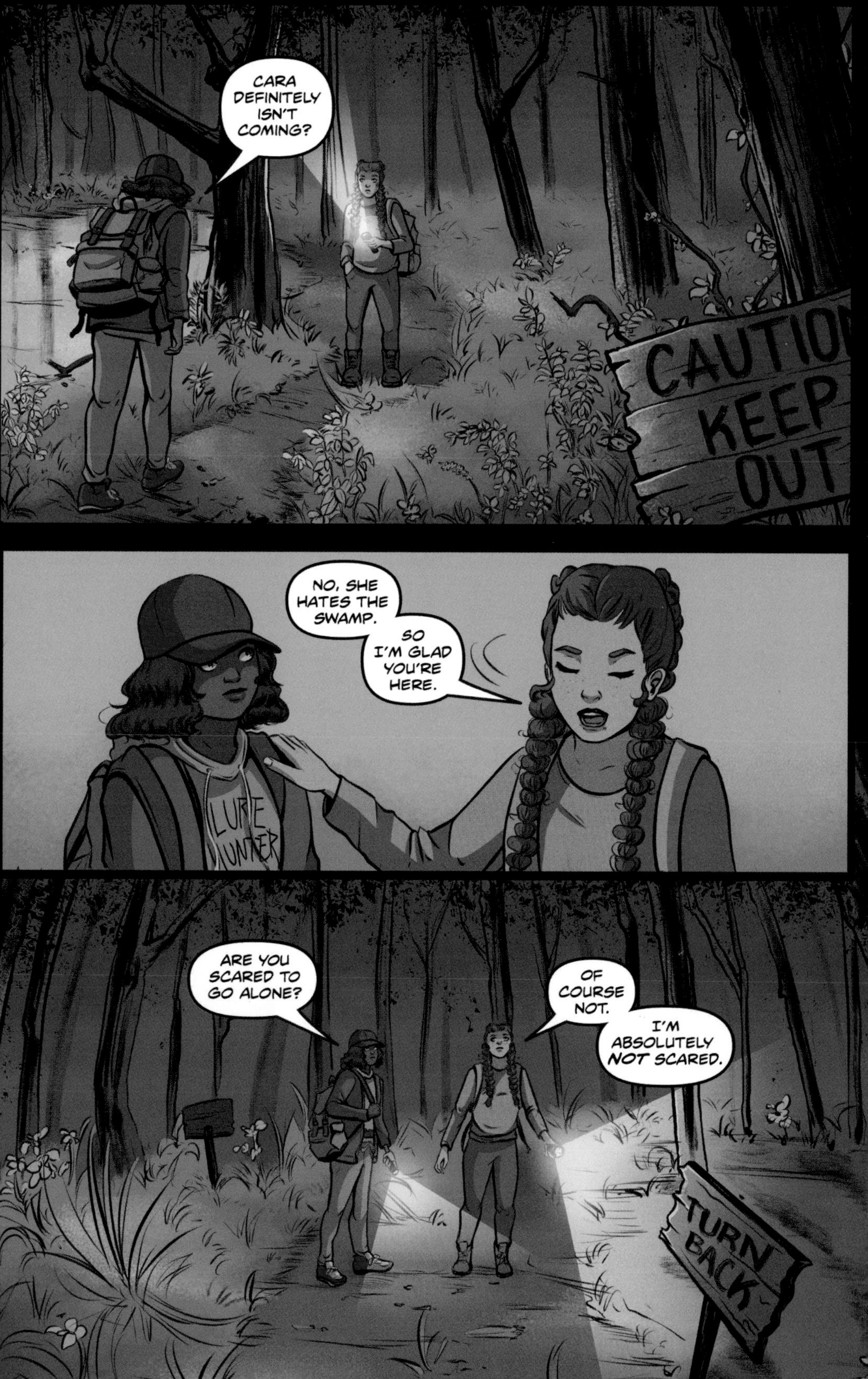
CARA DEFINITELY ISN'T COMING?
CAUTION KEEP OUT
NO, SHE HATES THE SWAMP.
SO I'M GLAD YOU'RE HERE.
ARE YOU SCARED TO GO ALONE?
OF COURSE NOT.
I'M ABSOLUTELY *NOT* SCARED.
TURN BACK

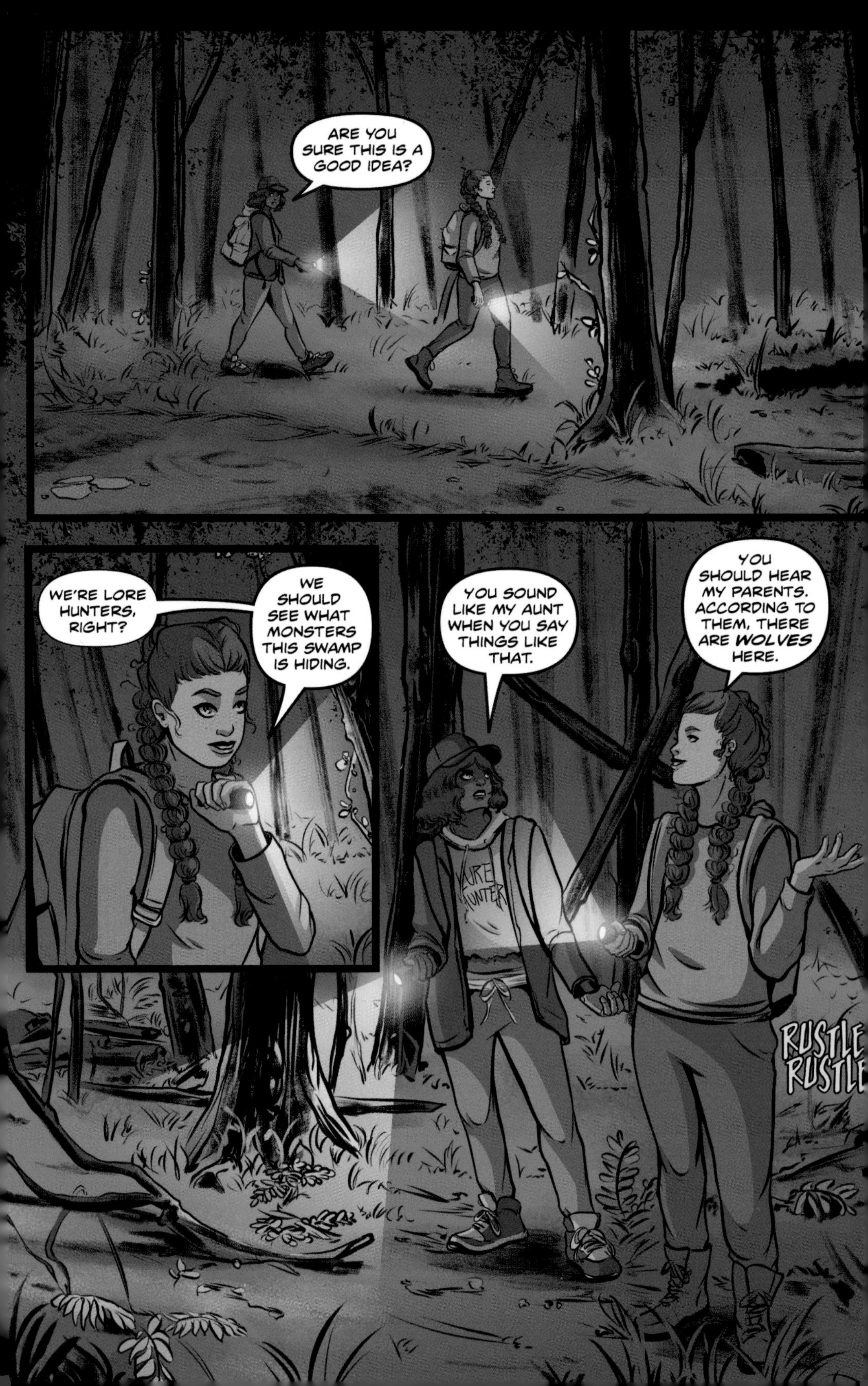
ARE YOU SURE THIS IS A GOOD IDEA?
WE'RE LORE HUNTERS, RIGHT?
WE SHOULD SEE WHAT MONSTERS THIS SWAMP IS HIDING.
YOU SOUND LIKE MY AUNT WHEN YOU SAY THINGS LIKE THAT.
YOU SHOULD HEAR MY PARENTS. ACCORDING TO THEM, THERE ARE **WOLVES** HERE.
RUSTLE RUSTLE

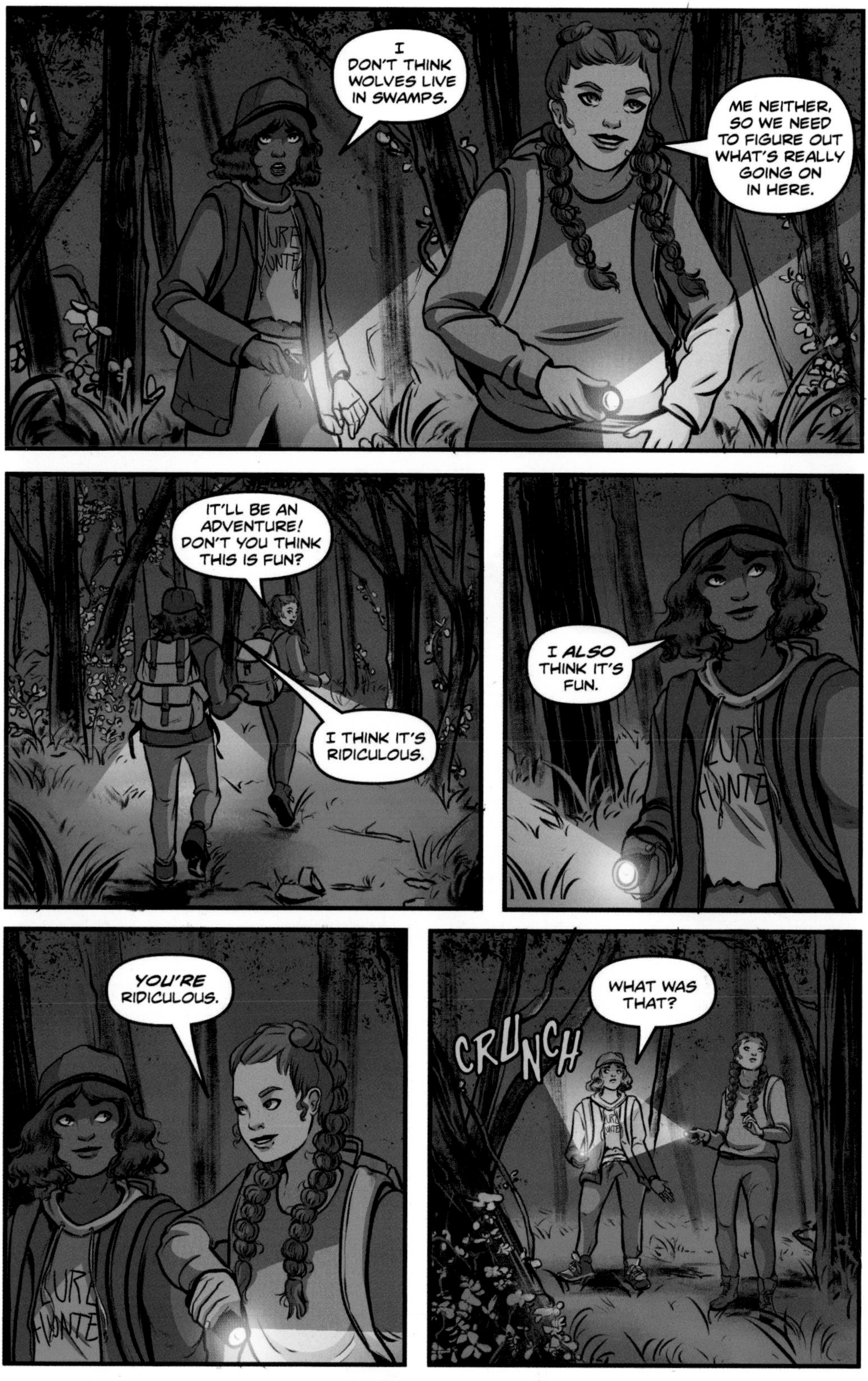
I DON'T THINK WOLVES LIVE IN SWAMPS.
ME NEITHER, SO WE NEED TO FIGURE OUT WHAT'S REALLY GOING ON IN HERE.
IT'LL BE AN ADVENTURE! DON'T YOU THINK THIS IS FUN?
I THINK IT'S RIDICULOUS.
I *ALSO* THINK IT'S FUN.
YOU'RE RIDICULOUS.
CRUNCH
WHAT WAS THAT?

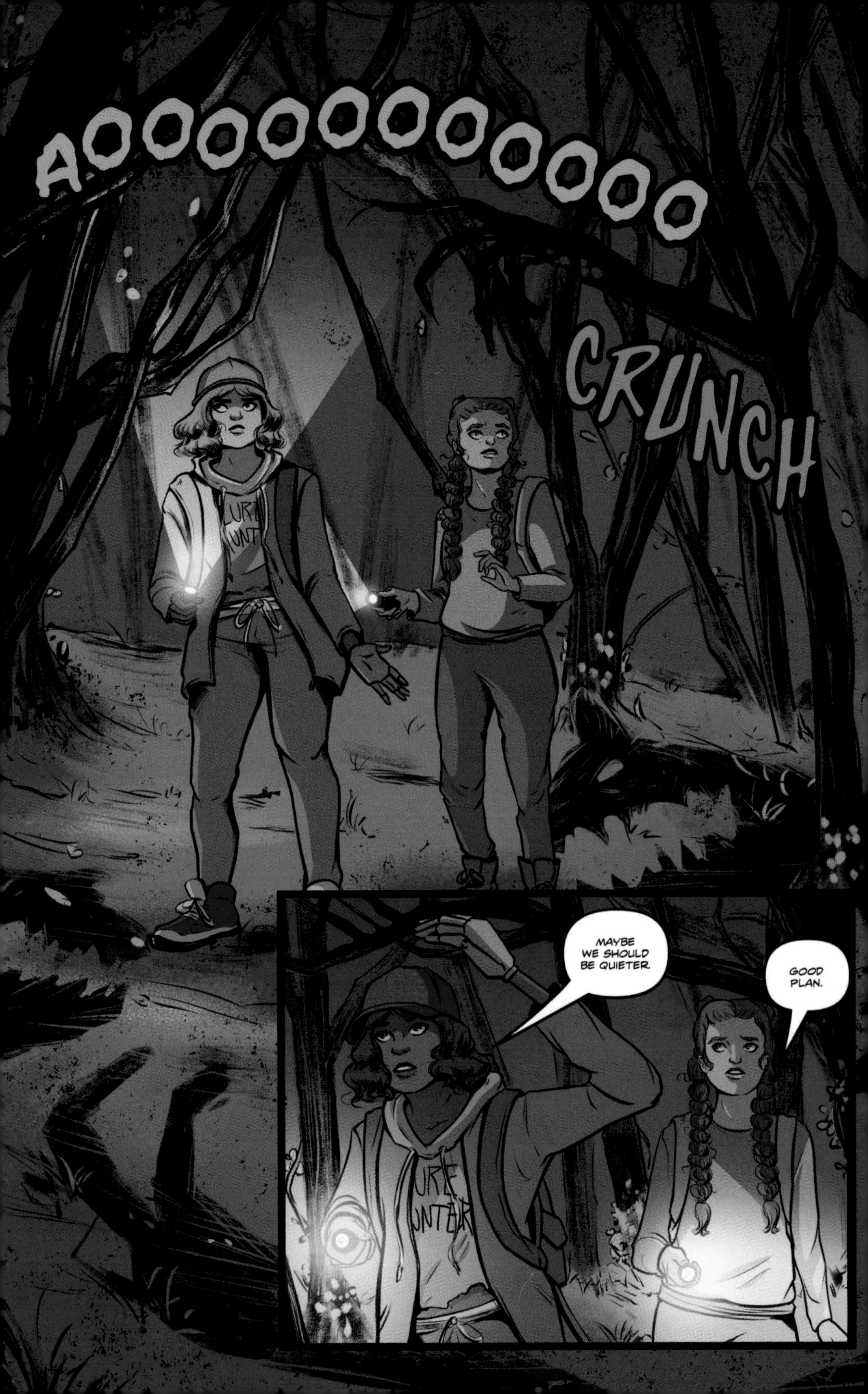
AOOOOOOOOOOO
CRUNCH
MAYBE WE SHOULD BE QUIETER.
GOOD PLAN.

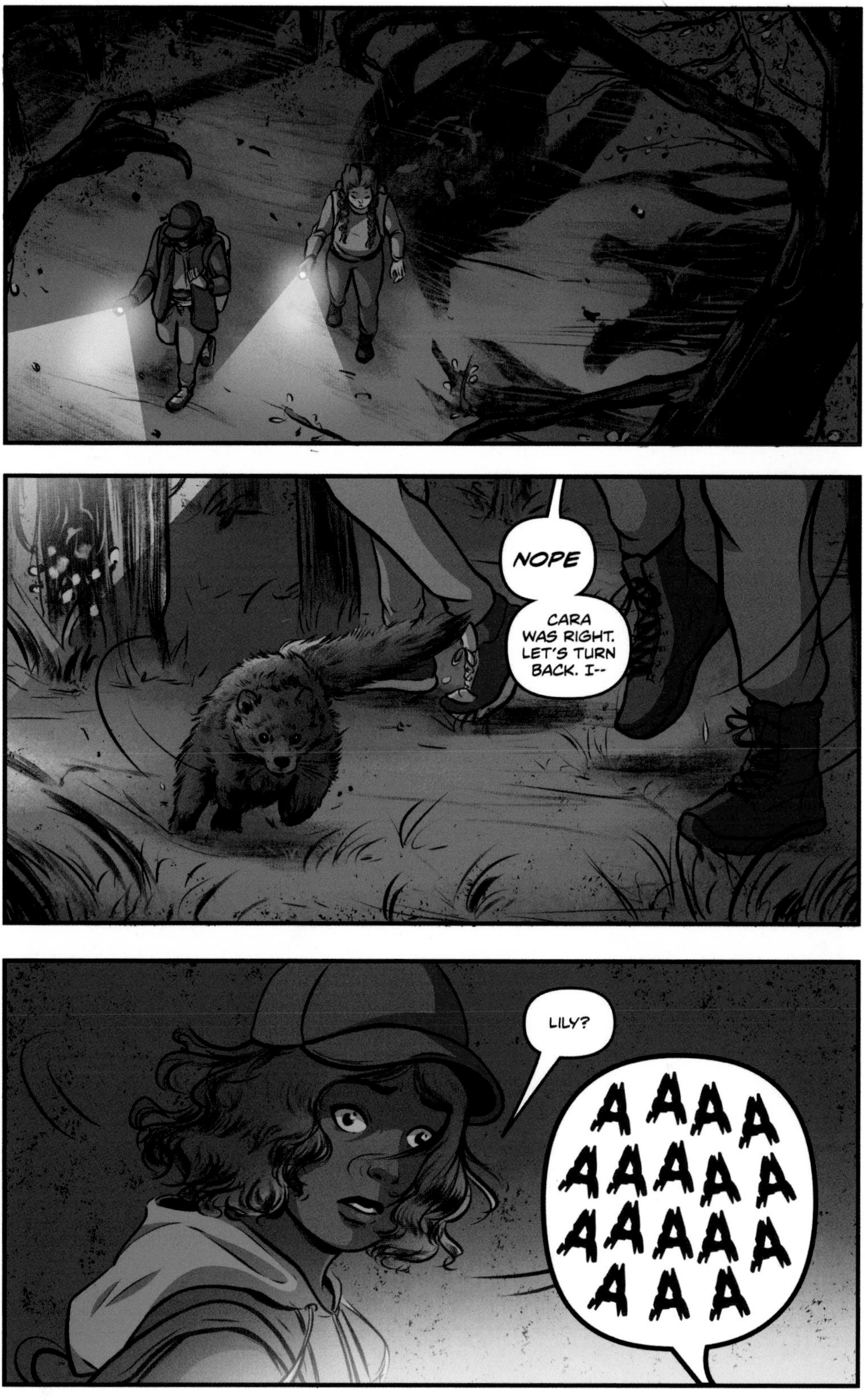
NOPE
CARA WAS RIGHT. LET'S TURN BACK. I--
LILY?
AAAAAAAAAAAAAAAAAA

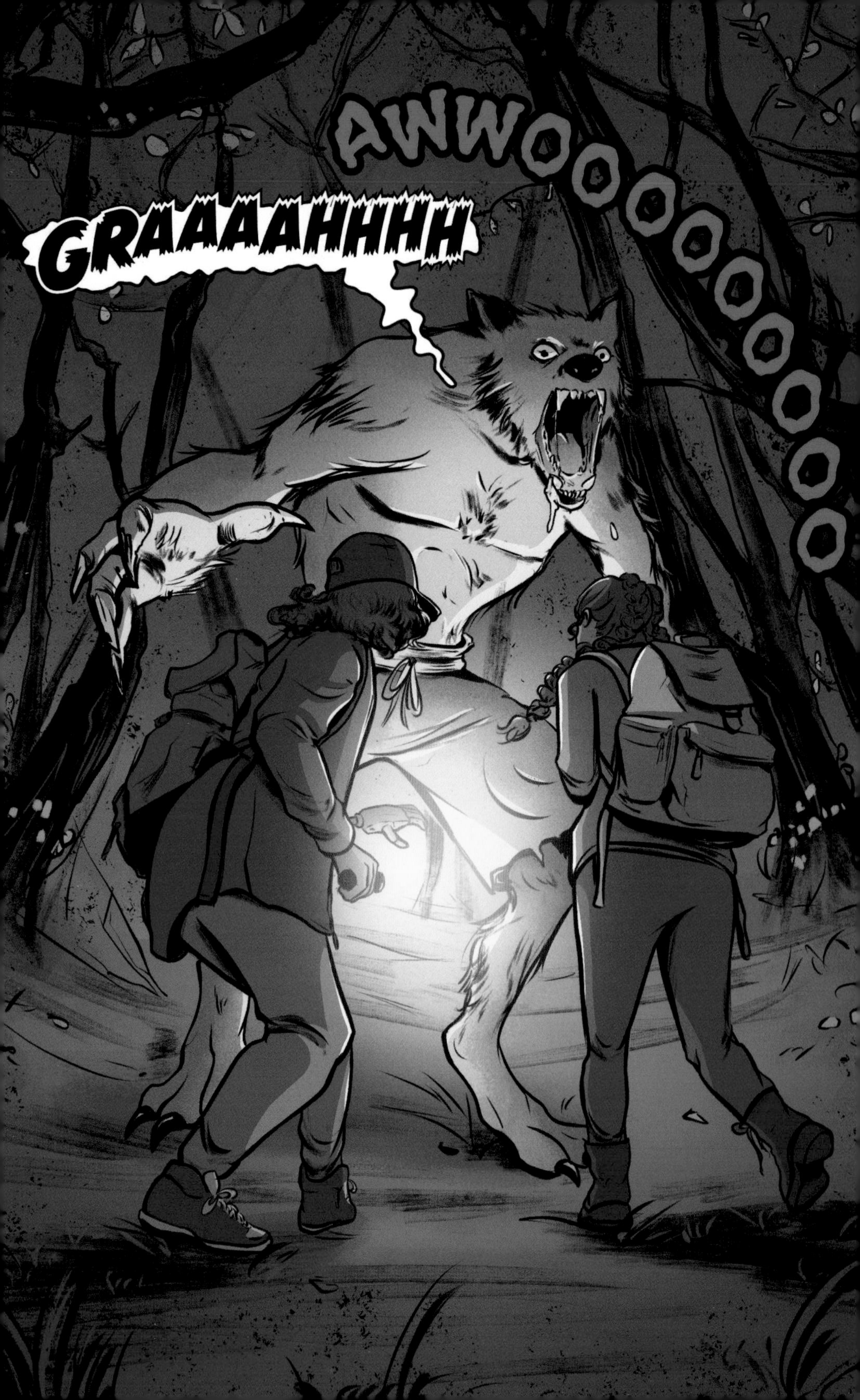
AWWOOOOOOOOOOOO
GRAAAAAHHHH

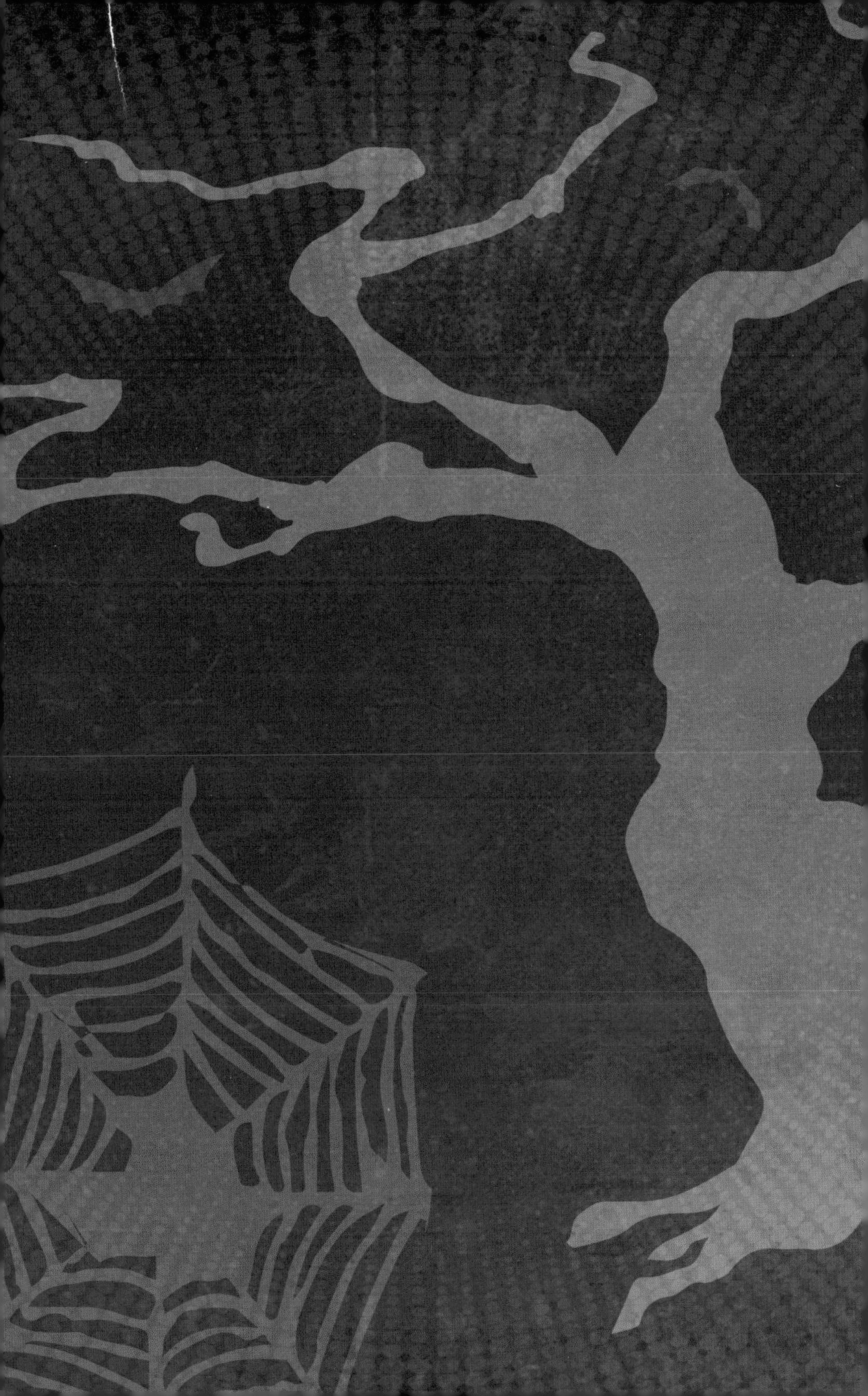

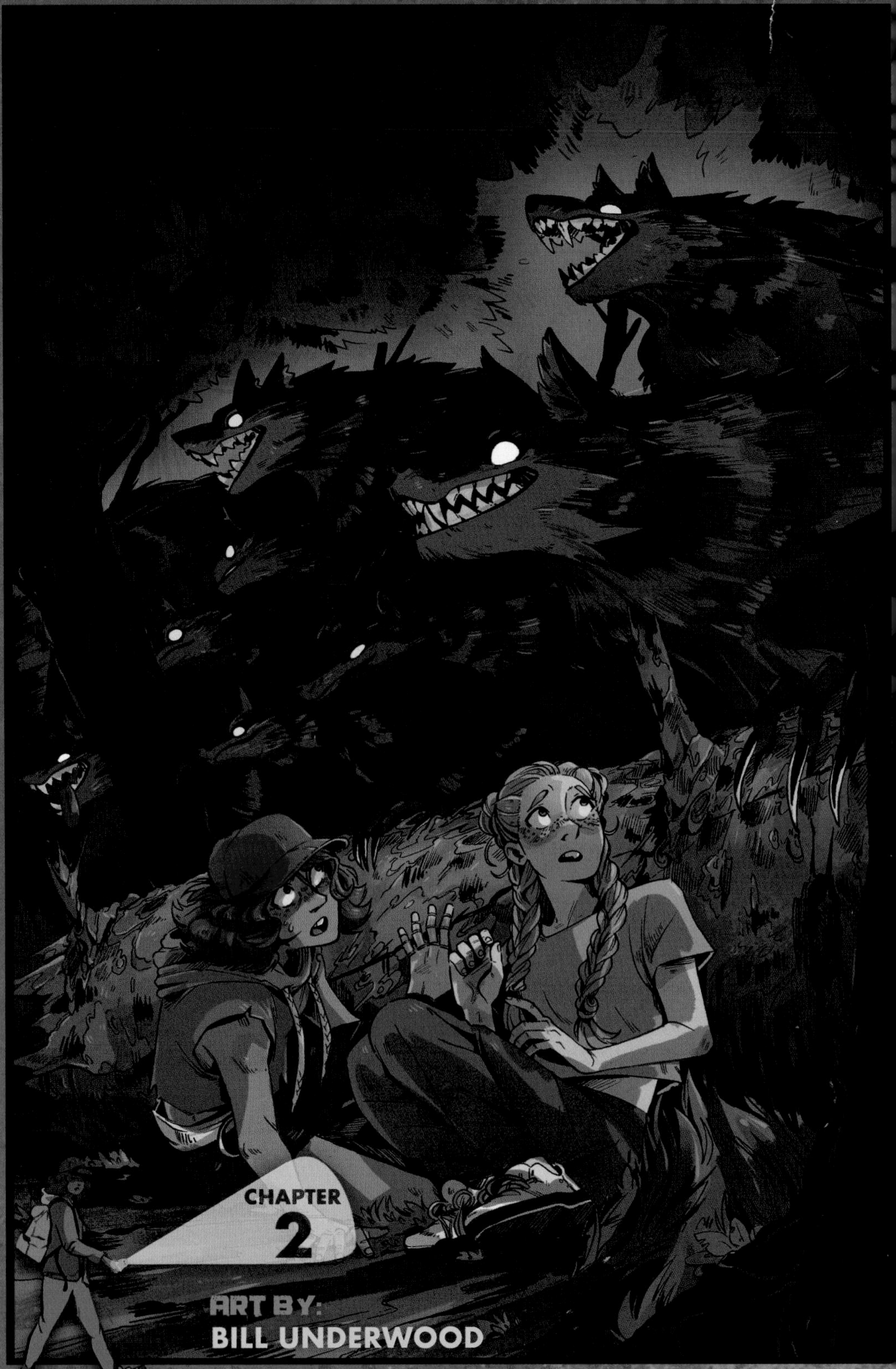
CHAPTER
2
ART BY:
BILL UNDERWOOD

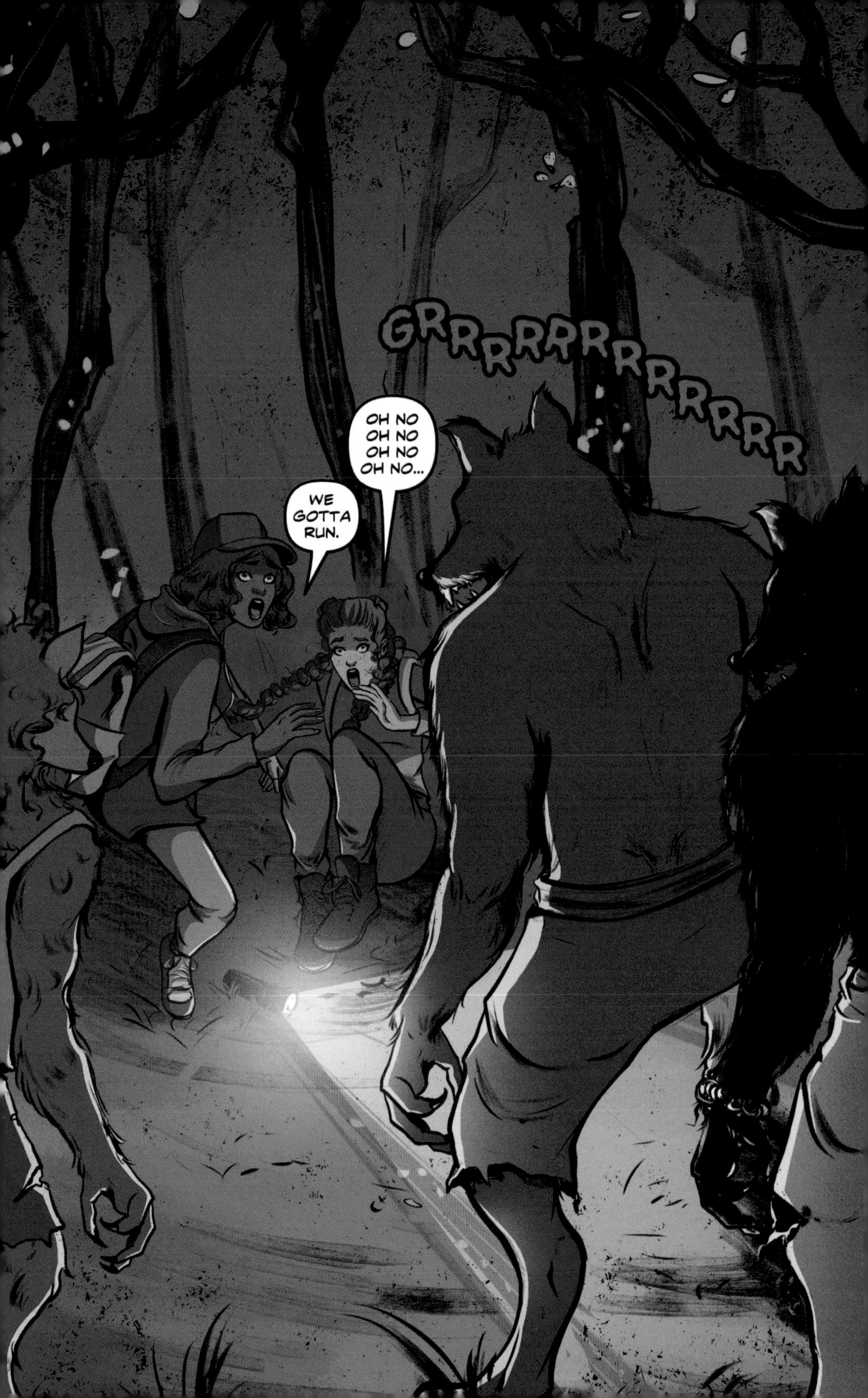
GRRRRRRRRRRRRRR
WE GOTTA RUN.
OH NO OH NO OH NO OH NO...

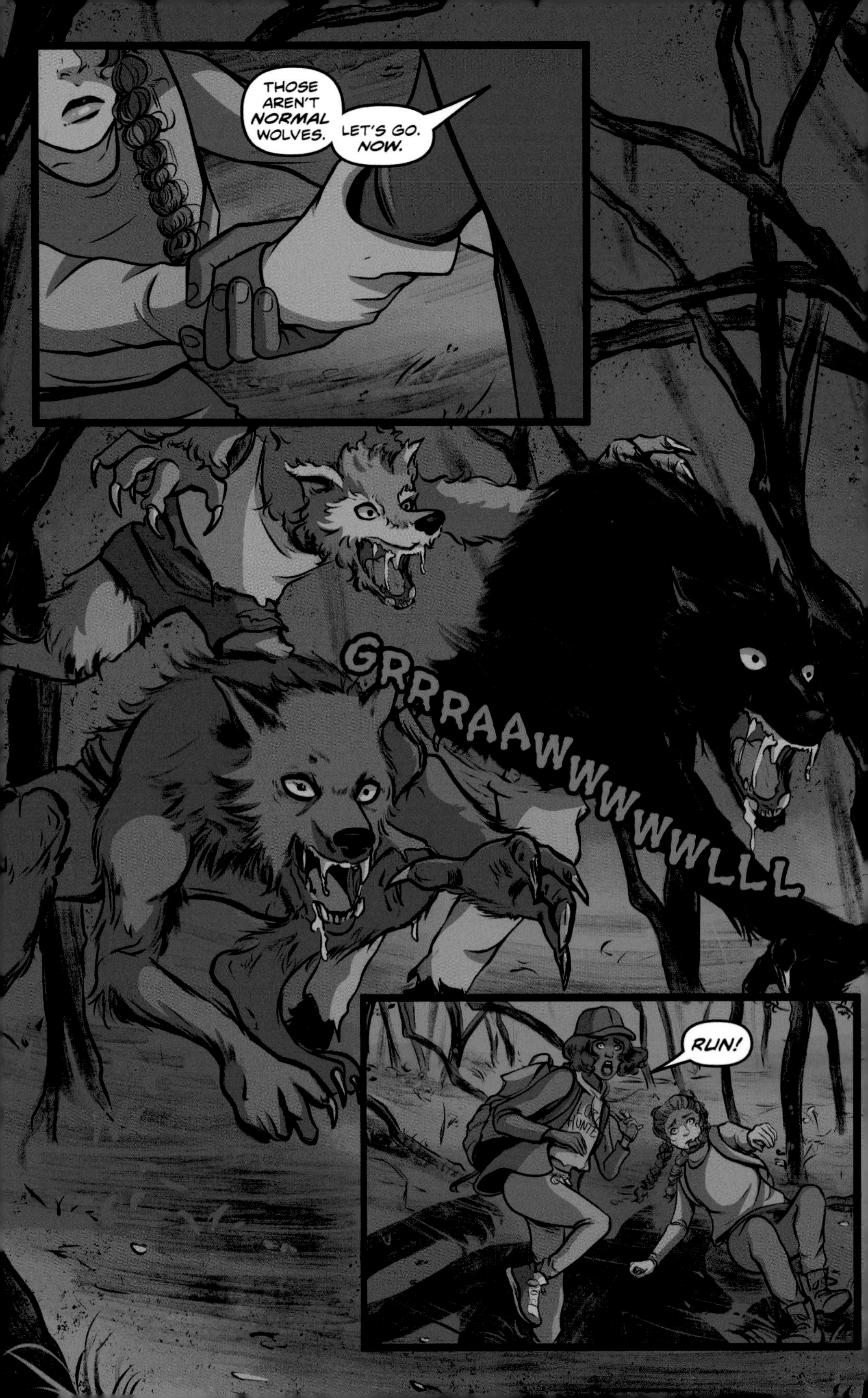
THOSE AREN'T NORMAL WOLVES.
LET'S GO. NOW.
GRRRAAWWWWWLLL
RUN!
LORE HUNTE

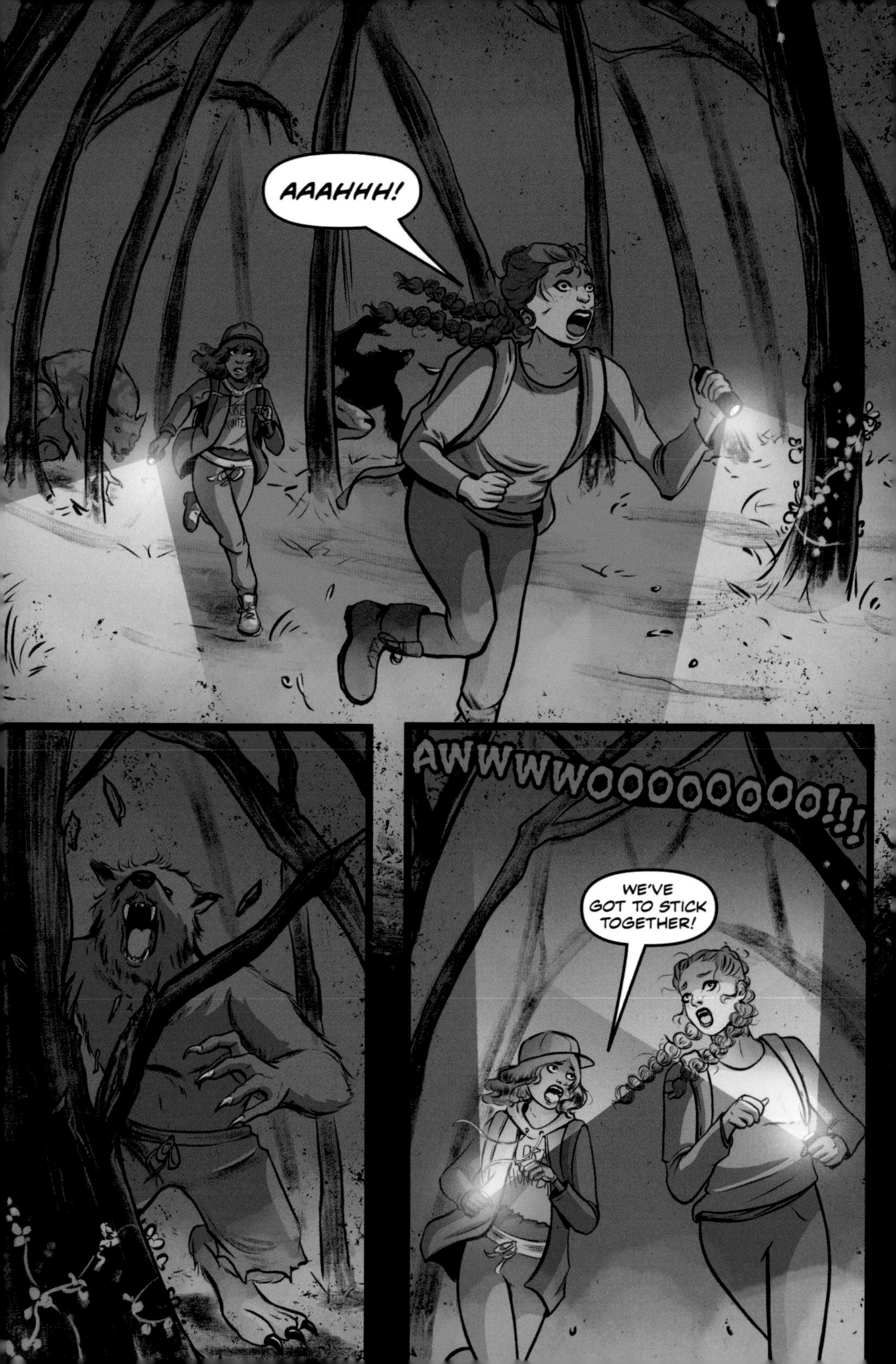
AAAHHH!
AWWWWOOOOOOOOOO!!!
WE'VE GOT TO STICK TOGETHER!

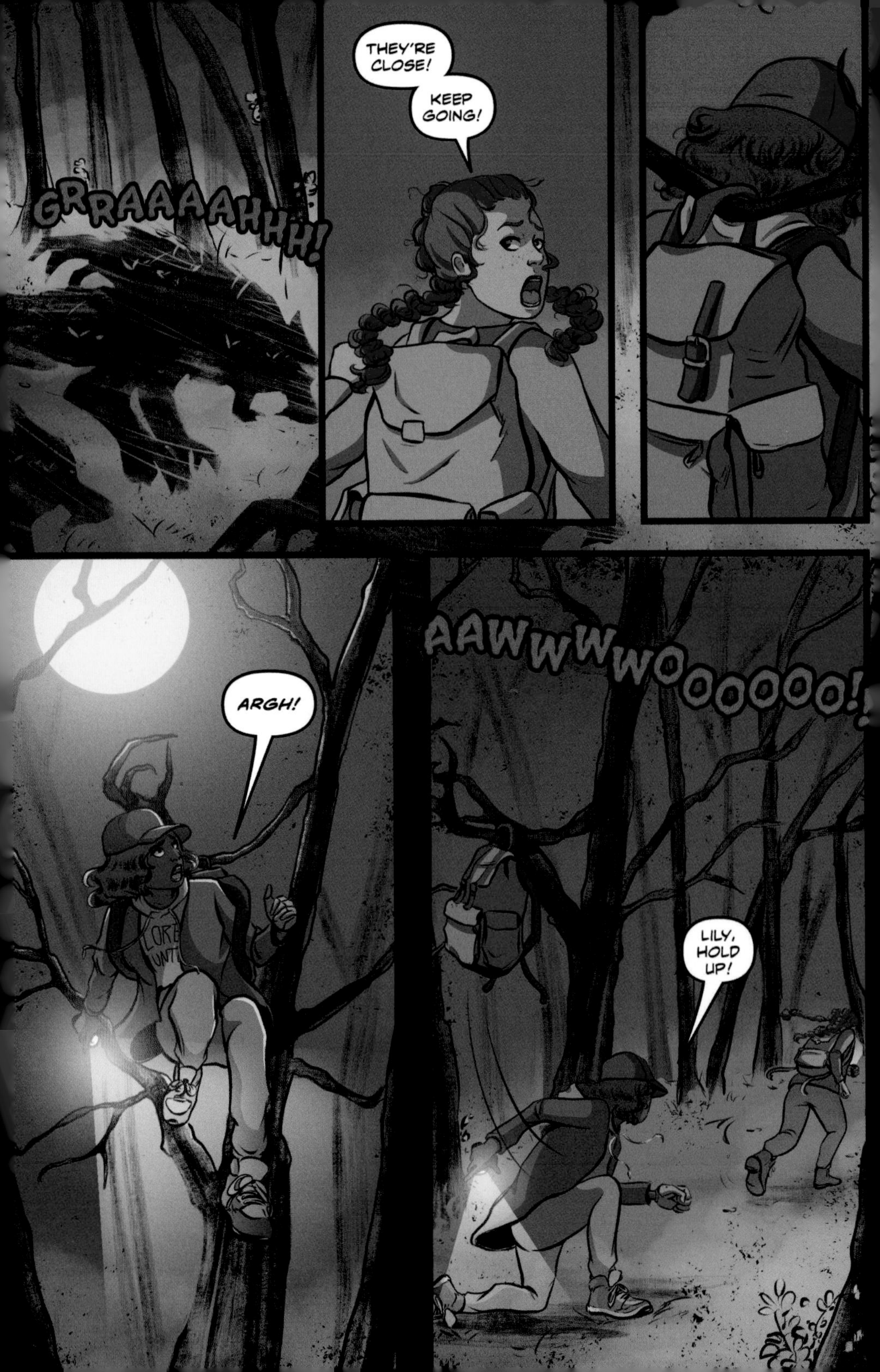
GRRAAAAAHHHH!
THEY'RE CLOSE!
KEEP GOING!
ARGH!
AAWWWWWOOOOOOO!!
LILY, HOLD UP!

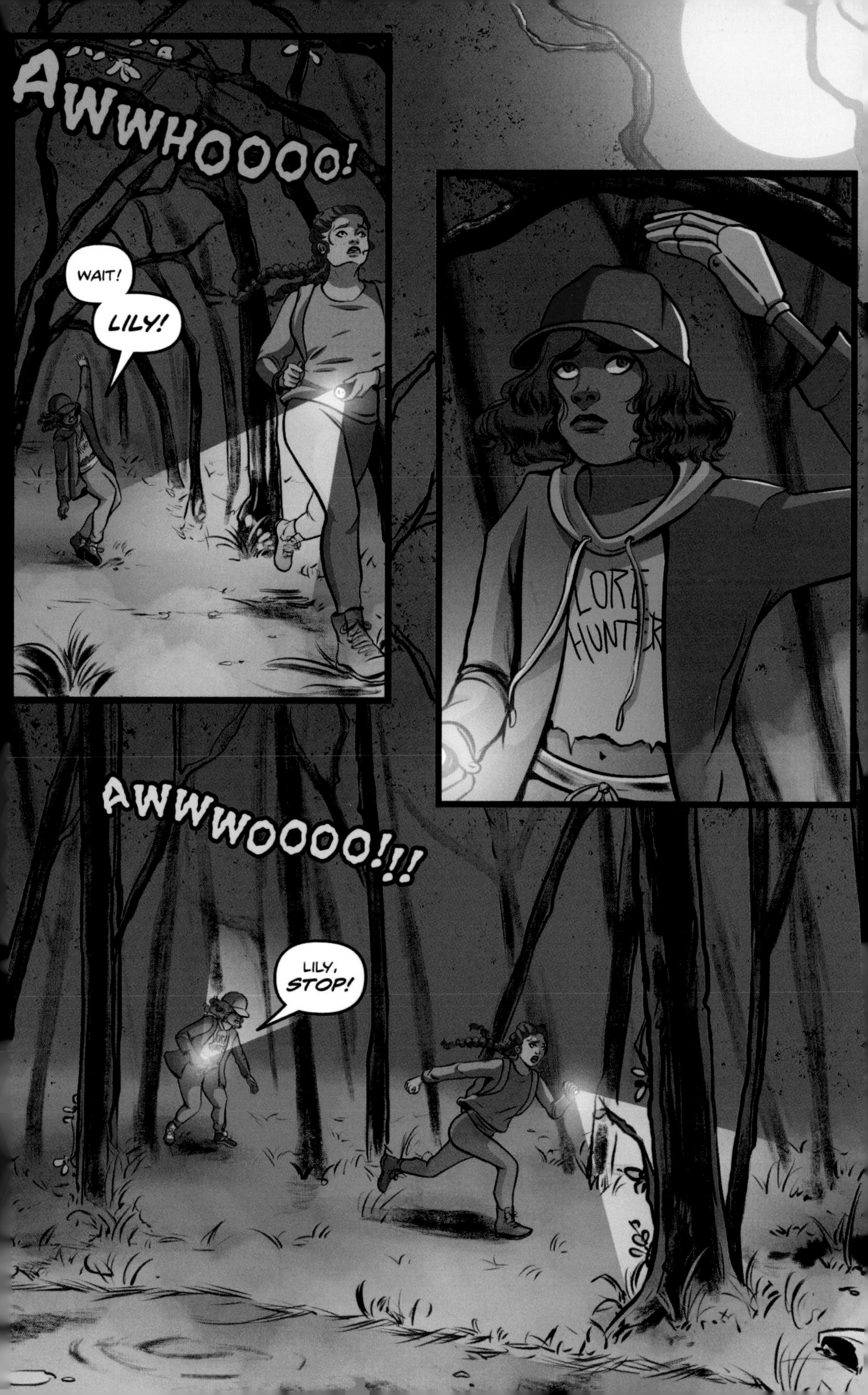
AWWHOOOO!
WAIT!
LILY!
LORE HUNTER
AWWWOOOO!!!
LILY, STOP!

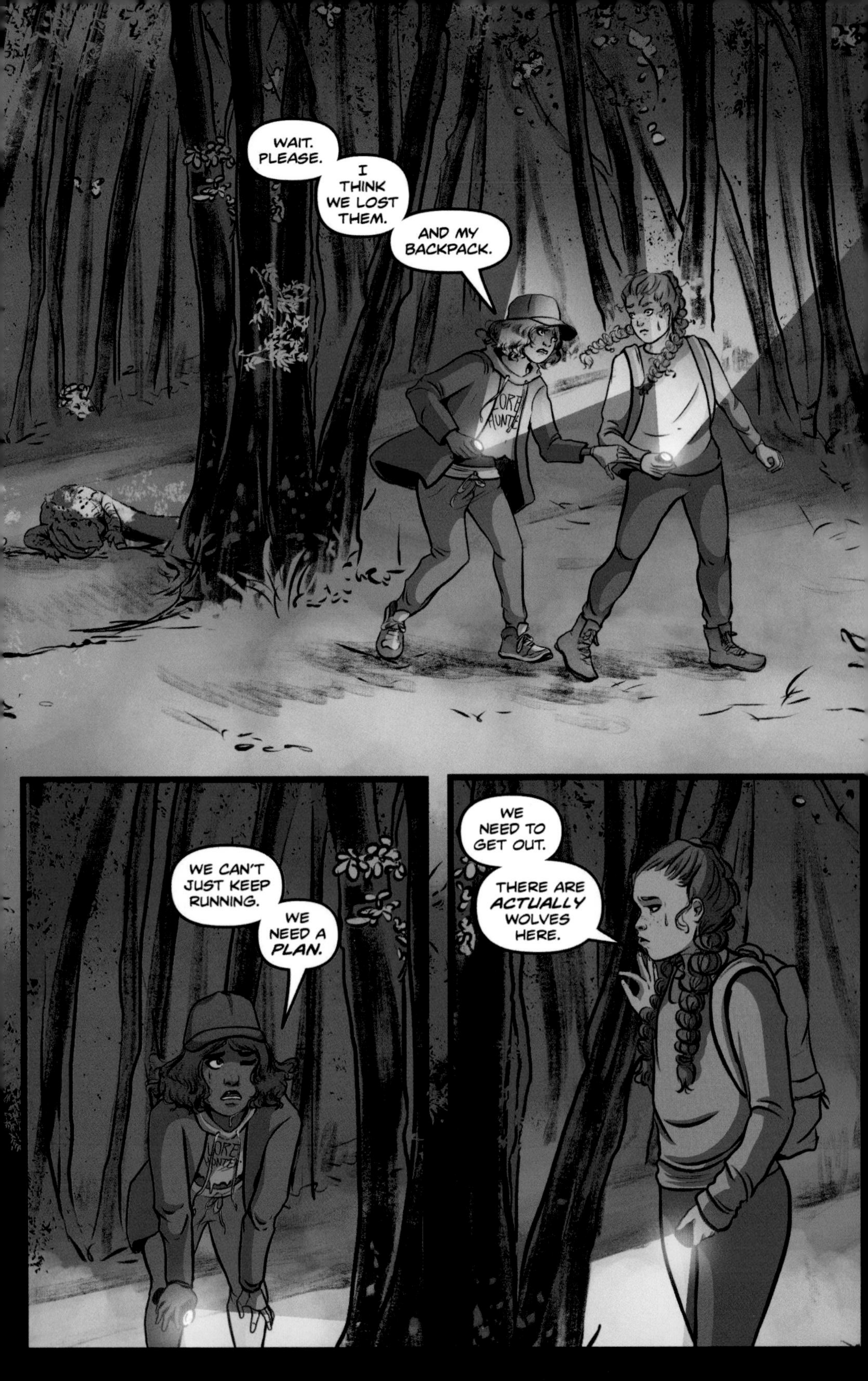
WAIT. PLEASE.
I THINK WE LOST THEM.
AND MY BACKPACK.
WE CAN'T JUST KEEP RUNNING.
WE NEED A *PLAN.*
WE NEED TO GET OUT.
THERE ARE *ACTUALLY* WOLVES HERE.

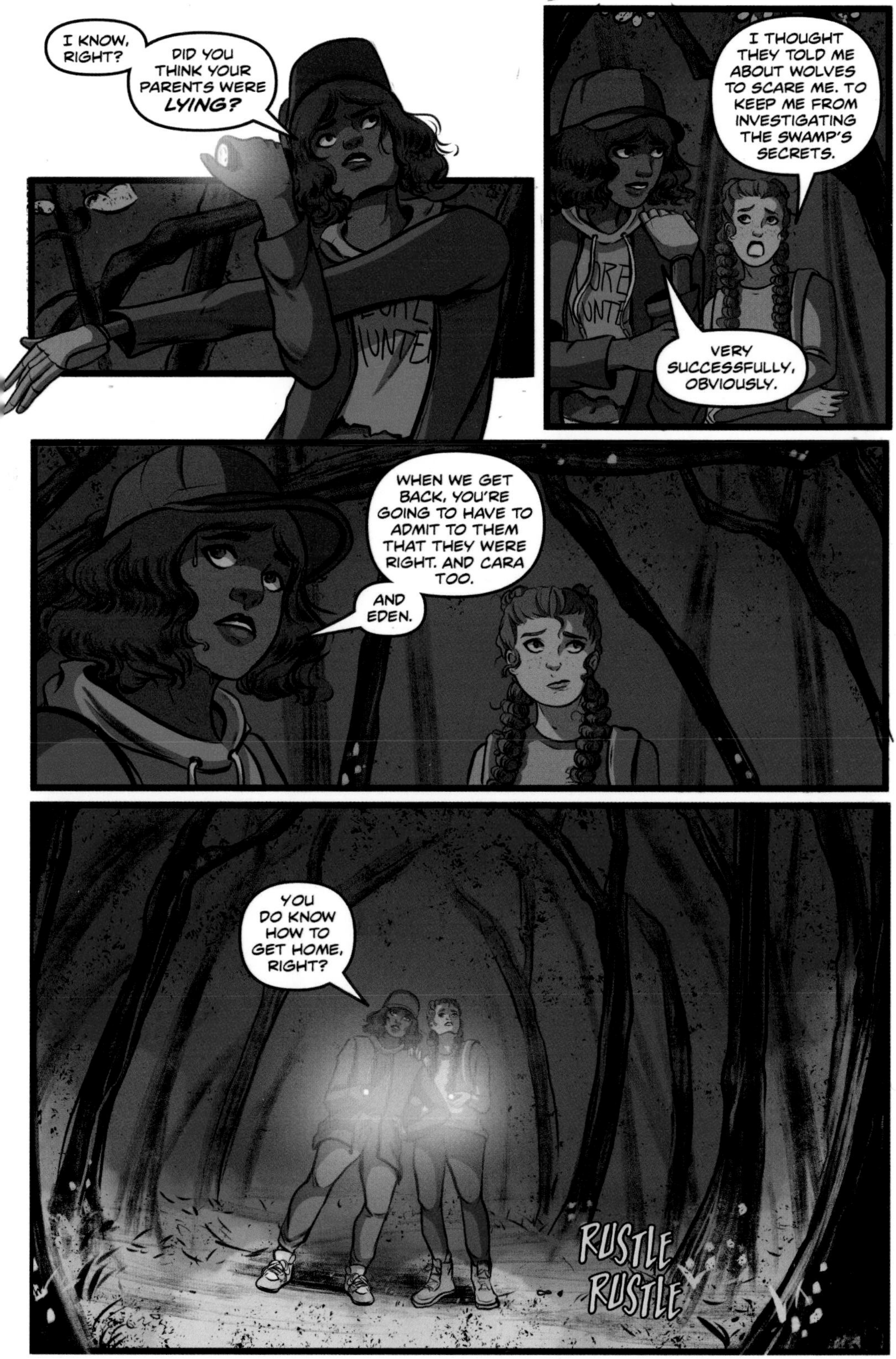
I KNOW, RIGHT?
DID YOU THINK YOUR PARENTS WERE *LYING?*
I THOUGHT THEY TOLD ME ABOUT WOLVES TO SCARE ME. TO KEEP ME FROM INVESTIGATING THE SWAMP'S SECRETS.
VERY SUCCESSFULLY, OBVIOUSLY.
WHEN WE GET BACK, YOU'RE GOING TO HAVE TO ADMIT TO THEM THAT THEY WERE RIGHT. AND CARA TOO.
AND EDEN.
YOU DO KNOW HOW TO GET HOME, RIGHT?
RUSTLE RUSTLE

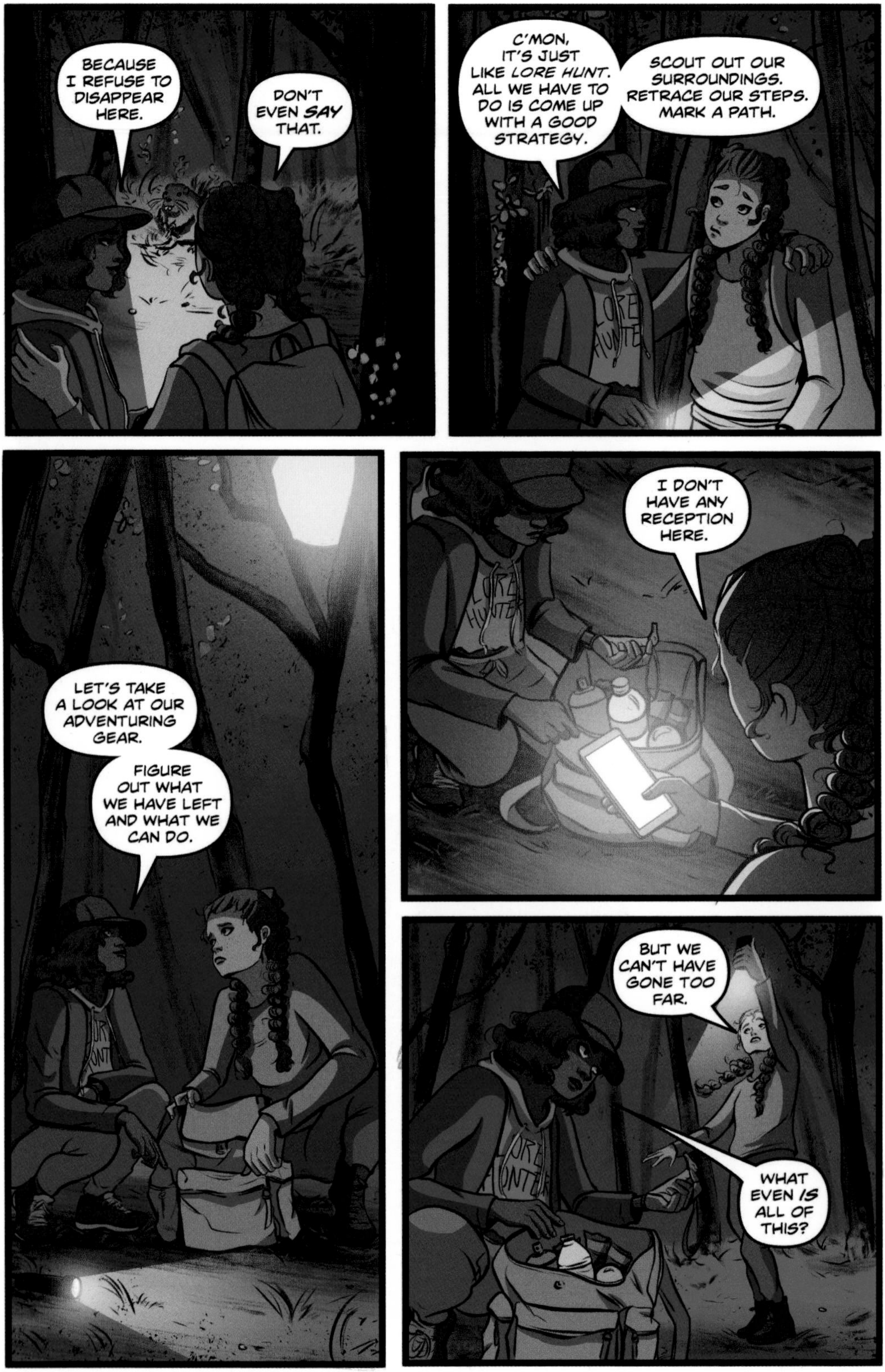
BECAUSE I REFUSE TO DISAPPEAR HERE.
DON'T EVEN *SAY* THAT.
C'MON, IT'S JUST LIKE *LORE HUNT*. ALL WE HAVE TO DO IS COME UP WITH A GOOD STRATEGY.
SCOUT OUT OUR SURROUNDINGS. RETRACE OUR STEPS. MARK A PATH.
LORE HUNTER
LET'S TAKE A LOOK AT OUR ADVENTURING GEAR.
FIGURE OUT WHAT WE HAVE LEFT AND WHAT WE CAN DO.
I DON'T HAVE ANY RECEPTION HERE.
BUT WE CAN'T HAVE GONE TOO FAR.
WHAT EVEN *IS* ALL OF THIS?

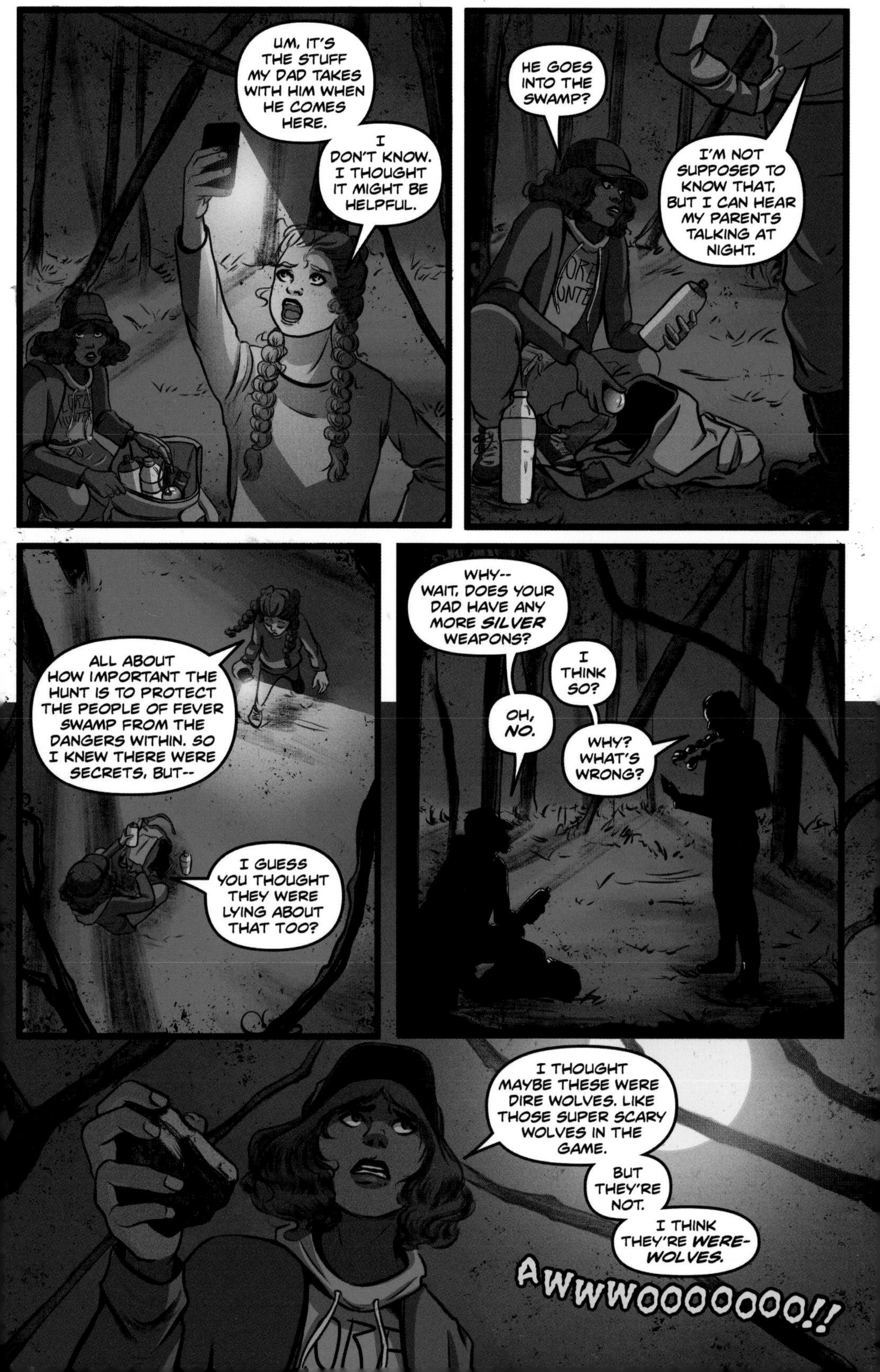
UM, IT'S THE STUFF MY DAD TAKES WITH HIM WHEN HE COMES HERE.
I DON'T KNOW. I THOUGHT IT MIGHT BE HELPFUL.
HE GOES INTO THE SWAMP?
I'M NOT SUPPOSED TO KNOW THAT, BUT I CAN HEAR MY PARENTS TALKING AT NIGHT.
ALL ABOUT HOW IMPORTANT THE HUNT IS TO PROTECT THE PEOPLE OF FEVER SWAMP FROM THE DANGERS WITHIN. SO I KNEW THERE WERE SECRETS, BUT--
I GUESS YOU THOUGHT THEY WERE LYING ABOUT THAT TOO?
WHY-- WAIT, DOES YOUR DAD HAVE ANY MORE *SILVER* WEAPONS?
I THINK SO?
OH, *NO.*
WHY? WHAT'S WRONG?
I THOUGHT MAYBE THESE WERE DIRE WOLVES. LIKE THOSE SUPER SCARY WOLVES IN THE GAME.
BUT THEY'RE NOT.
I THINK THEY'RE *WERE-WOLVES.*
AWWWOOOOOOO!!

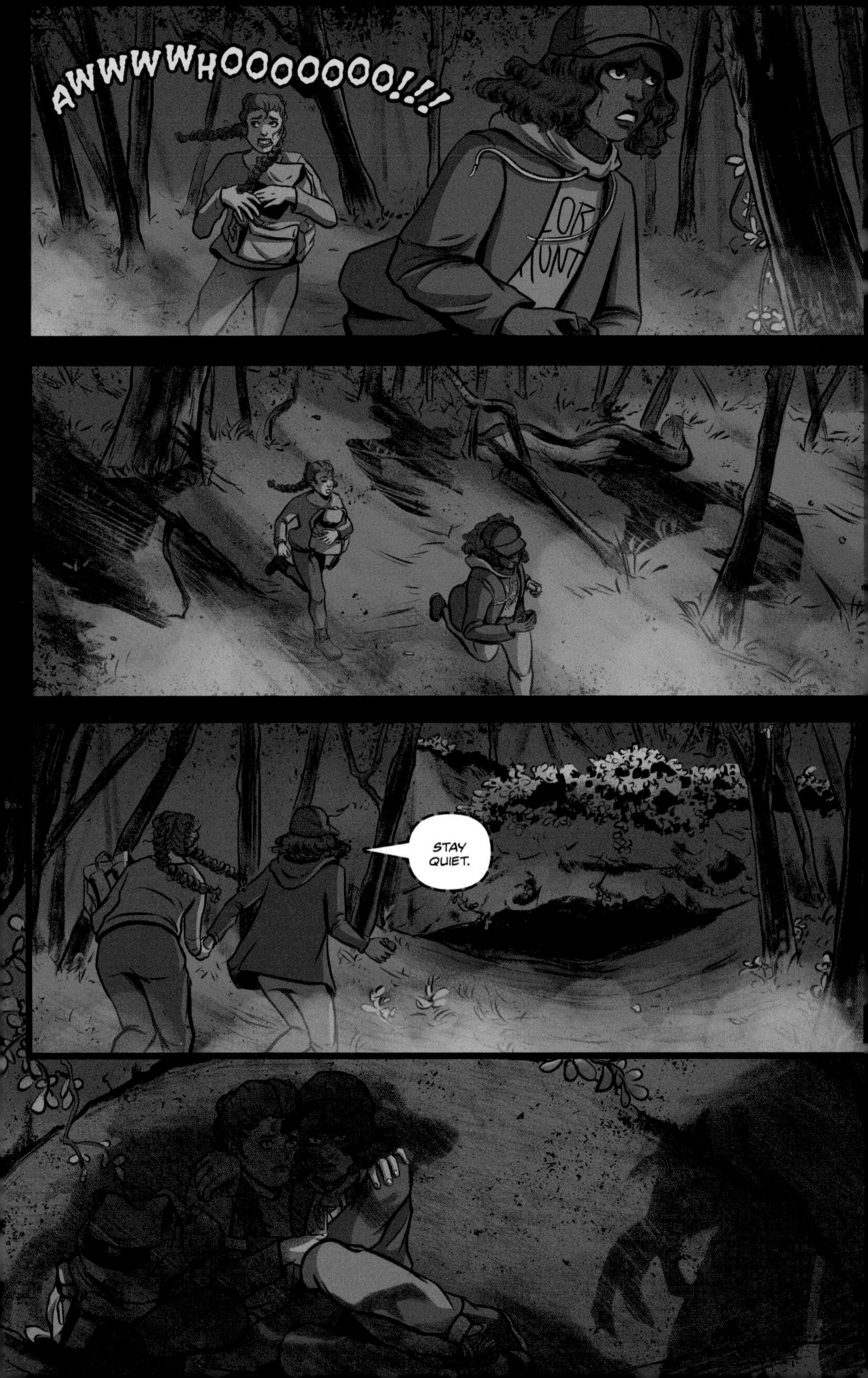
AWWWWHOOOOOOOO!!!!
STAY QUIET.

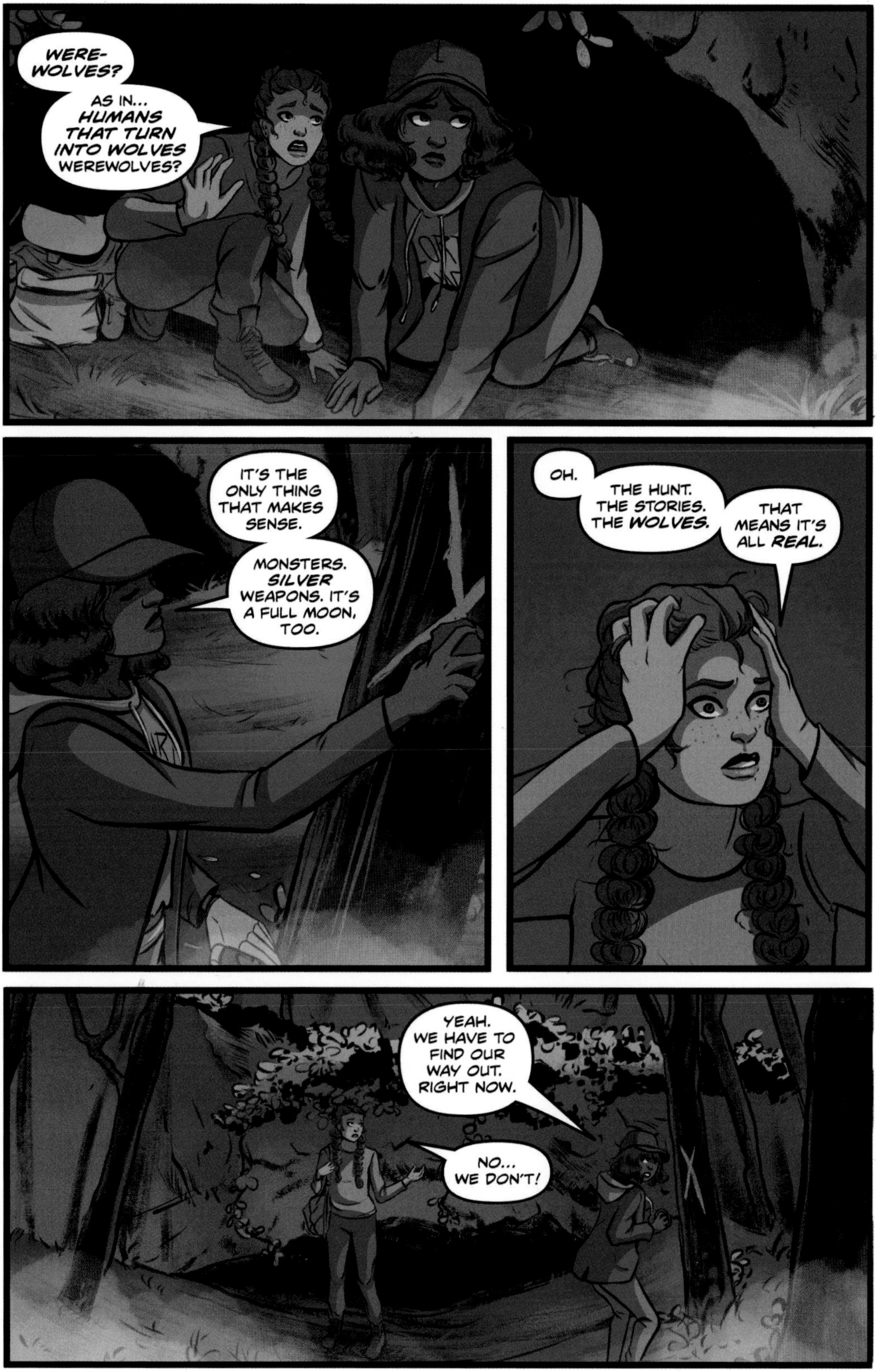
WERE-WOLVES?
AS IN... HUMANS THAT TURN INTO WOLVES WEREWOLVES?
IT'S THE ONLY THING THAT MAKES SENSE.
MONSTERS. SILVER WEAPONS. IT'S A FULL MOON, TOO.
OH.
THE HUNT. THE STORIES. THE WOLVES.
THAT MEANS IT'S ALL REAL.
YEAH. WE HAVE TO FIND OUR WAY OUT. RIGHT NOW.
NO... WE DON'T!

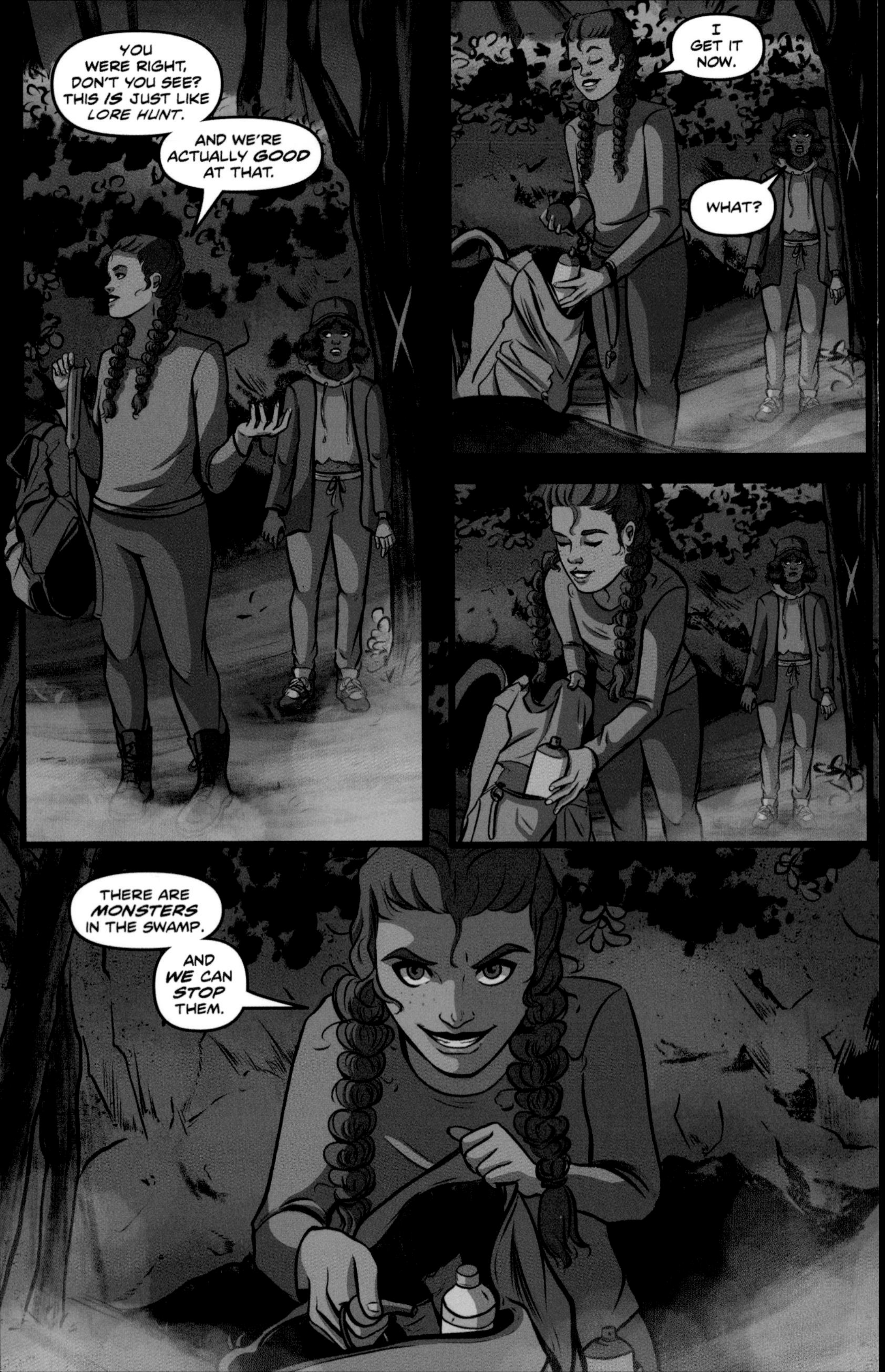
YOU WERE RIGHT, DON'T YOU SEE? THIS *IS* JUST LIKE *LORE HUNT*.
AND WE'RE ACTUALLY **GOOD** AT THAT.
I GET IT NOW.
WHAT?
THERE ARE **MONSTERS** IN THE SWAMP.
AND **WE** CAN **STOP** THEM.

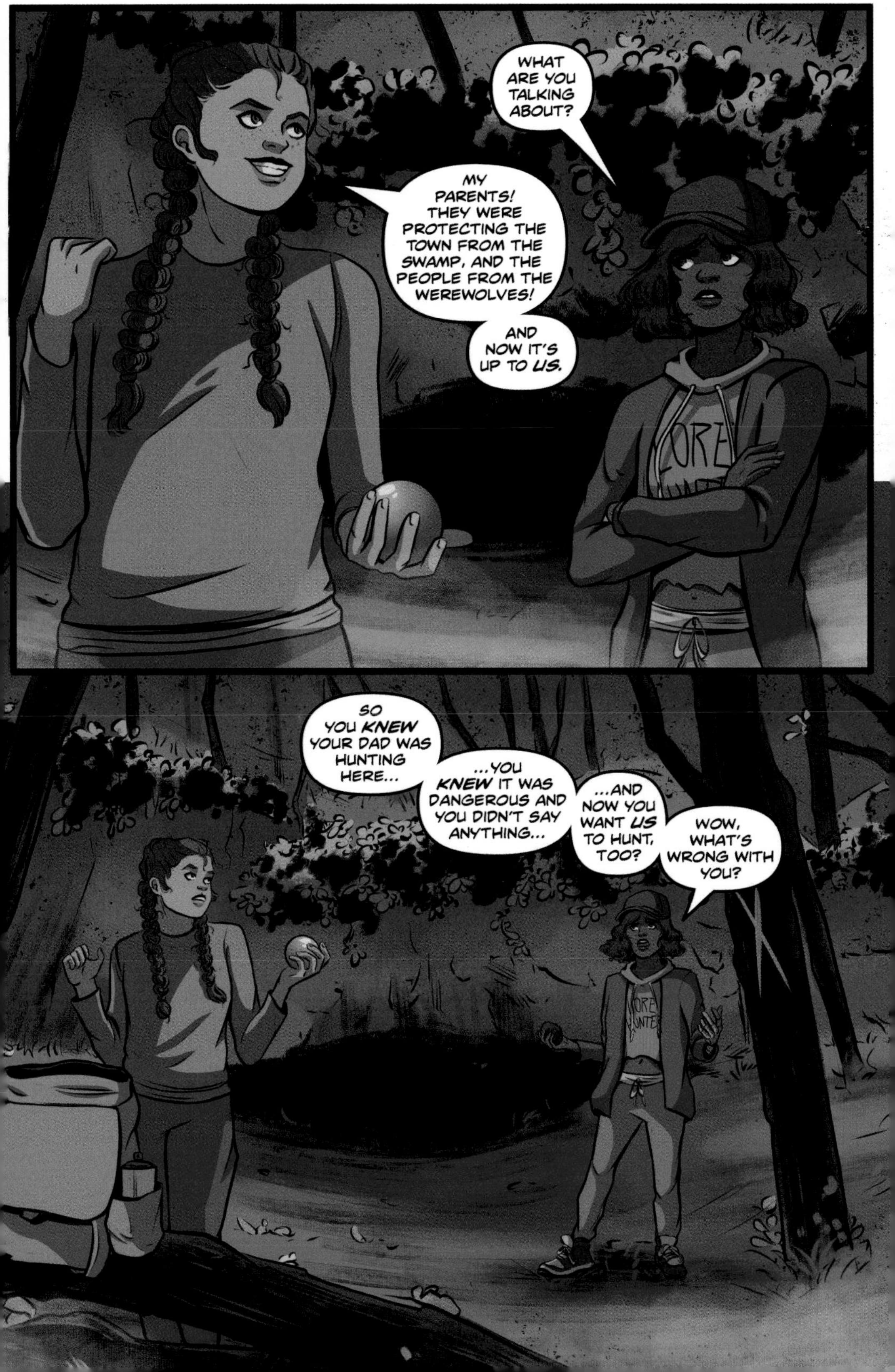

WHAT ARE YOU TALKING ABOUT?
MY PARENTS! THEY WERE PROTECTING THE TOWN FROM THE SWAMP, AND THE PEOPLE FROM THE WEREWOLVES!
AND NOW IT'S UP TO *US*.
SO YOU *KNEW* YOUR DAD WAS HUNTING HERE...
...YOU *KNEW* IT WAS DANGEROUS AND YOU DIDN'T SAY ANYTHING...
...AND NOW YOU WANT *US* TO HUNT, TOO?
WOW, WHAT'S WRONG WITH YOU?

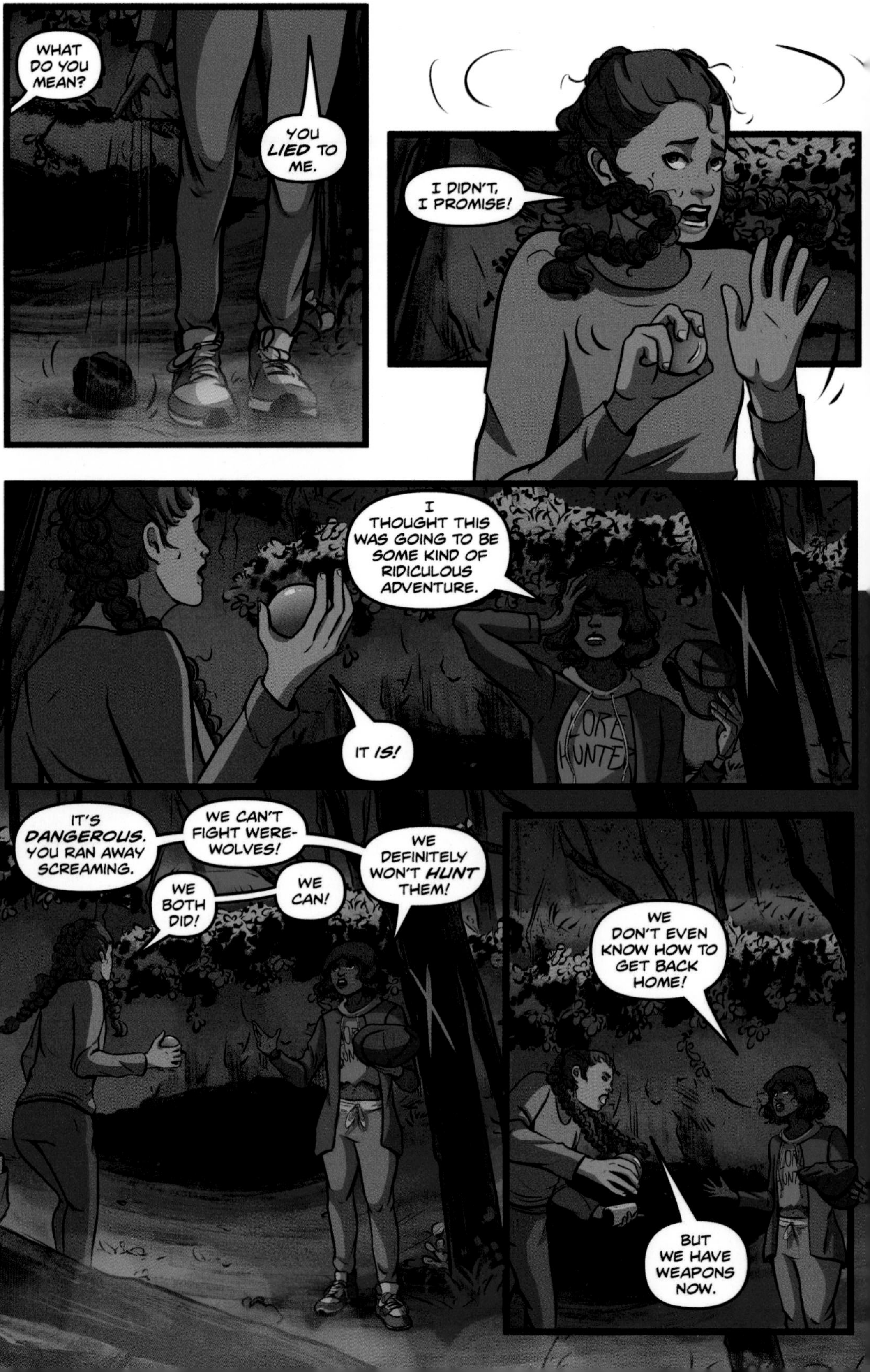
WHAT DO YOU MEAN?
YOU LIED TO ME.
I DIDN'T, I PROMISE!
I THOUGHT THIS WAS GOING TO BE SOME KIND OF RIDICULOUS ADVENTURE.
IT IS!
IT'S DANGEROUS. YOU RAN AWAY SCREAMING.
WE BOTH DID!
WE CAN'T FIGHT WERE-WOLVES!
WE CAN!
WE DEFINITELY WON'T HUNT THEM!
WE DON'T EVEN KNOW HOW TO GET BACK HOME!
BUT WE HAVE WEAPONS NOW.

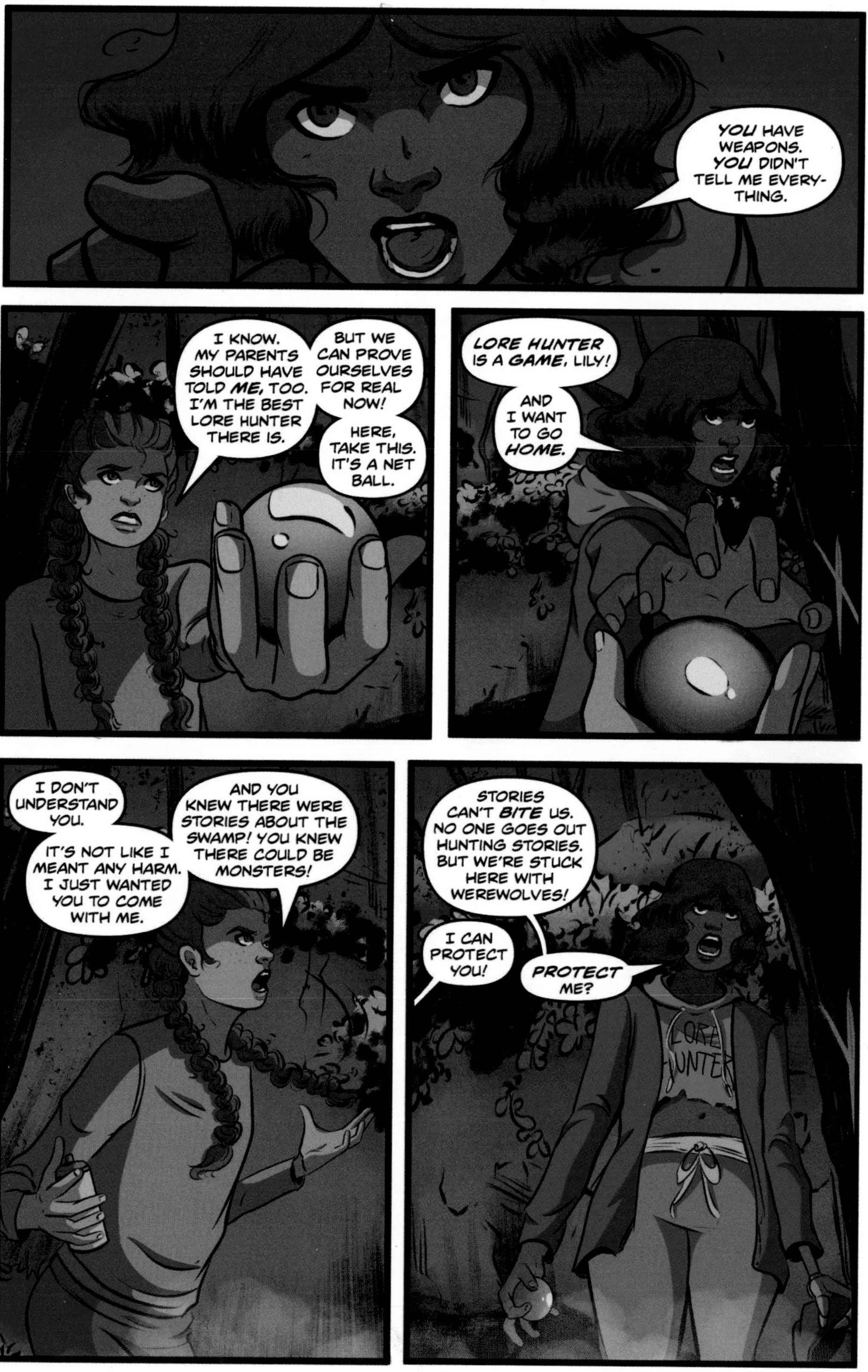
YOU HAVE WEAPONS. YOU DIDN'T TELL ME EVERY-THING.
I KNOW. MY PARENTS SHOULD HAVE TOLD ME, TOO. I'M THE BEST LORE HUNTER THERE IS.
BUT WE CAN PROVE OURSELVES FOR REAL NOW!
HERE, TAKE THIS. IT'S A NET BALL.
LORE HUNTER IS A GAME, LILY!
AND I WANT TO GO HOME.
I DON'T UNDERSTAND YOU.
IT'S NOT LIKE I MEANT ANY HARM. I JUST WANTED YOU TO COME WITH ME.
AND YOU KNEW THERE WERE STORIES ABOUT THE SWAMP! YOU KNEW THERE COULD BE MONSTERS!
STORIES CAN'T BITE US. NO ONE GOES OUT HUNTING STORIES. BUT WE'RE STUCK HERE WITH WEREWOLVES!
I CAN PROTECT YOU!
PROTECT ME?
LORE HUNTER

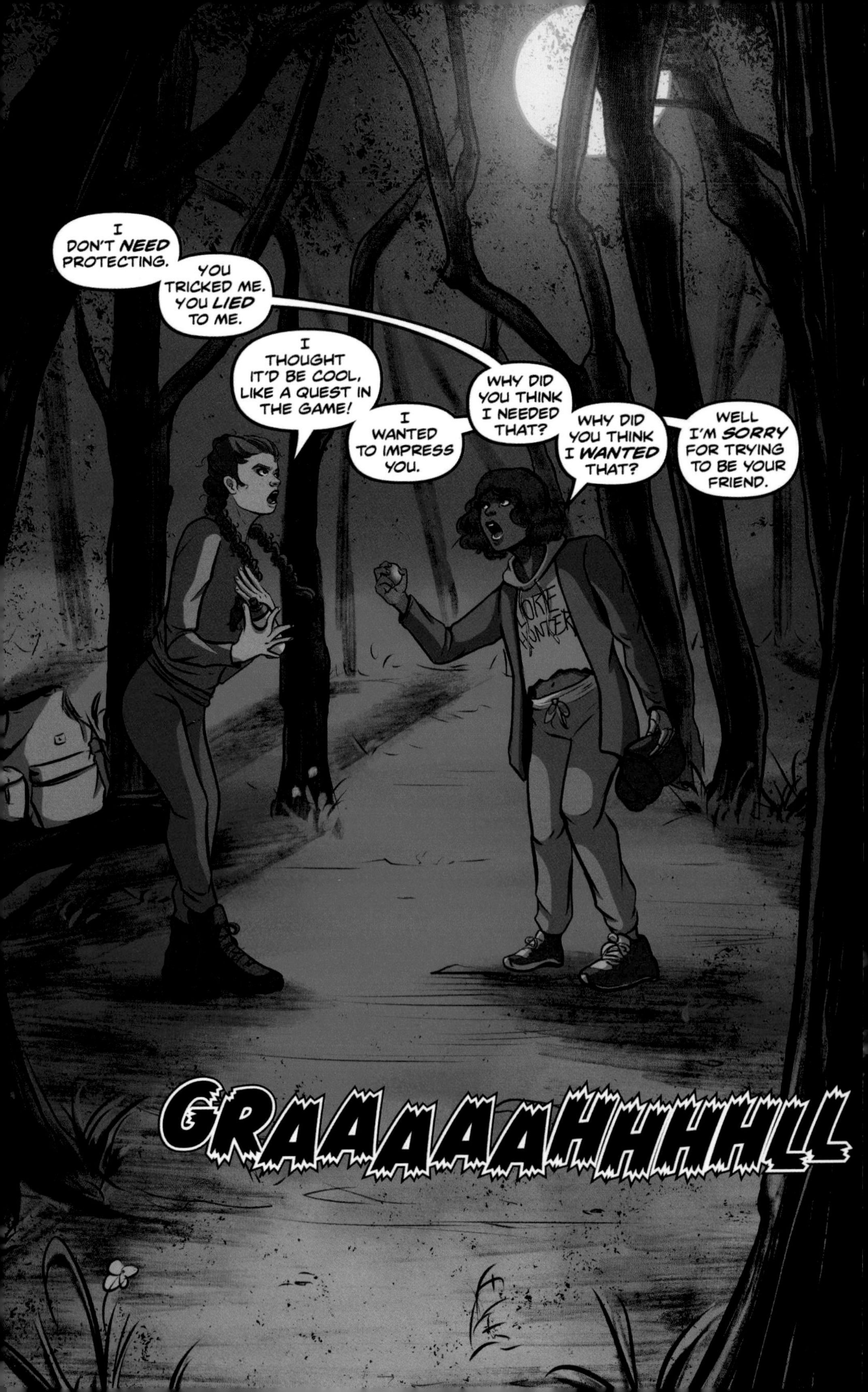

I DON'T NEED PROTECTING.
YOU TRICKED ME. YOU LIED TO ME.
I THOUGHT IT'D BE COOL, LIKE A QUEST IN THE GAME!
I WANTED TO IMPRESS YOU.
WHY DID YOU THINK I NEEDED THAT?
WHY DID YOU THINK I WANTED THAT?
WELL I'M SORRY FOR TRYING TO BE YOUR FRIEND.
LORE HUNTER
GRAAAAAAHHHHLL

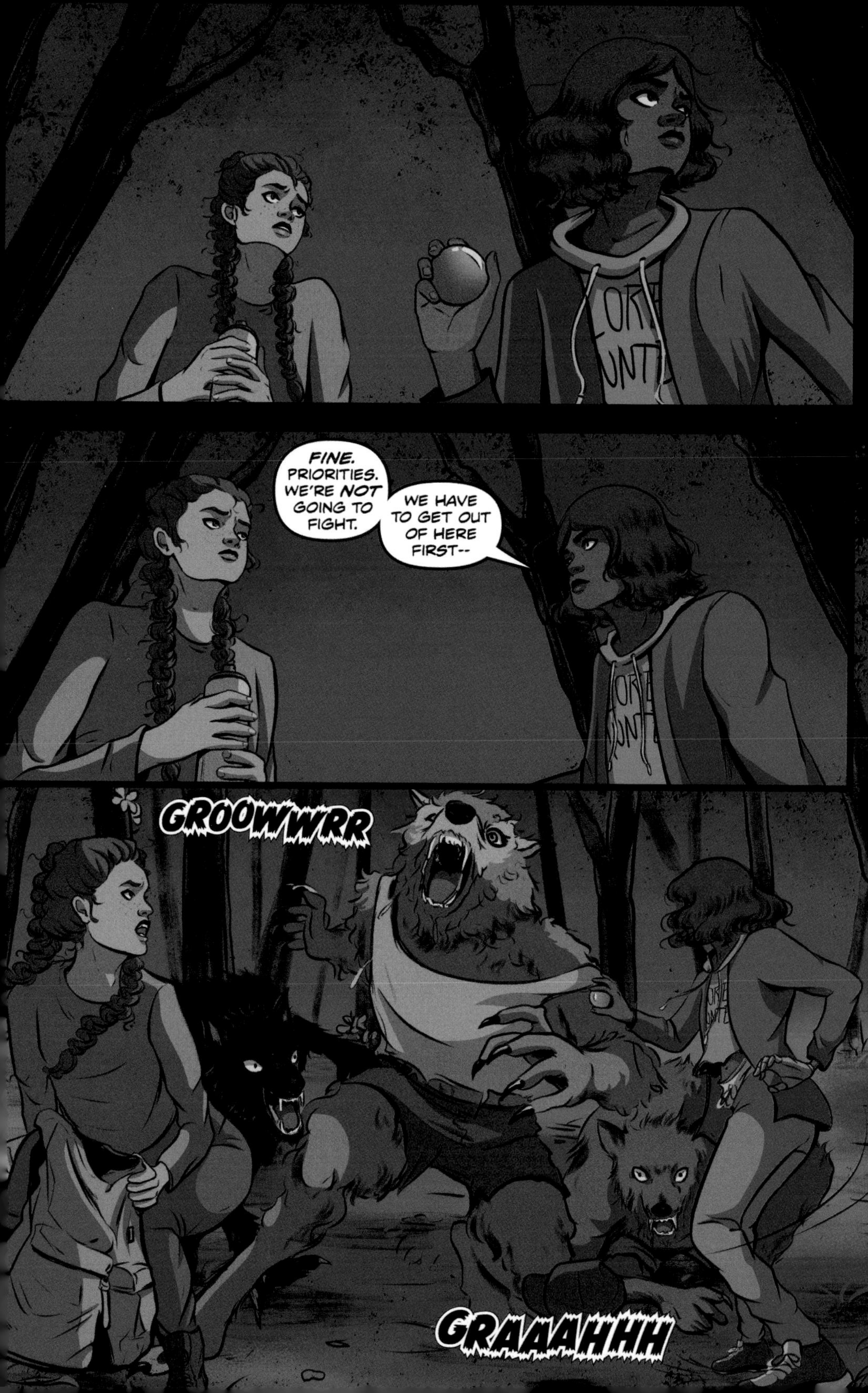
FINE. PRIORITIES. WE'RE NOT GOING TO FIGHT.
WE HAVE TO GET OUT OF HERE FIRST--
GROOWWRR
GRAAAHHH

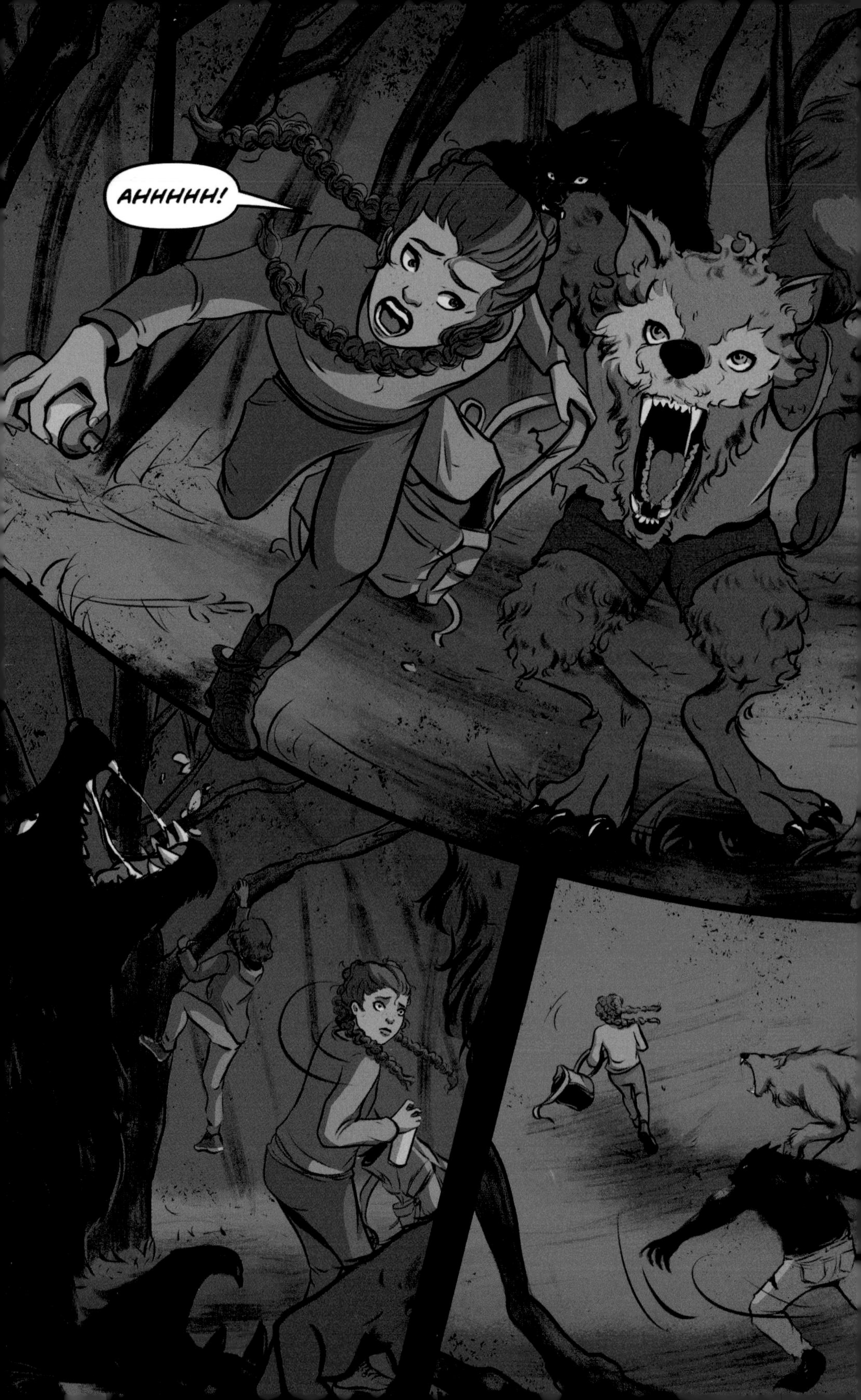
AHHHHH!

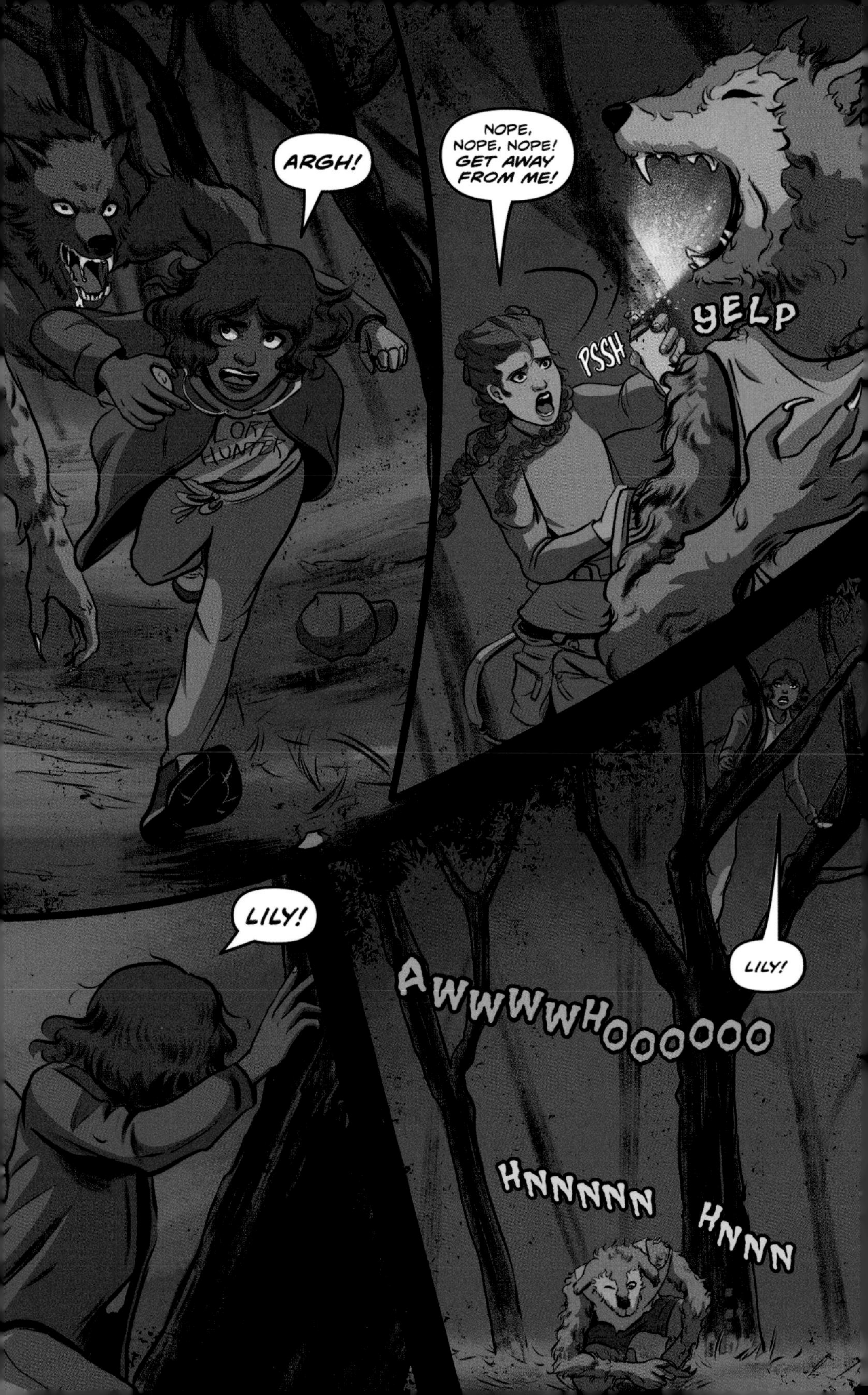
ARGH!
NOPE, NOPE, NOPE! GET AWAY FROM ME!
PSSH
YELP
LORE HUNTER
LILY!
AWWWWWHOOOOOO
LILY!
HNNNNNN
HNNN

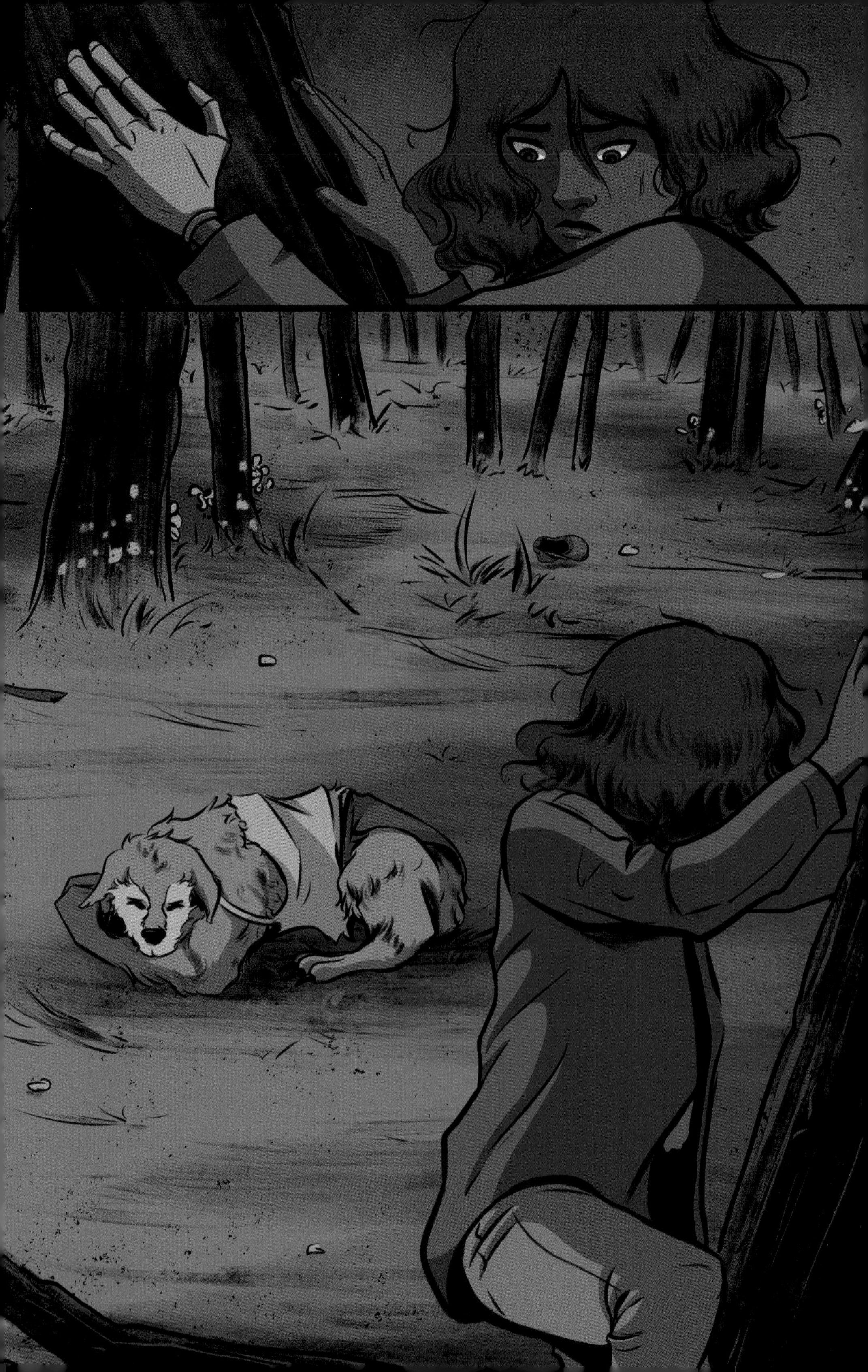

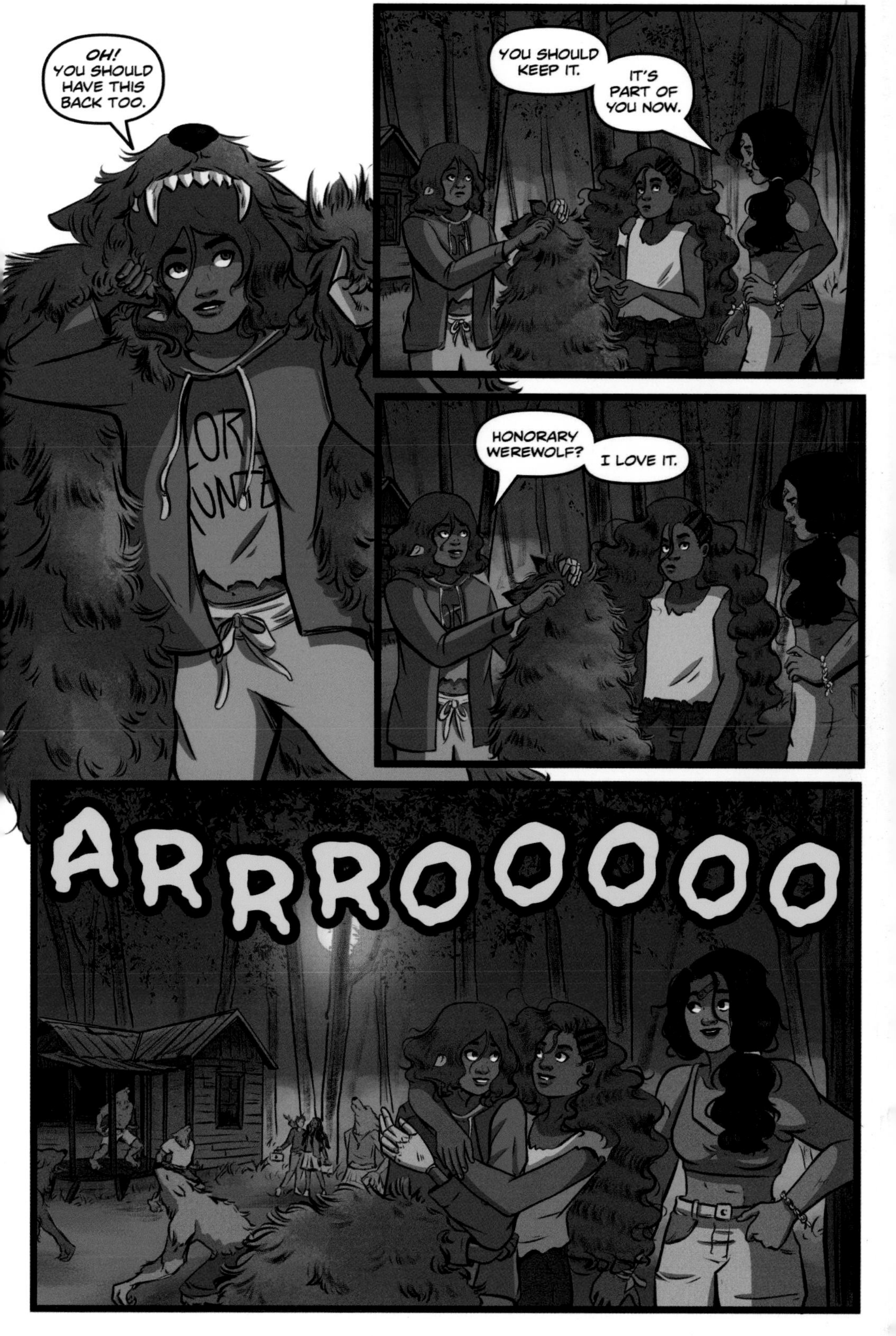
OH! YOU SHOULD HAVE THIS BACK TOO.
YOU SHOULD KEEP IT.
IT'S PART OF YOU NOW.
HONORARY WEREWOLF?
I LOVE IT.
ARRROOOOO

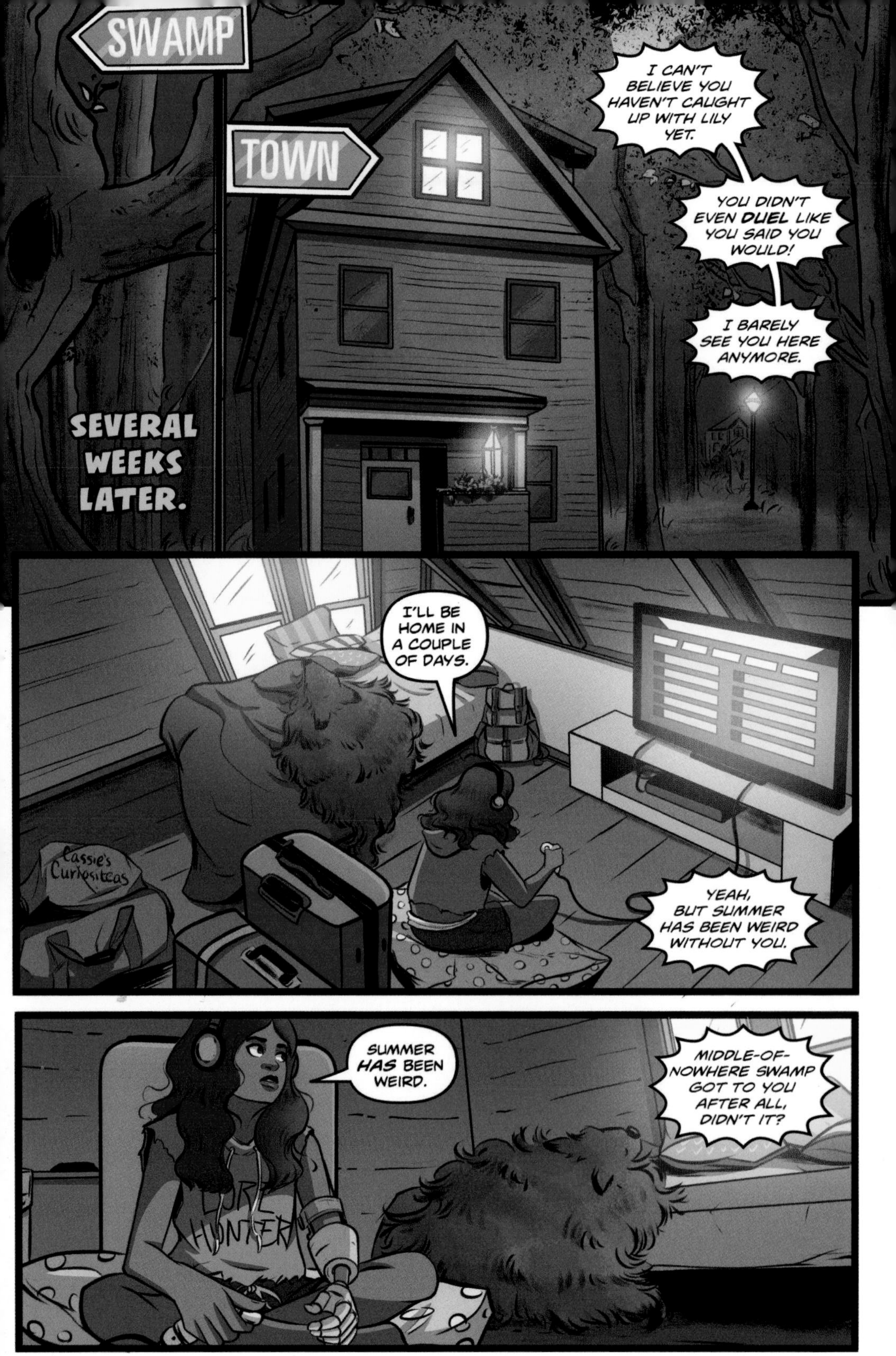
SWAMP
TOWN
SEVERAL WEEKS LATER.
I CAN'T BELIEVE YOU HAVEN'T CAUGHT UP WITH LILY YET.
YOU DIDN'T EVEN DUEL LIKE YOU SAID YOU WOULD!
I BARELY SEE YOU HERE ANYMORE.
I'LL BE HOME IN A COUPLE OF DAYS.
YEAH, BUT SUMMER HAS BEEN WEIRD WITHOUT YOU.
Cassie's Curiosities
SUMMER HAS BEEN WEIRD.
MIDDLE-OF-NOWHERE SWAMP GOT TO YOU AFTER ALL, DIDN'T IT?
LORE HUNTER

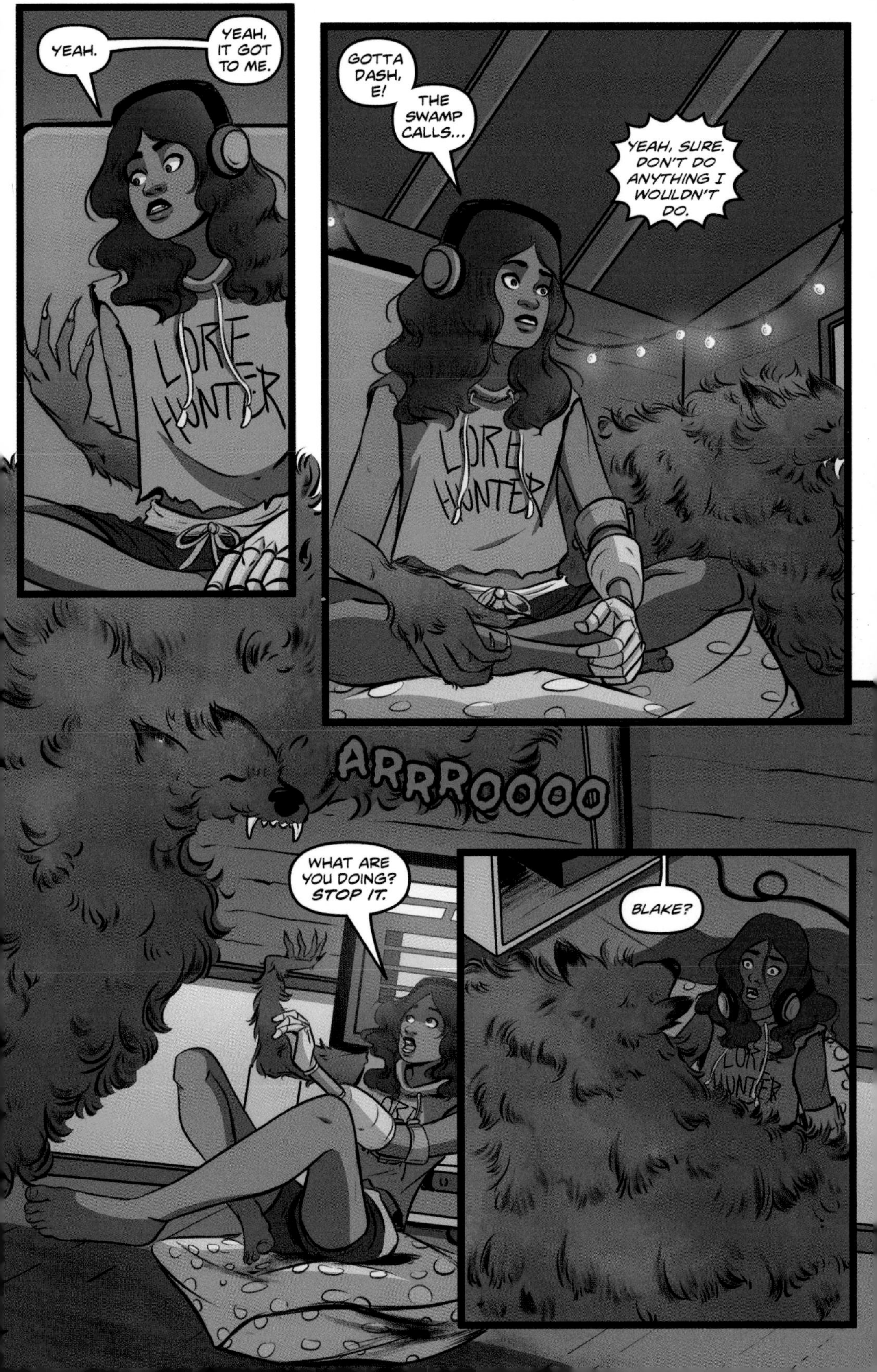
YEAH.
YEAH, IT GOT TO ME.
LORE HUNTER
GOTTA DASH, E!
THE SWAMP CALLS...
YEAH, SURE. DON'T DO ANYTHING I WOULDN'T DO.
LORE HUNTER
ARRROOOO
WHAT ARE YOU DOING? STOP IT.
BLAKE?
LORE HUNTER

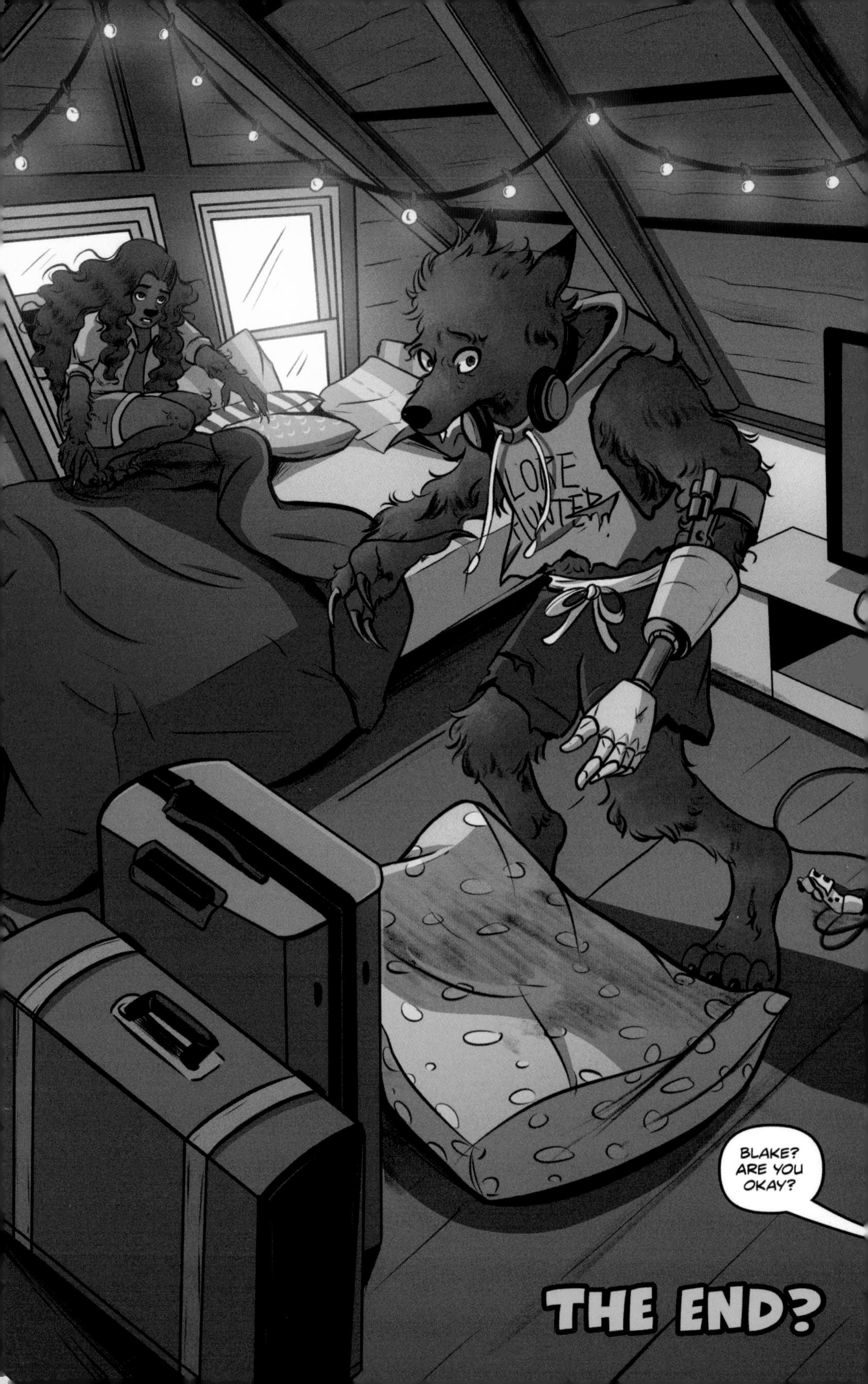
LORE HUNTER
BLAKE? ARE YOU OKAY?
THE END?

Goosebumps

COVER GALLERY

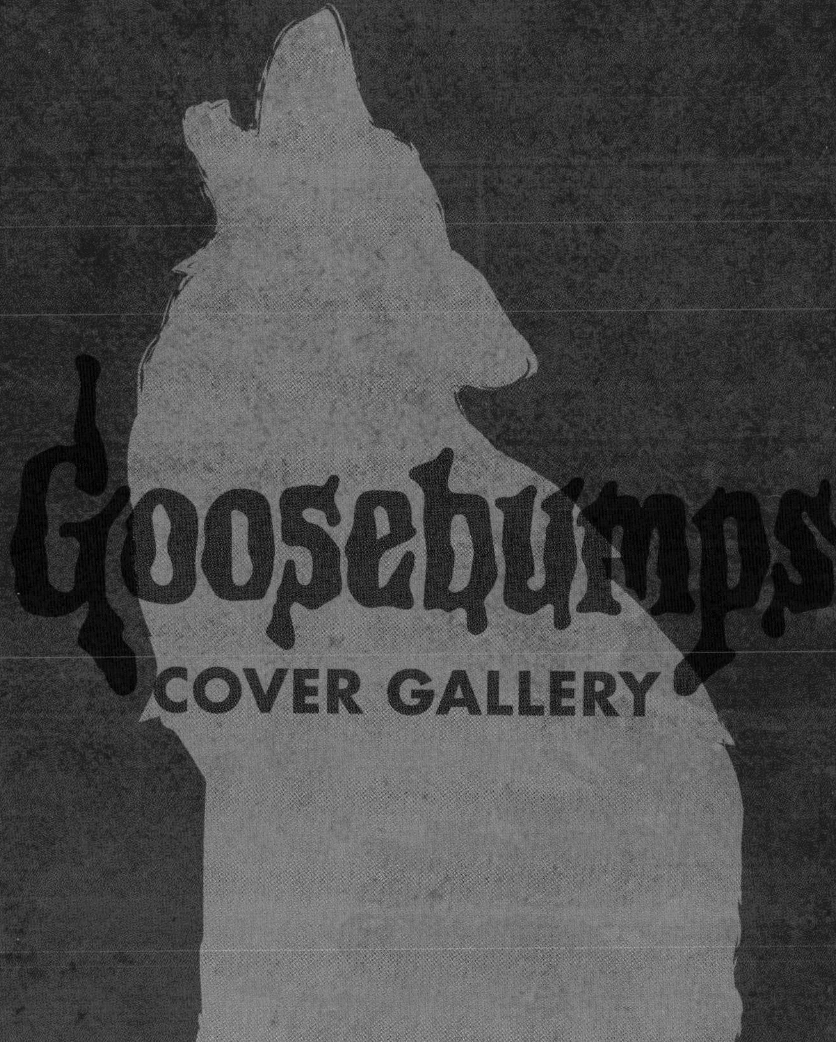

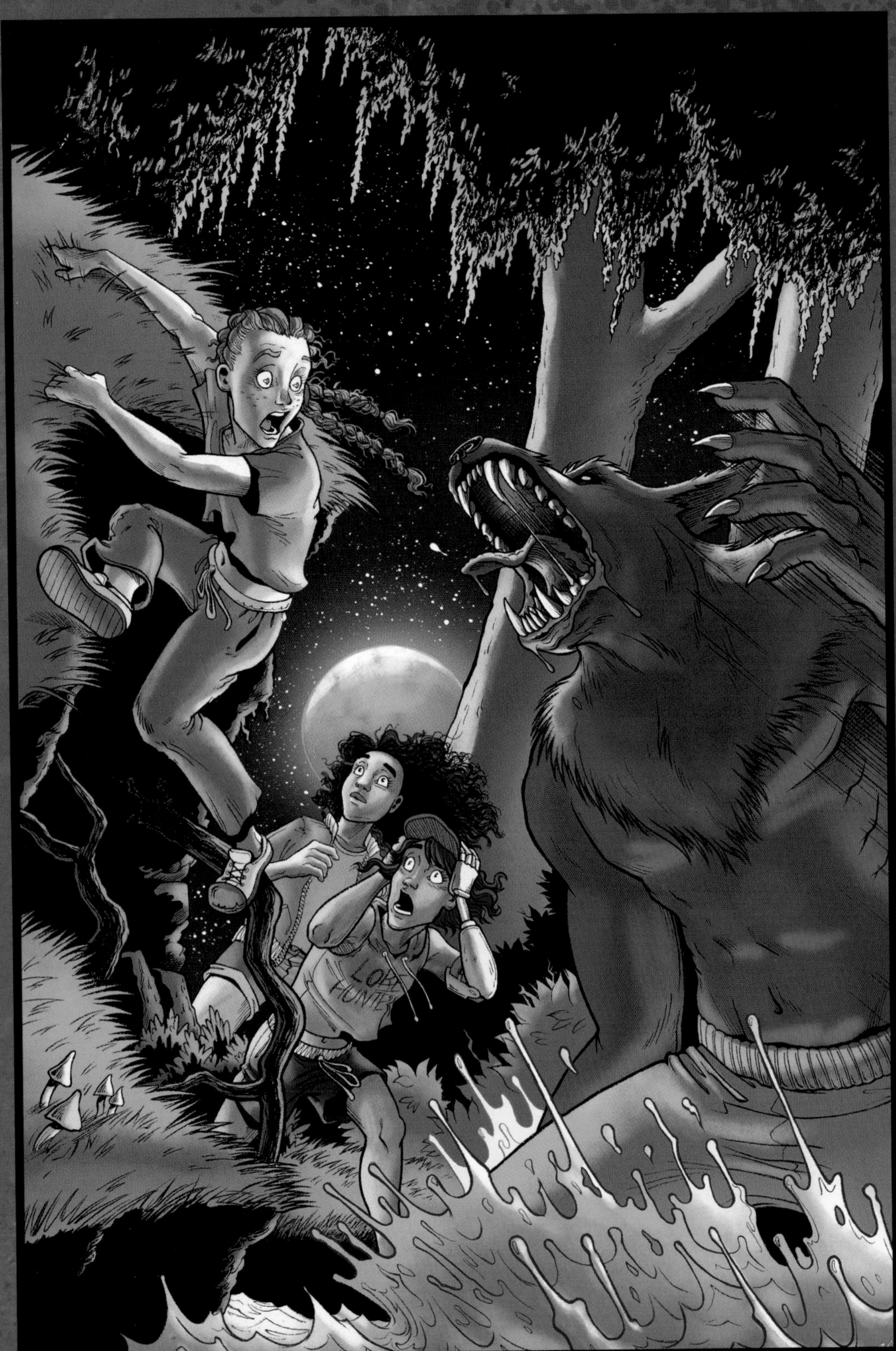

ART BY: CLARA MEATH **COLORS BY:** DJ CHAVIS

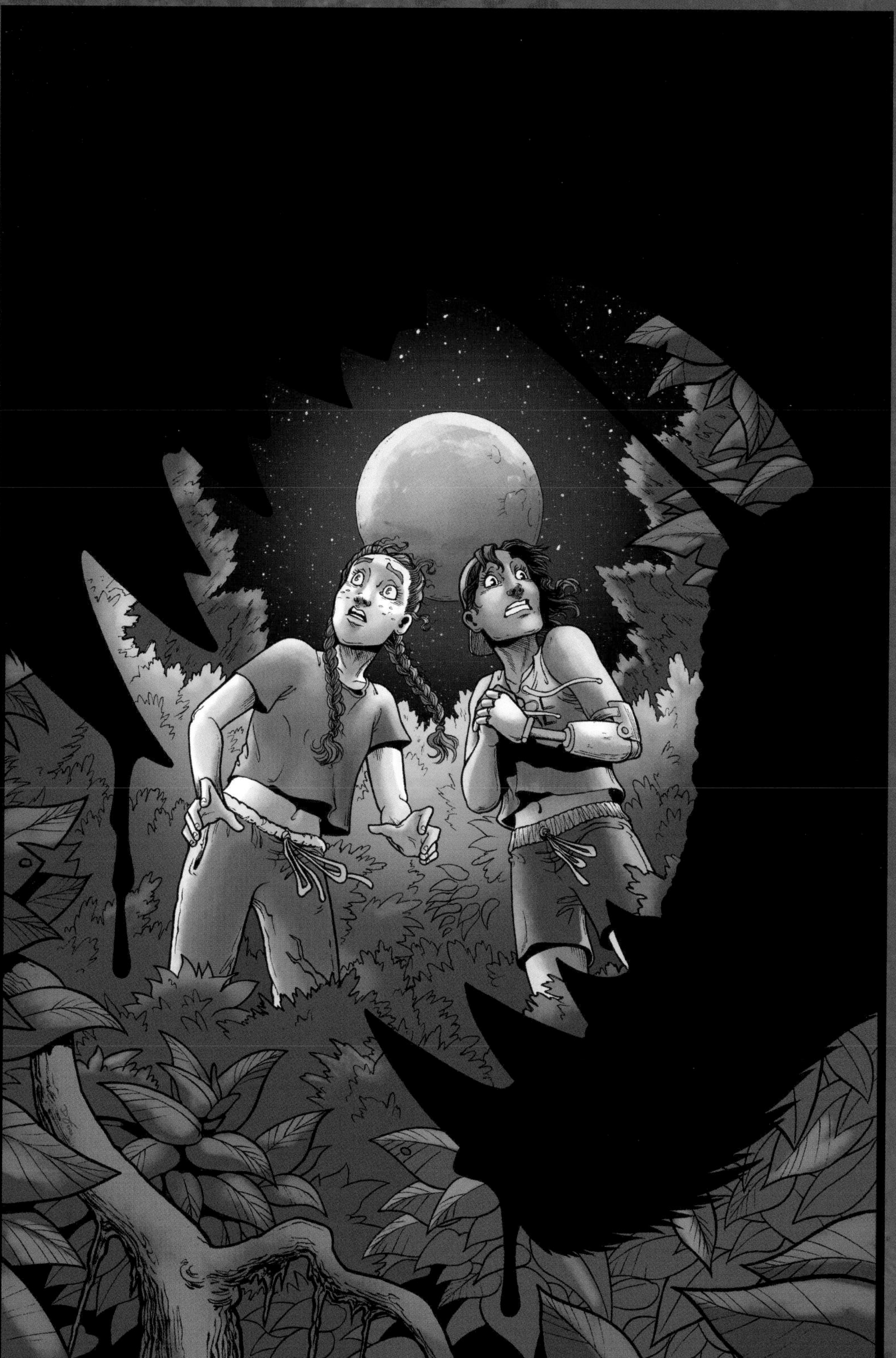

ART BY: CLARA MEATH COLORS BY: DJ CHAVIS

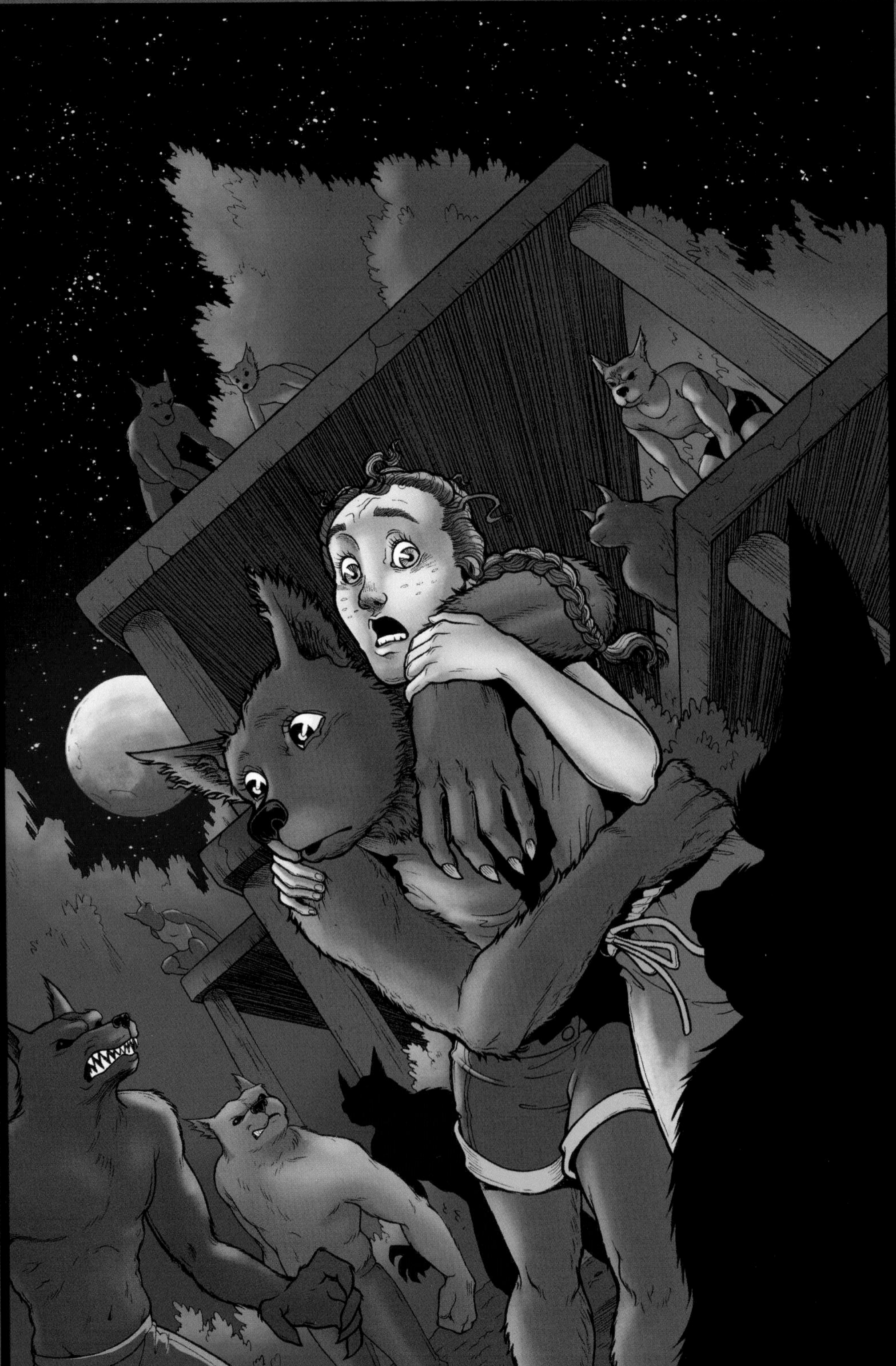

ART BY: CLARA MEATH COLORS BY: DJ CHAVIS

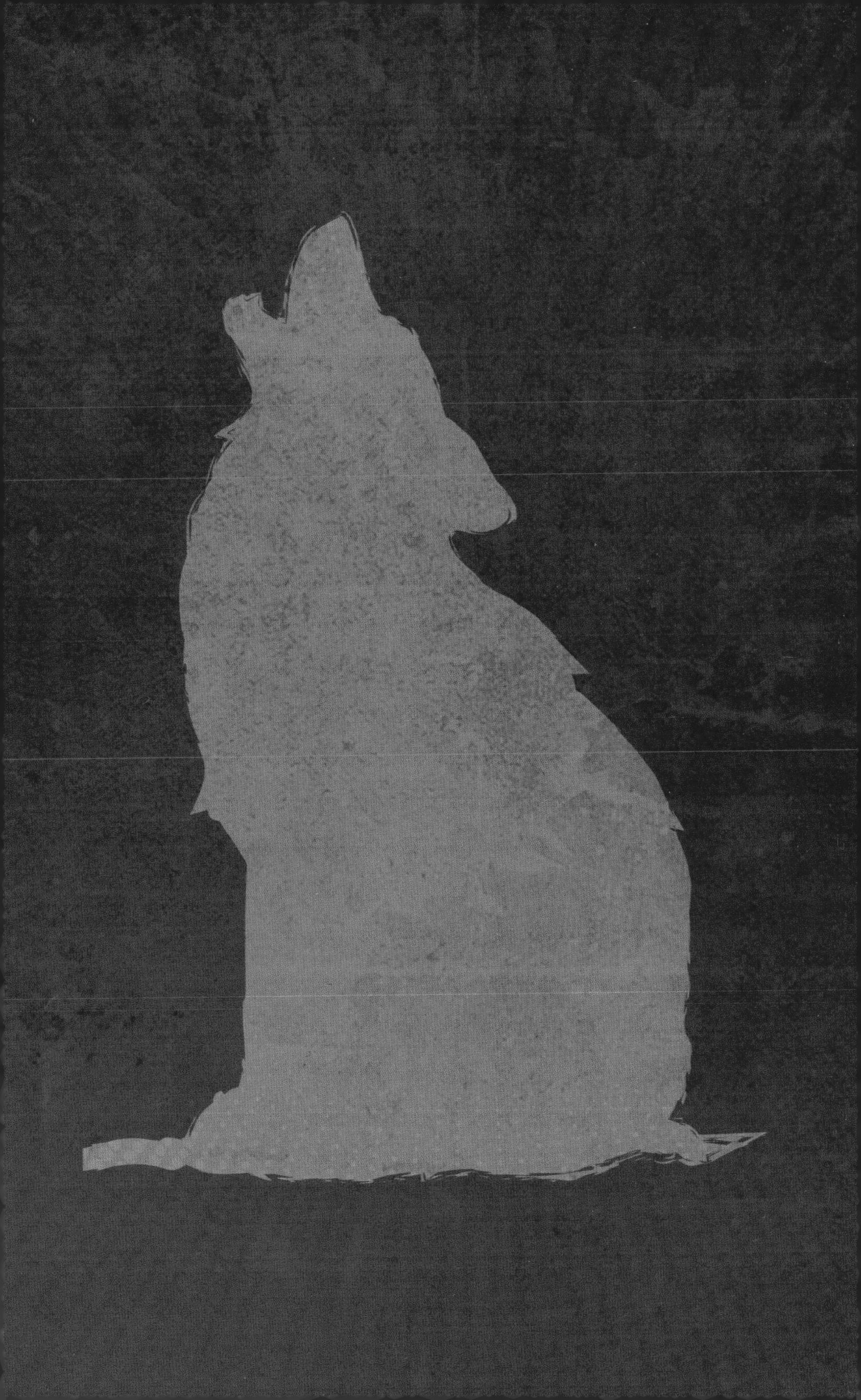

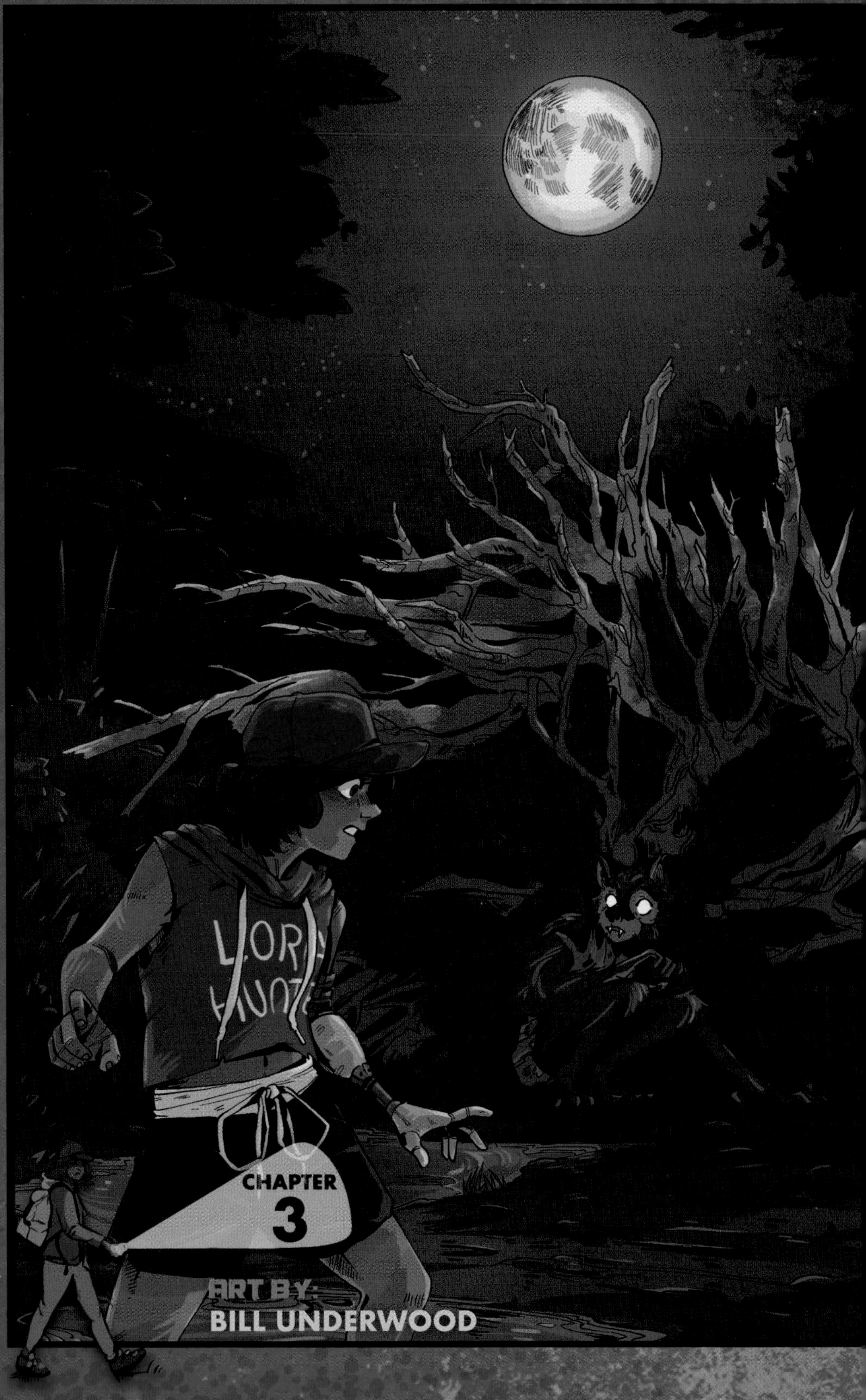
CHAPTER
3
ART BY:
BILL UNDERWOOD

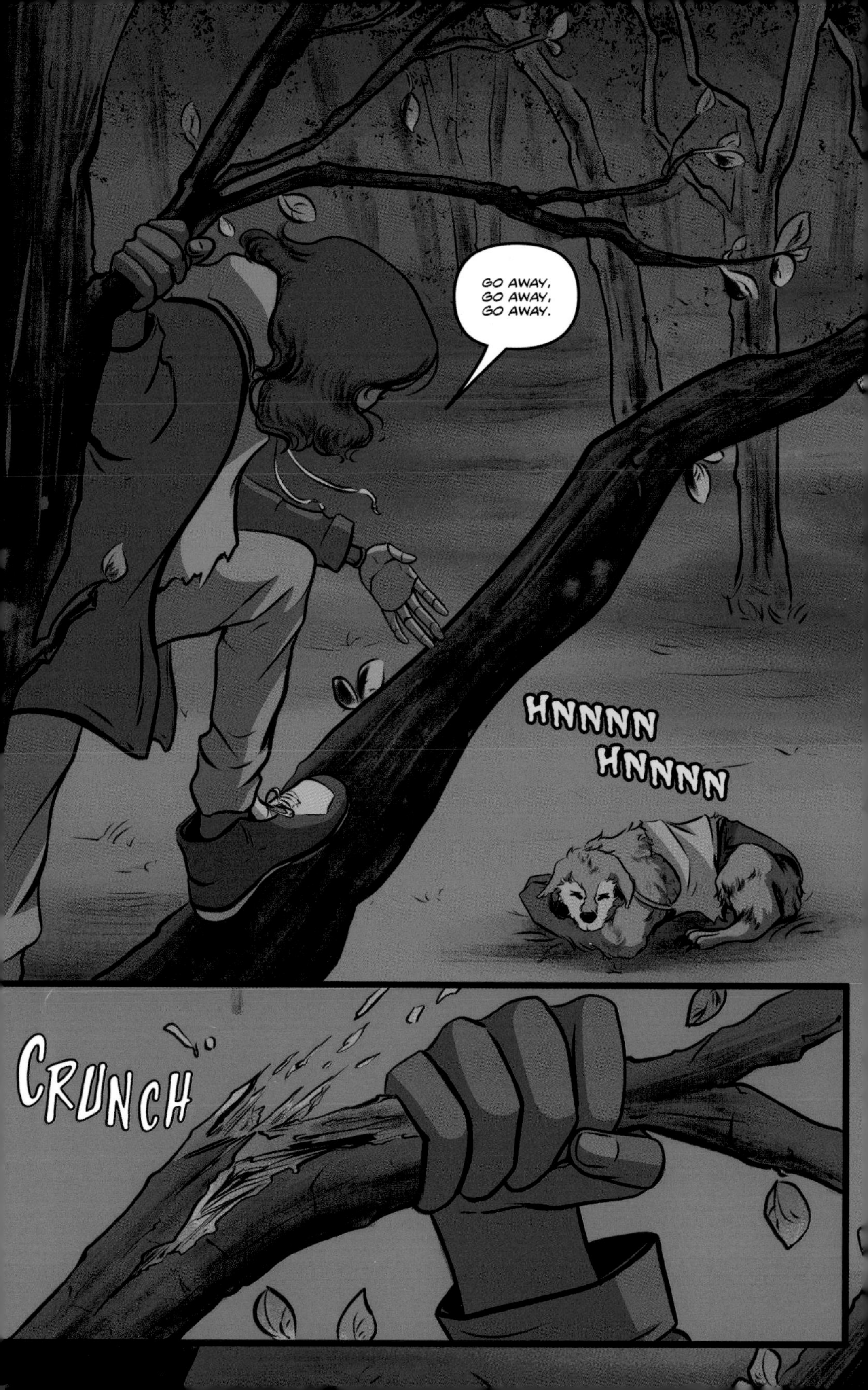
GO AWAY, GO AWAY, GO AWAY.
HNNNN HNNNNN
CRUNCH

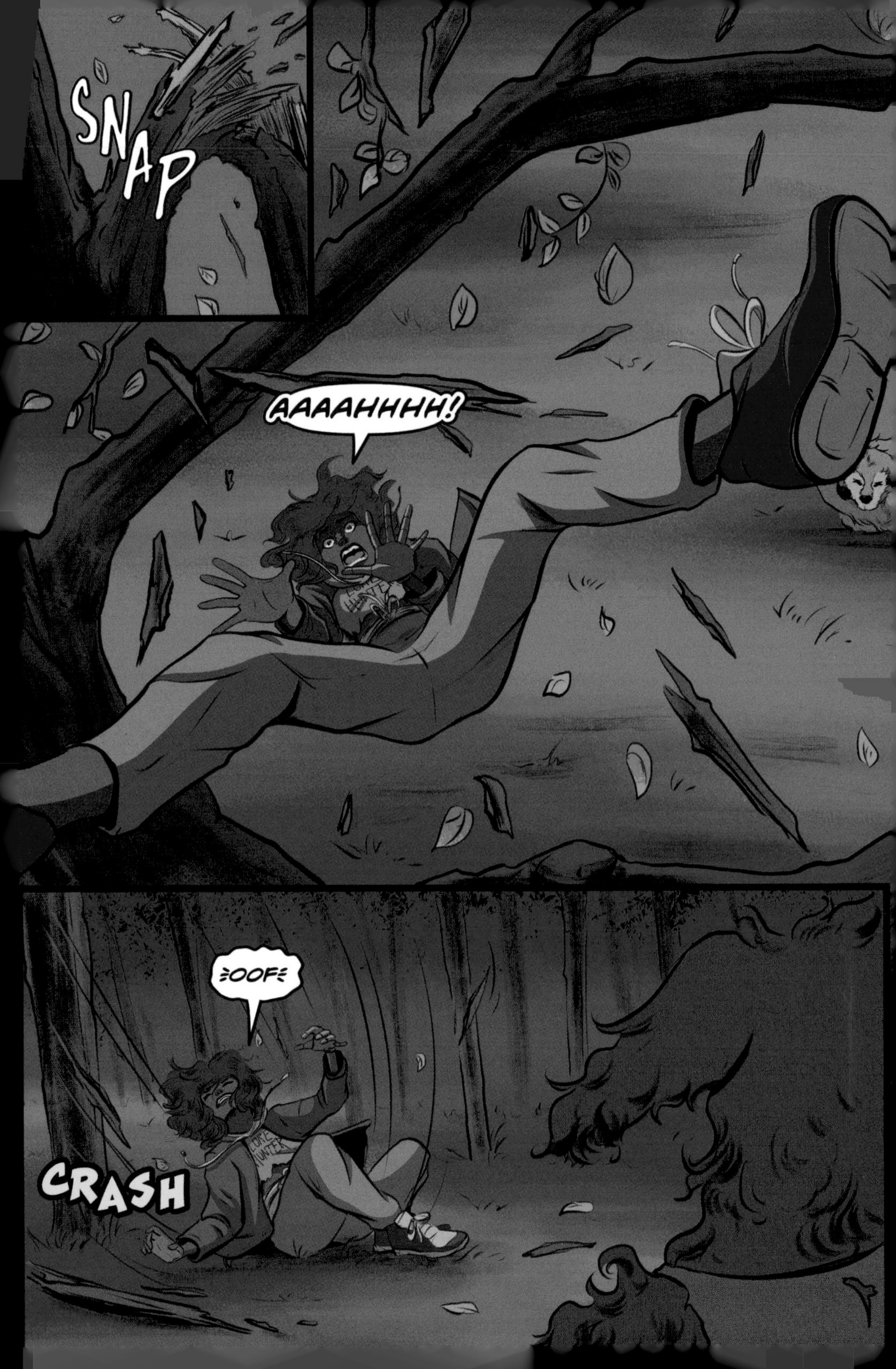
SNAP
AAAAHHHH!
OOF
CRASH

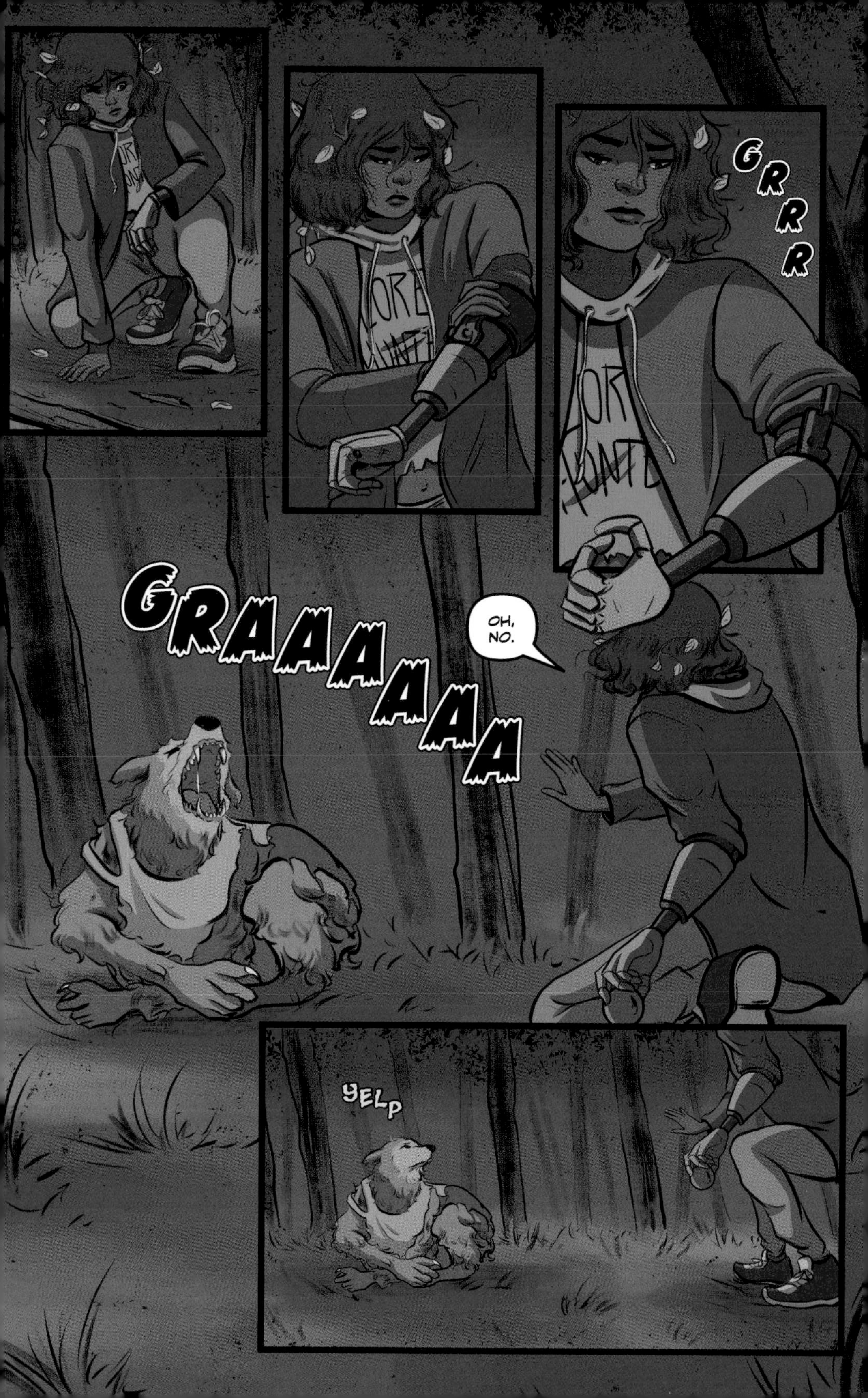
GRRR
GRAAAAAAAA
OH, NO.
YELP

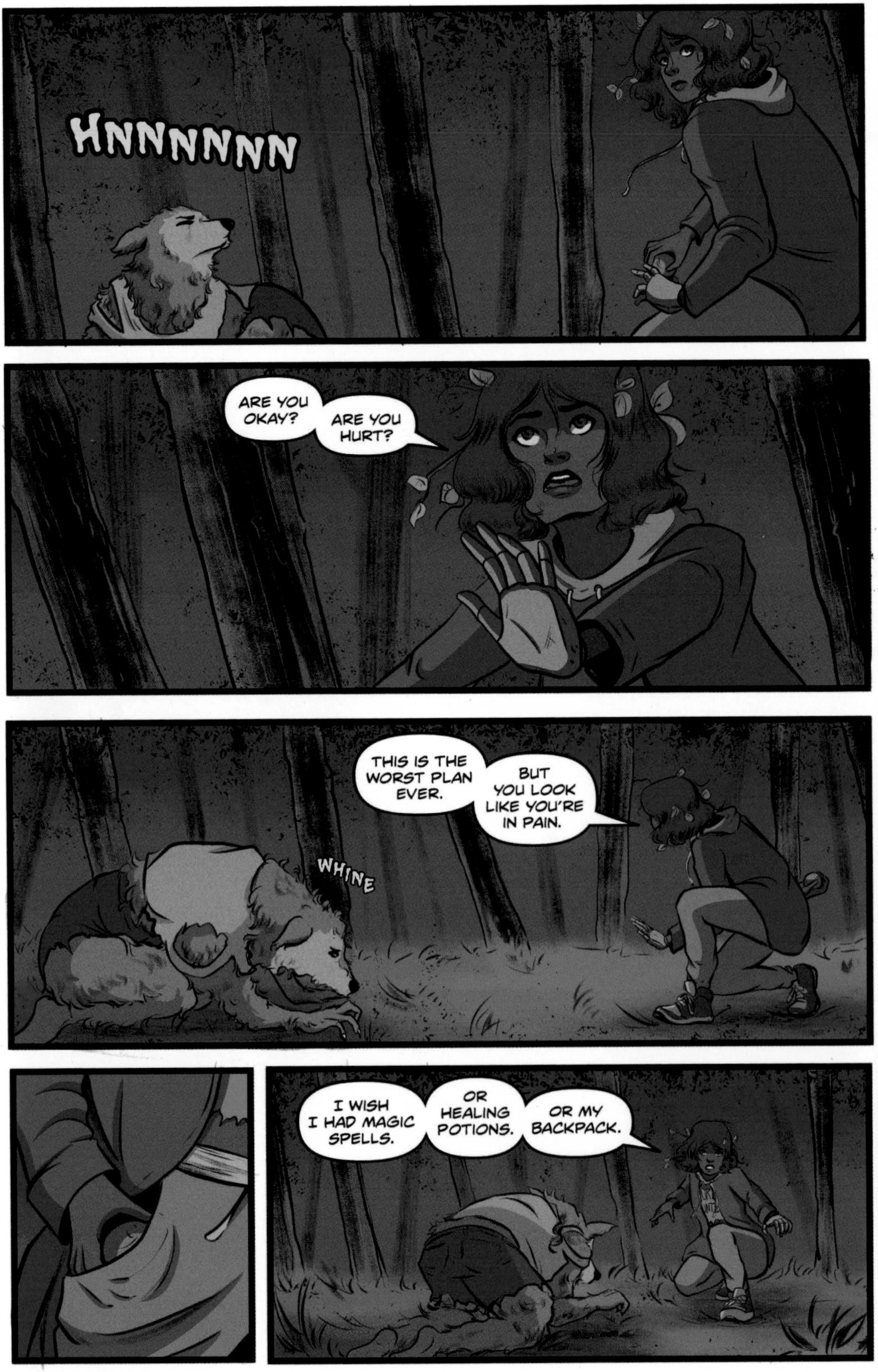
HNNNNNNN
ARE YOU OKAY?
ARE YOU HURT?
THIS IS THE WORST PLAN EVER.
BUT YOU LOOK LIKE YOU'RE IN PAIN.
WHINE
I WISH I HAD MAGIC SPELLS.
OR HEALING POTIONS.
OR MY BACKPACK.

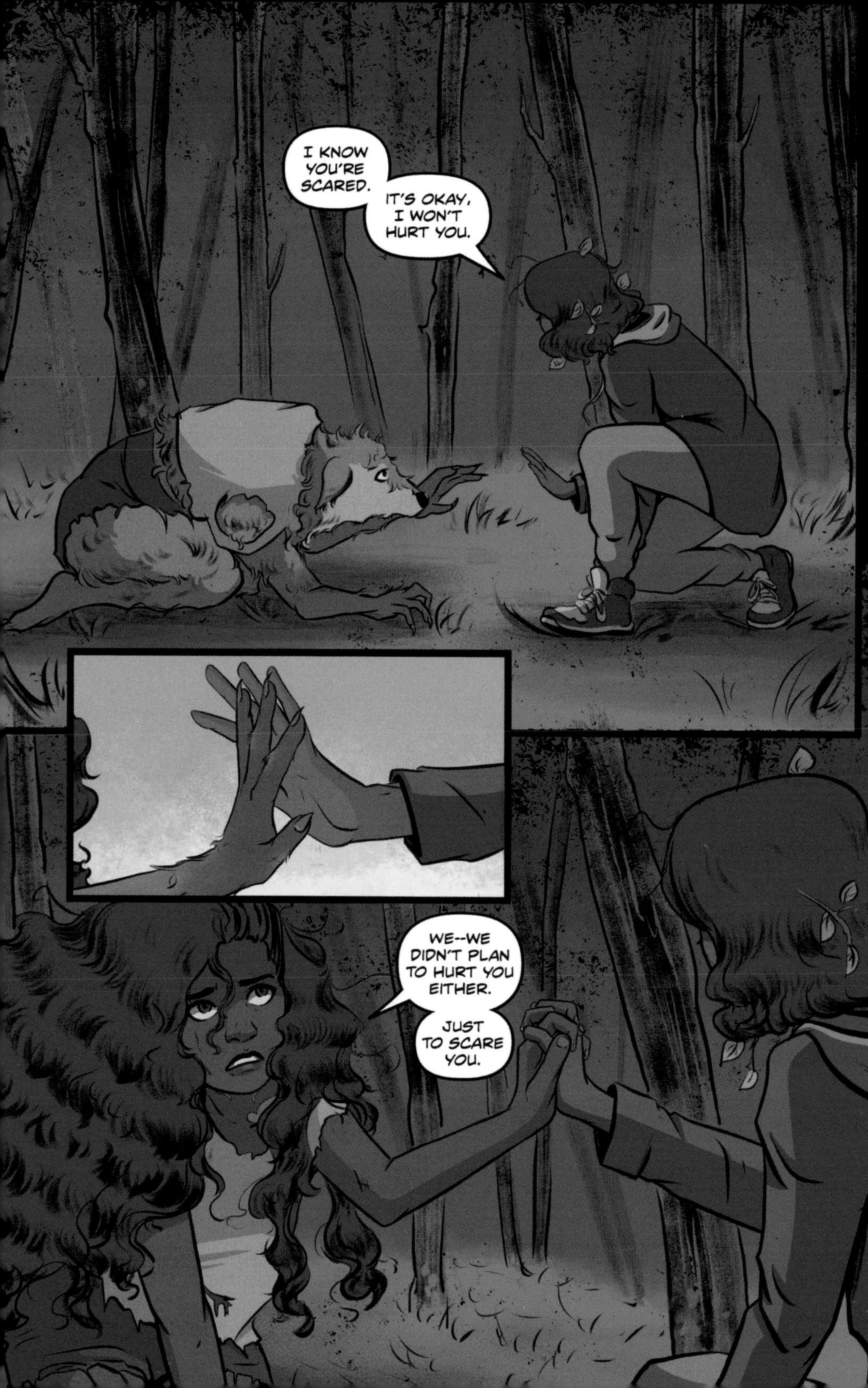
I KNOW YOU'RE SCARED.
IT'S OKAY, I WON'T HURT YOU.
WE--WE DIDN'T PLAN TO HURT YOU EITHER.
JUST TO SCARE YOU.

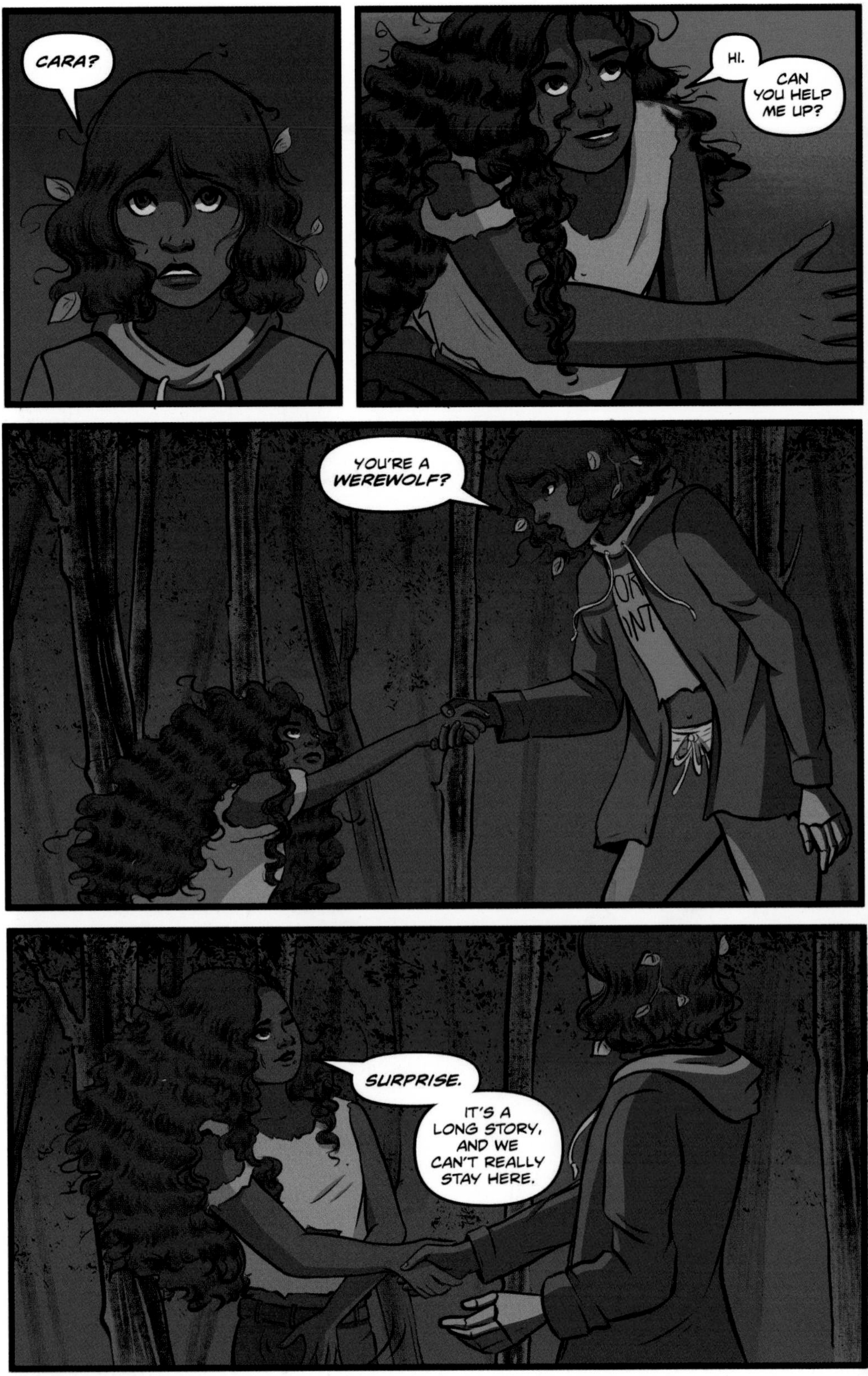

CARA?
HI.
CAN YOU HELP ME UP?
YOU'RE A WEREWOLF?
SURPRISE.
IT'S A LONG STORY, AND WE CAN'T REALLY STAY HERE.

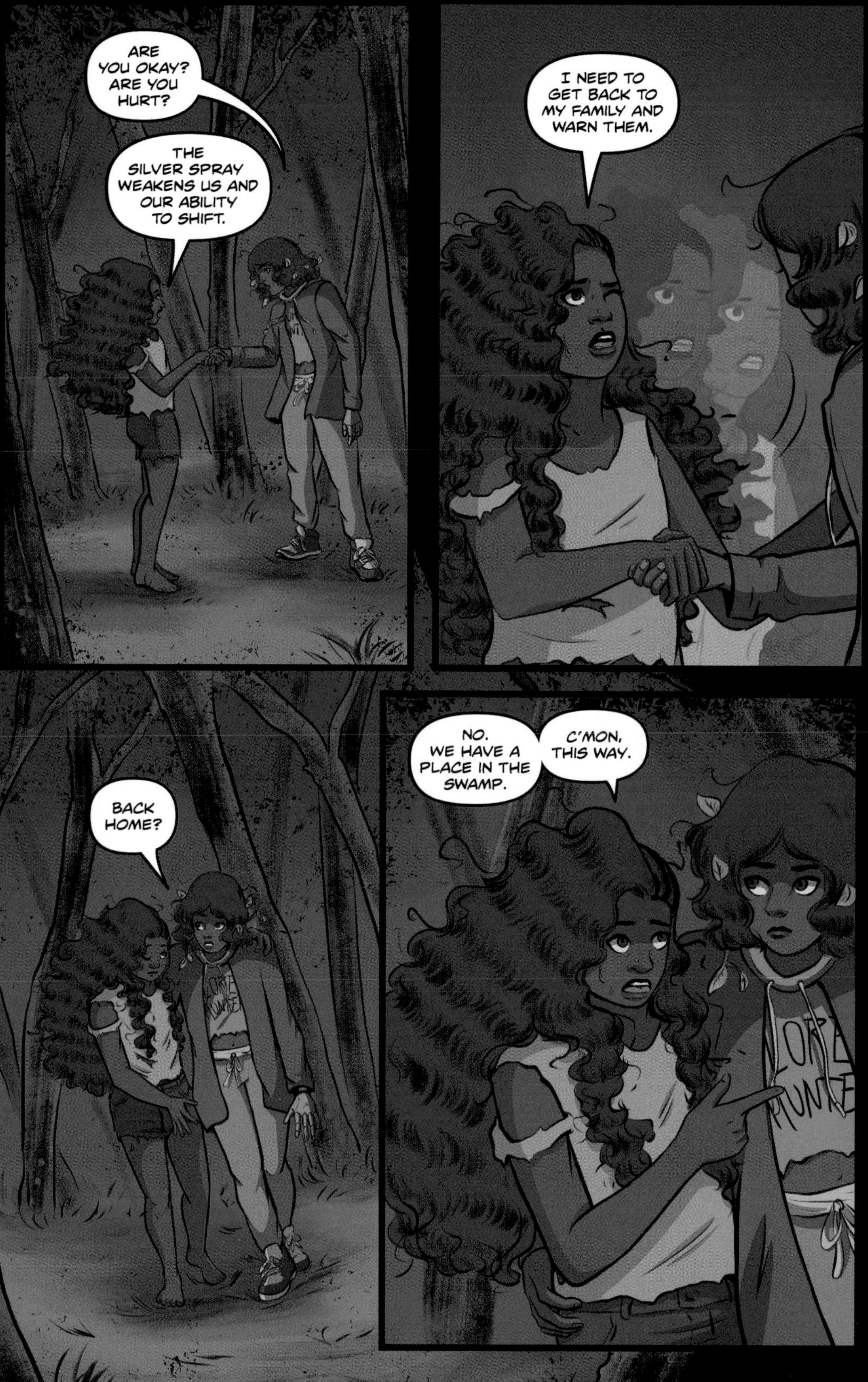
ARE YOU OKAY? ARE YOU HURT?
THE SILVER SPRAY WEAKENS US AND OUR ABILITY TO SHIFT.
I NEED TO GET BACK TO MY FAMILY AND WARN THEM.
BACK HOME?
NO. WE HAVE A PLACE IN THE SWAMP.
C'MON, THIS WAY.

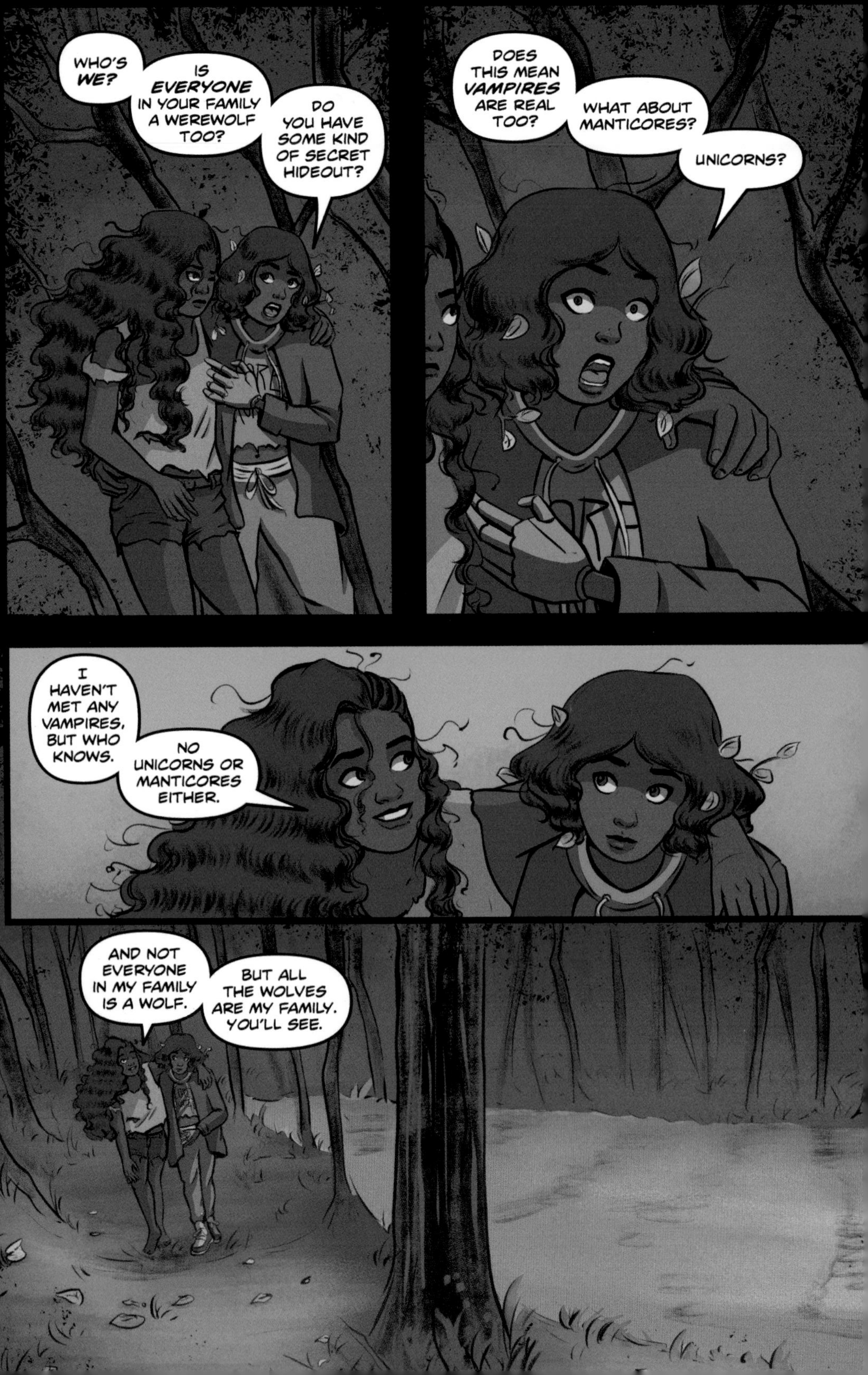
WHO'S *WE*?
IS *EVERYONE* IN YOUR FAMILY A WEREWOLF TOO?
DO YOU HAVE SOME KIND OF SECRET HIDEOUT?
DOES THIS MEAN *VAMPIRES* ARE REAL TOO?
WHAT ABOUT MANTICORES?
UNICORNS?
I HAVEN'T MET ANY VAMPIRES, BUT WHO KNOWS.
NO UNICORNS OR MANTICORES EITHER.
AND NOT EVERYONE IN MY FAMILY IS A WOLF.
BUT ALL THE WOLVES ARE MY FAMILY. YOU'LL SEE.

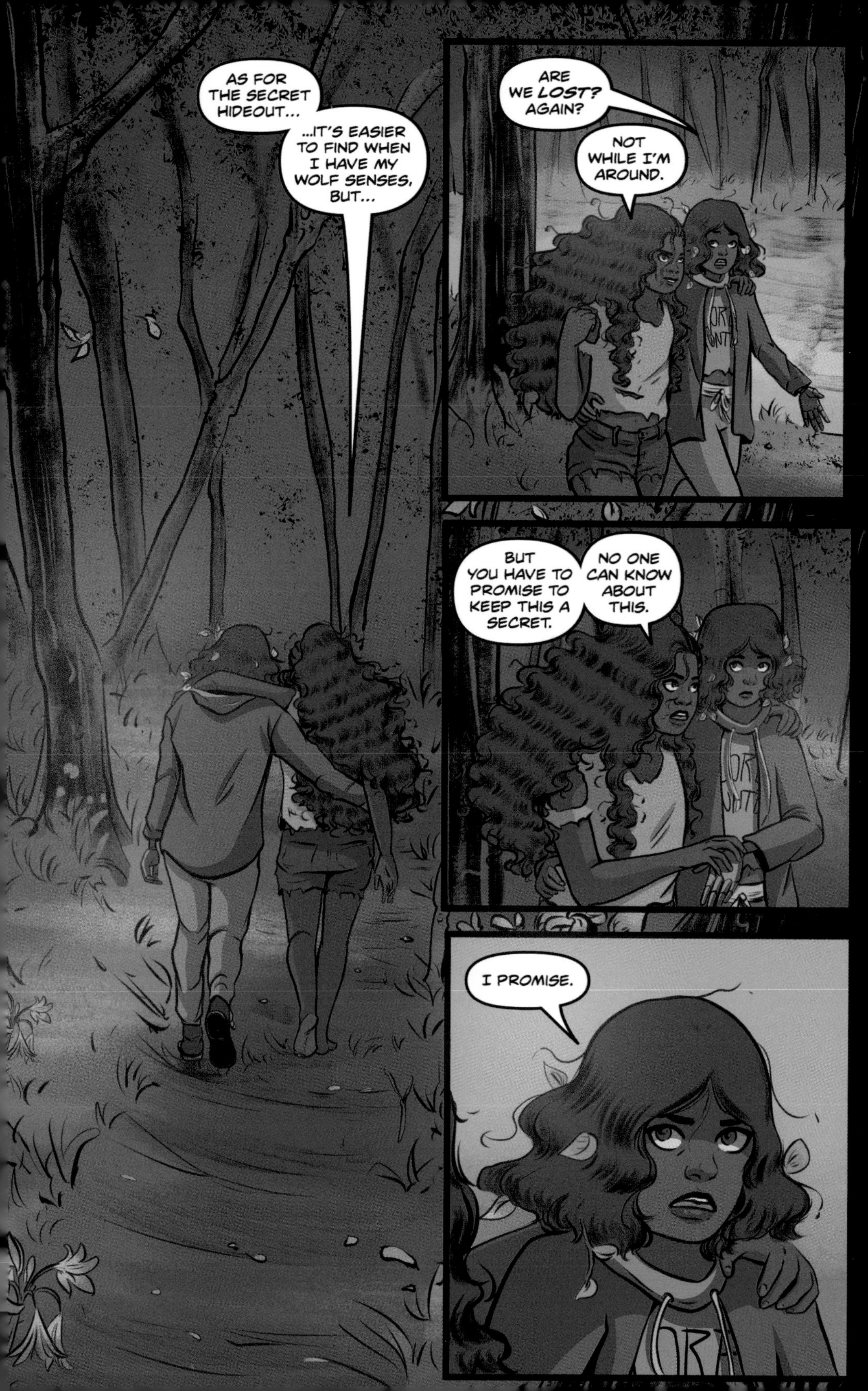
AS FOR THE SECRET HIDEOUT...
...IT'S EASIER TO FIND WHEN I HAVE MY WOLF SENSES, BUT...
ARE WE *LOST?* AGAIN?
NOT WHILE I'M AROUND.
BUT YOU HAVE TO PROMISE TO KEEP THIS A SECRET.
NO ONE CAN KNOW ABOUT THIS.
I PROMISE.

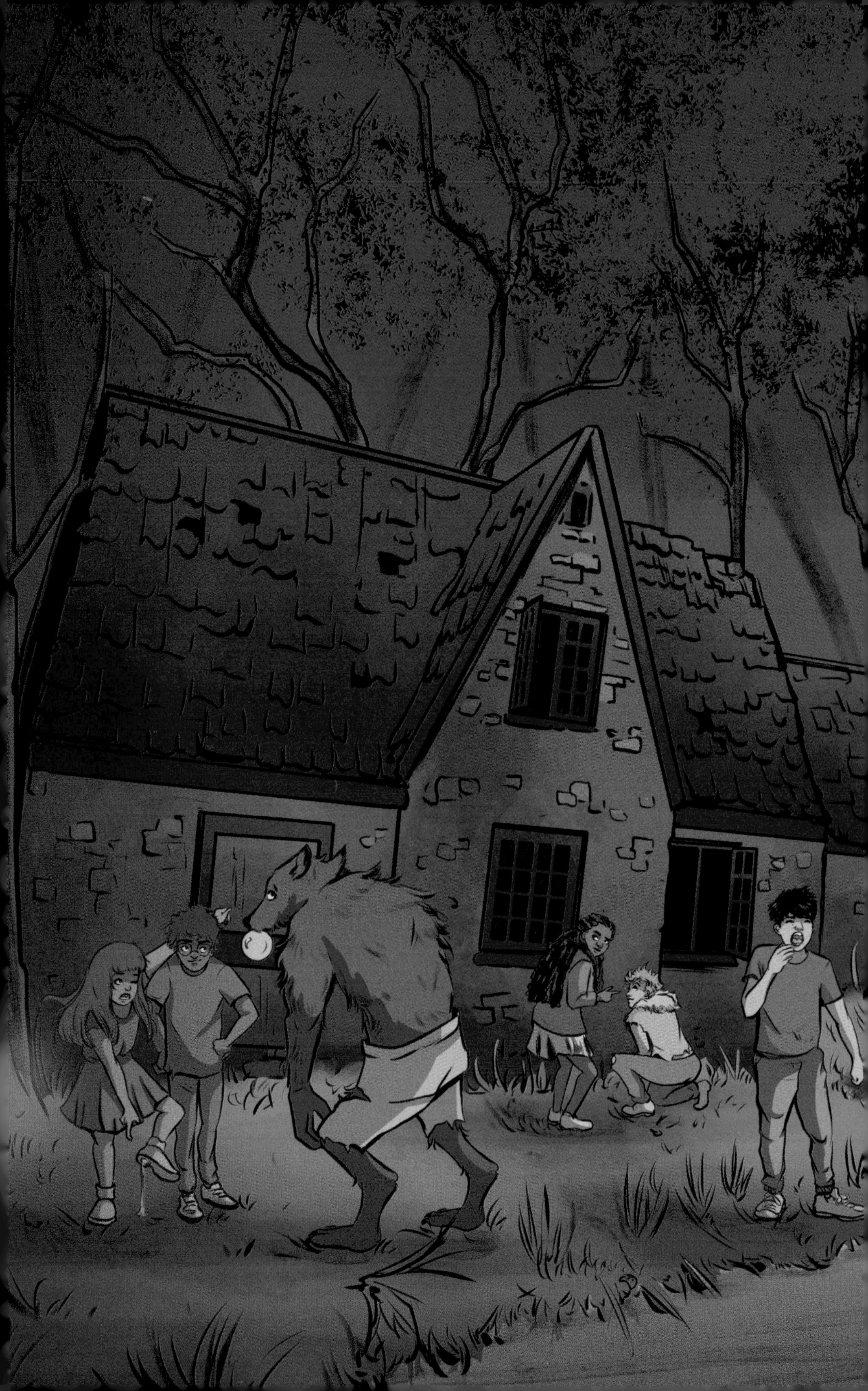

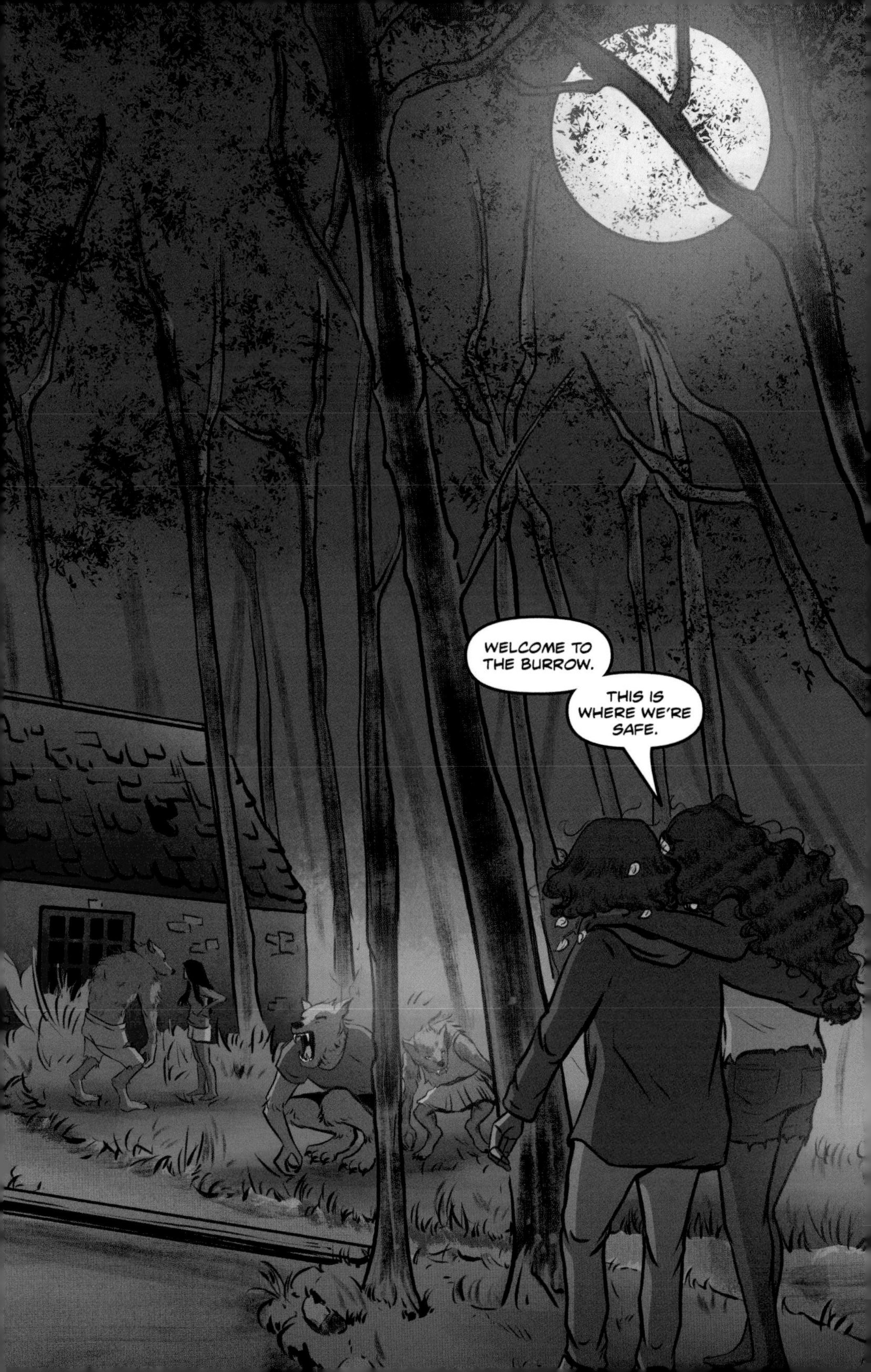
WELCOME TO THE BURROW.
THIS IS WHERE WE'RE SAFE.

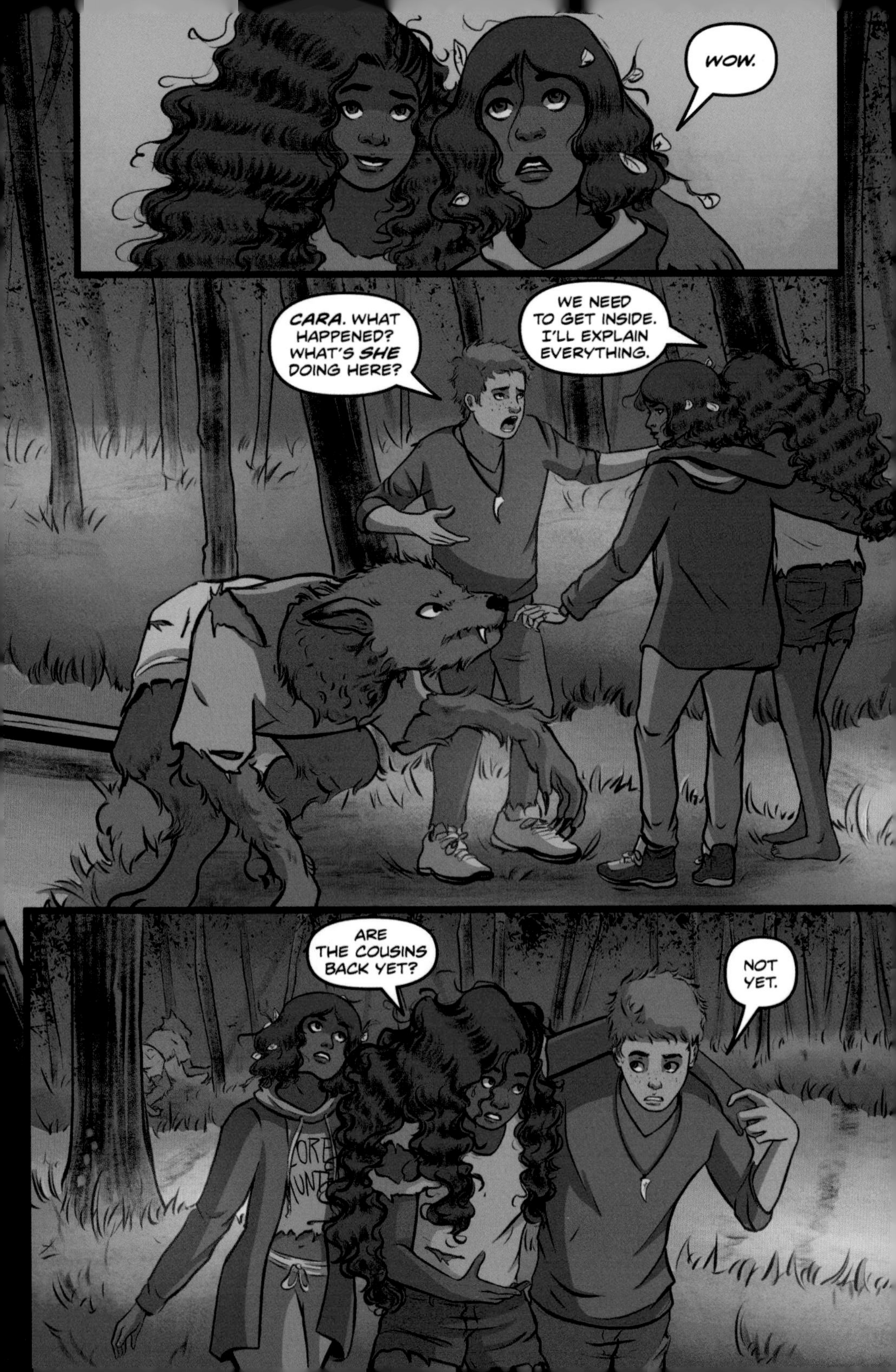
WOW.
CARA. WHAT HAPPENED? WHAT'S SHE DOING HERE?
WE NEED TO GET INSIDE. I'LL EXPLAIN EVERYTHING.
ARE THE COUSINS BACK YET?
NOT YET.

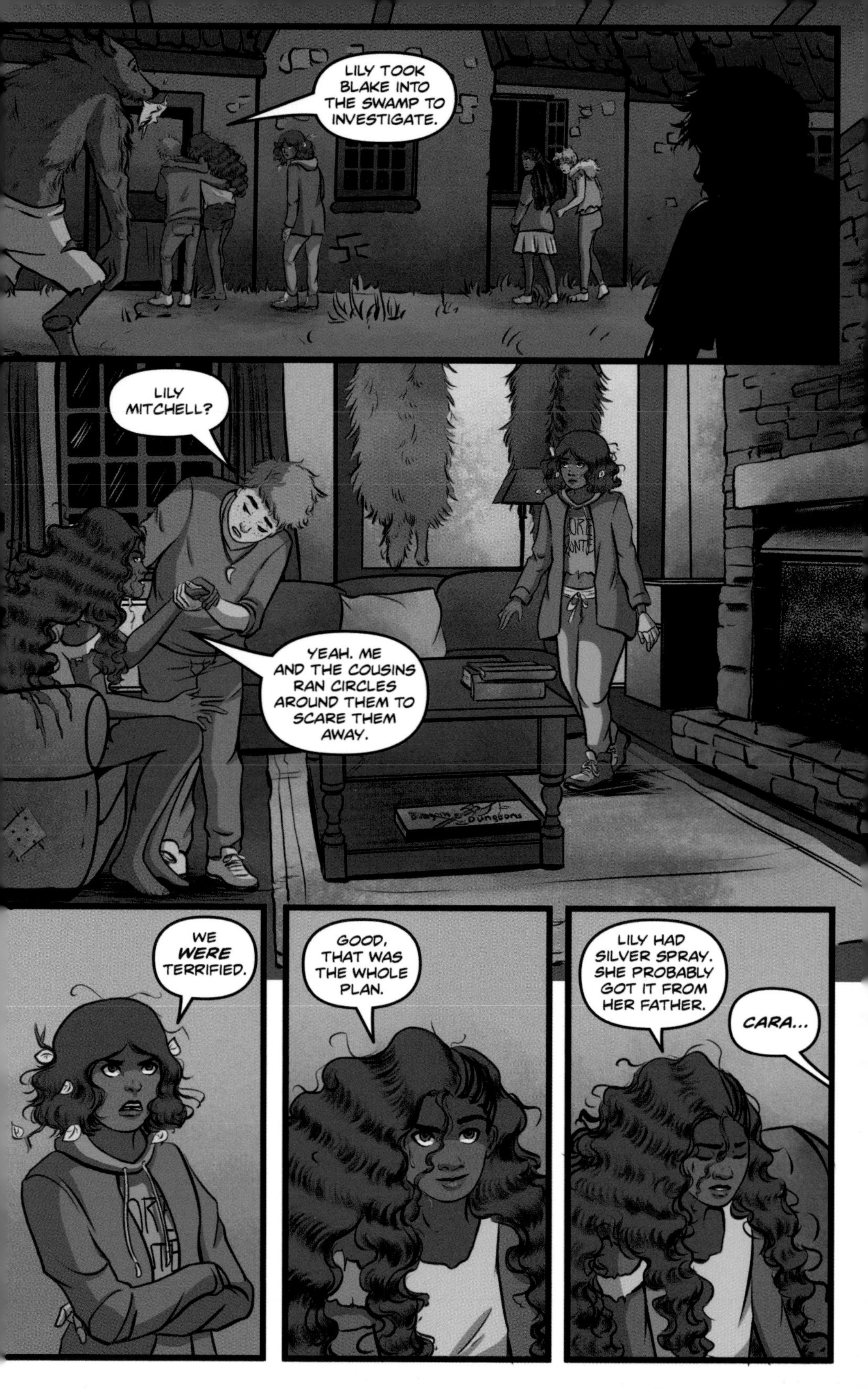
LILY TOOK BLAKE INTO THE SWAMP TO INVESTIGATE.
LILY MITCHELL?
YEAH. ME AND THE COUSINS RAN CIRCLES AROUND THEM TO SCARE THEM AWAY.
WE *WERE* TERRIFIED.
GOOD, THAT WAS THE WHOLE PLAN.
LILY HAD SILVER SPRAY. SHE PROBABLY GOT IT FROM HER FATHER.
CARA...

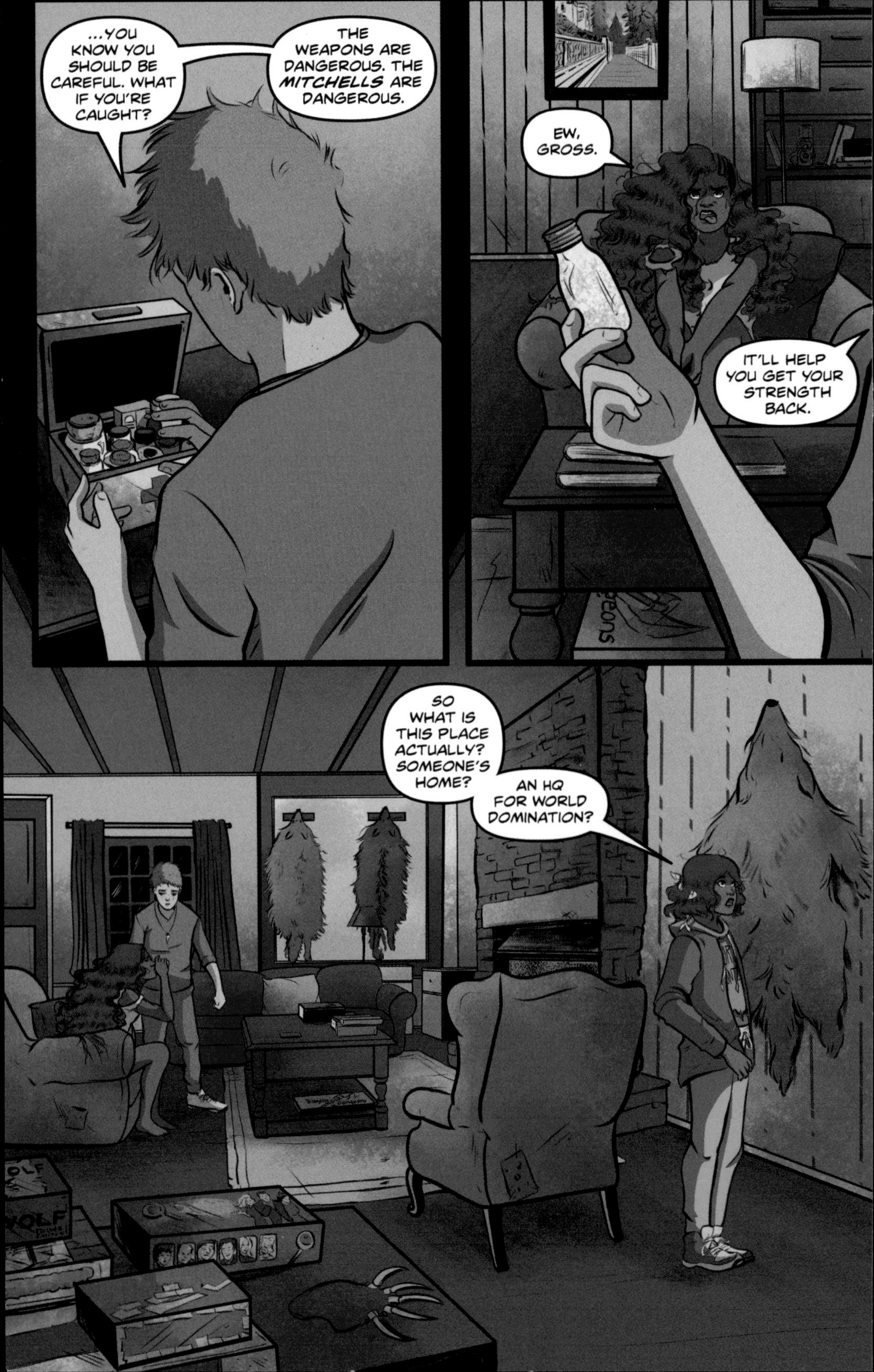
...YOU KNOW YOU SHOULD BE CAREFUL. WHAT IF YOU'RE CAUGHT?
THE WEAPONS ARE DANGEROUS. THE MITCHELLS ARE DANGEROUS.
EW, GROSS.
IT'LL HELP YOU GET YOUR STRENGTH BACK.
SO WHAT IS THIS PLACE ACTUALLY? SOMEONE'S HOME?
AN HQ FOR WORLD DOMINATION?

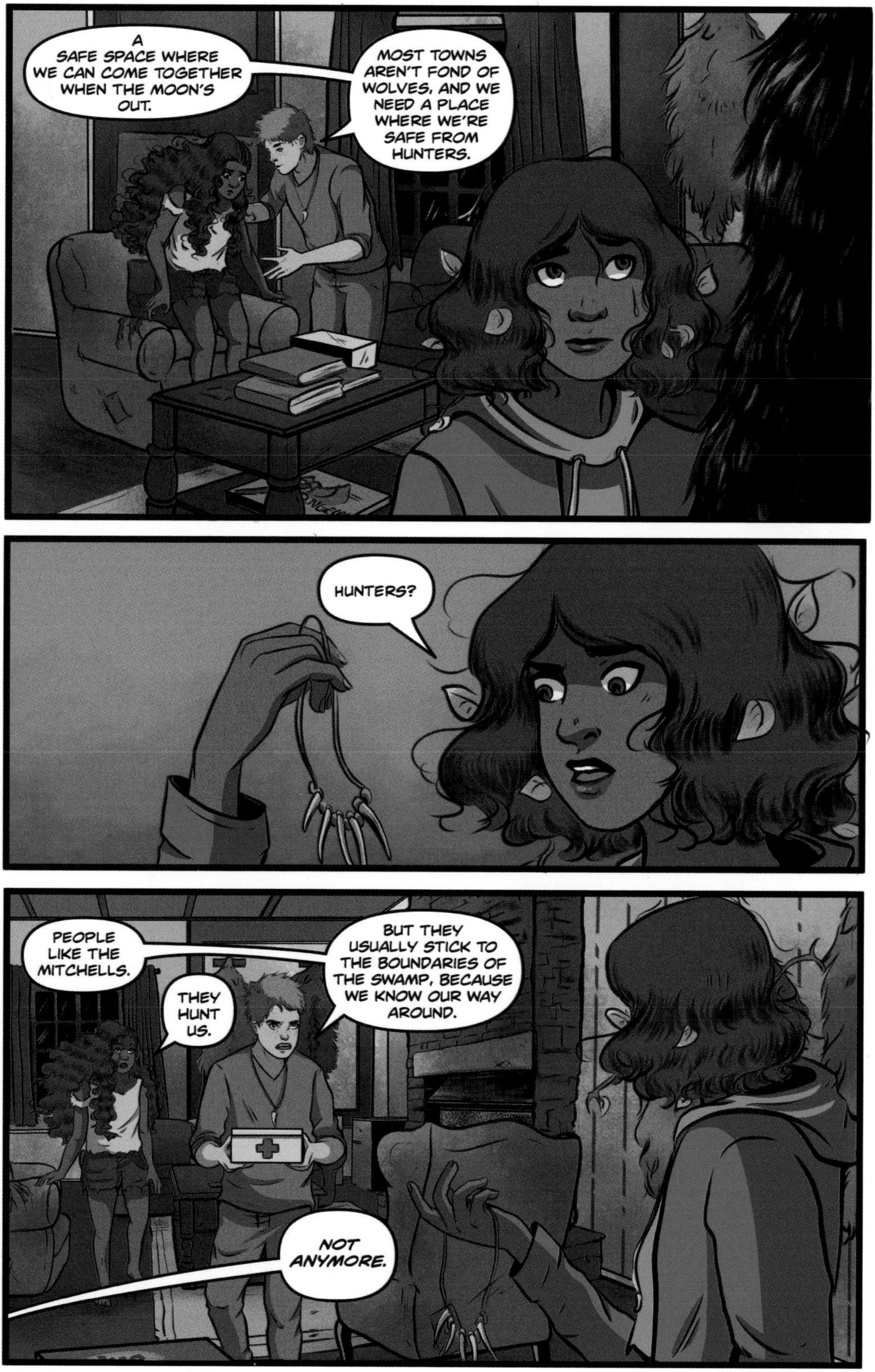
A SAFE SPACE WHERE WE CAN COME TOGETHER WHEN THE MOON'S OUT.
MOST TOWNS AREN'T FOND OF WOLVES, AND WE NEED A PLACE WHERE WE'RE SAFE FROM HUNTERS.
HUNTERS?
PEOPLE LIKE THE MITCHELLS.
THEY HUNT US.
BUT THEY USUALLY STICK TO THE BOUNDARIES OF THE SWAMP, BECAUSE WE KNOW OUR WAY AROUND.
NOT ANYMORE.

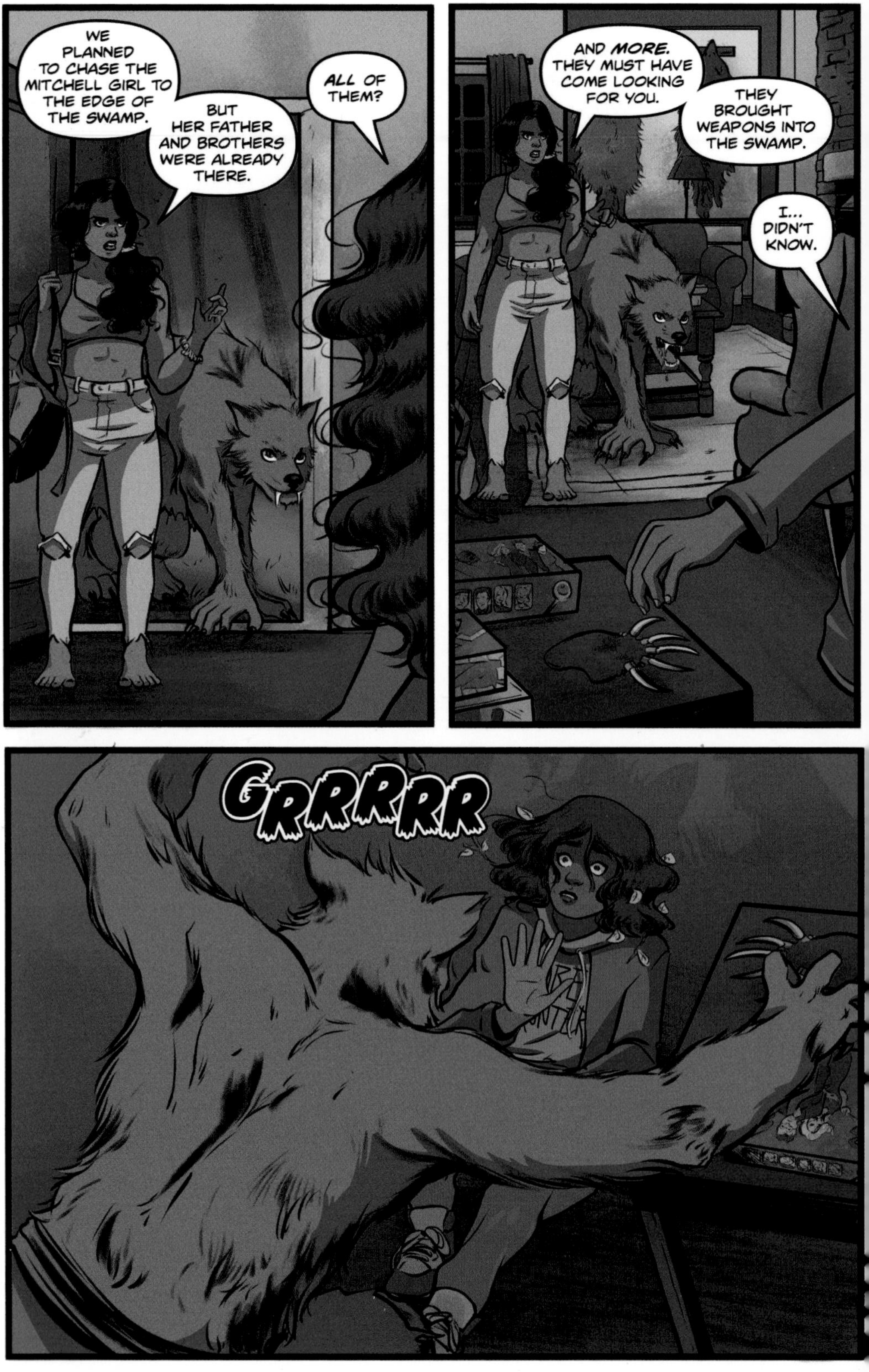
WE PLANNED TO CHASE THE MITCHELL GIRL TO THE EDGE OF THE SWAMP.
BUT HER FATHER AND BROTHERS WERE ALREADY THERE.
ALL OF THEM?
AND MORE. THEY MUST HAVE COME LOOKING FOR YOU.
THEY BROUGHT WEAPONS INTO THE SWAMP.
I... DIDN'T KNOW.
GRRRRR

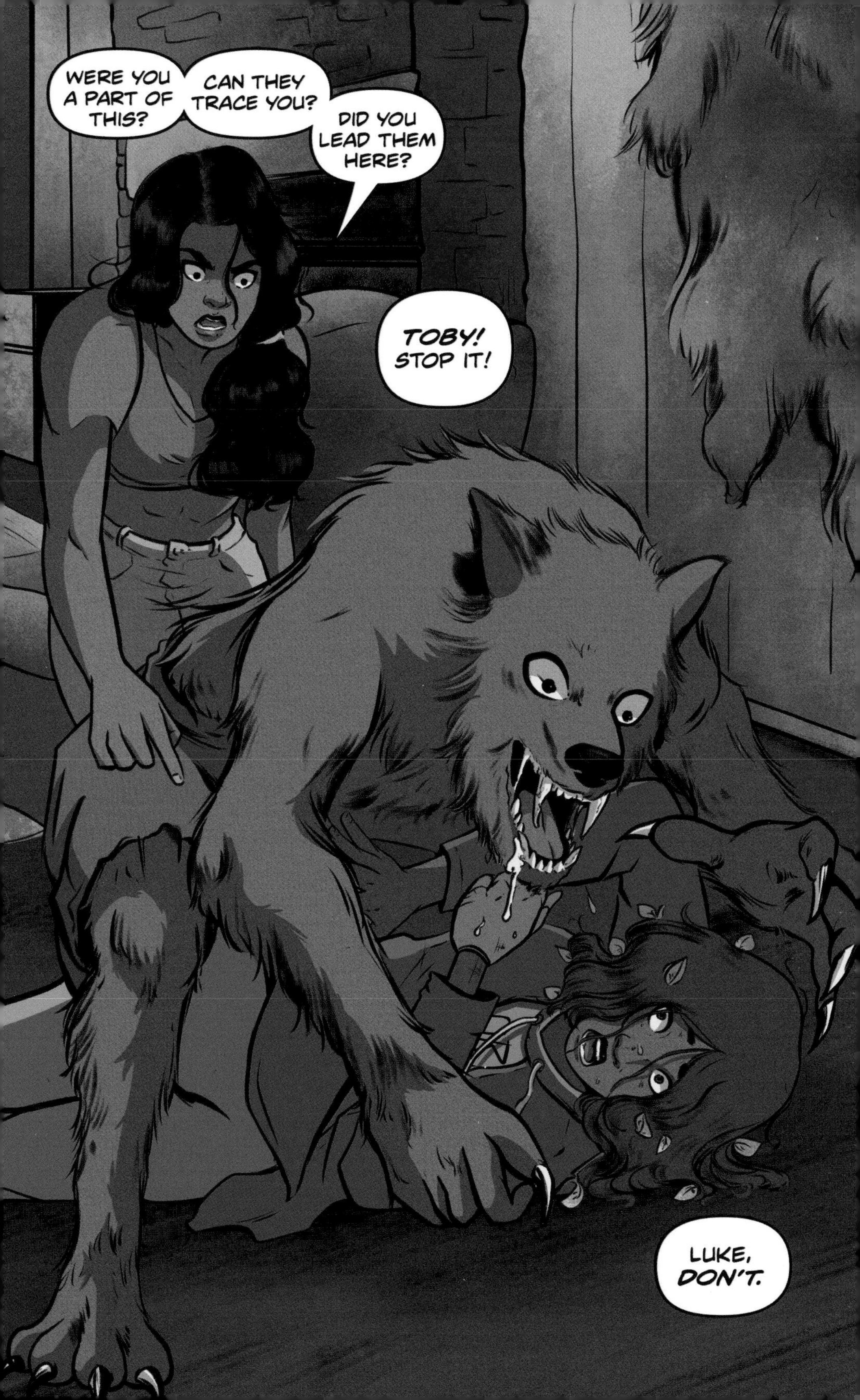
WERE YOU A PART OF THIS?
CAN THEY TRACE YOU?
DID YOU LEAD THEM HERE?
TOBY! STOP IT!
LUKE, DON'T.

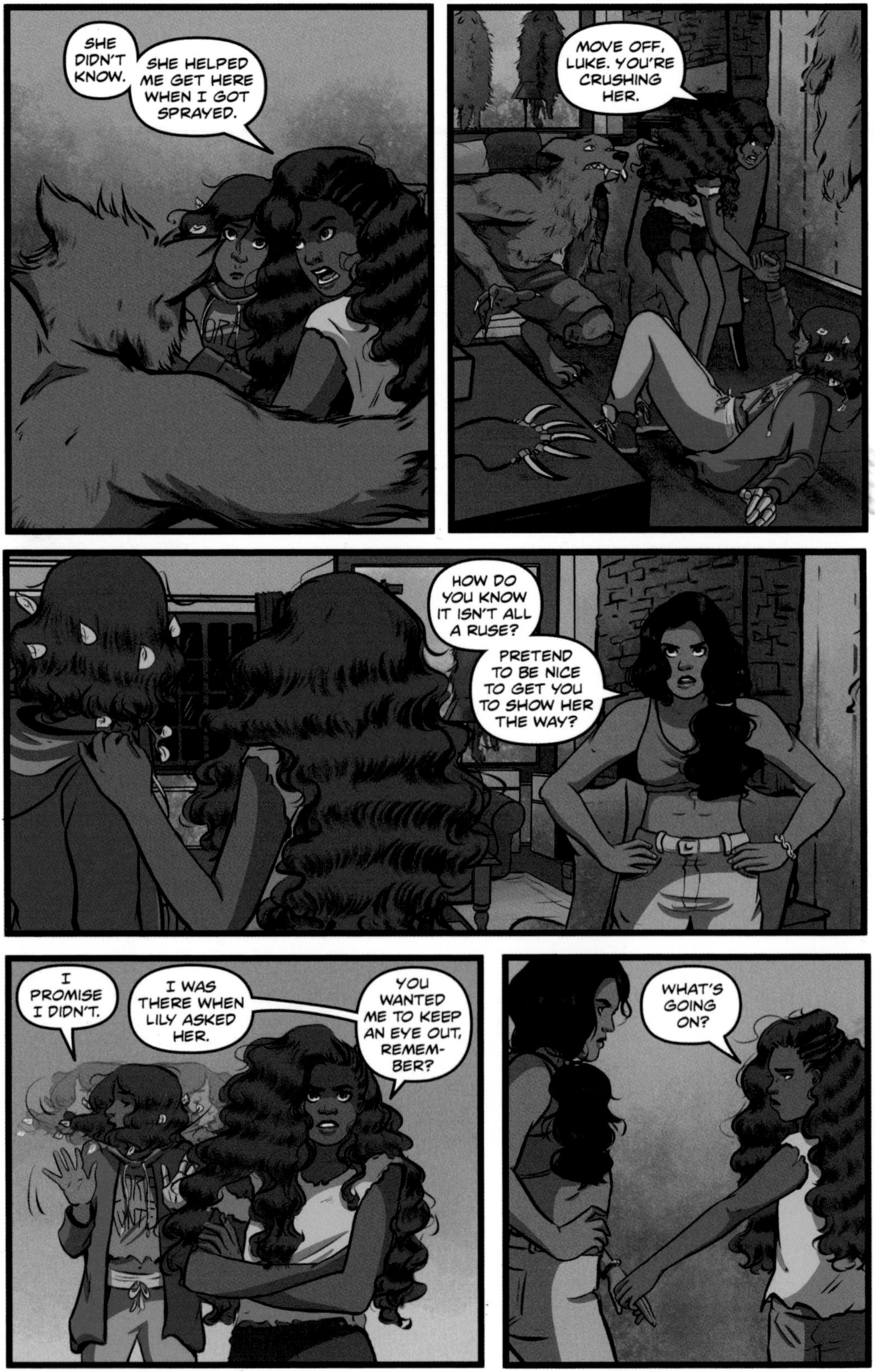
SHE DIDN'T KNOW.
SHE HELPED ME GET HERE WHEN I GOT SPRAYED.
MOVE OFF, LUKE. YOU'RE CRUSHING HER.
HOW DO YOU KNOW IT ISN'T ALL A RUSE?
PRETEND TO BE NICE TO GET YOU TO SHOW HER THE WAY?
I PROMISE I DIDN'T.
I WAS THERE WHEN LILY ASKED HER.
YOU WANTED ME TO KEEP AN EYE OUT, REMEMBER?
WHAT'S GOING ON?

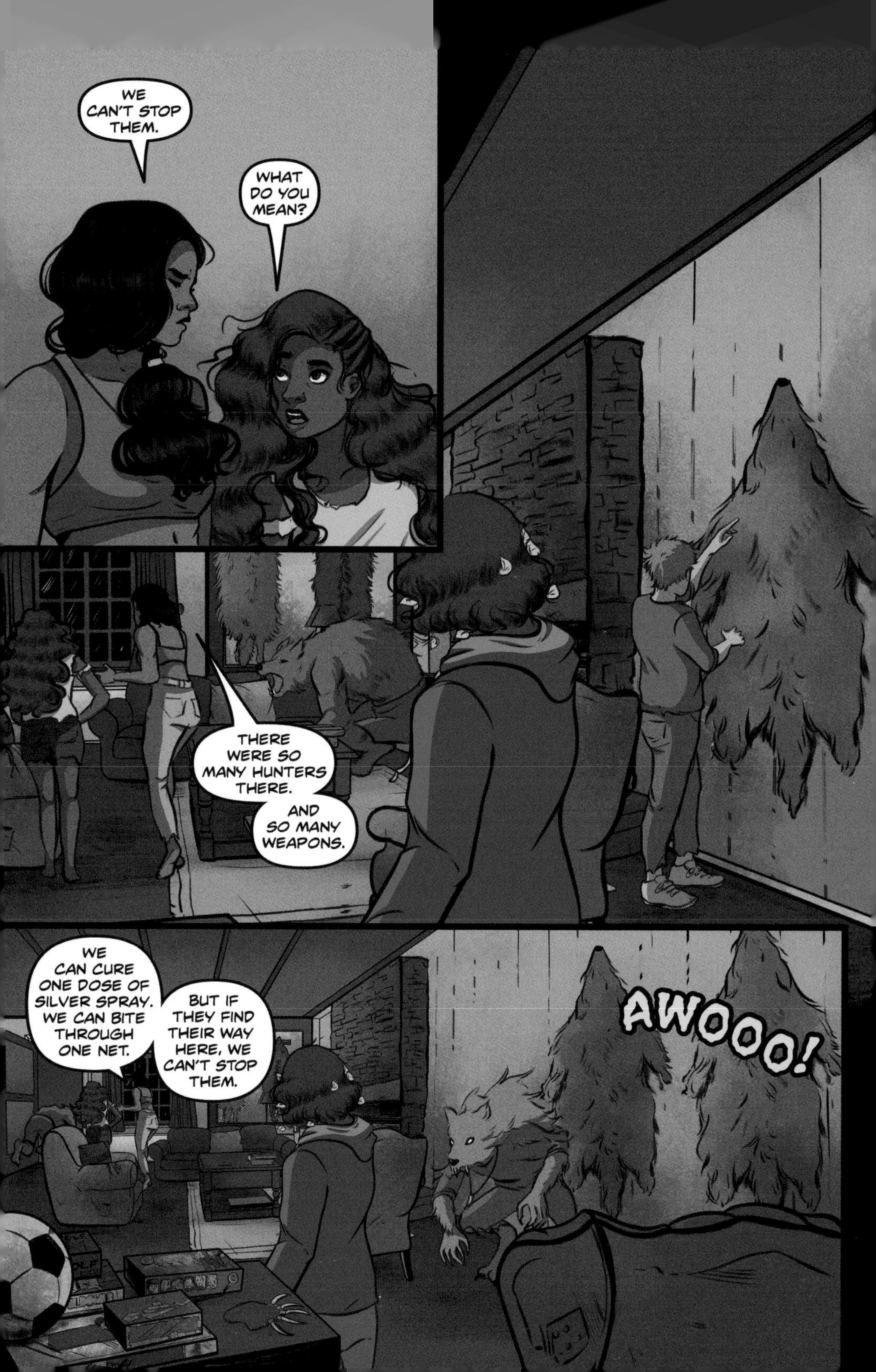
WE CAN'T STOP THEM.
WHAT DO YOU MEAN?
THERE WERE SO MANY HUNTERS THERE.
AND SO MANY WEAPONS.
WE CAN CURE ONE DOSE OF SILVER SPRAY. WE CAN BITE THROUGH ONE NET.
BUT IF THEY FIND THEIR WAY HERE, WE CAN'T STOP THEM.
AWOOOO!

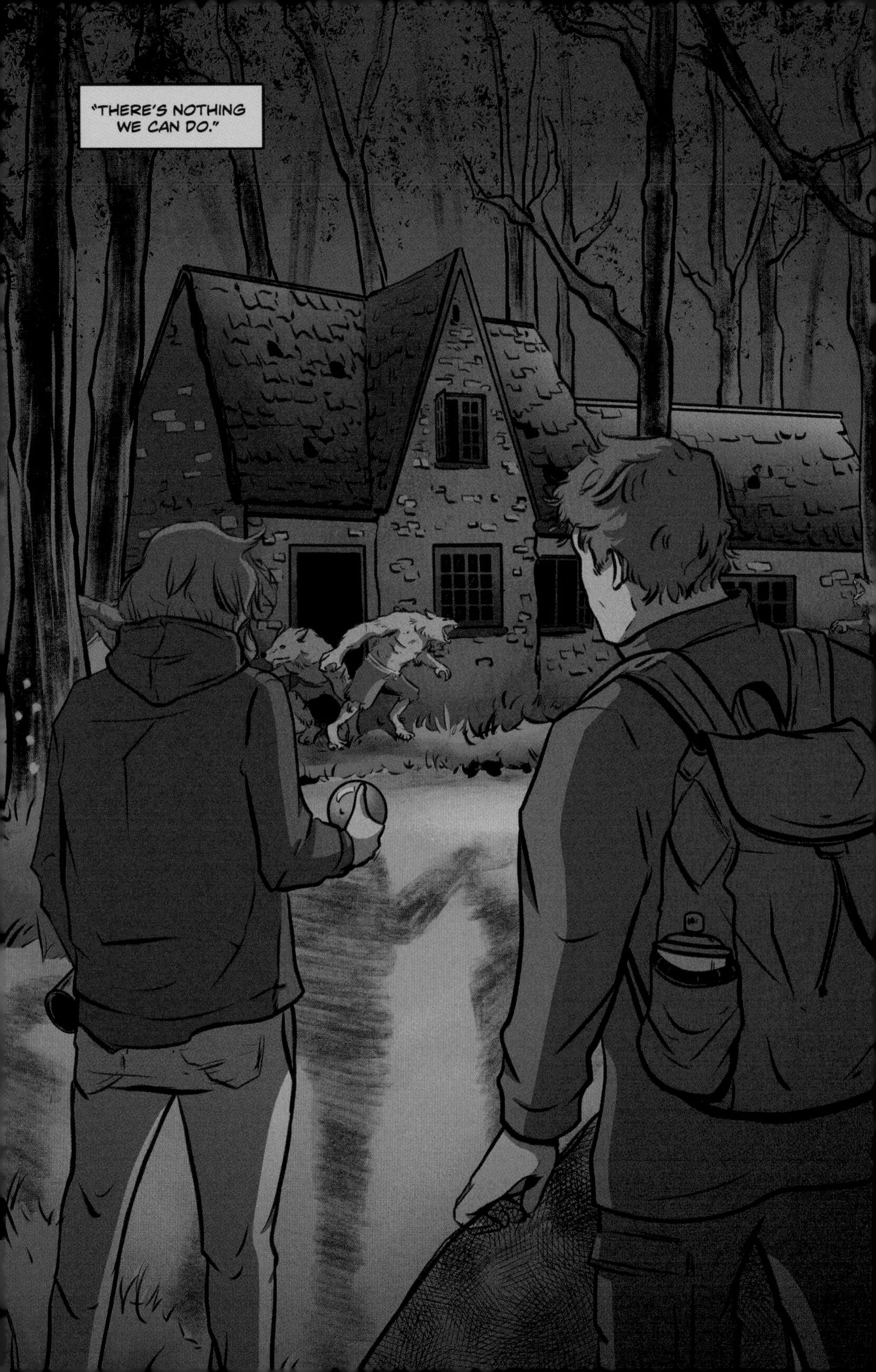
"THERE'S NOTHING WE CAN DO."

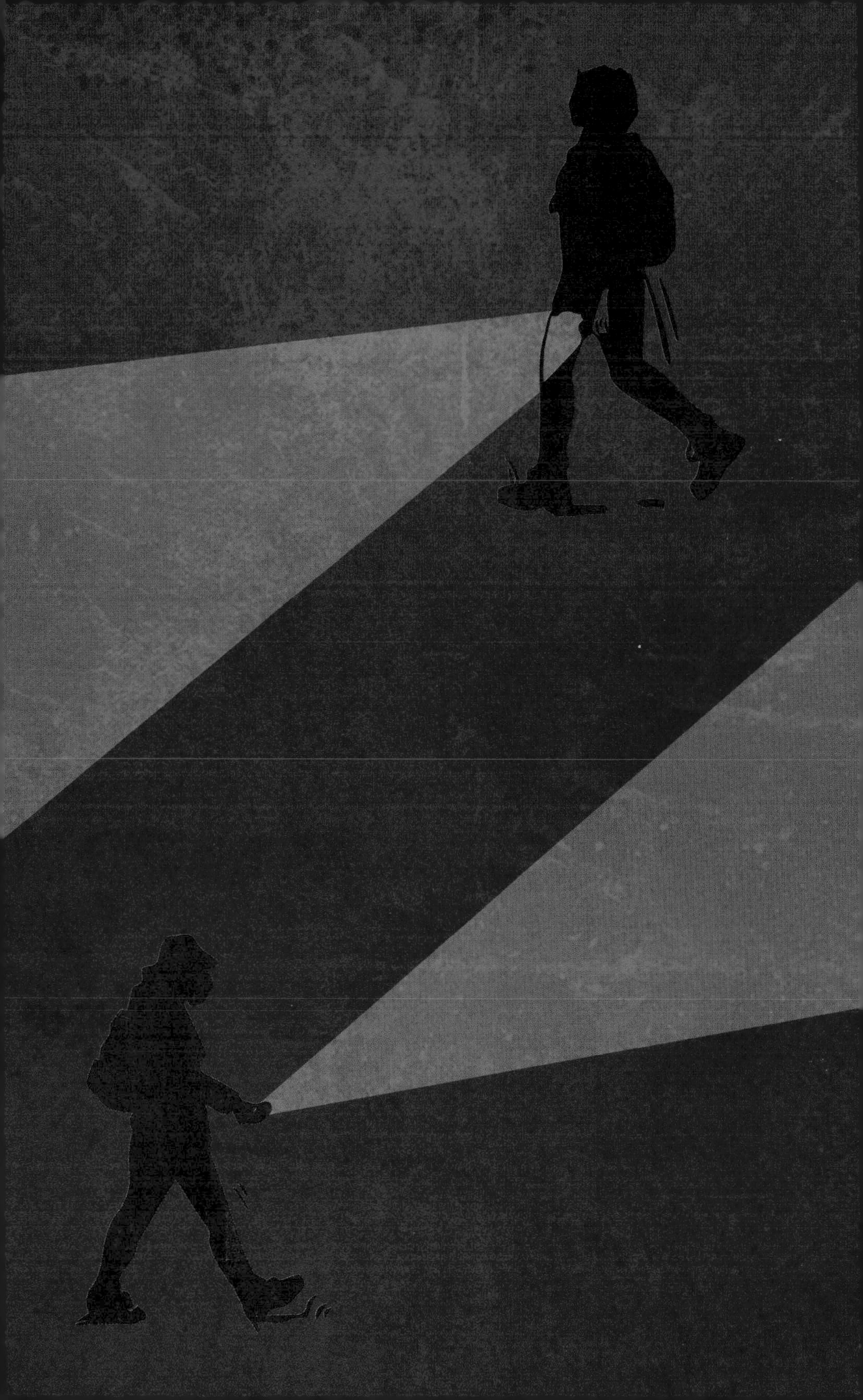

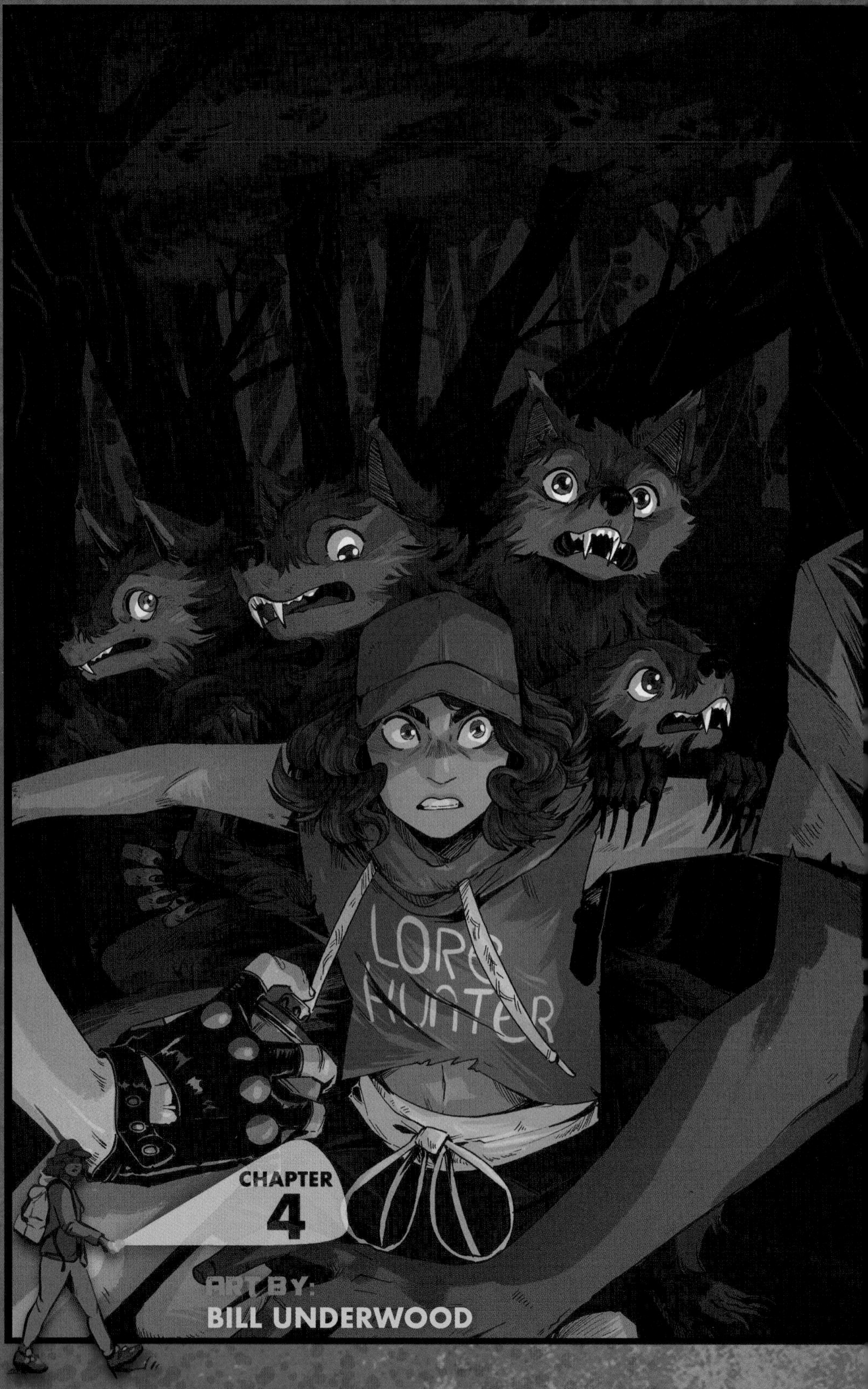
LORE HUNTER
CHAPTER
4
ART BY:
BILL UNDERWOOD

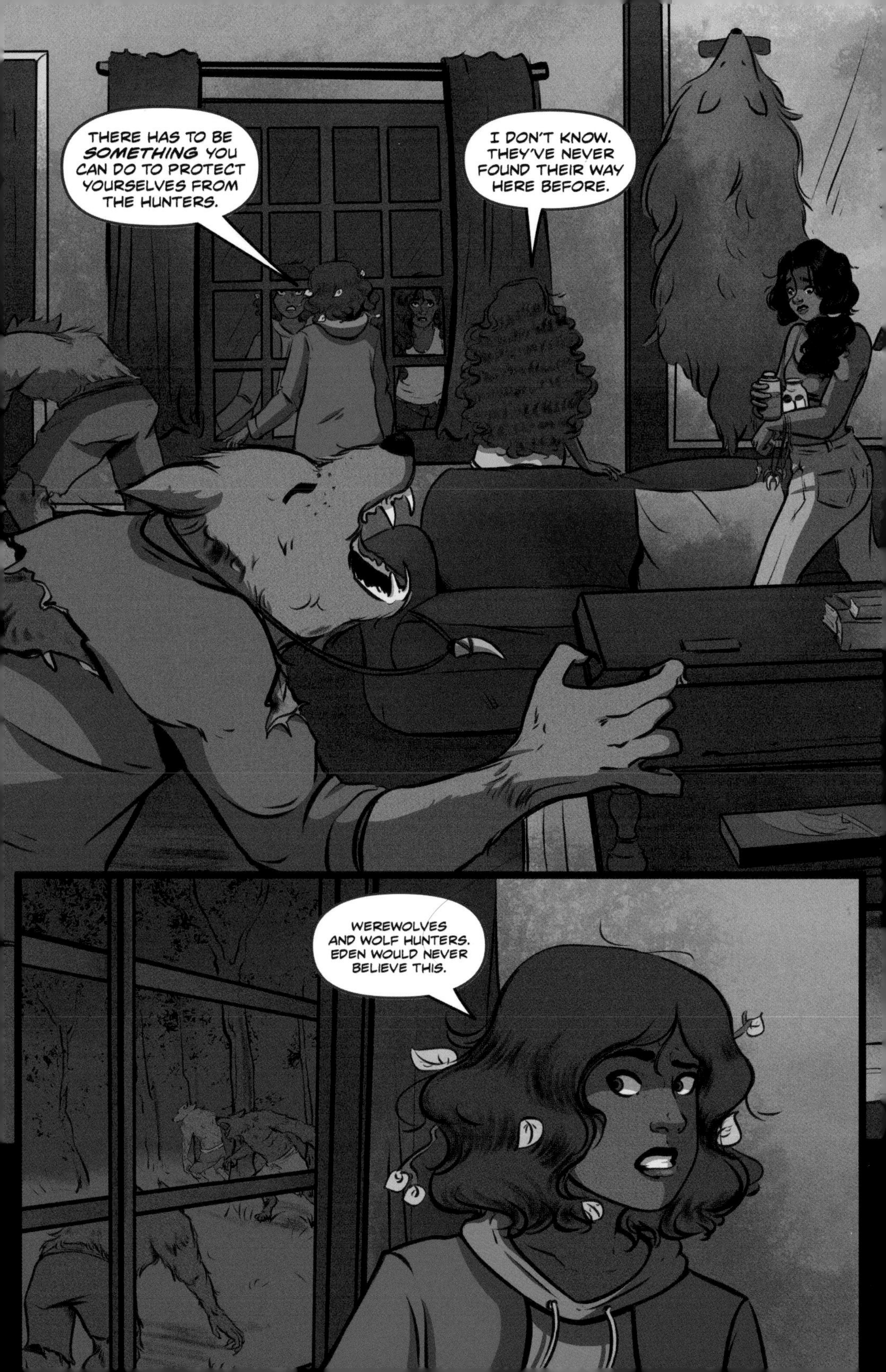
THERE HAS TO BE *SOMETHING* YOU CAN DO TO PROTECT YOURSELVES FROM THE HUNTERS.
I DON'T KNOW. THEY'VE NEVER FOUND THEIR WAY HERE BEFORE.
WEREWOLVES AND WOLF HUNTERS. EDEN WOULD NEVER BELIEVE THIS.

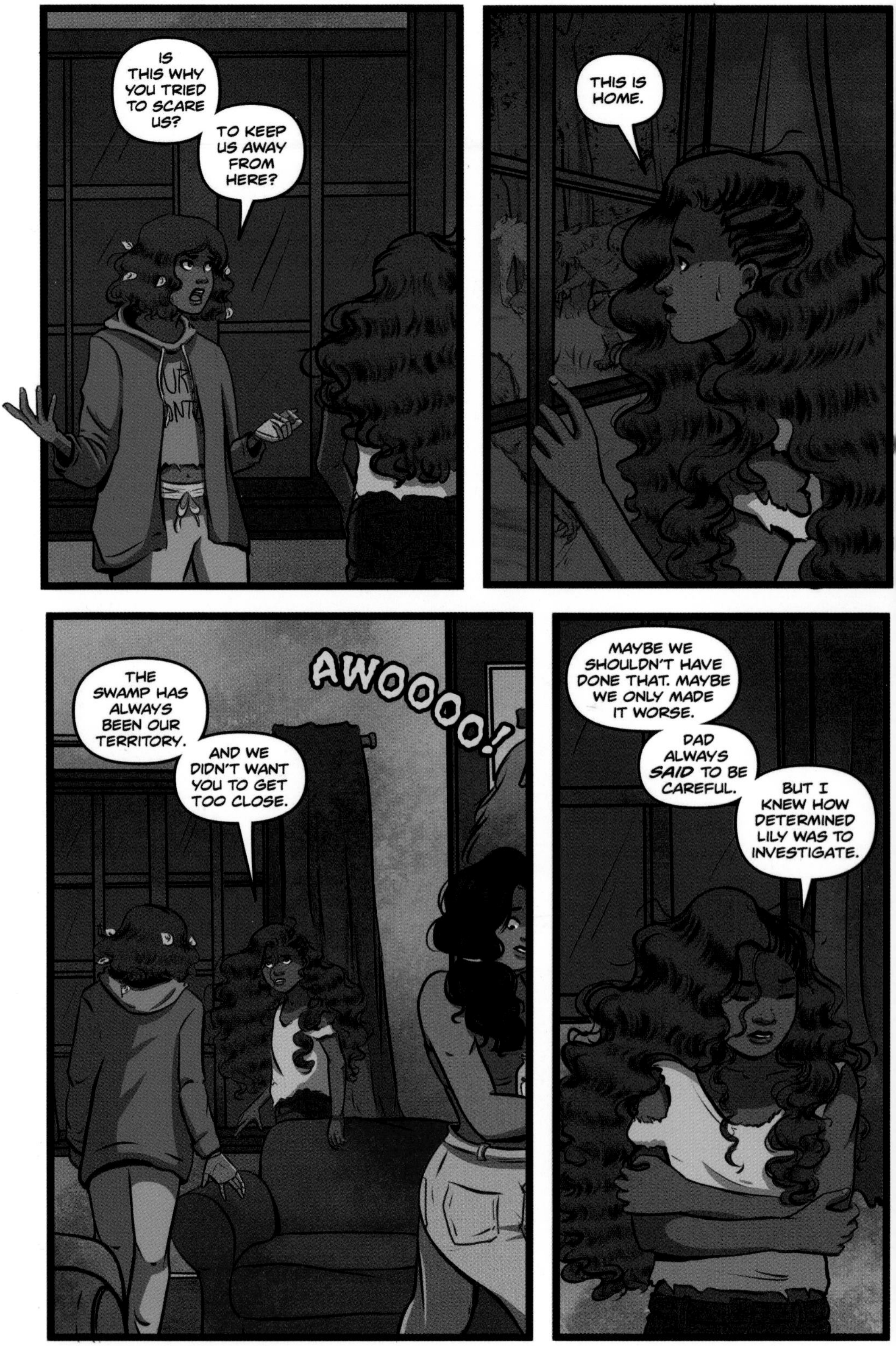
IS THIS WHY YOU TRIED TO SCARE US?
TO KEEP US AWAY FROM HERE?
THIS IS HOME.
THE SWAMP HAS ALWAYS BEEN OUR TERRITORY.
AND WE DIDN'T WANT YOU TO GET TOO CLOSE.
AWOOOO!
MAYBE WE SHOULDN'T HAVE DONE THAT. MAYBE WE ONLY MADE IT WORSE.
DAD ALWAYS *SAID* TO BE CAREFUL.
BUT I KNEW HOW DETERMINED LILY WAS TO INVESTIGATE.

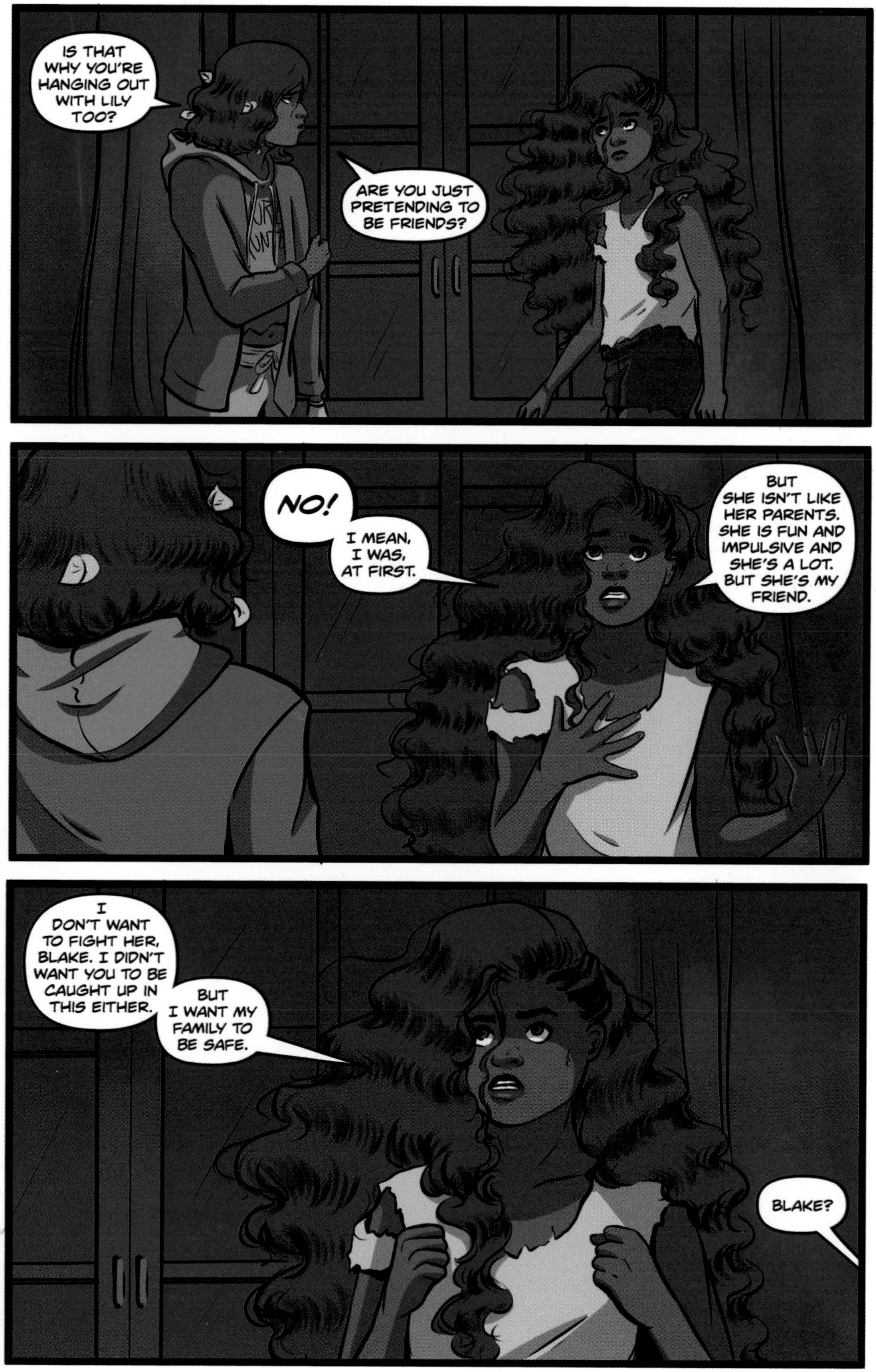
IS THAT WHY YOU'RE HANGING OUT WITH LILY TOO?
ARE YOU JUST PRETENDING TO BE FRIENDS?
NO!
I MEAN, I WAS, AT FIRST.
BUT SHE ISN'T LIKE HER PARENTS. SHE IS FUN AND IMPULSIVE AND SHE'S A LOT. BUT SHE'S MY FRIEND.
I DON'T WANT TO FIGHT HER, BLAKE. I DIDN'T WANT YOU TO BE CAUGHT UP IN THIS EITHER.
BUT I WANT MY FAMILY TO BE SAFE.
BLAKE?

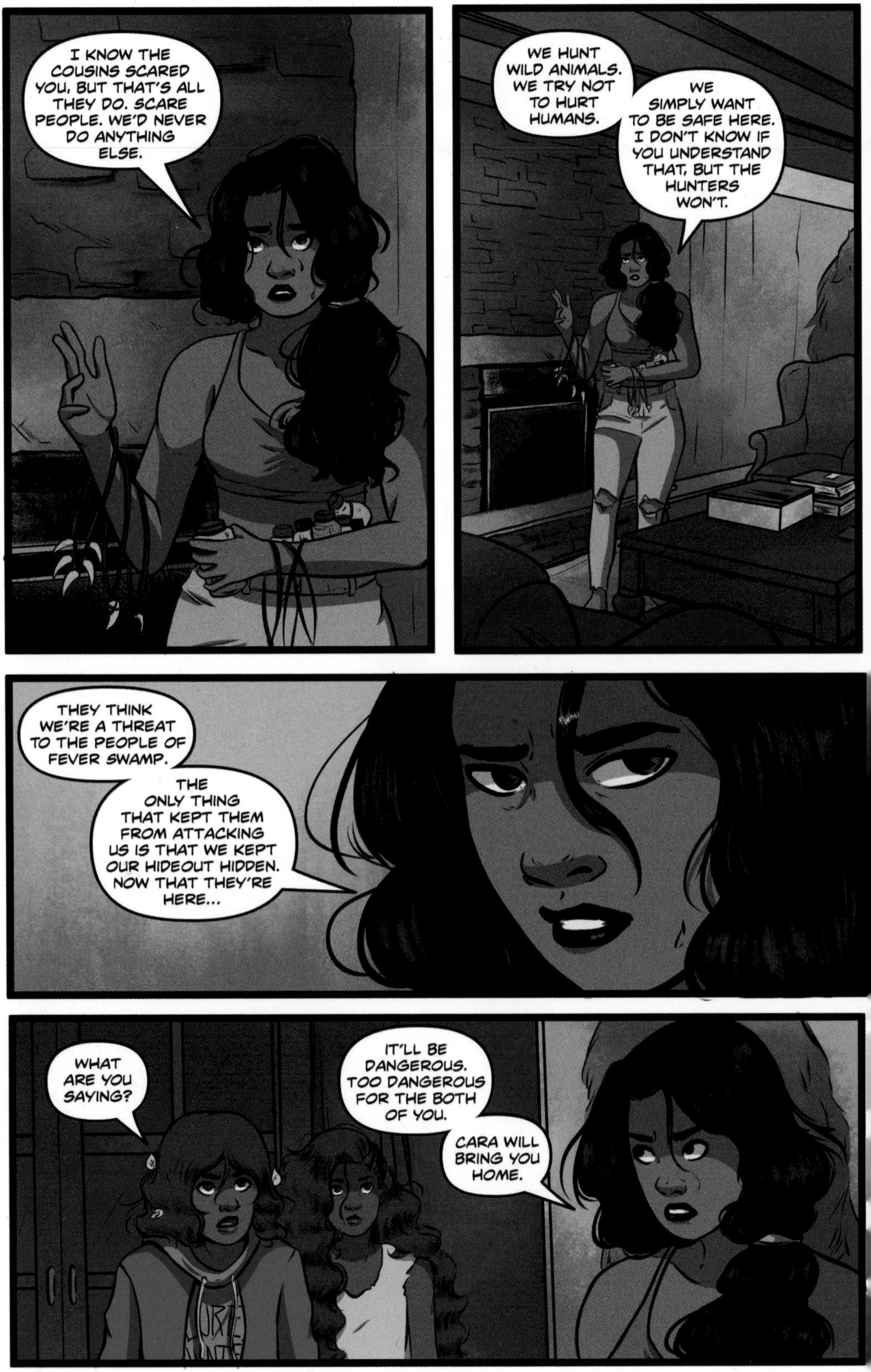
I KNOW THE COUSINS SCARED YOU, BUT THAT'S ALL THEY DO. SCARE PEOPLE. WE'D NEVER DO ANYTHING ELSE.
WE HUNT WILD ANIMALS. WE TRY NOT TO HURT HUMANS.
WE SIMPLY WANT TO BE SAFE HERE. I DON'T KNOW IF YOU UNDERSTAND THAT, BUT THE HUNTERS WON'T.
THEY THINK WE'RE A THREAT TO THE PEOPLE OF FEVER SWAMP.
THE ONLY THING THAT KEPT THEM FROM ATTACKING US IS THAT WE KEPT OUR HIDEOUT HIDDEN. NOW THAT THEY'RE HERE...
WHAT ARE YOU SAYING?
IT'LL BE DANGEROUS. TOO DANGEROUS FOR THE BOTH OF YOU.
CARA WILL BRING YOU HOME.

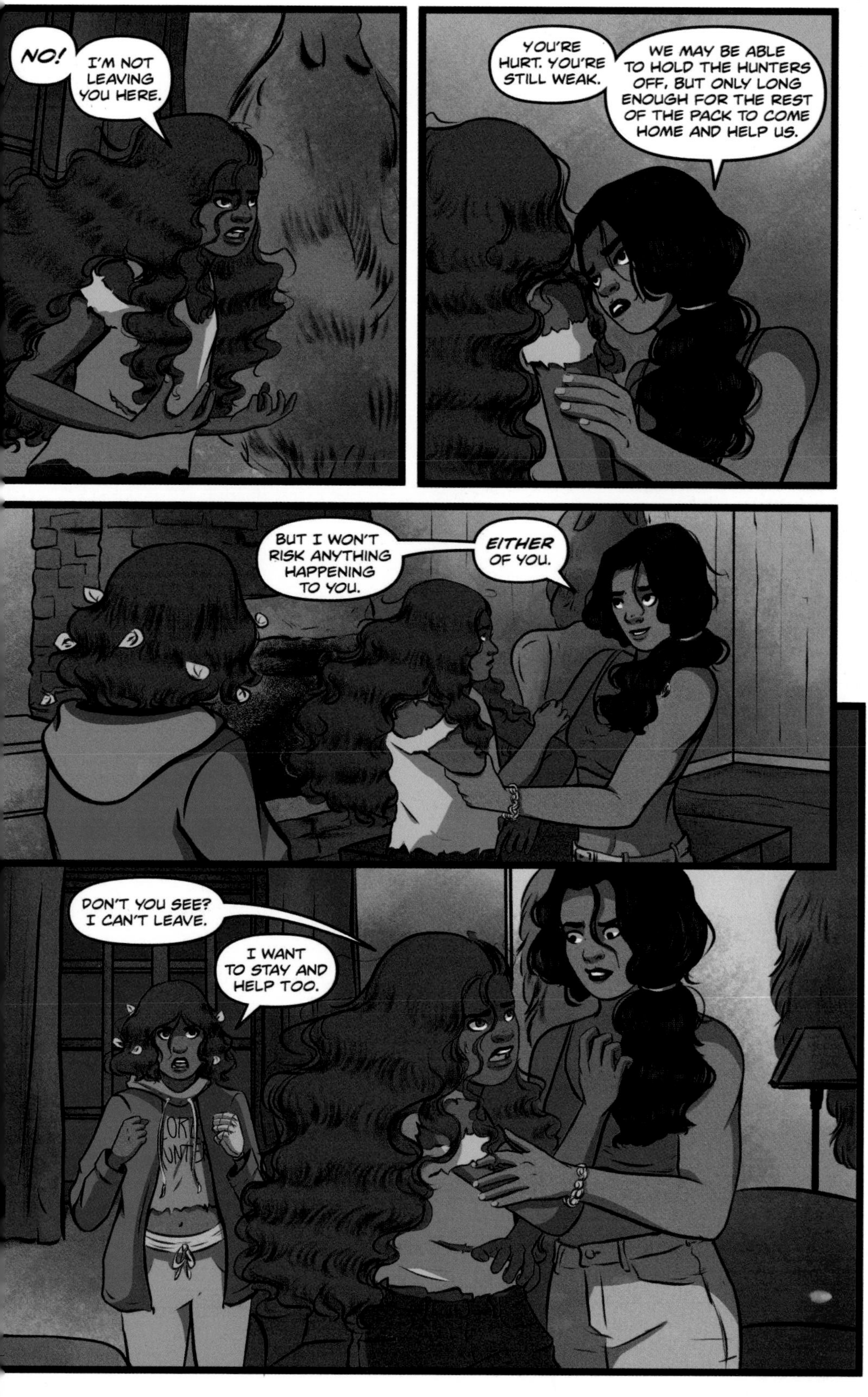
NO!
I'M NOT LEAVING YOU HERE.
YOU'RE HURT. YOU'RE STILL WEAK.
WE MAY BE ABLE TO HOLD THE HUNTERS OFF, BUT ONLY LONG ENOUGH FOR THE REST OF THE PACK TO COME HOME AND HELP US.
BUT I WON'T RISK ANYTHING HAPPENING TO YOU.
EITHER OF YOU.
DON'T YOU SEE? I CAN'T LEAVE.
I WANT TO STAY AND HELP TOO.

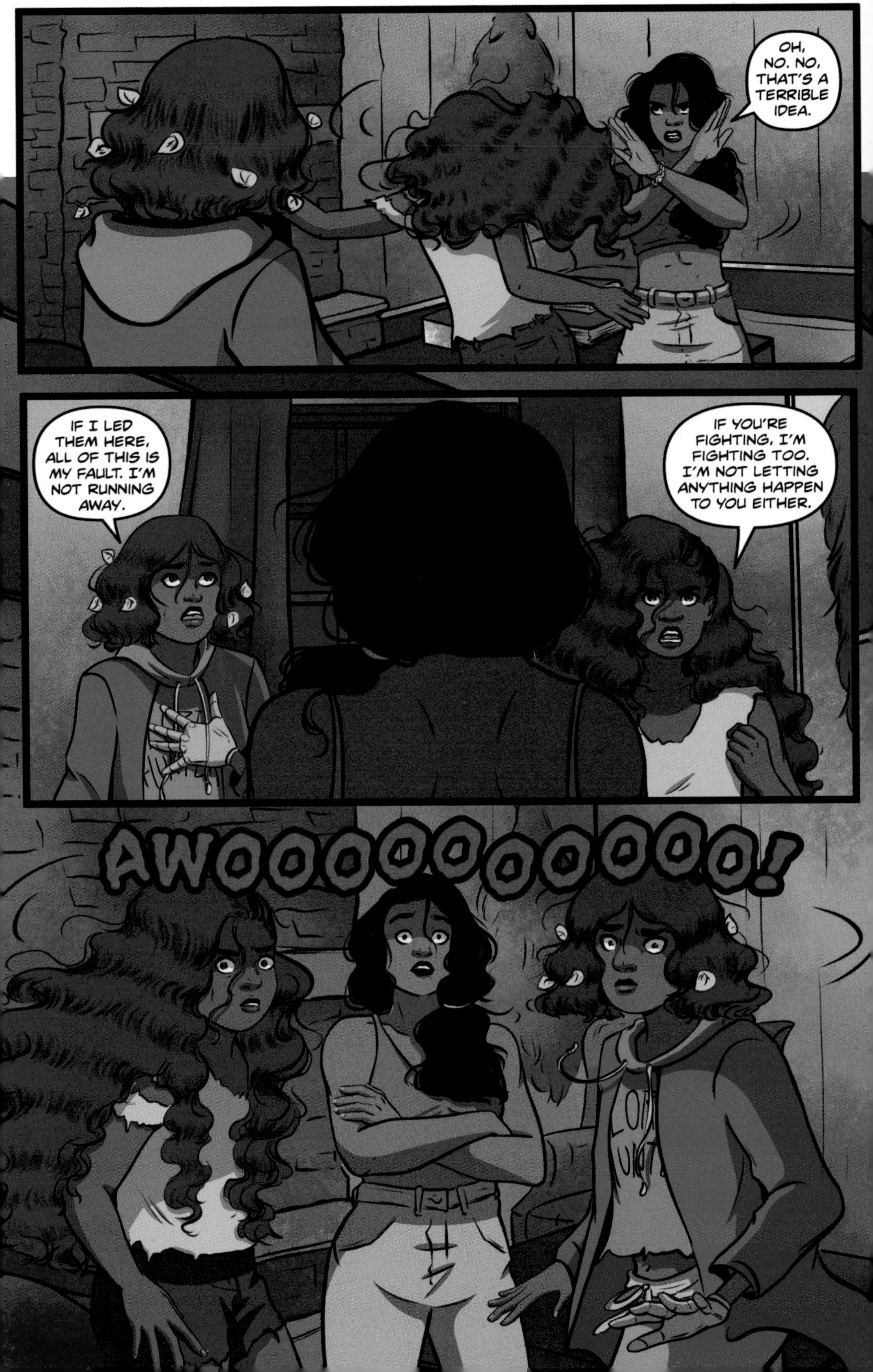
OH, NO. NO, THAT'S A TERRIBLE IDEA.
IF I LED THEM HERE, ALL OF THIS IS MY FAULT. I'M NOT RUNNING AWAY.
IF YOU'RE FIGHTING, I'M FIGHTING TOO. I'M NOT LETTING ANYTHING HAPPEN TO YOU EITHER.
AWOOOOOOOOOO!

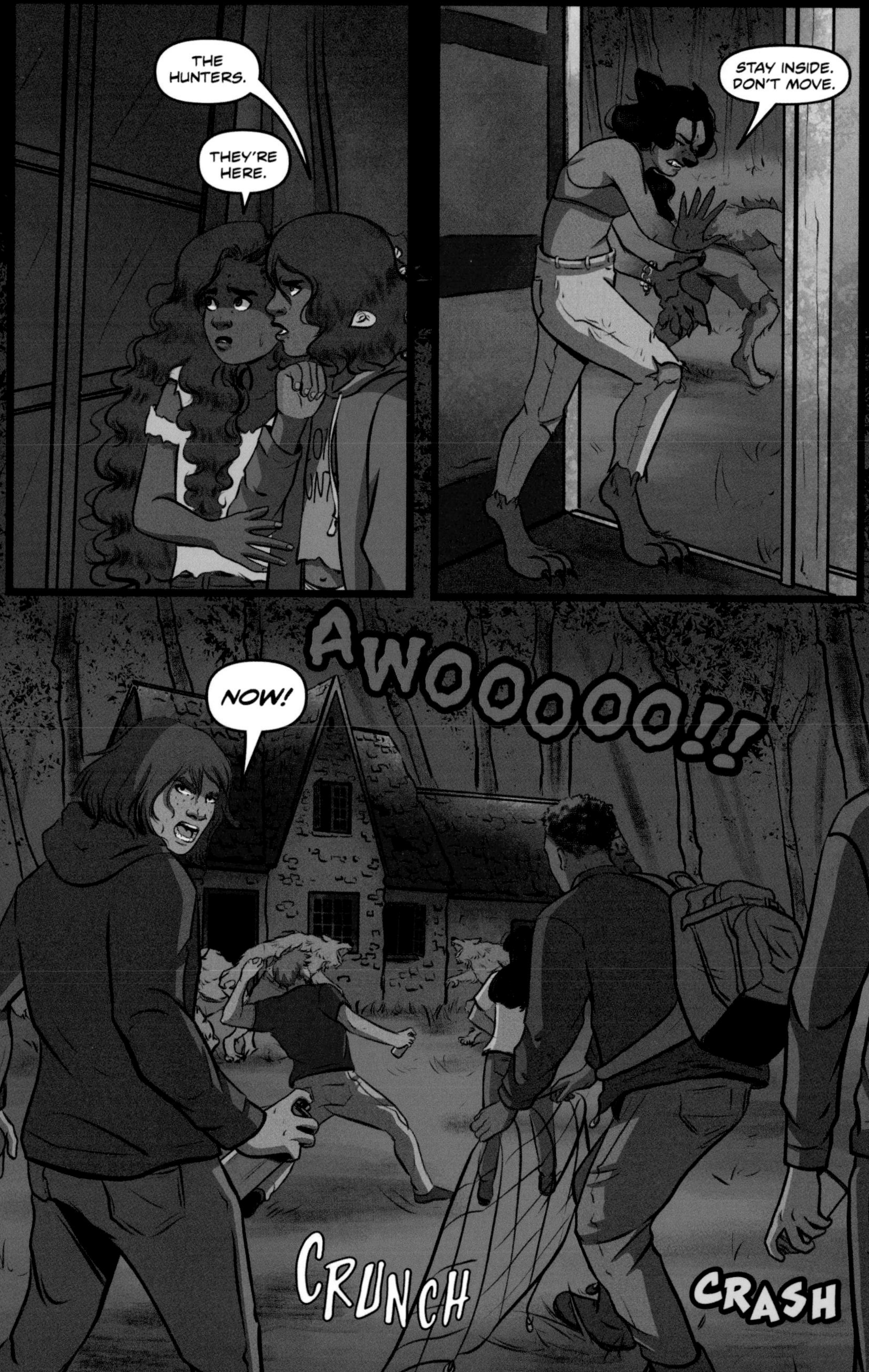
THE HUNTERS.
THEY'RE HERE.
STAY INSIDE. DON'T MOVE.
AWOOOOOO!!
NOW!
CRUNCH
CRASH

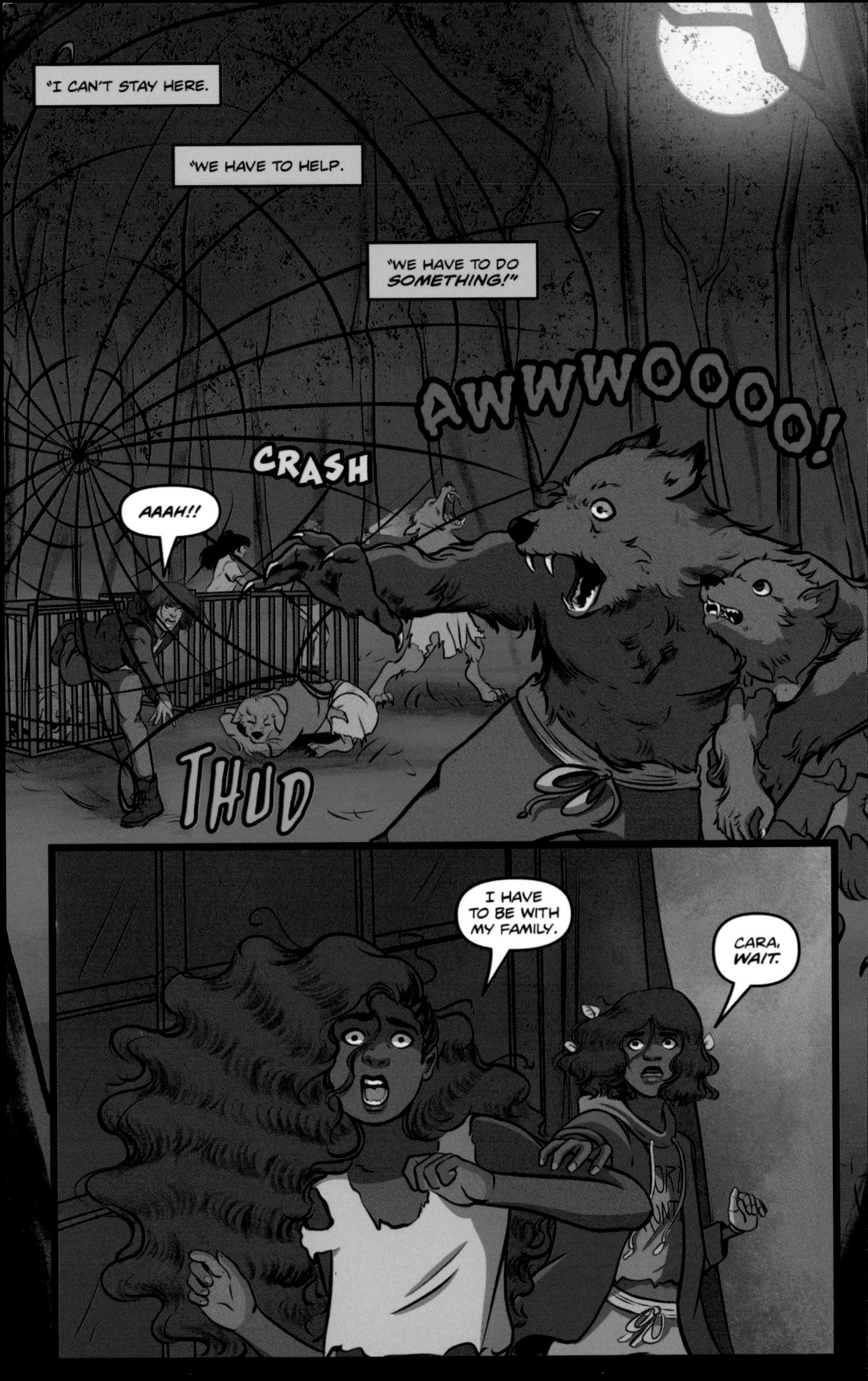
"I CAN'T STAY HERE.
"WE HAVE TO HELP.
"WE HAVE TO DO *SOMETHING!*"
AWWWOOOO!
CRASH
AAAH!!
THUD
I HAVE TO BE WITH MY FAMILY.
CARA, *WAIT.*

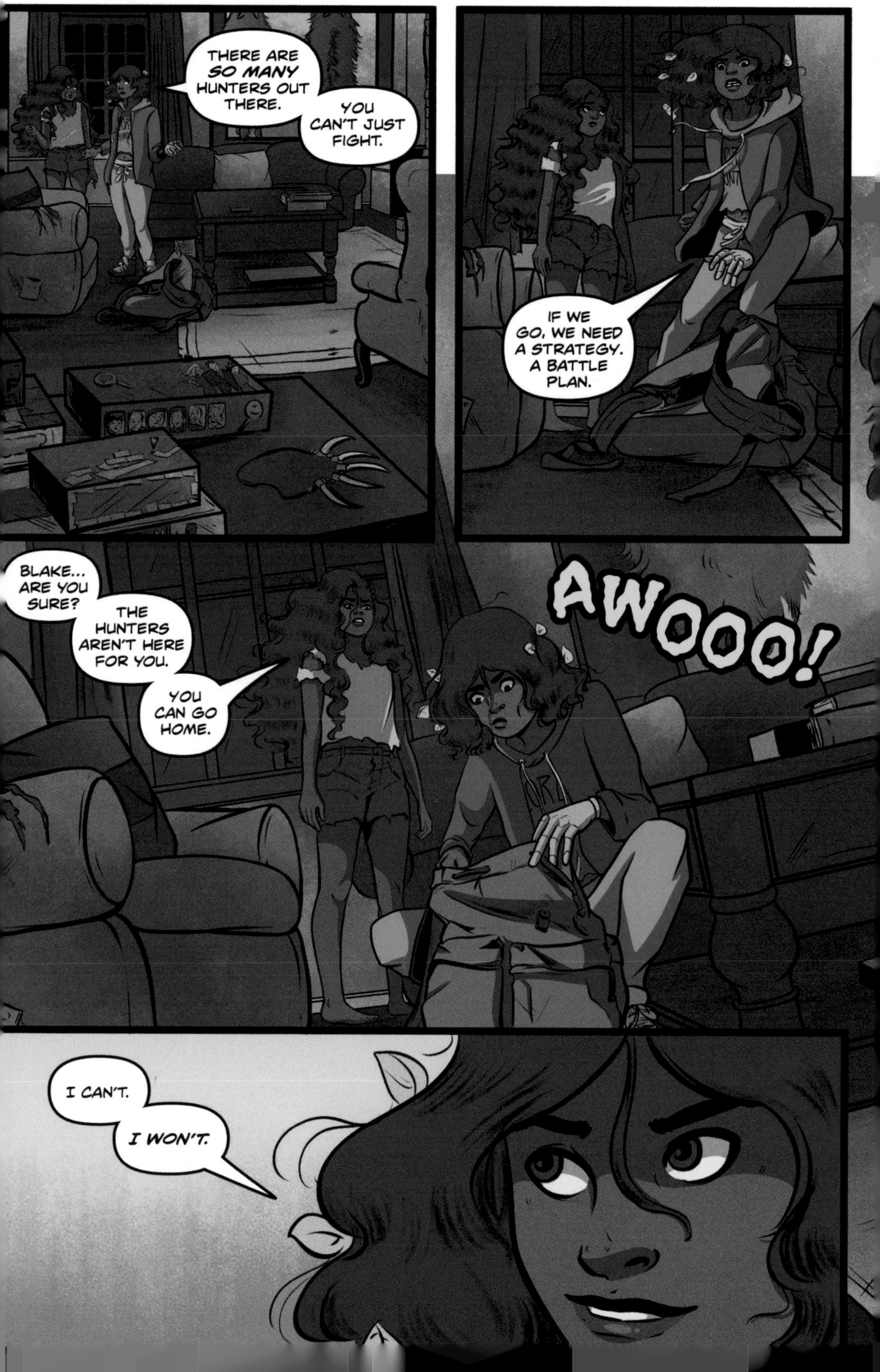
THERE ARE *SO MANY* HUNTERS OUT THERE.
YOU CAN'T JUST FIGHT.
IF WE GO, WE NEED A STRATEGY. A BATTLE PLAN.
BLAKE... ARE YOU SURE?
THE HUNTERS AREN'T HERE FOR YOU.
YOU CAN GO HOME.
AWOOO!
I CAN'T.
I WON'T.

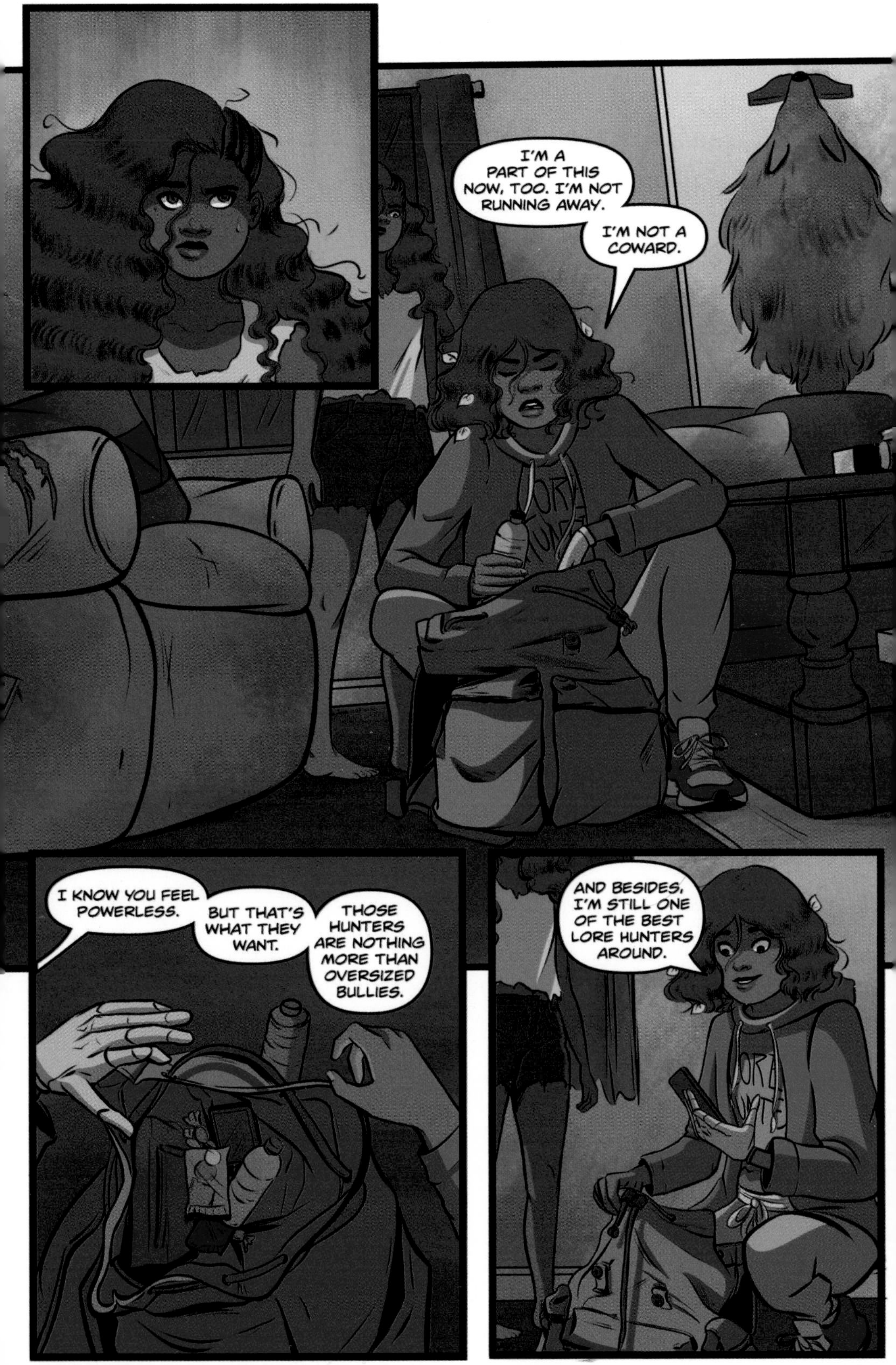

I'M A PART OF THIS NOW, TOO. I'M NOT RUNNING AWAY.
I'M NOT A COWARD.
I KNOW YOU FEEL POWERLESS.
BUT THAT'S WHAT THEY WANT.
THOSE HUNTERS ARE NOTHING MORE THAN OVERSIZED BULLIES.
AND BESIDES, I'M STILL ONE OF THE BEST LORE HUNTERS AROUND.

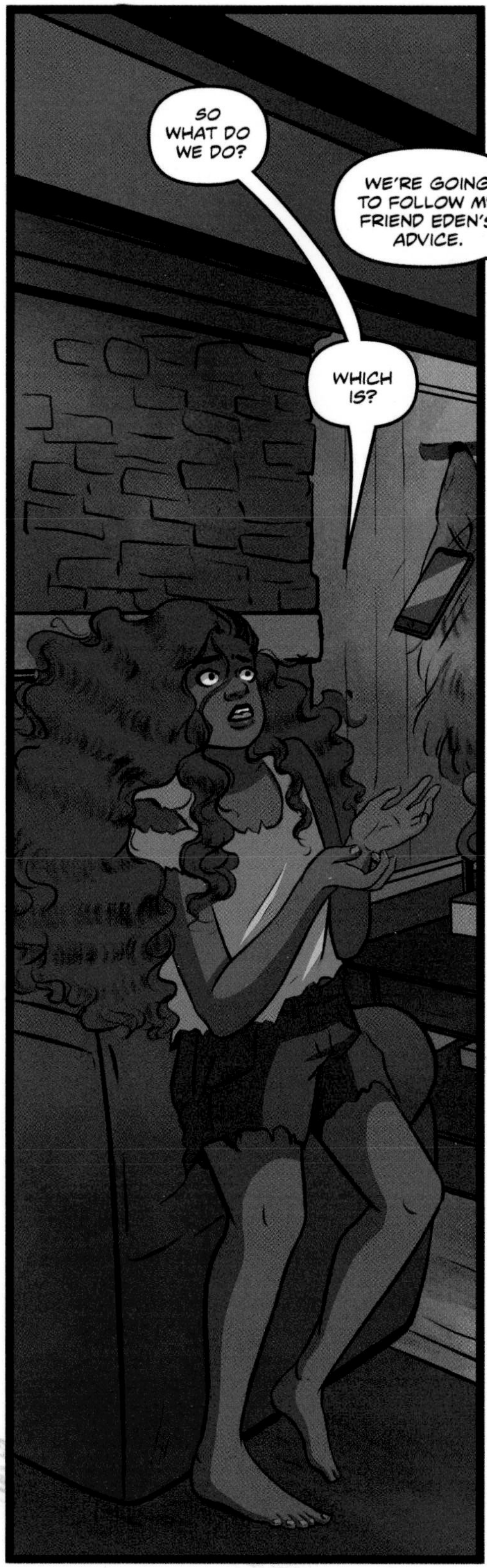
SO WHAT DO WE DO?
WE'RE GOING TO FOLLOW MY FRIEND EDEN'S ADVICE.
WHICH IS?

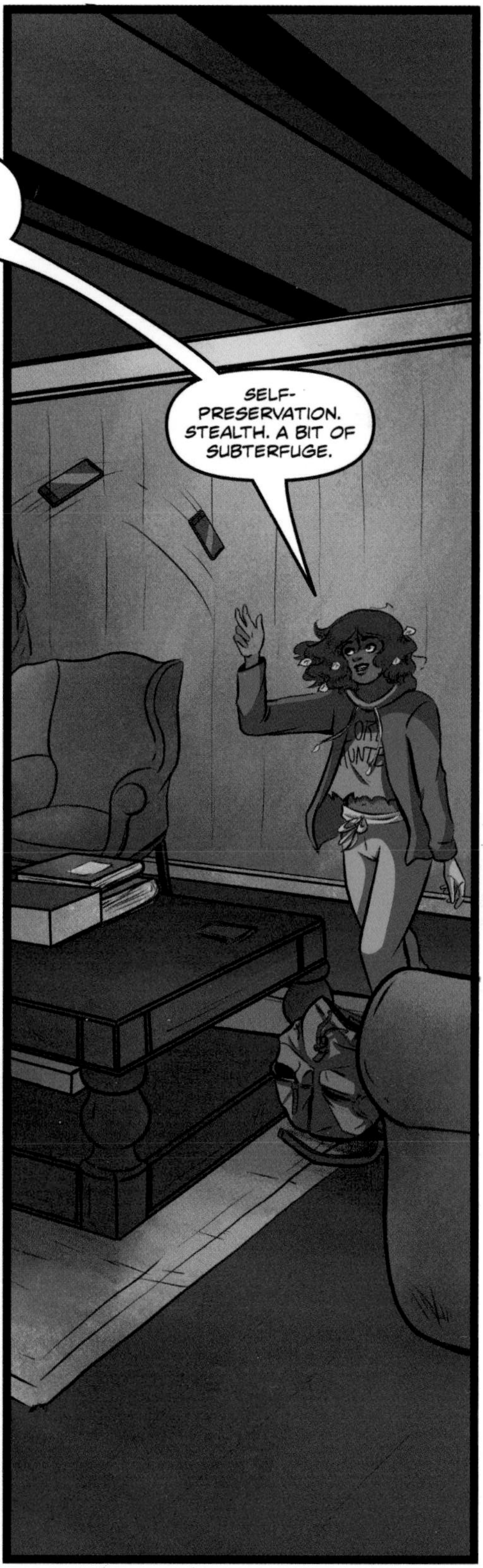
SELF-PRESERVATION. STEALTH. A BIT OF SUBTERFUGE.

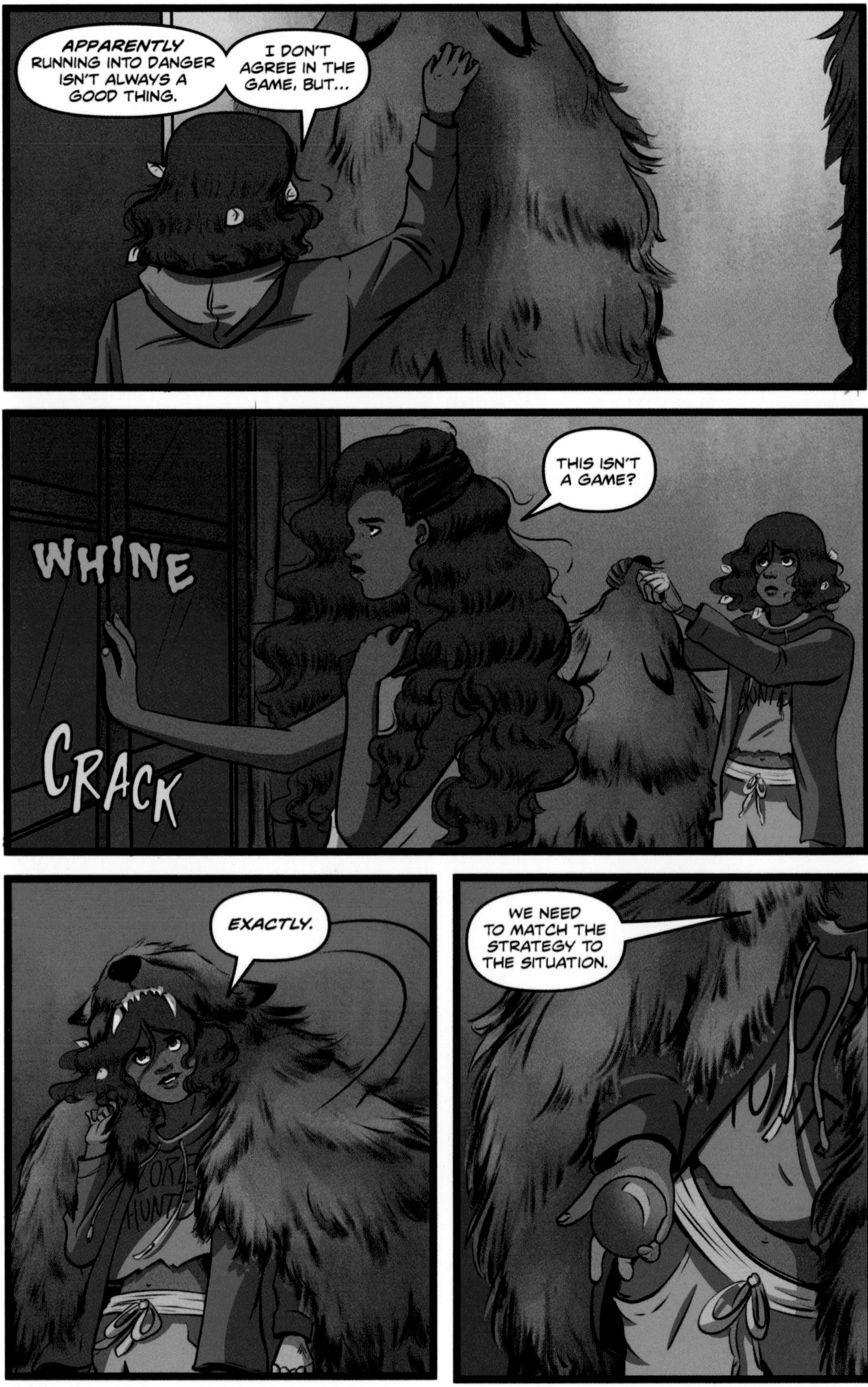
APPARENTLY RUNNING INTO DANGER ISN'T ALWAYS A GOOD THING.
I DON'T AGREE IN THE GAME, BUT...
THIS ISN'T A GAME?
WHINE
CRACK
EXACTLY.
WE NEED TO MATCH THE STRATEGY TO THE SITUATION.

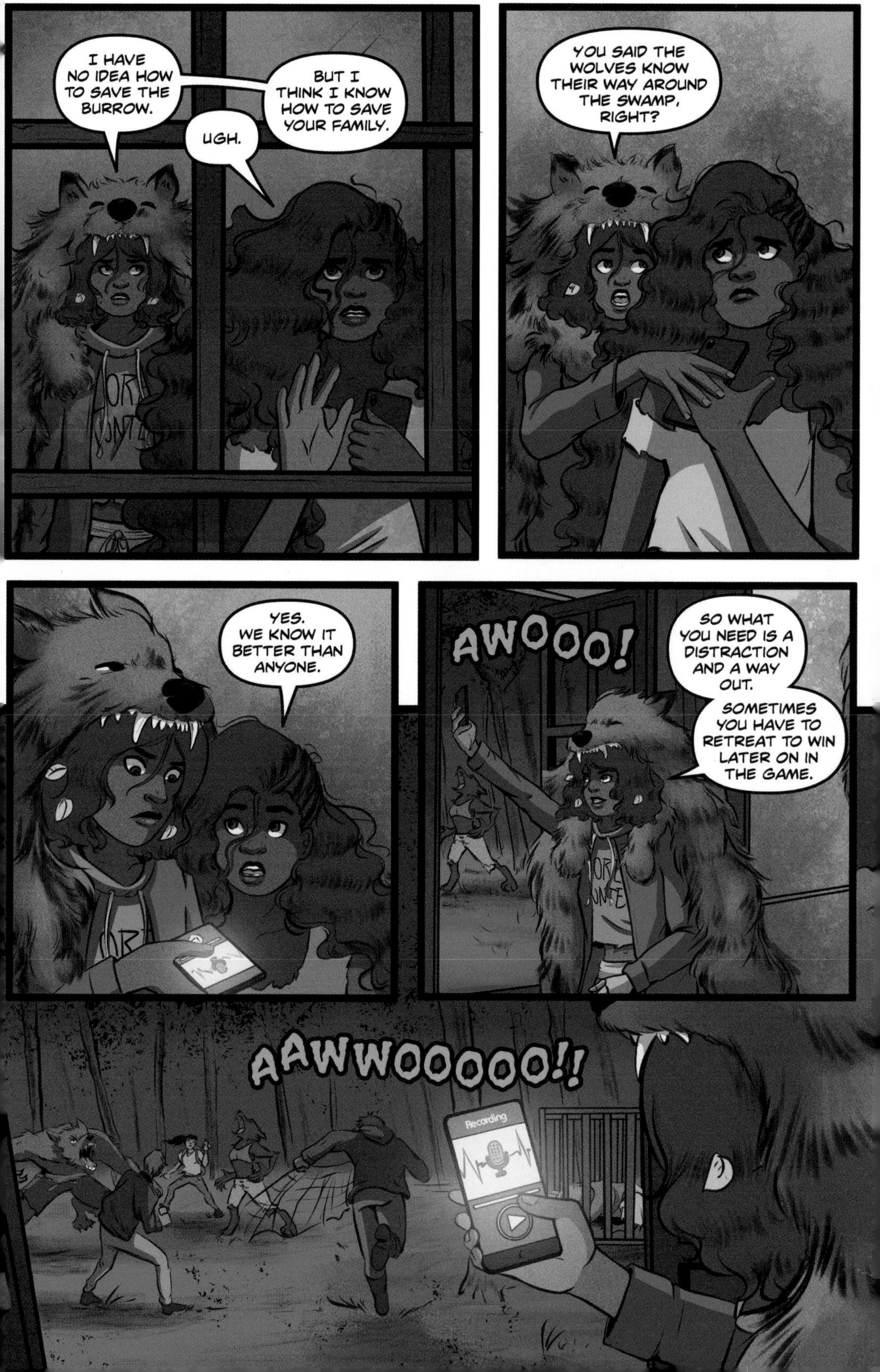
I HAVE NO IDEA HOW TO SAVE THE BURROW.
BUT I THINK I KNOW HOW TO SAVE YOUR FAMILY.
UGH.
YOU SAID THE WOLVES KNOW THEIR WAY AROUND THE SWAMP, RIGHT?
YES. WE KNOW IT BETTER THAN ANYONE.
AWOOO!
SO WHAT YOU NEED IS A DISTRACTION AND A WAY OUT.
SOMETIMES YOU HAVE TO RETREAT TO WIN LATER ON IN THE GAME.
AAWWOOOOOO!!
Recording

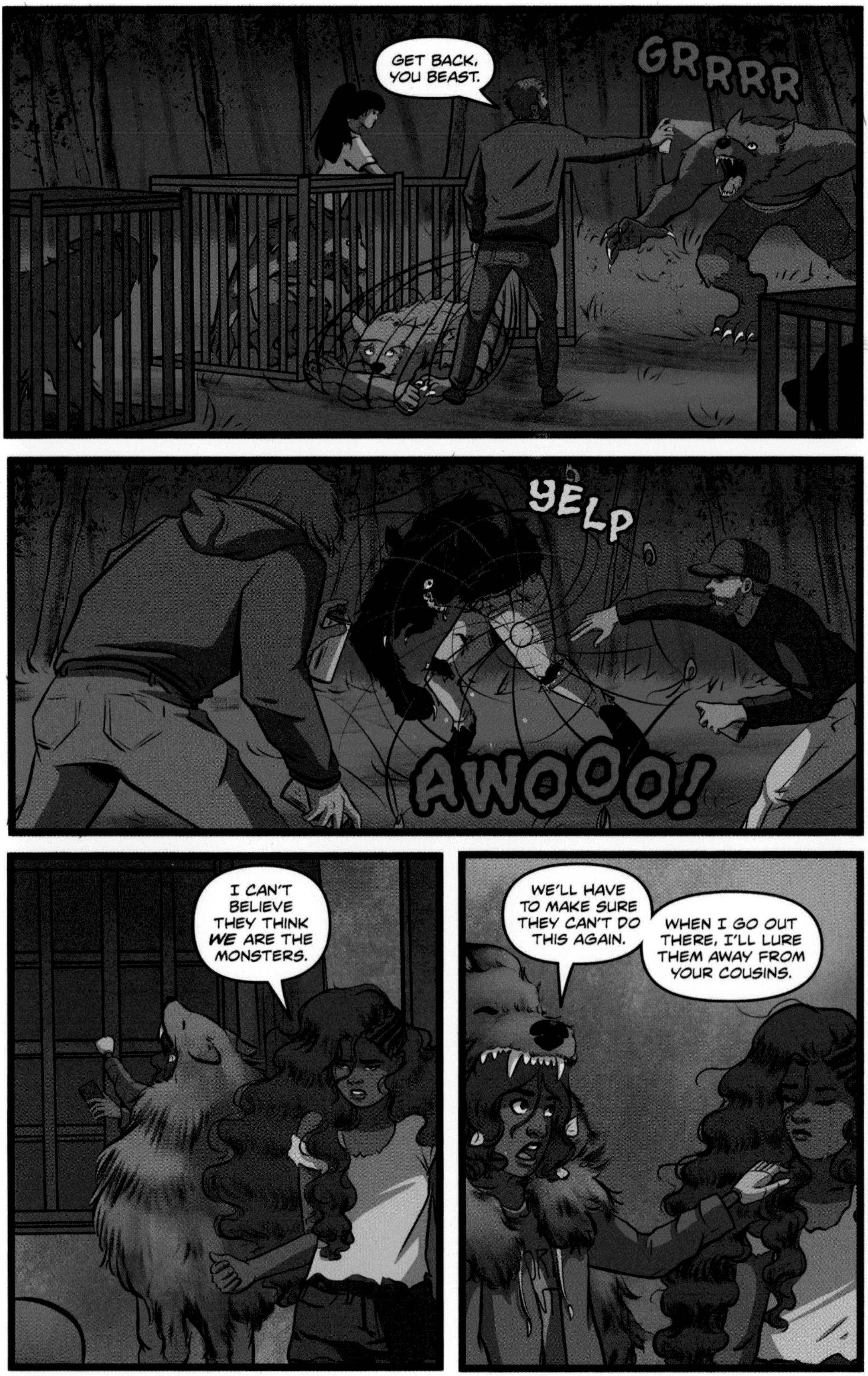
GET BACK, YOU BEAST.
GRRRRR
YELP
AWOOO!
I CAN'T BELIEVE THEY THINK WE ARE THE MONSTERS.
WE'LL HAVE TO MAKE SURE THEY CAN'T DO THIS AGAIN.
WHEN I GO OUT THERE, I'LL LURE THEM AWAY FROM YOUR COUSINS.

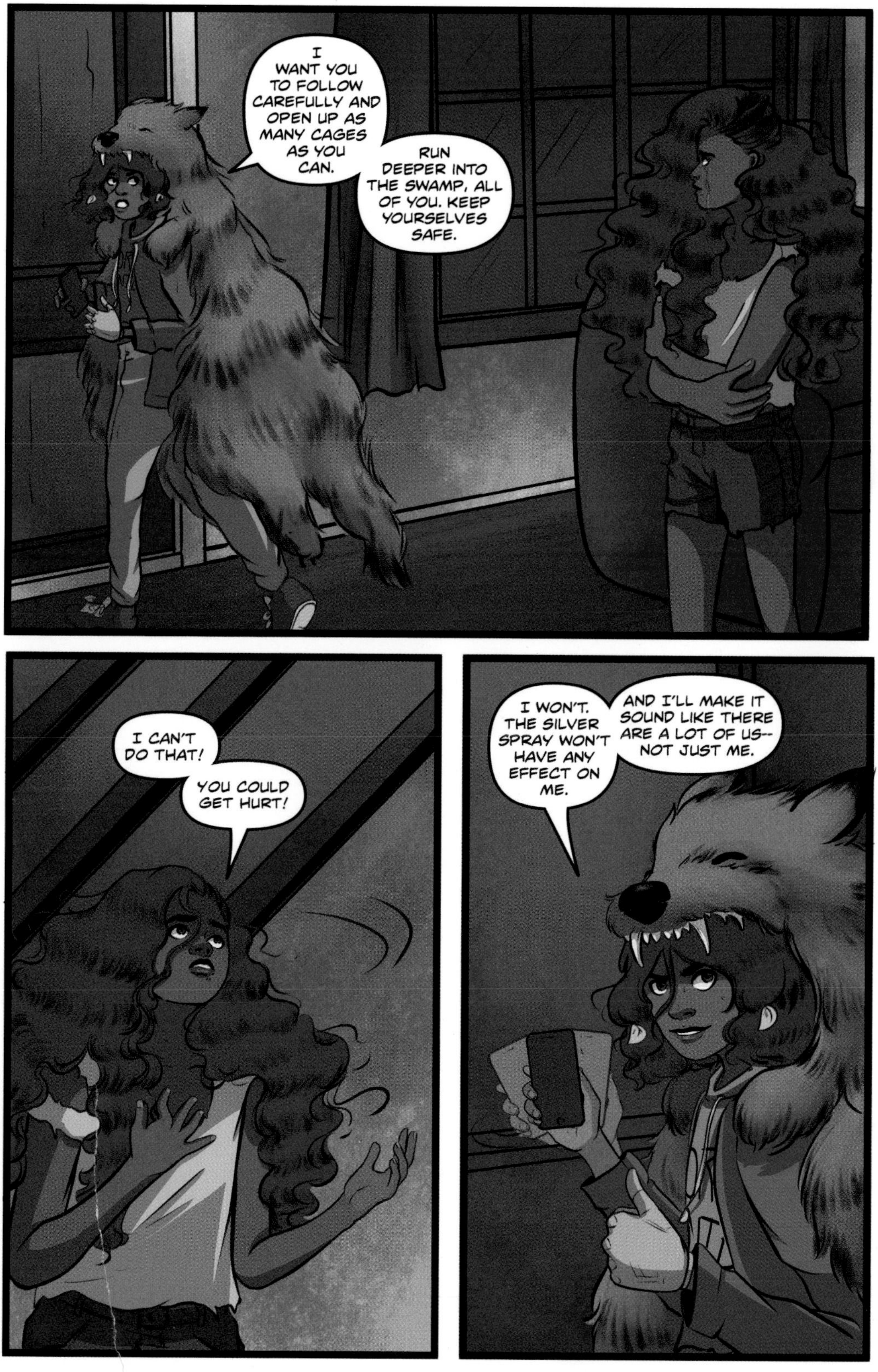
I WANT YOU TO FOLLOW CAREFULLY AND OPEN UP AS MANY CAGES AS YOU CAN.
RUN DEEPER INTO THE SWAMP, ALL OF YOU. KEEP YOURSELVES SAFE.
I CAN'T DO THAT!
YOU COULD GET HURT!
I WON'T. THE SILVER SPRAY WON'T HAVE ANY EFFECT ON ME.
AND I'LL MAKE IT SOUND LIKE THERE ARE A LOT OF US-- NOT JUST ME.

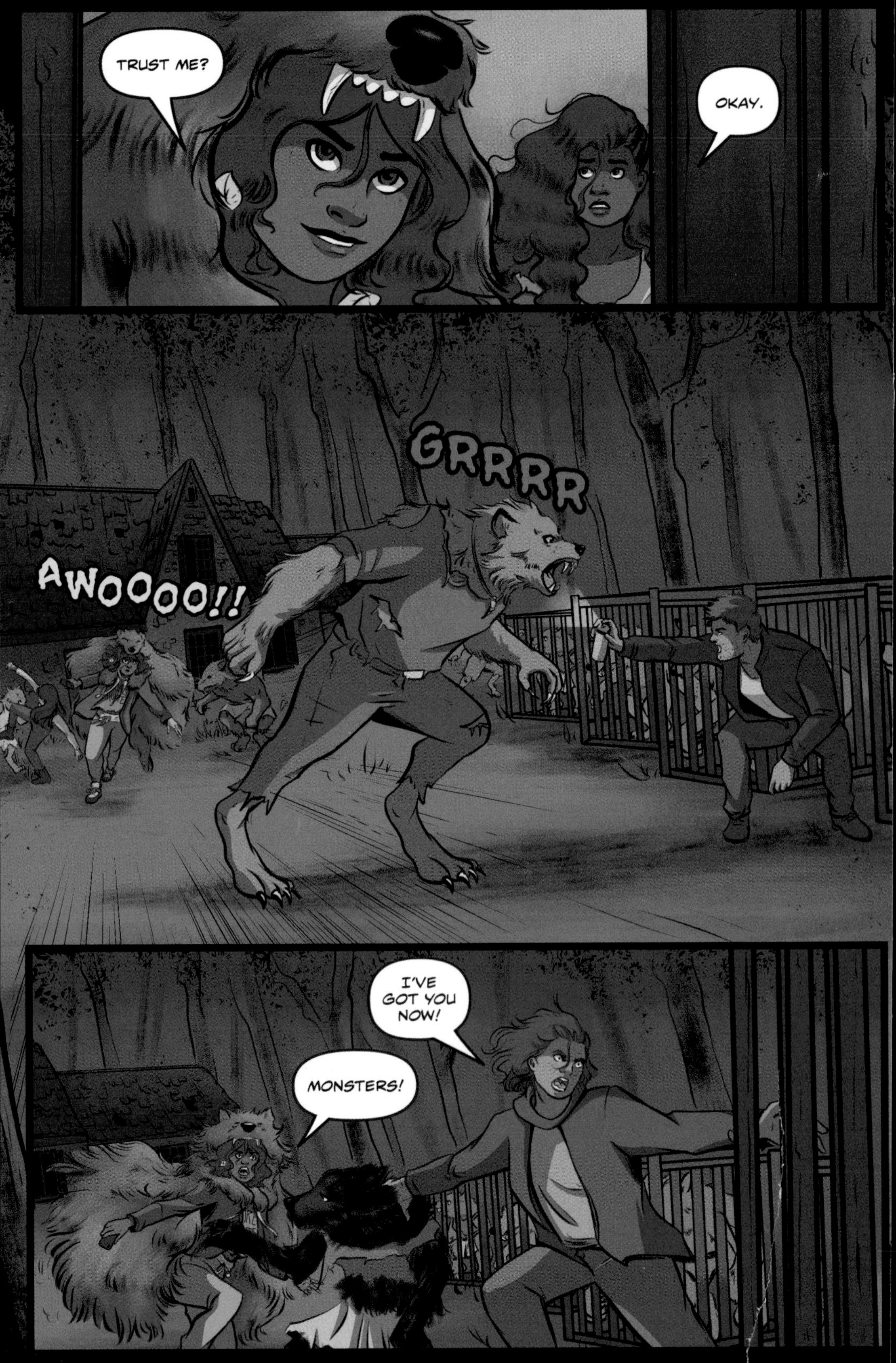
TRUST ME?
OKAY.
GRRRRR
AWOOOO!!
I'VE GOT YOU NOW!
MONSTERS!

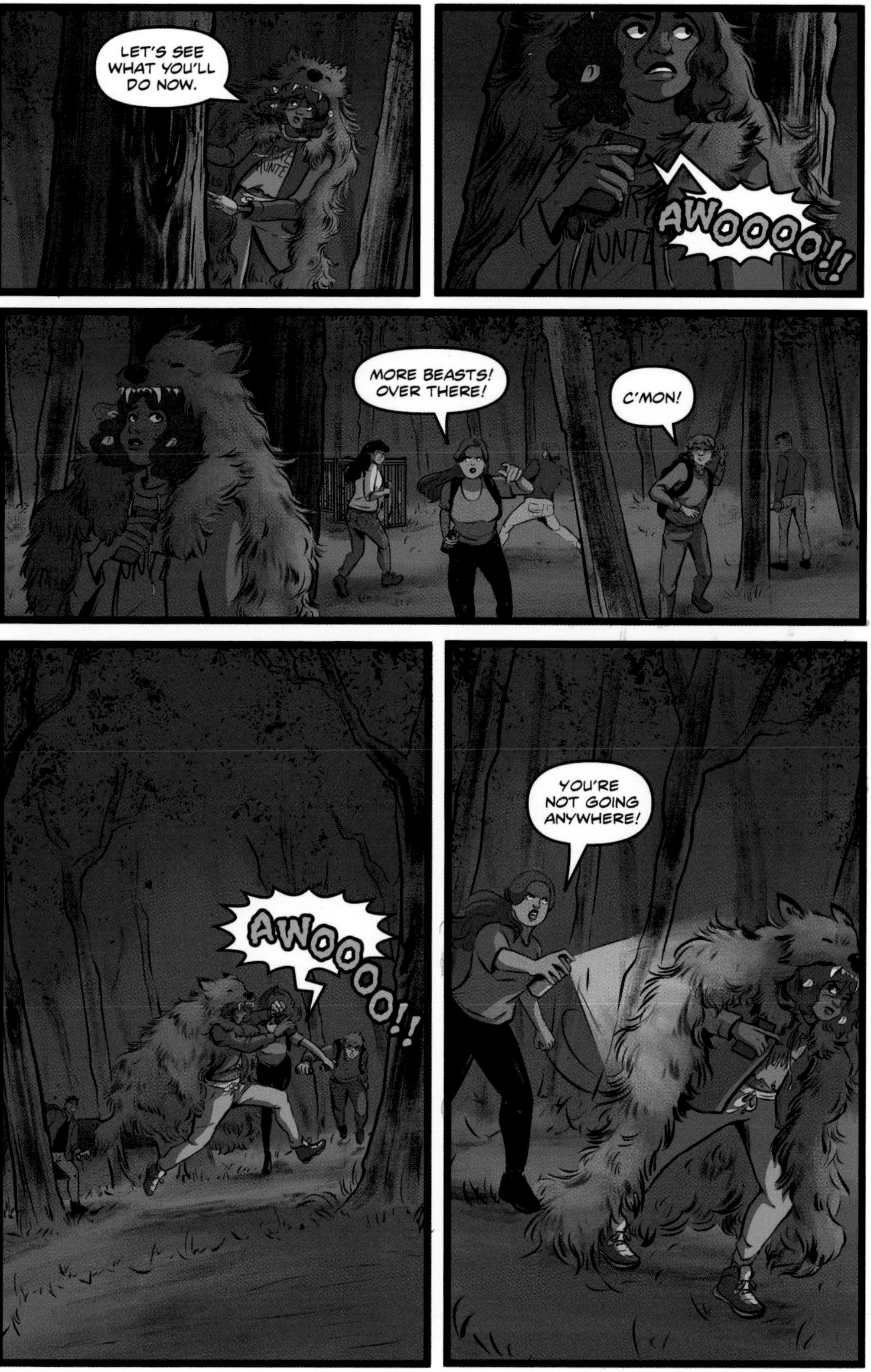
LET'S SEE WHAT YOU'LL DO NOW.
AWOOOO!!
MORE BEASTS! OVER THERE!
C'MON!
AWOOOO!!
YOU'RE NOT GOING ANYWHERE!

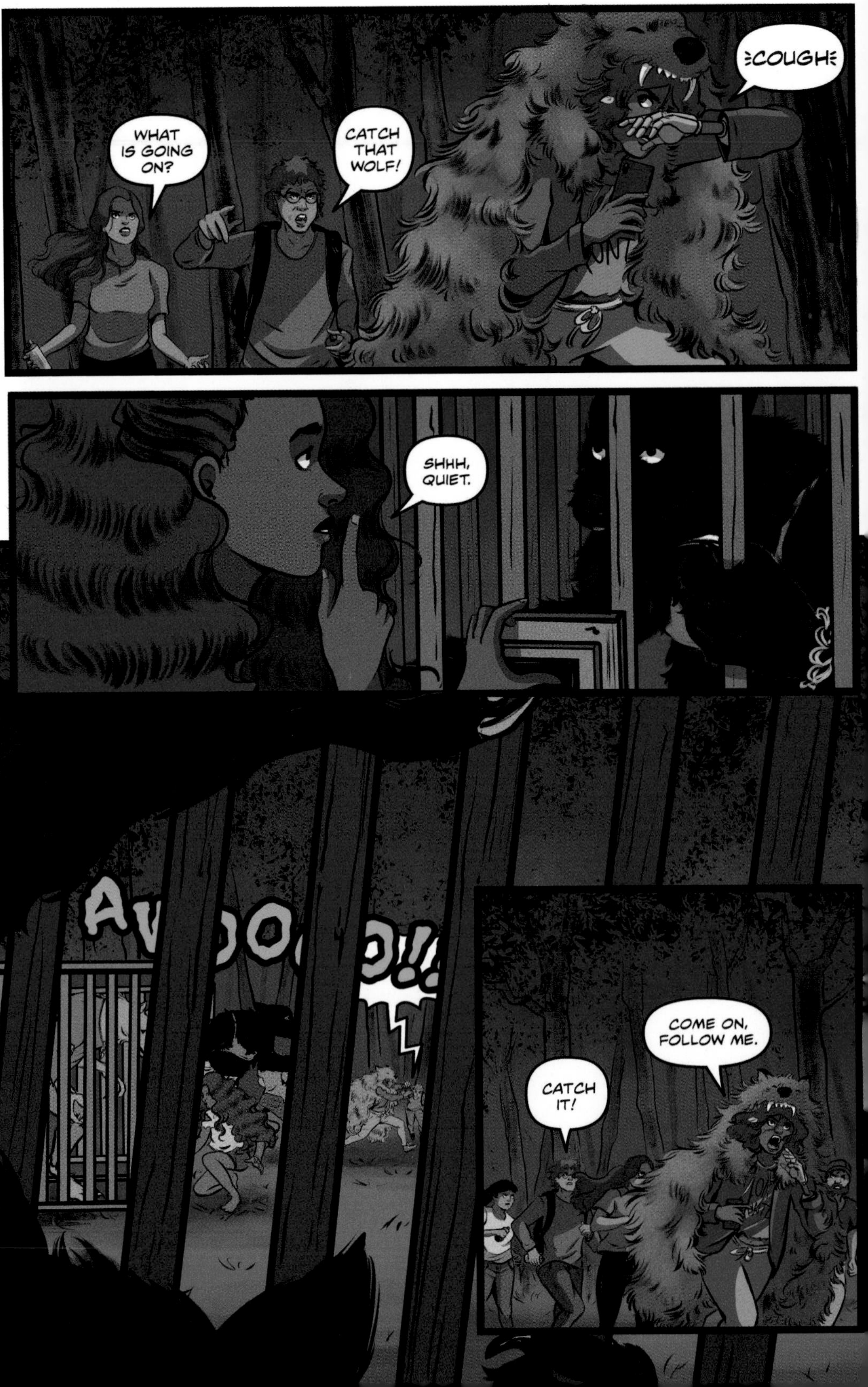
WHAT IS GOING ON?
CATCH THAT WOLF!
:COUGH:
SHHH, QUIET.
AWOOOO!!
CATCH IT!
COME ON, FOLLOW ME.

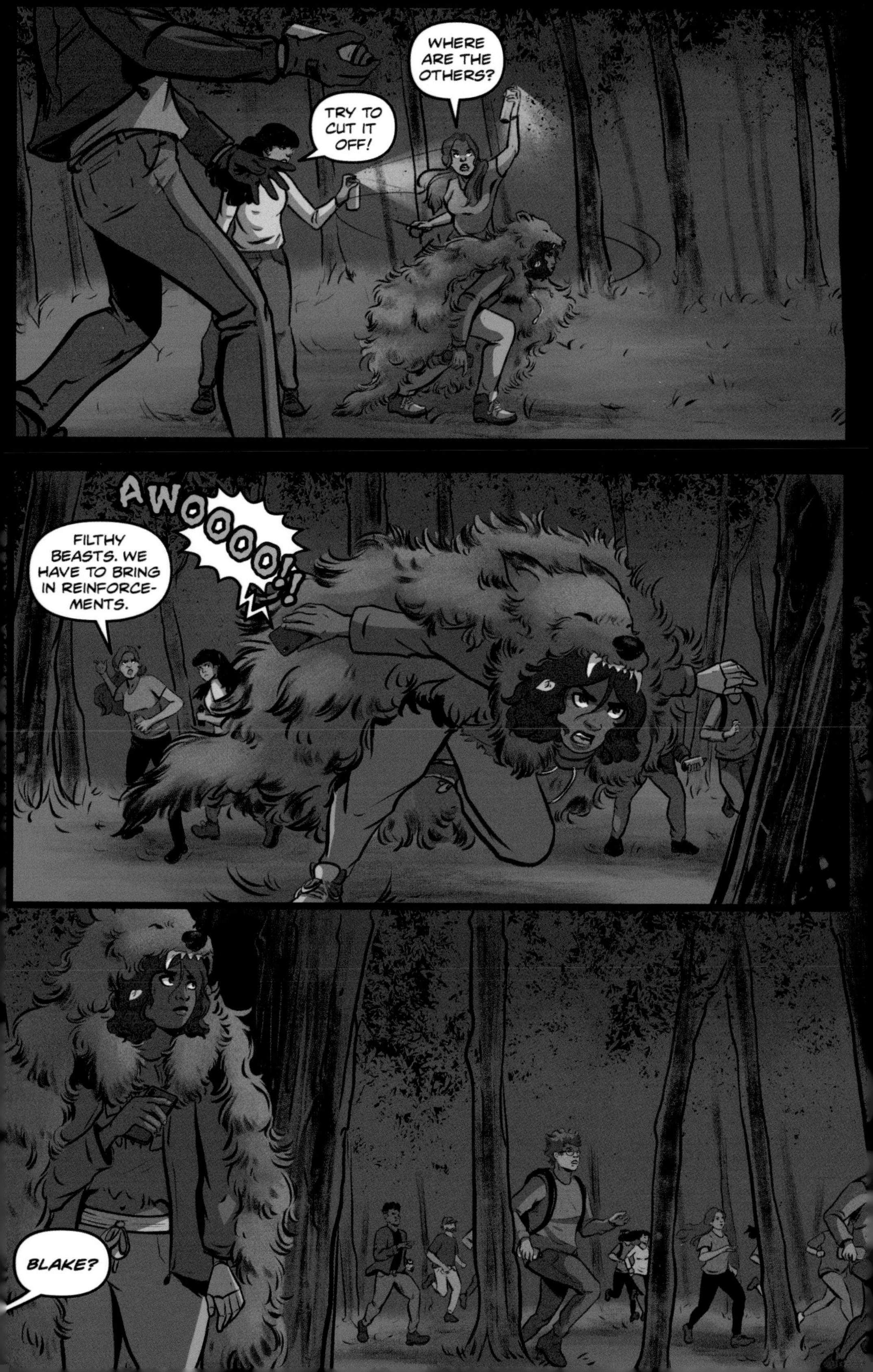
WHERE ARE THE OTHERS?
TRY TO CUT IT OFF!
FILTHY BEASTS. WE HAVE TO BRING IN REINFORCE-MENTS.
AWOOOOO!!
BLAKE?

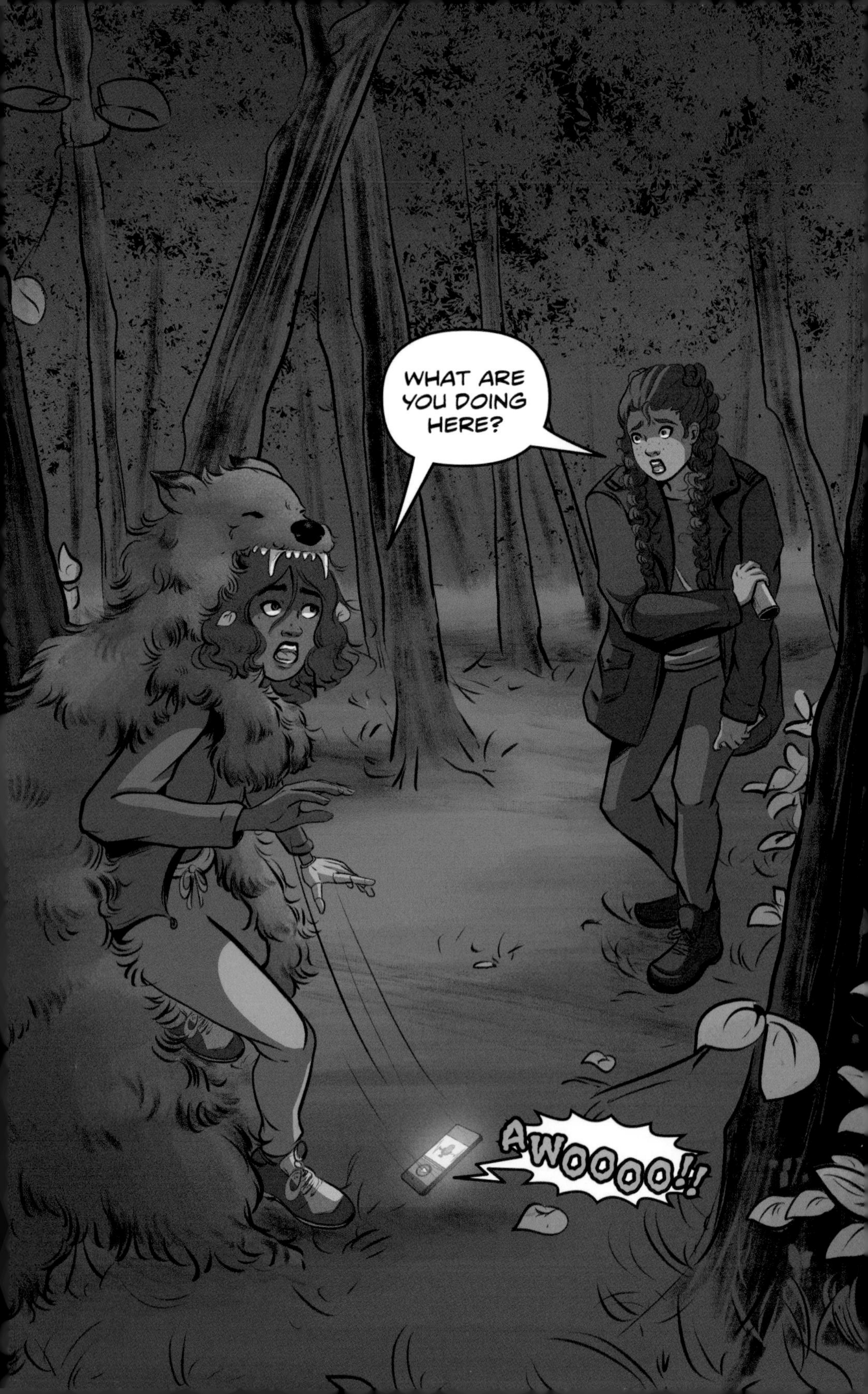
WHAT ARE YOU DOING HERE?
AWOOOOO!!

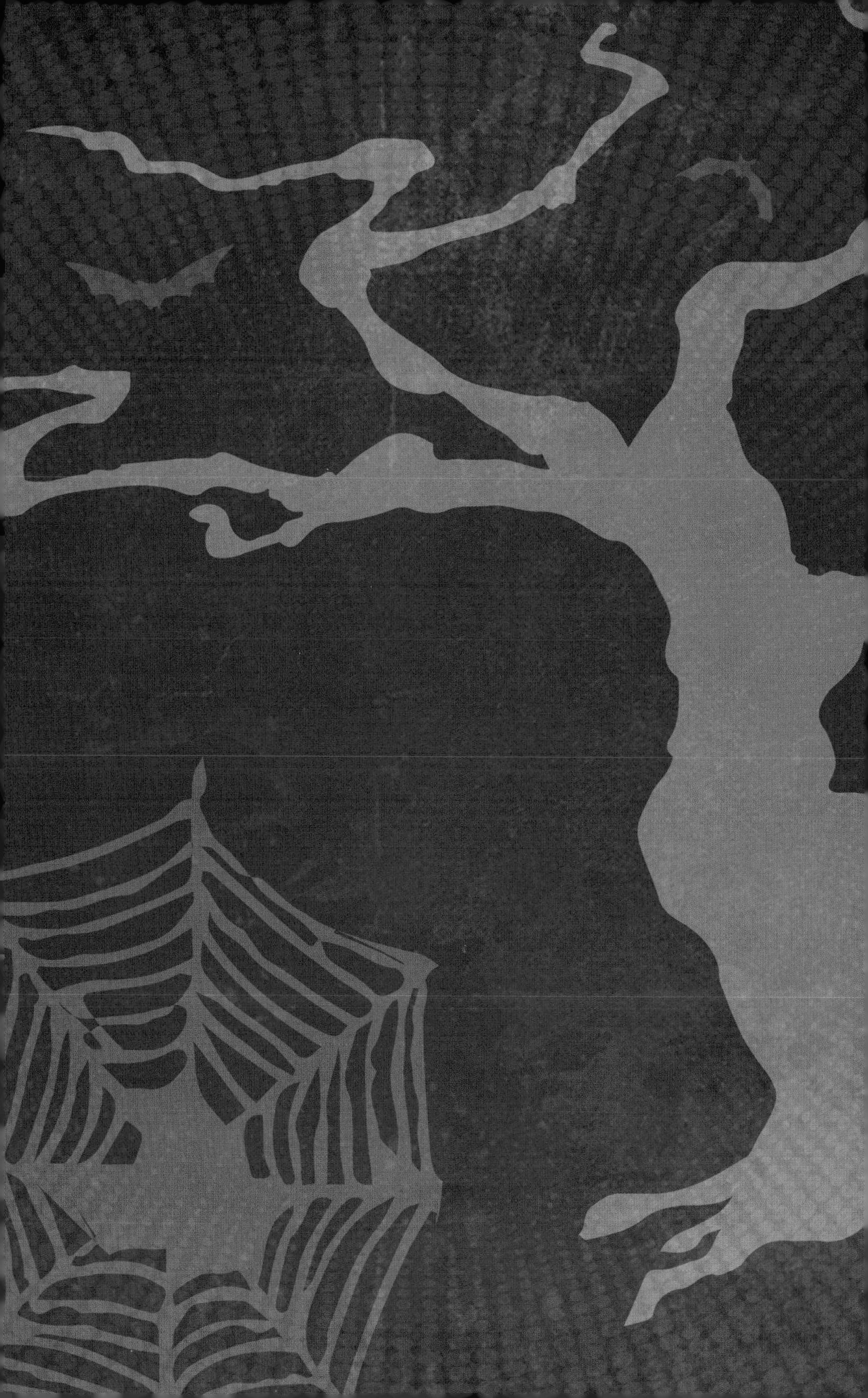

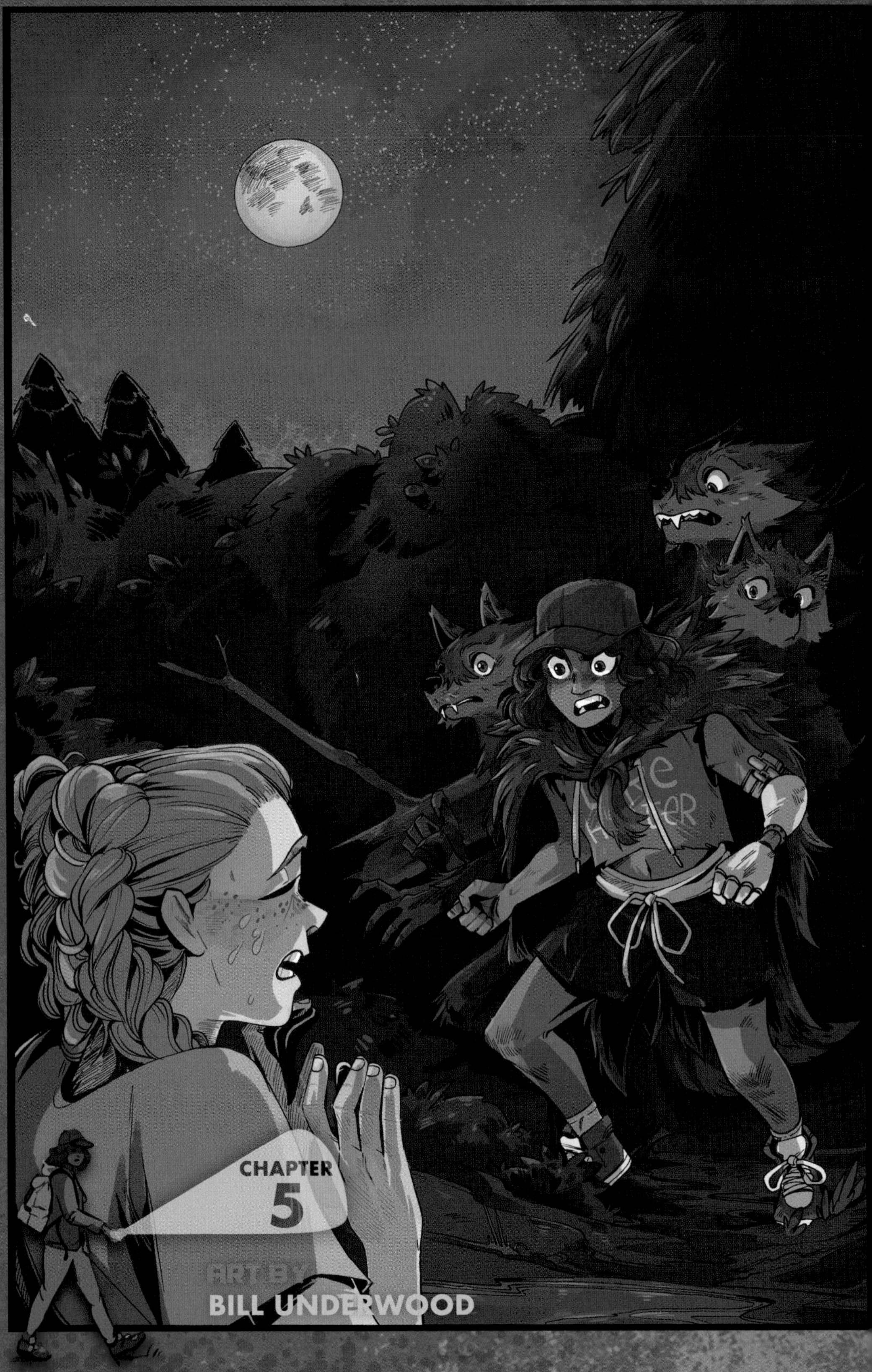
CHAPTER
5
ART BY
BILL UNDERWOOD

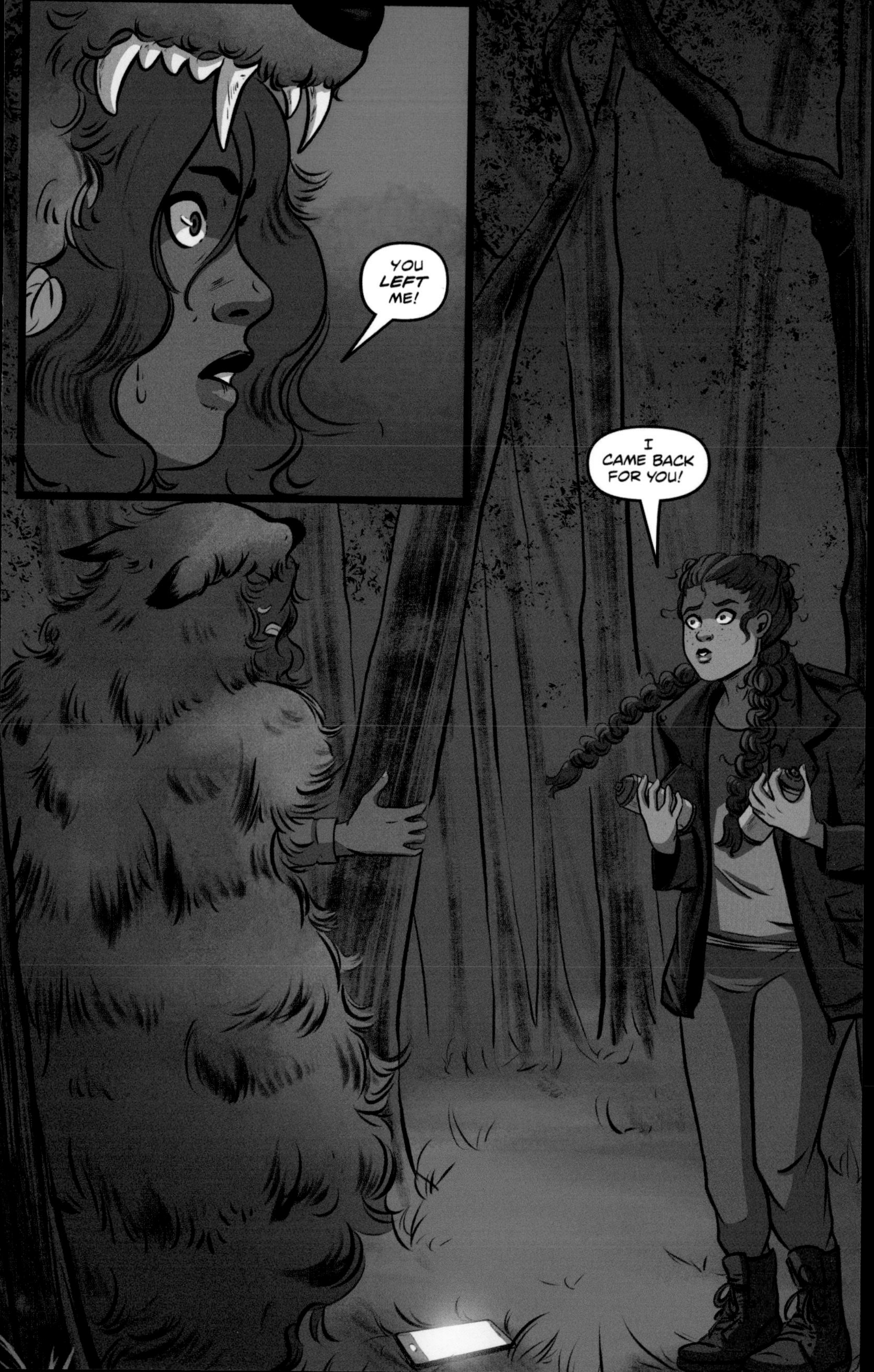
YOU LEFT ME!
I CAME BACK FOR YOU!

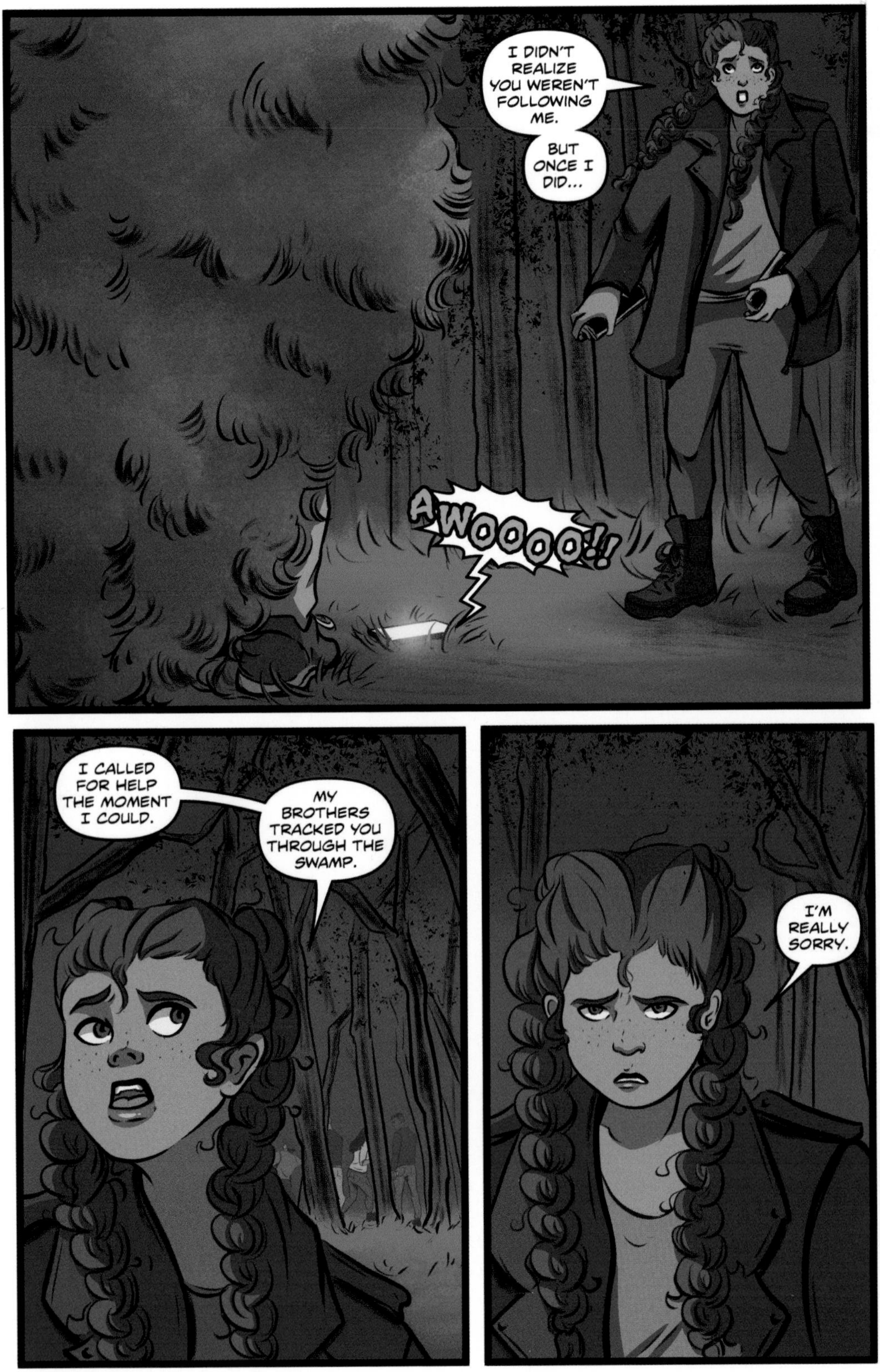
I DIDN'T REALIZE YOU WEREN'T FOLLOWING ME.
BUT ONCE I DID...
AWOOOOO!!
I CALLED FOR HELP THE MOMENT I COULD.
MY BROTHERS TRACKED YOU THROUGH THE SWAMP.
I'M REALLY SORRY.

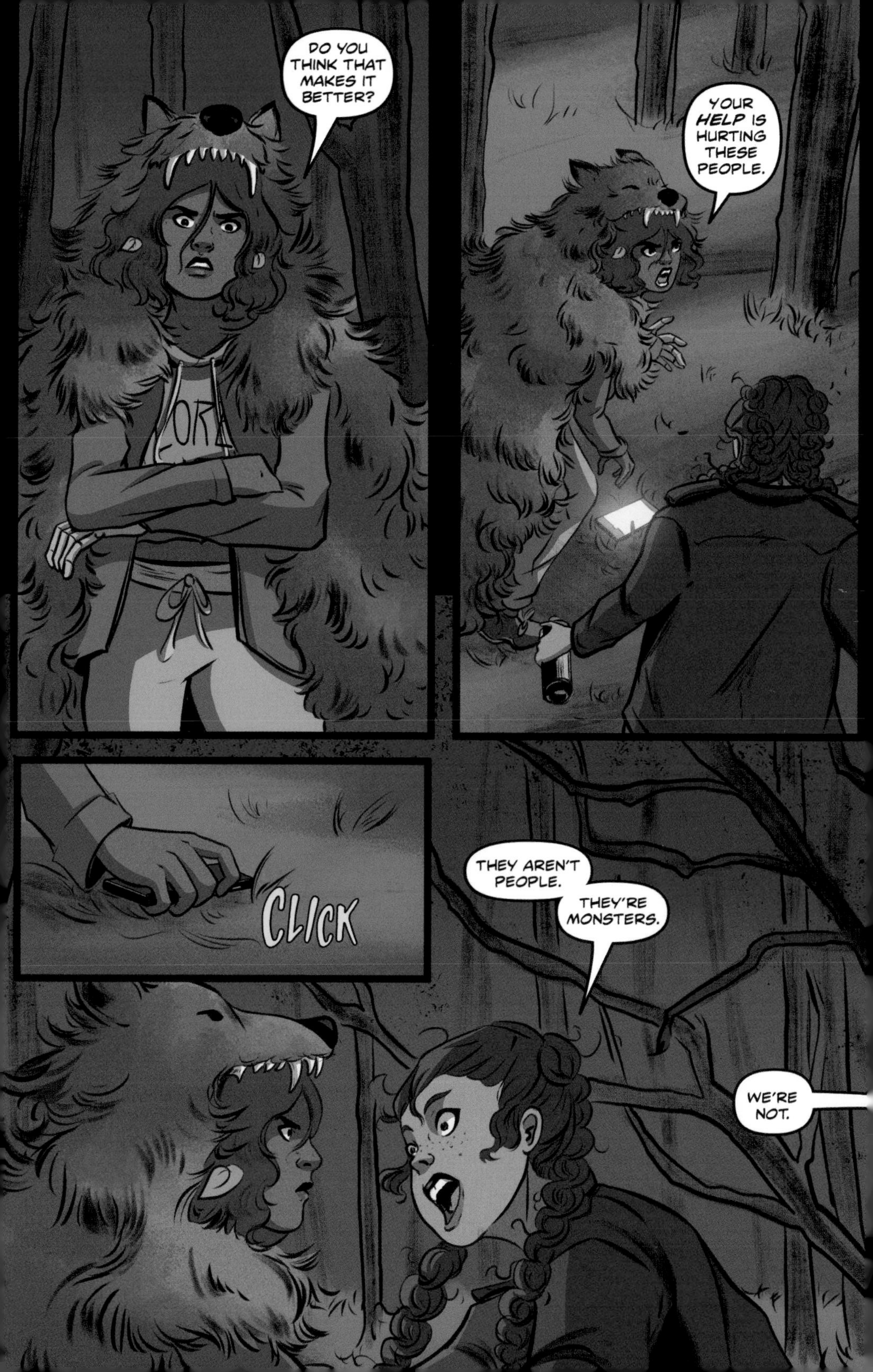
DO YOU THINK THAT MAKES IT BETTER?
YOUR HELP IS HURTING THESE PEOPLE.
CLICK
THEY AREN'T PEOPLE.
THEY'RE MONSTERS.
WE'RE NOT.

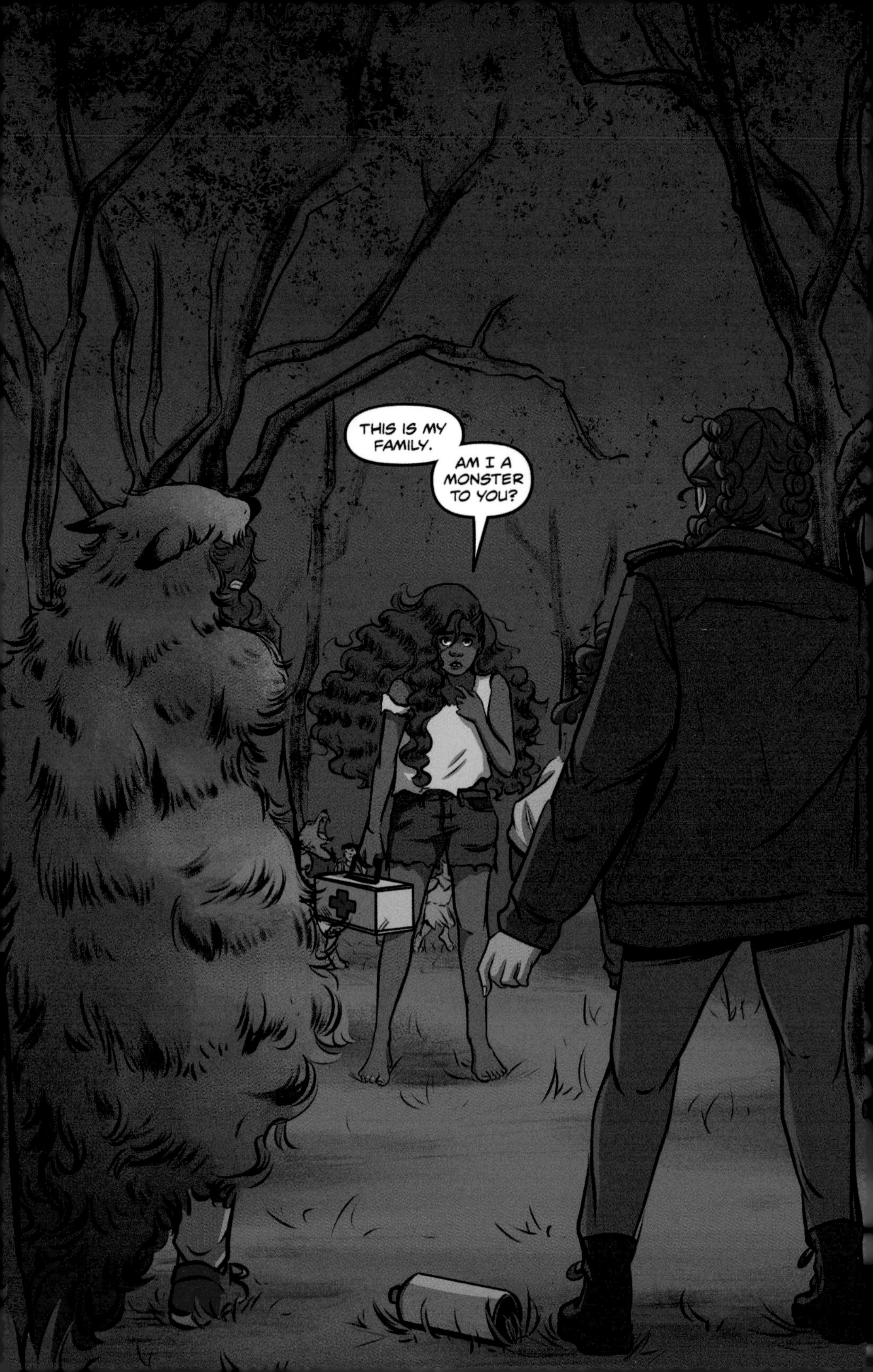
THIS IS MY FAMILY.
AM I A MONSTER TO YOU?

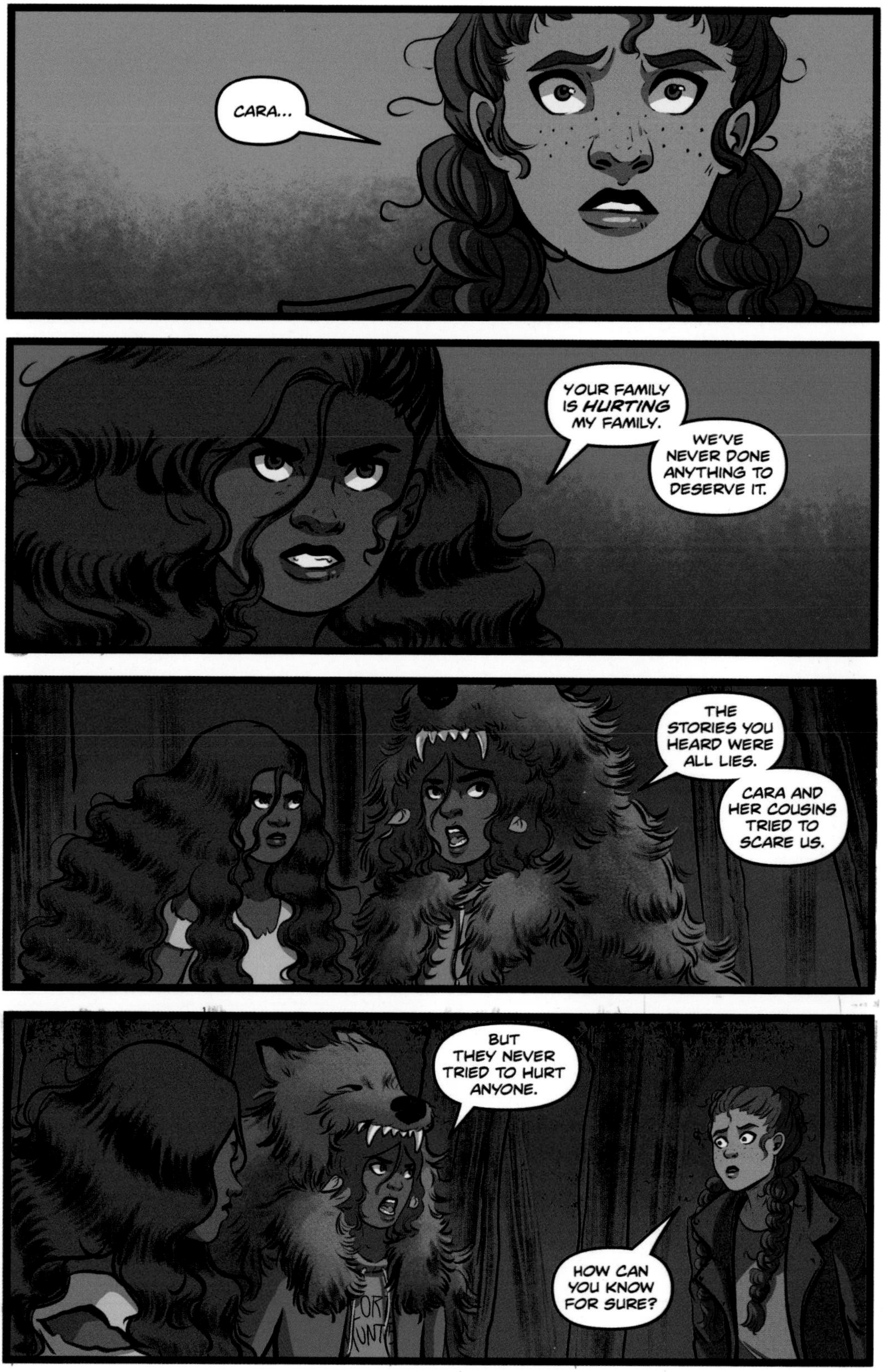
CARA...
YOUR FAMILY IS *HURTING* MY FAMILY.
WE'VE NEVER DONE ANYTHING TO DESERVE IT.
THE STORIES YOU HEARD WERE ALL LIES.
CARA AND HER COUSINS TRIED TO SCARE US.
BUT THEY NEVER TRIED TO HURT ANYONE.
HOW CAN YOU KNOW FOR SURE?

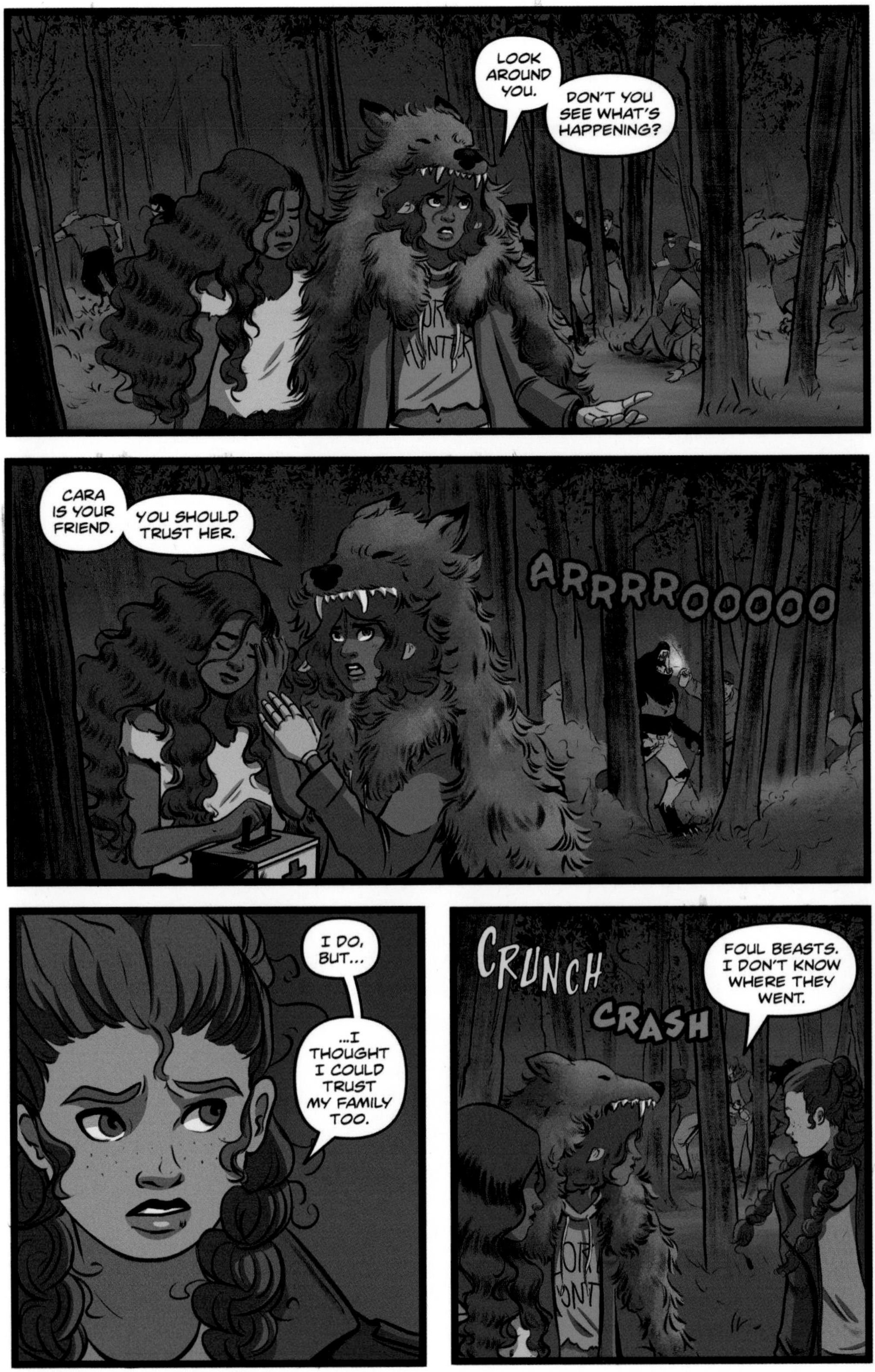
LOOK AROUND YOU.
DON'T YOU SEE WHAT'S HAPPENING?
CARA IS YOUR FRIEND.
YOU SHOULD TRUST HER.
ARRRRROOOOO
I DO, BUT...
...I THOUGHT I COULD TRUST MY FAMILY TOO.
CRUNCH
CRASH
FOUL BEASTS. I DON'T KNOW WHERE THEY WENT.

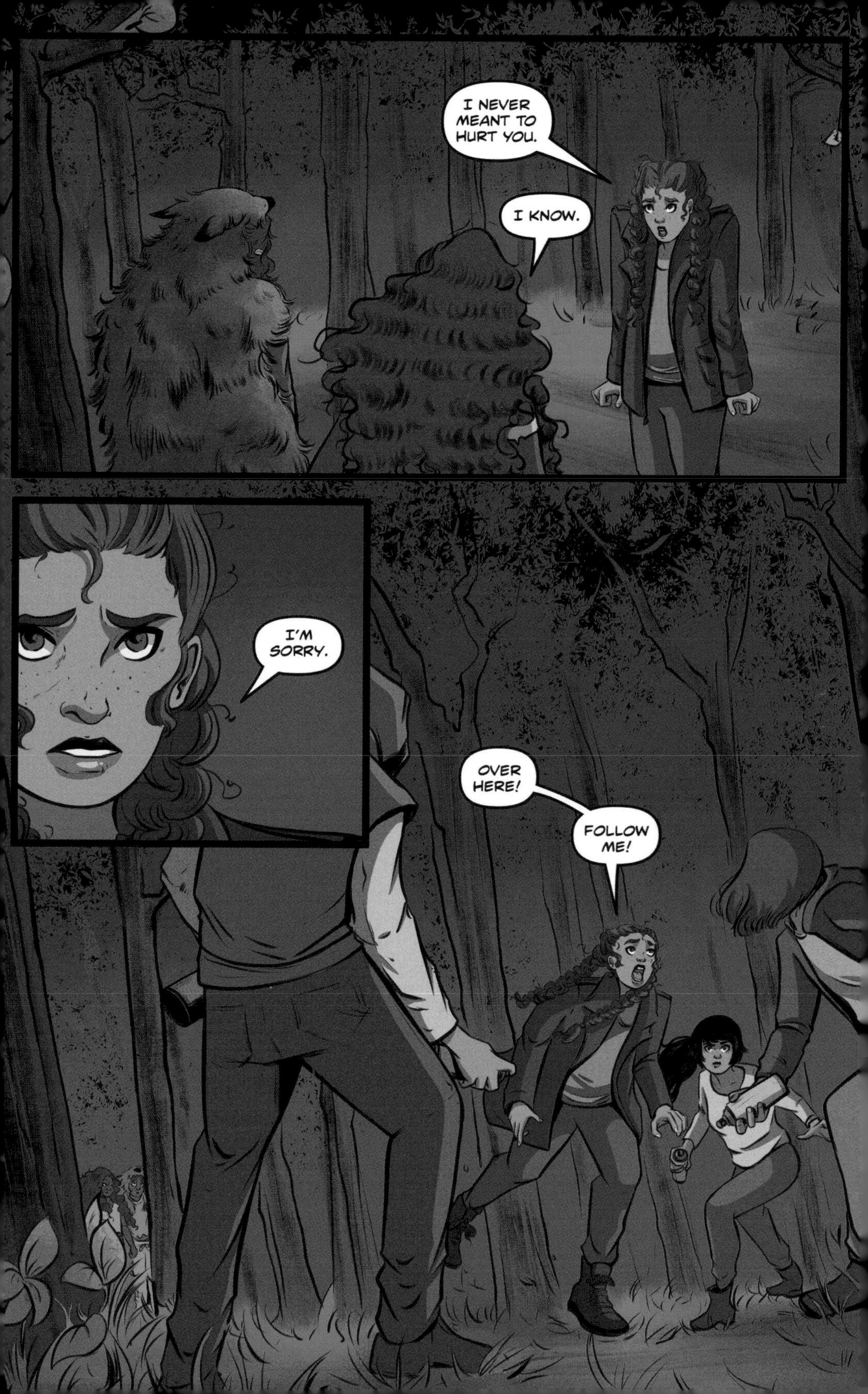

I NEVER MEANT TO HURT YOU.
I KNOW.
I'M SORRY.
OVER HERE!
FOLLOW ME!

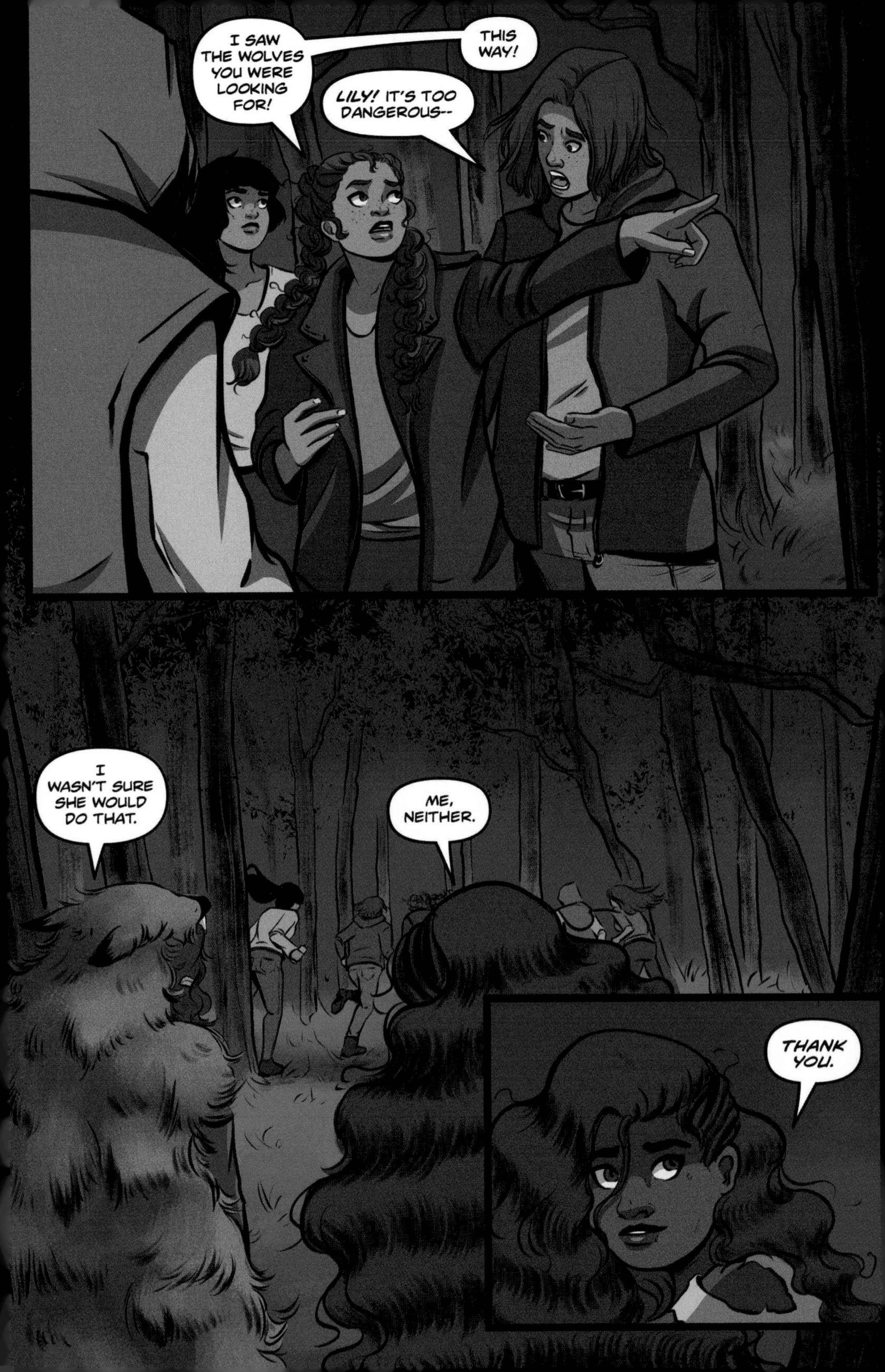
I SAW THE WOLVES YOU WERE LOOKING FOR!
THIS WAY!
LILY! IT'S TOO DANGEROUS--
I WASN'T SURE SHE WOULD DO THAT.
ME, NEITHER.
THANK YOU.

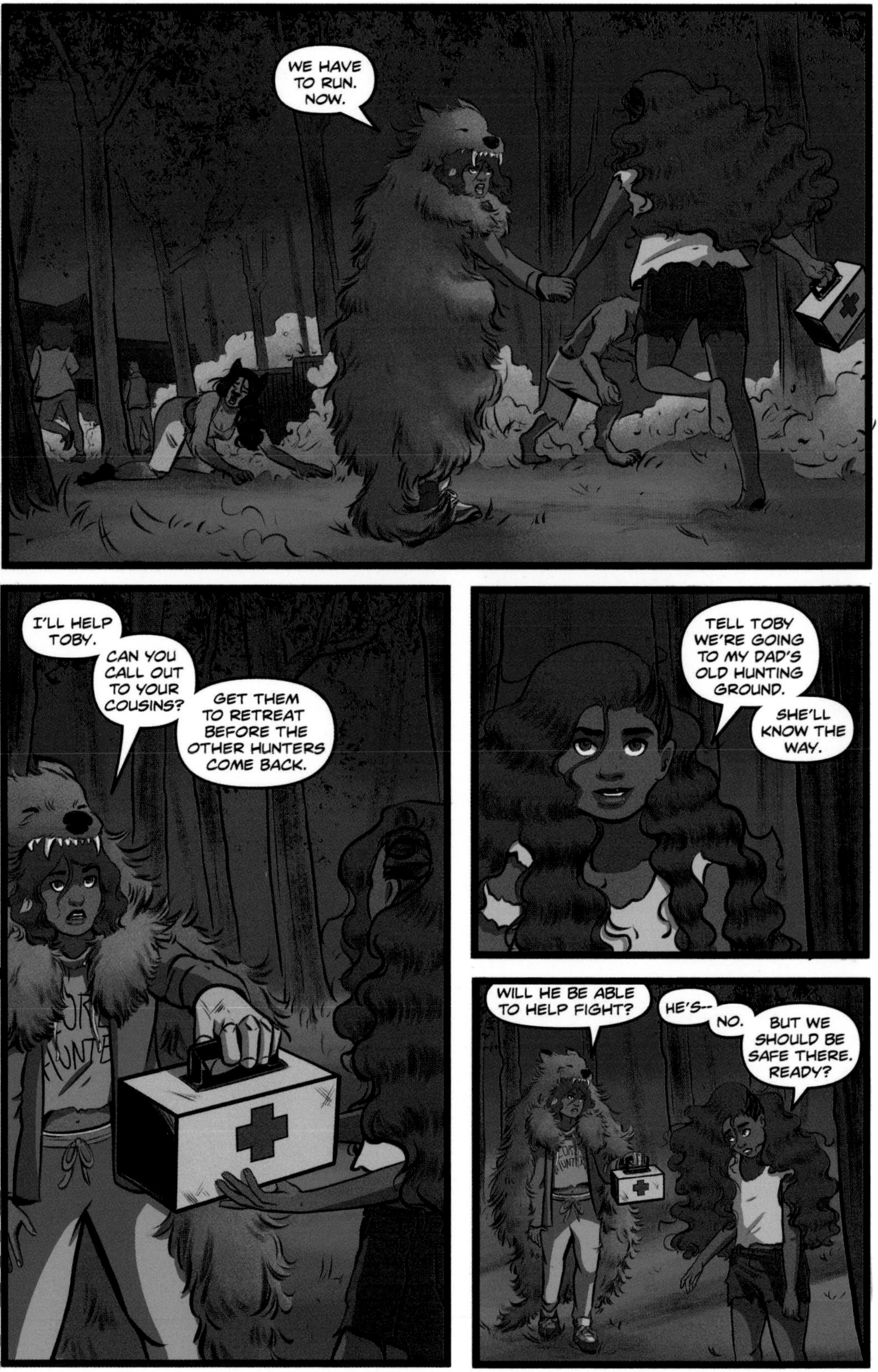
WE HAVE TO RUN. NOW.
I'LL HELP TOBY.
CAN YOU CALL OUT TO YOUR COUSINS?
GET THEM TO RETREAT BEFORE THE OTHER HUNTERS COME BACK.
TELL TOBY WE'RE GOING TO MY DAD'S OLD HUNTING GROUND.
SHE'LL KNOW THE WAY.
WILL HE BE ABLE TO HELP FIGHT?
HE'S--
NO.
BUT WE SHOULD BE SAFE THERE. READY?

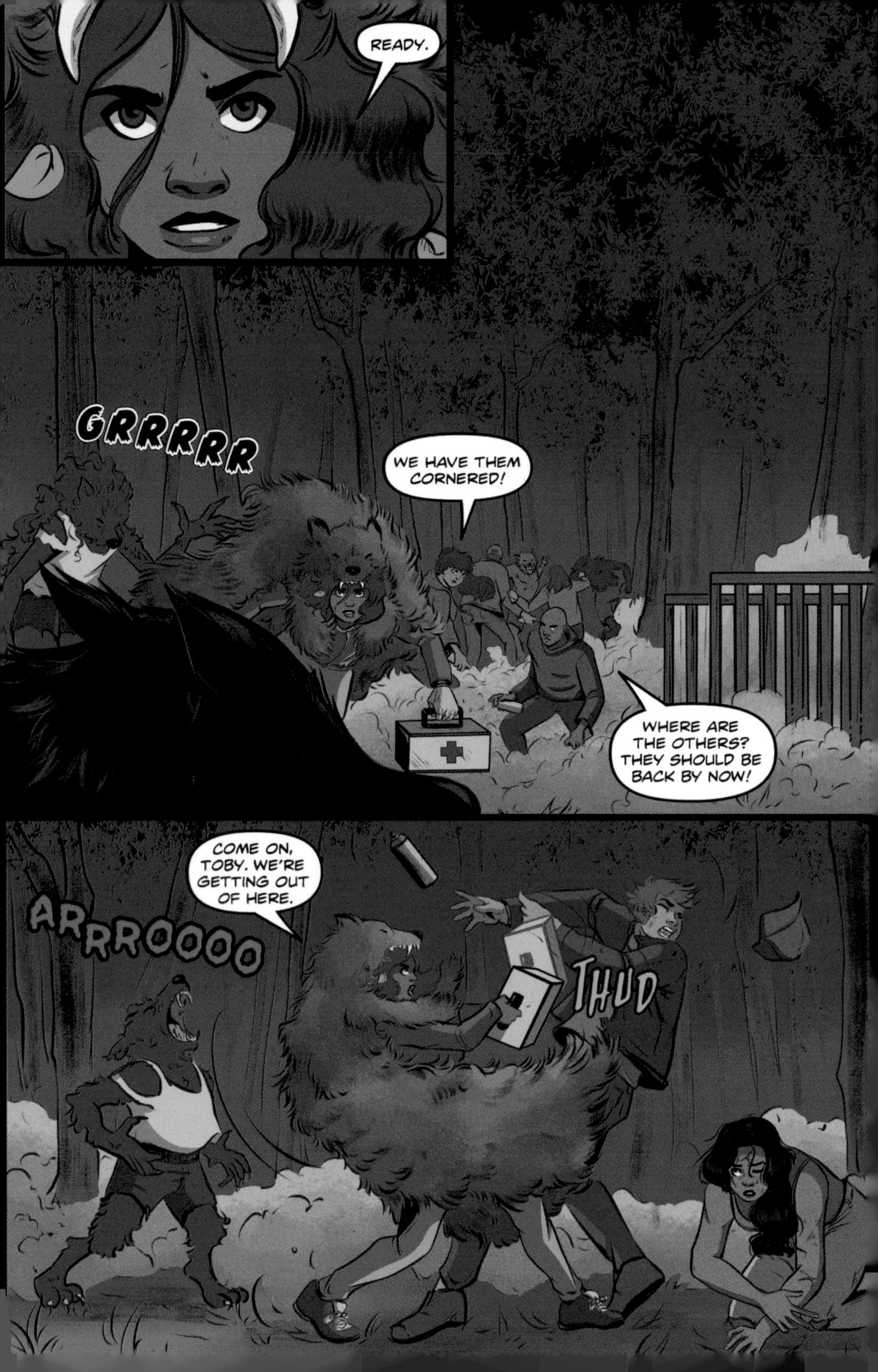
READY.
GRRRRRR
WE HAVE THEM CORNERED!
WHERE ARE THE OTHERS? THEY SHOULD BE BACK BY NOW!
ARRROOOO
COME ON, TOBY. WE'RE GETTING OUT OF HERE.
THUD

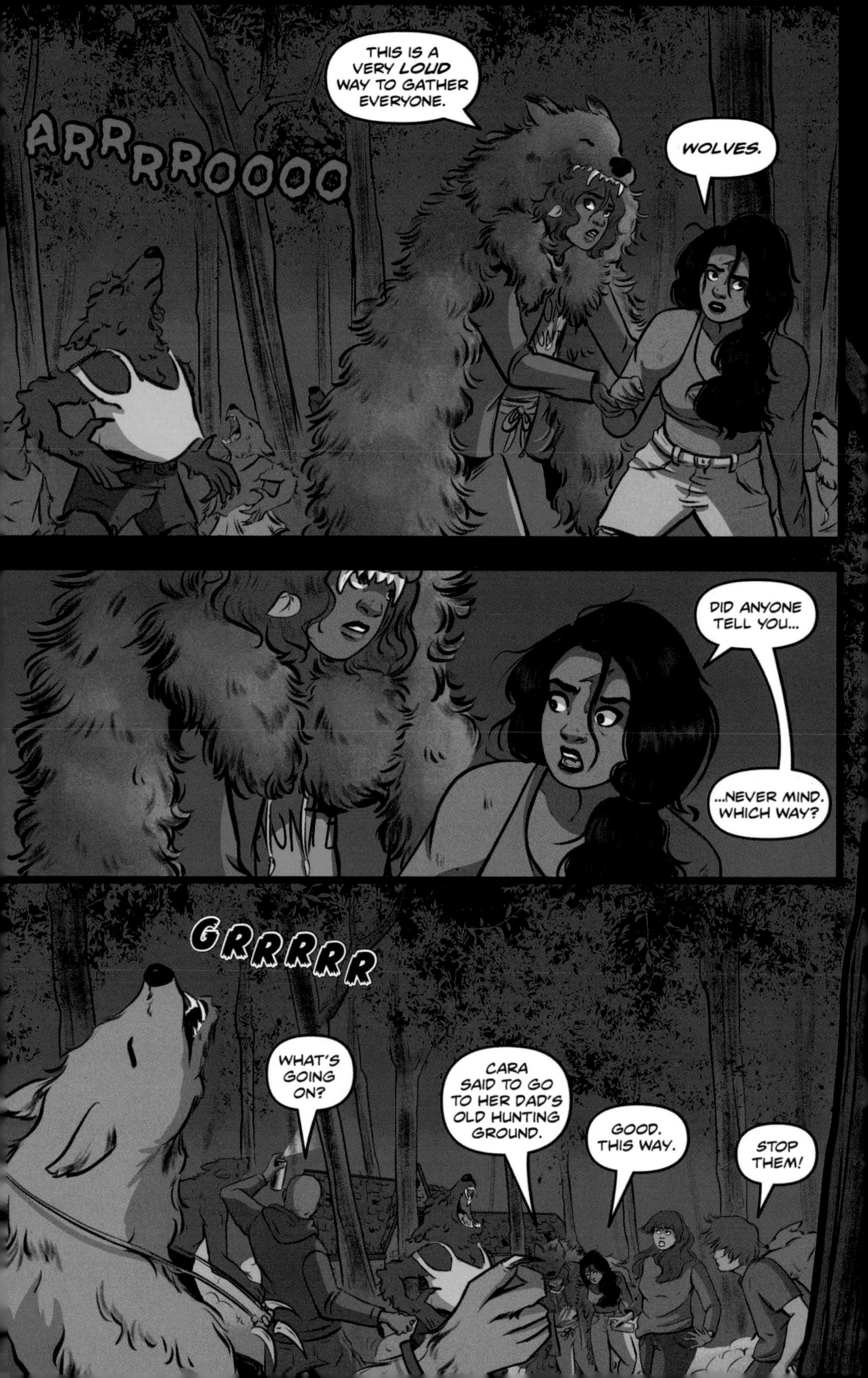

ARRRROOOOO
THIS IS A VERY LOUD WAY TO GATHER EVERYONE.
WOLVES.
DID ANYONE TELL YOU...
...NEVER MIND. WHICH WAY?
GRRRRRR
WHAT'S GOING ON?
CARA SAID TO GO TO HER DAD'S OLD HUNTING GROUND.
GOOD. THIS WAY.
STOP THEM!

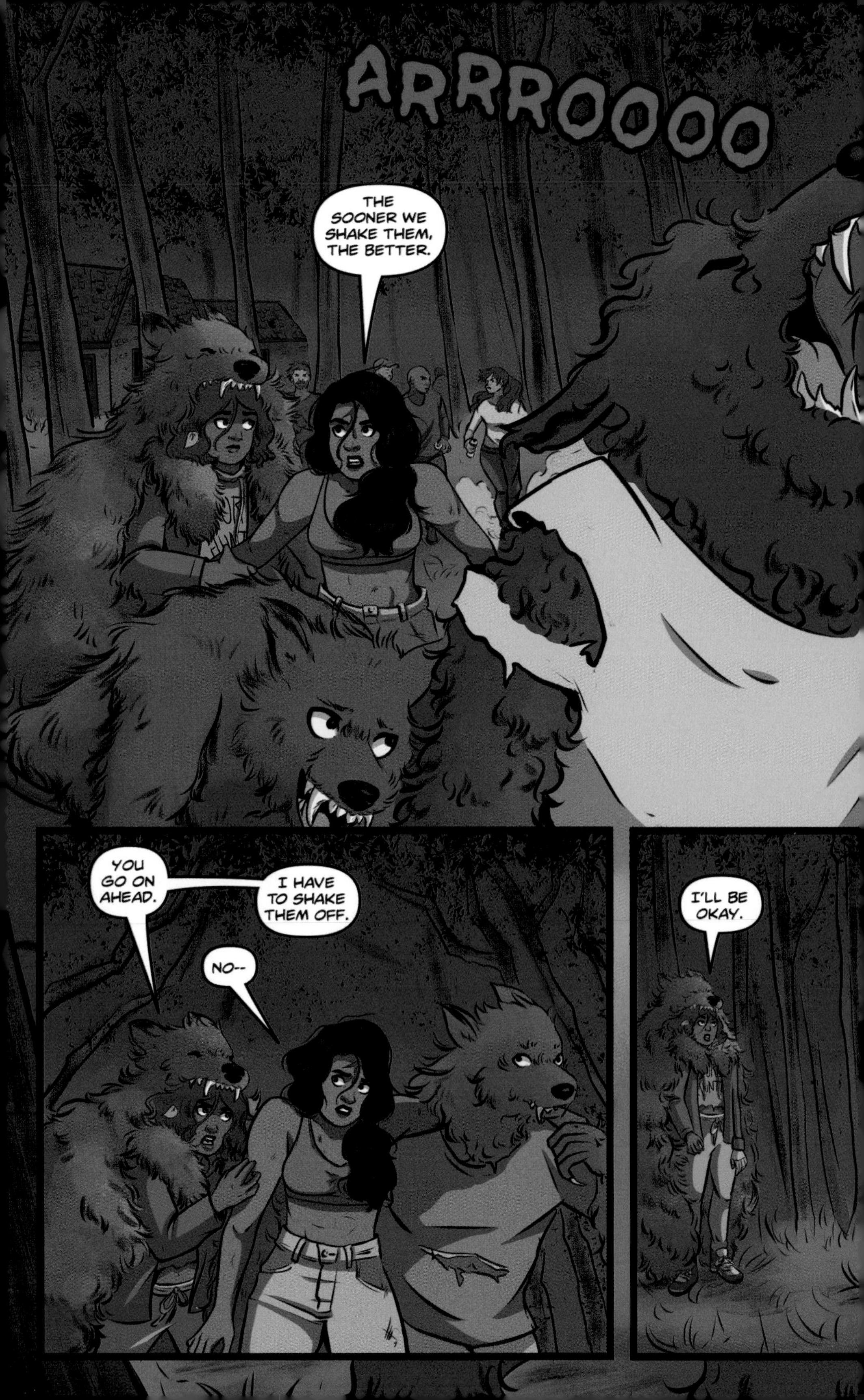
ARRROOOO
THE SOONER WE SHAKE THEM, THE BETTER.
YOU GO ON AHEAD.
I HAVE TO SHAKE THEM OFF.
NO--
I'LL BE OKAY.

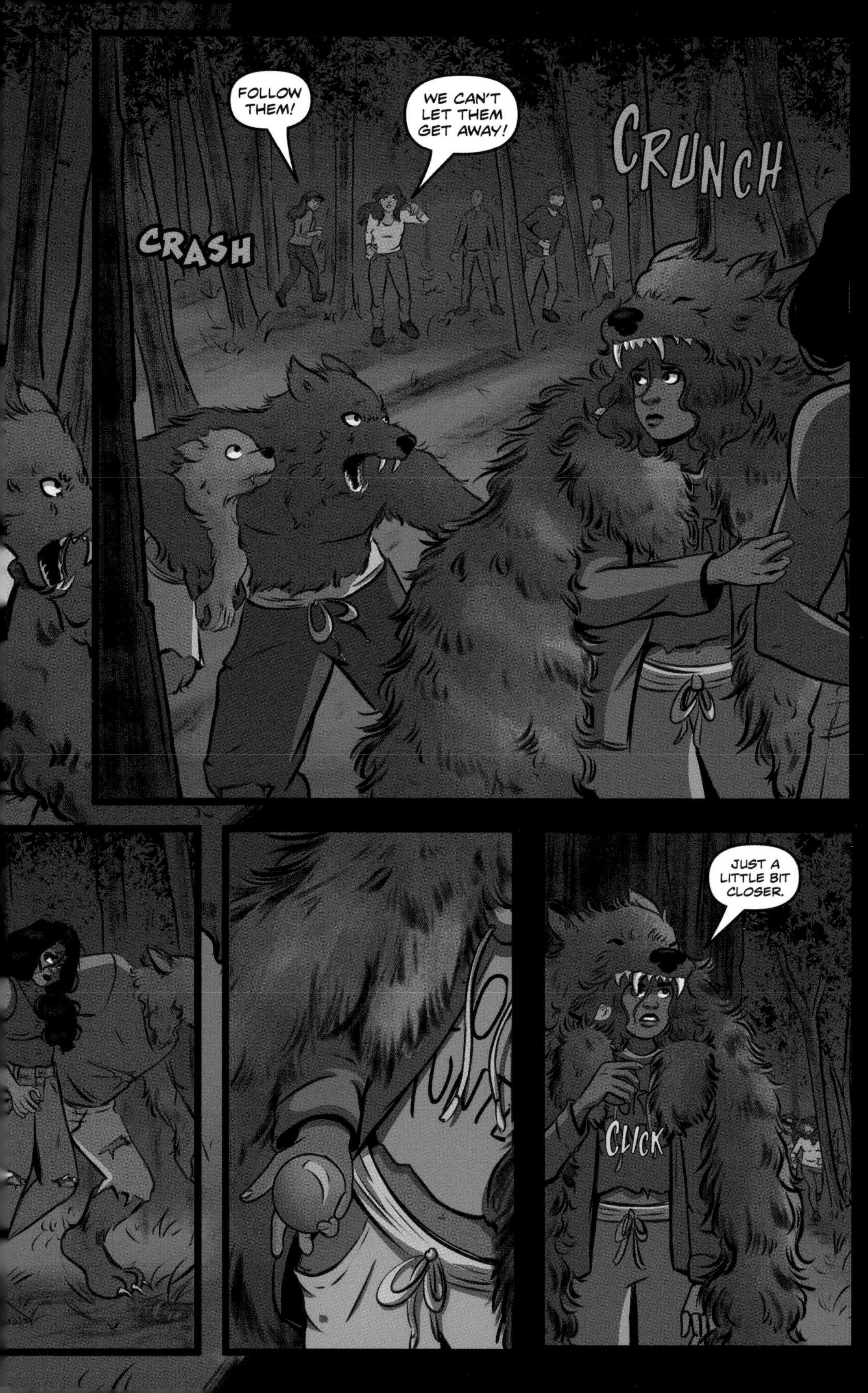
FOLLOW THEM!
WE CAN'T LET THEM GET AWAY!
CRUNCH
CRASH
JUST A LITTLE BIT CLOSER.
CLICK

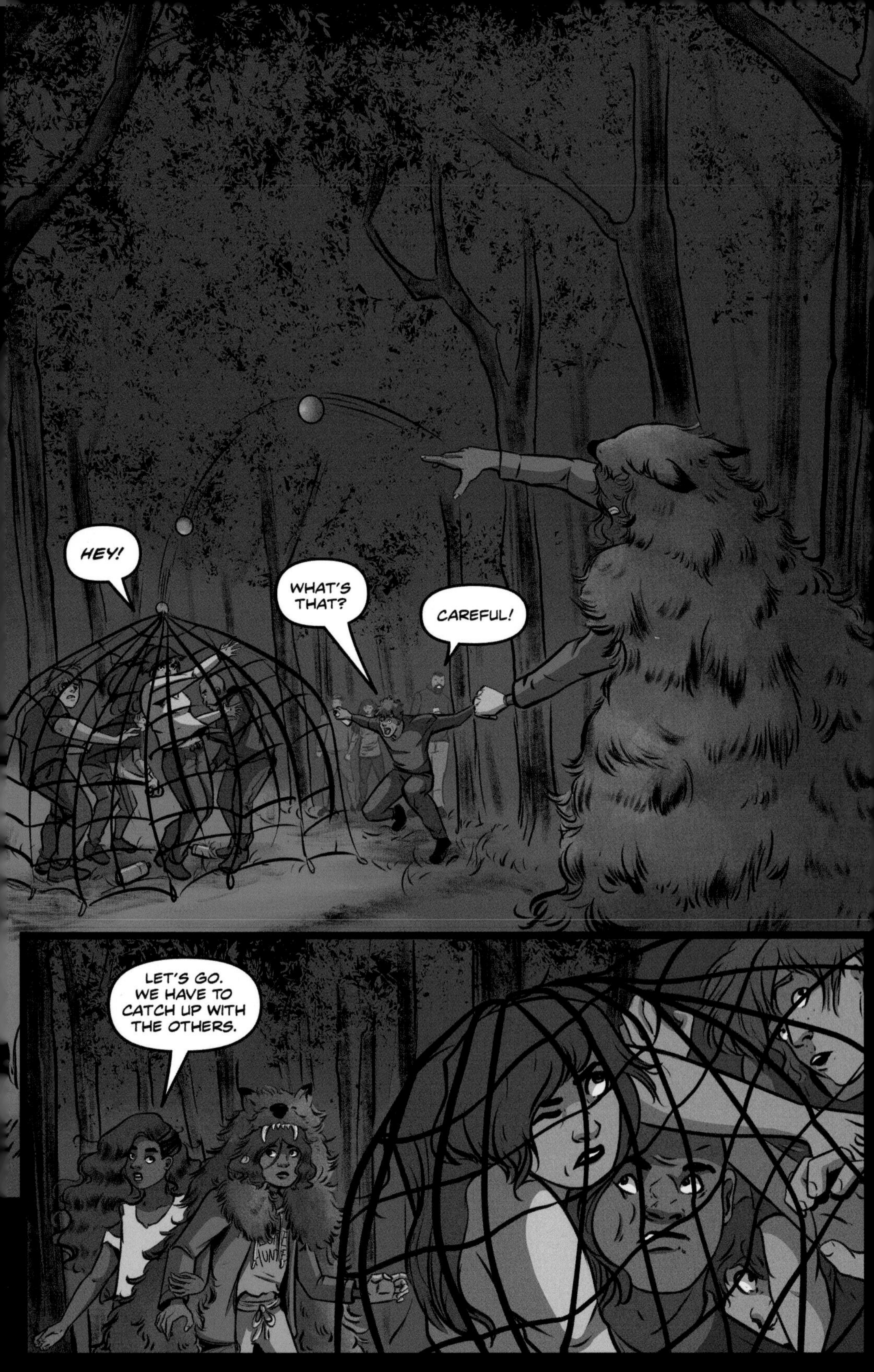
HEY!
WHAT'S THAT?
CAREFUL!
LET'S GO. WE HAVE TO CATCH UP WITH THE OTHERS.

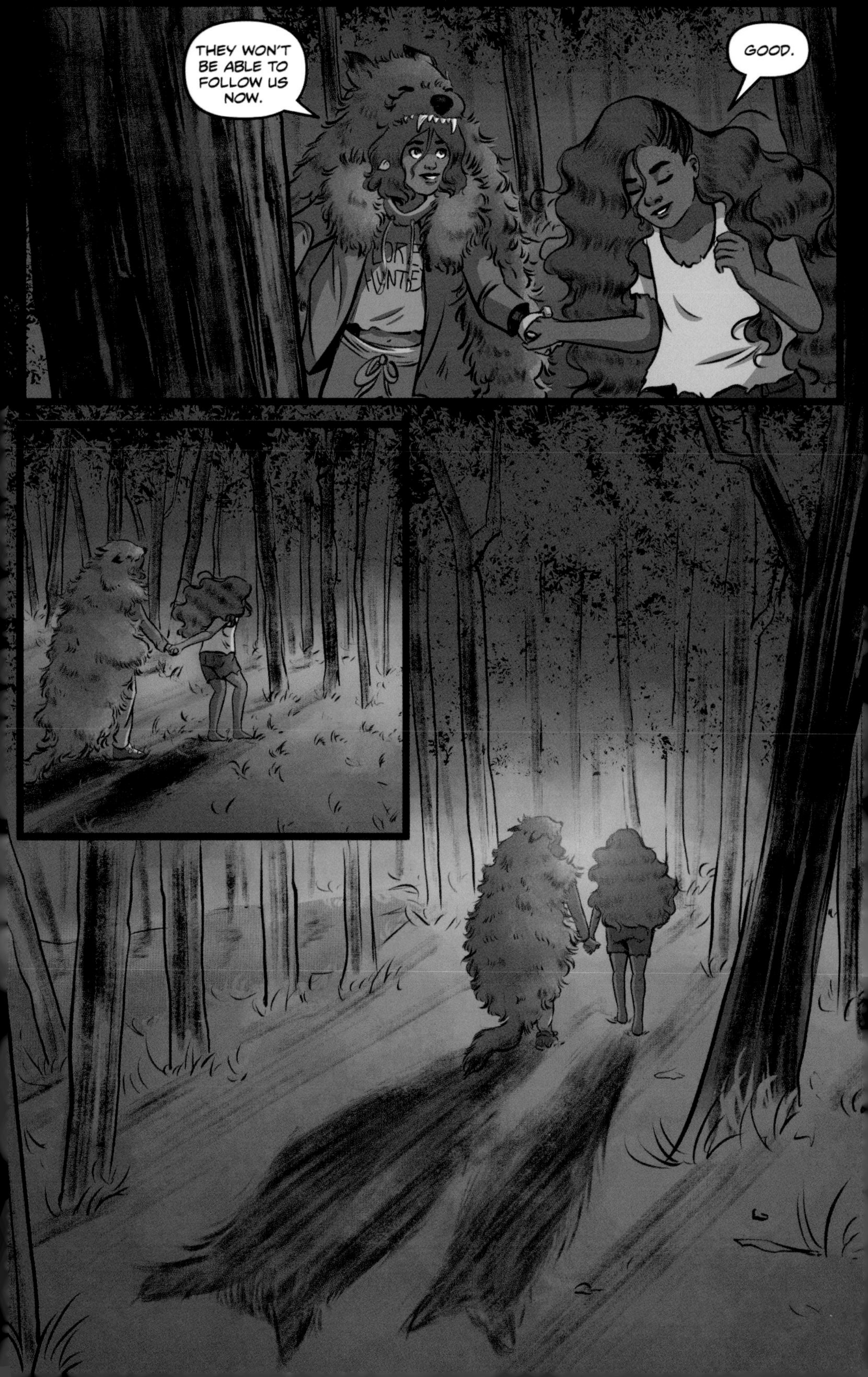
THEY WON'T BE ABLE TO FOLLOW US NOW.
GOOD.

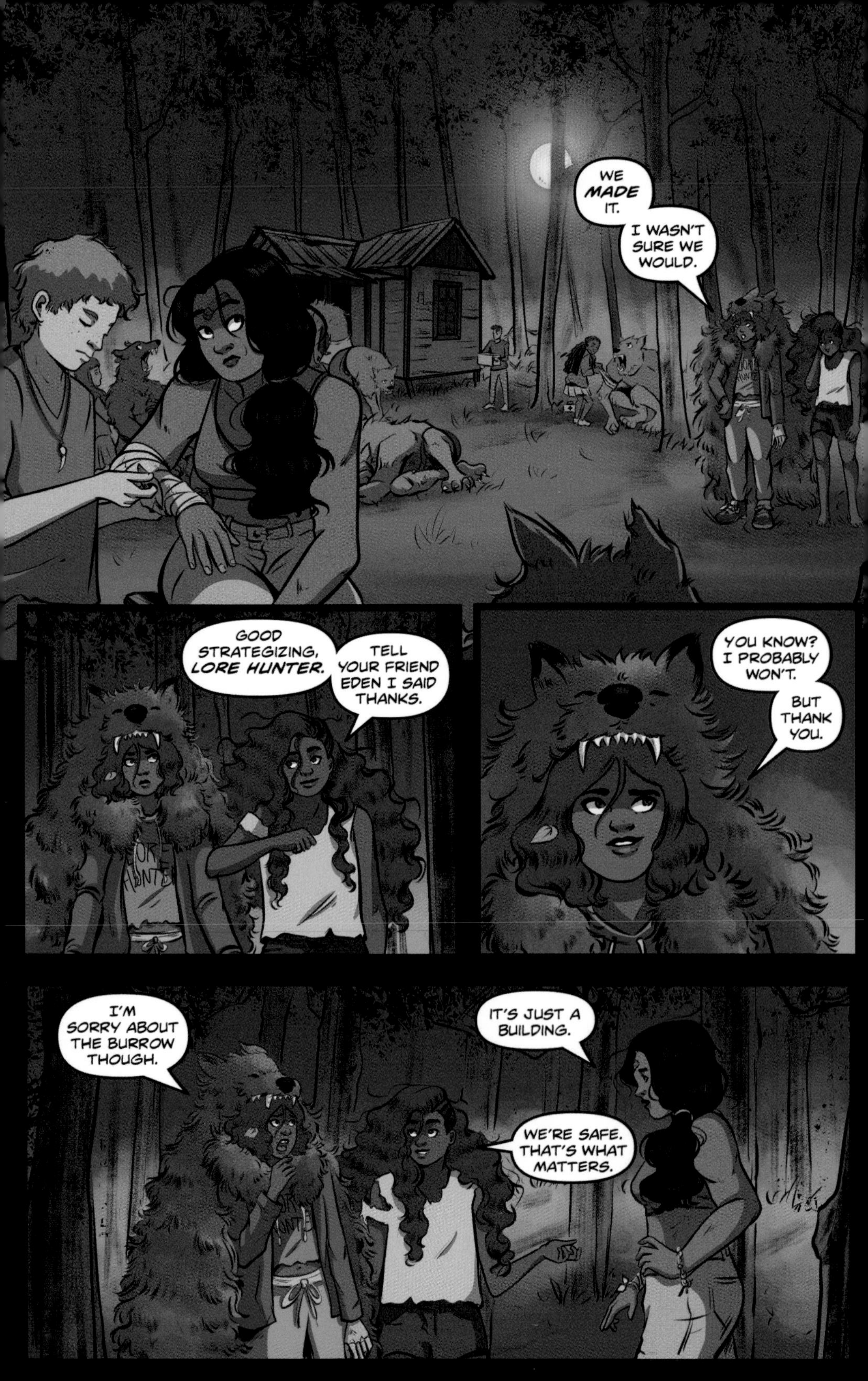
WE MADE IT.
I WASN'T SURE WE WOULD.
GOOD STRATEGIZING, LORE HUNTER.
TELL YOUR FRIEND EDEN I SAID THANKS.
YOU KNOW? I PROBABLY WON'T.
BUT THANK YOU.
I'M SORRY ABOUT THE BURROW THOUGH.
IT'S JUST A BUILDING.
WE'RE SAFE. THAT'S WHAT MATTERS.

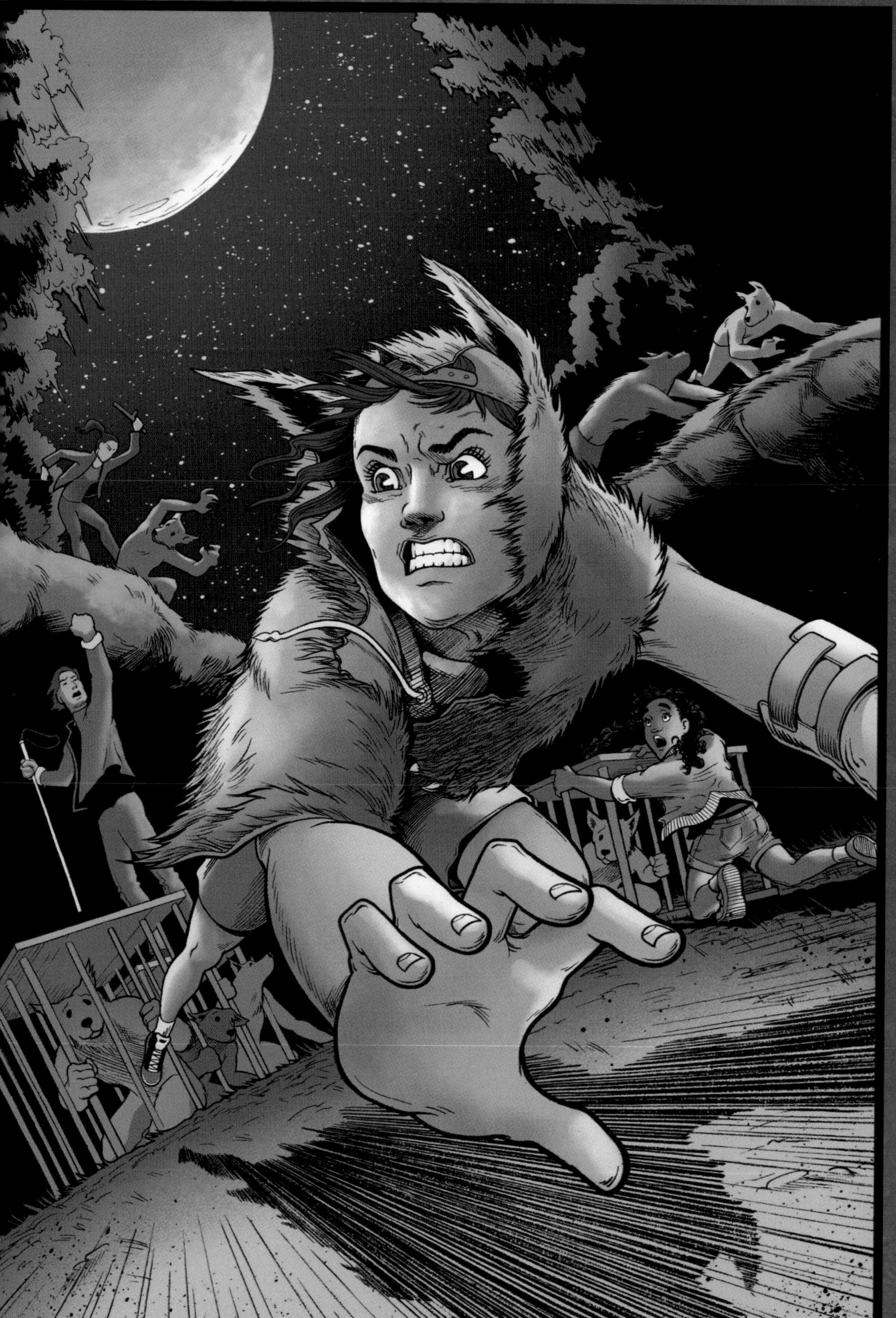

ART BY: CLARA MEATH **COLORS BY:** DJ CHAVIS

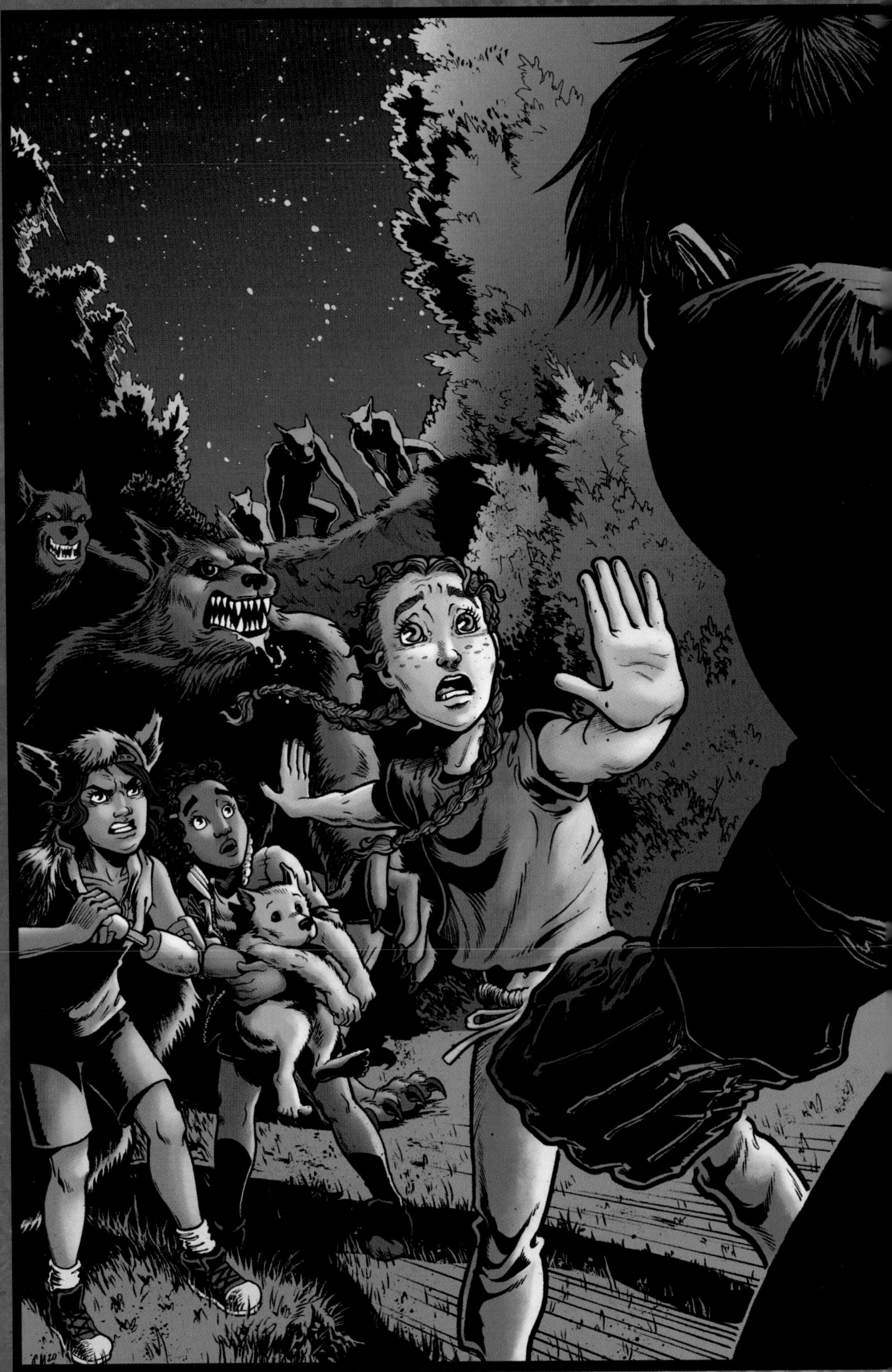

ART BY: CLARA MEATH COLORS BY: DJ CHAVIS

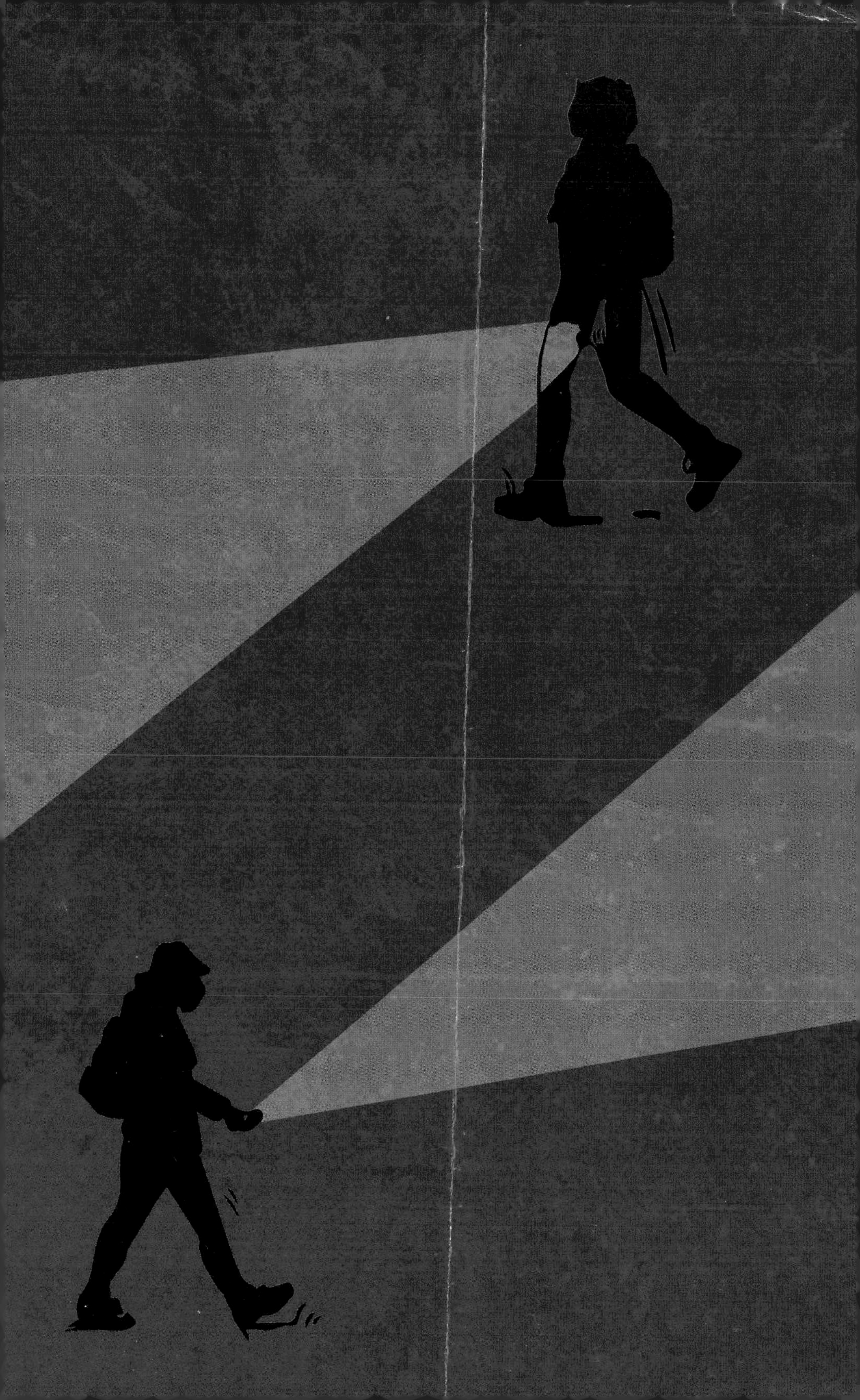

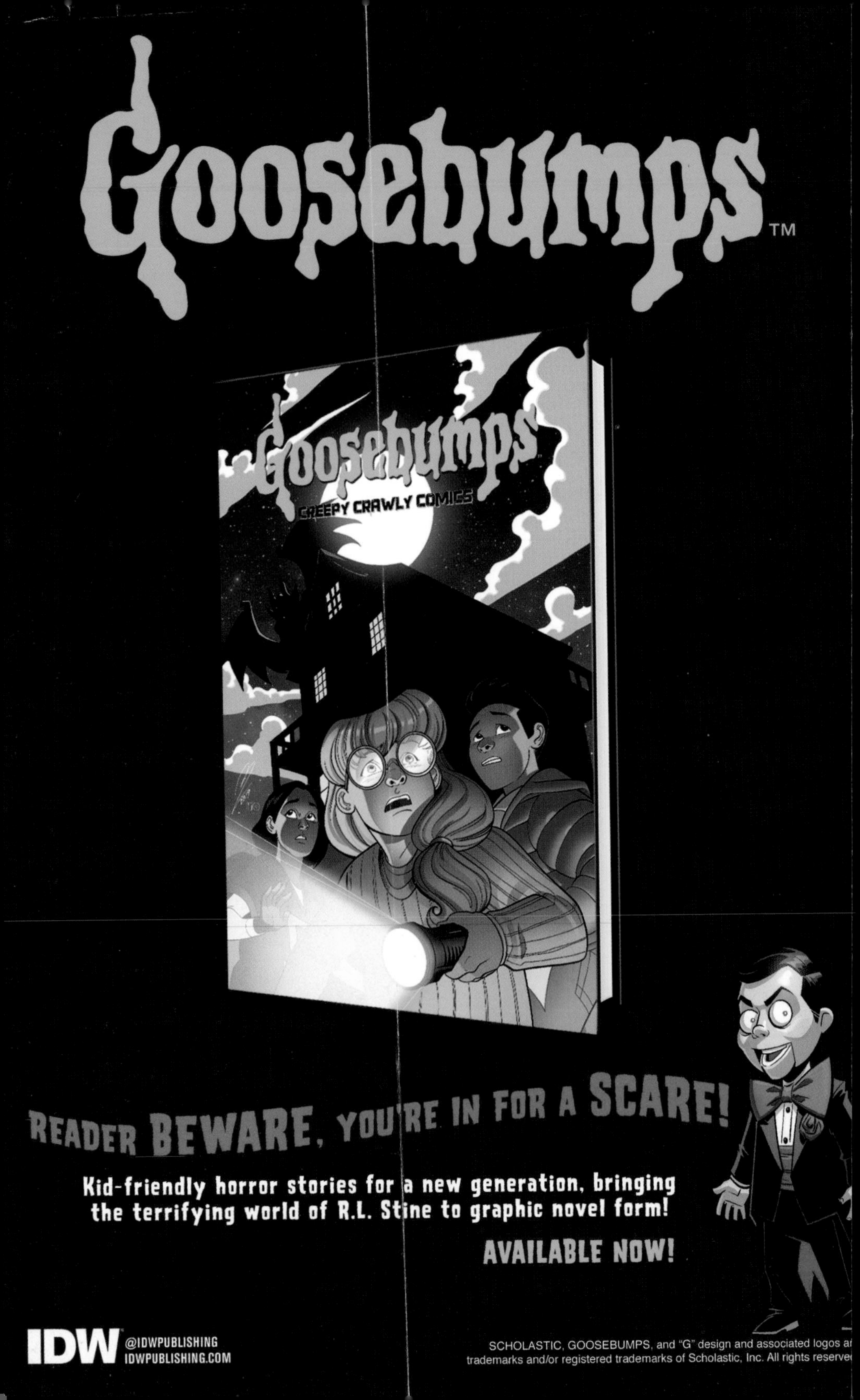

Goosebumps™
Goosebumps
CREEPY CRAWLY COMICS
READER BEWARE, YOU'RE IN FOR A SCARE!
Kid-friendly horror stories for a new generation, bringing the terrifying world of R.L. Stine to graphic novel form!
AVAILABLE NOW!
IDW @IDWPUBLISHING IDWPUBLISHING.COM
SCHOLASTIC, GOOSEBUMPS, and "G" design and associated logos are trademarks and/or registered trademarks of Scholastic, Inc. All rights reserved.